One small boy

BILL NAUGHTON

One small boy

LONDON

MACGIBBON & KEE

1957

First published 1957

© MACGIBBON & KEE 1957

MADE IN GREAT BRITAIN
PRINTED AT THE ST ANN'S PRESS
PARK ROAD, ALTRINCHAM

CONTENTS

BOOK ONE

CONTENTS—*continued*

CHAPTER ONE

The Father's Farewell

———

I HATE THE WAY she keeps me waiting to be tucked in, he thought. Every night she does it, thinking the sleep might get me first and save her the job. He turned from the candle flame and looked to the wall. Is that shadow *my* head? Maybe they're right and I do need a haircut after all. I hate that raw itchy neck you get from the short hard hair. I won't call her again. That shadow would nearly frighten you. He slid his fingers along the rosary beads to the Crucifix and then settled them on the bony figure. He whispered a Hail Mary and after it counted the coppers in his other hand. I'd be right now, he thought, if only she'd come. I'll count to ninety-seven, and if she's not here then I'll go down. She has time for the tinker lad that would come into the shop, but she leaves me to go to sleep alone. Counting slowly he listened for the mother's step, but heard only the voices of the men drinking in the room. He felt the hope desert him near the end of the count, and he let up a spasm of tears and wiped his eyes on his shirt-sleeve. I said I'd get up, he told himself aloud, and up I'll get. He got out of the warm bed, took his trousers off the bedrail and put them on, tying them with a strip of an old belt. He put the coppers in his pocket and hung the rosary beads over the brass bed-knob. He looked to the candle, and seeing it was burnt down to a stub he left it and went out of the room.

He looked into the front room that served for the shop. In the pale light of the lamp on the counter he could see the shawled head of an old woman whispering to his mother.

His brother Willie looked up from filling a can of oil and gave him a cross look, at the same time beckoning to the mother. She turned to him: 'Sure I'll be up with you in a minute, agraw,' she whispered. He felt the temper rise in him at the sight of her face, the face he had been waiting for in bed. He wanted to hurt her, but all he could think to say was 'Suff!' He turned from her and, pressing away the tears, looked into the room, watching warily for his father. Six men were in the room, drinking porter and talking. Jamesey, with the one arm, saw him and gave a wink for him to come in. He went in and stood near the man. 'Where is he?' he asked.

'Is it your father? Gone down to Father John for his blessin' before goin' off to England tomorrow, the Lord save us,' and he blessed himself.

The fire had been piled with sods of wet turf, and sweet heavy smoke rolled thickly into the room from the chimney-piece. He coughed and the man picked up a mug of stout from under his stool: 'God bless you—an' now take a good sup outa that an' divil the much you'll harm.' He held on to the man's hand, hairy and hard, as he drank the porter, gazing down into the depths of the mug, seeing the tunnel with a dark foamy swell within. 'Thanks,' he whispered. He felt Jamesey rub his stomach after it: 'You're swelled Mick-yeen,' he heard him say, laughing softly. It's easy to please a man, he thought.

'This time tomorrow night,' sighed one of the men, 'Mor-cheen will be away on the high sea.'

'He will so,' agreed others.

'I've heard told,' said an old man, 'that the English eat meat at every meal. If that's the case they must be powerful men altogether.'

'It is so,' said another, 'but for the most part they're stumpy fellows. But the women are a tremenjus size.'

A man spat into the fire: 'A thing I heard has me half kept from ever settin' foot there,' he said in a low voice. 'In all towns, so I was told, you'd see some kind of a yoke of a hut or the like, for any man that would want to use it.
8

Now isn't it an awful thing, an' I'm told it's true—that a man could be comin' out of a place like that an' meet face-to-face his own parish priest goin' in!'

'It's called a *gents*,' said one man, 'an' you could meet him inside, the two of yeez shoulder to shoulder.'

'Oh, I'd split with the shame,' said the other.

'Arra what kind of coarse talk is at ye at all?' said Jamesey, taking the jug and filling out drinks. Then he sat down again and drew the boy between his knees and gave him another drink. 'Ye'd be as well have a puff of the pipe,' he said, and he held the stunted pipe to the boy's lips. He took a suck at the hot clay stem and felt his mind twirl as he drew in the smoke. He quickly drew away from the pipe as he saw his father come into the room.

'Arra that's a bad fire ye have, men,' said the father, his blue eyes staring round the room 'an' a damn' bad fire at that.' He crossed to the hearth and stooping down he re-arranged the turf with his hands.

'I was after sayin',' said a man, 'that this time tomorrow you'll be on the high sea.'

'I will,' said the father, savagely building up the sods as they fell, 'an' well on the bloody high sea, God forgive me.' He turned to the boy: 'Are you up at this hour of the night, Mickyeen? What's on your mother to let you? Is everyone here goin' flamin' mad?'

The boy slipped out from between Jamesey's knees and went from the room feeling wobbly. He turned into the shop and went behind the counter to his mother, who was count-ing eggs into a case. 'I'll be up with you in a minute, agraw,' she said.

'You said that before.'

The figure of a tall man hesitated at the shop door, and then came in softly. 'You wouldn't have a package of "Gold Flake" for me, ma'am?' he whispered, leaning over the counter and smiling weakly.

'Indeed I would, Peter,' she said, turning and deftly slip-ping the yellow packet into his hand, 'an' ten more if you needed them.'

'I'll be in, ma'am' he said nervously.

'Don't I know well you will?' she said. 'That's a great evenin' now, thanks be to God.

'It is surely, ma'am,' said the man, slipping to the door, 'an' thank you very much, ma'am, for that.'

'Not at all,' said the mother, 'not at all.'

The boy drew back as he saw his father appear round the door: 'Was that that hangman Flaherty after cursed cigarettes?' he asked.

The mother didn't speak, but hummed loudly and watched the figure pass the window. 'He was in here earlier, the trick o' the loop,' went on the father, 'but he knew well he'd get none from me—the bloody curraghbuck that hasn't paid one penny piece over that counter this twelvemonth. Is it to that slunger would drink all before him you have cigarettes given?'

'I'll sink through that floor in shame,' said the mother, 'if you let that poor misfortunate man hear a word——'

'Misfortunate bloody rogue.'

'That man's father, Fergus Flaherty, an' his father before him, God rest their souls, an' his mother too, Anne Haynes, an' all ever belongin' him,' said the mother, 'were ever the decent an' respectable people.'

'I never knew a Flaherty yet,' said the father, his yellow teeth biting his lower lip, 'wasn't a plunderer an' thief.'

'I wouldn't put shame on that one,' said the mother firmly, 'or one of his name, for a thousand pounds—an' that's a great deal of money. Nor would I try but be decent to——'

'Decency, decency, decency,' said the father, 'is there nothin' in your head but decency? Give, give, give, to every eejit enterin' the shopdoor, an' no question whether they'll pay or not. Your decency will drive us to the poorhouse—an' indeed it has me driven to England tomorrow.'

'You had no place to say that, sir,' said the mother, softly. She turned to the boy: 'I'll take you up to bed now,' she said.

'If you don't,' said the father, 'I'll kick him into bed, s'help me God.'

10

'I defy you,' said the boy, though not loud enough for the man to hear. 'The candle's gone, mother,' he said.

She took one from the shelf, struck a match and lighted it, and pushed him on ahead. When they got to the room she said to him: 'You had to come down though you knew well I'd come—an' knowin' what night it is with the house full.'

A reply came to his lips, but he held it back as he recalled the father's words and how she had seemed hurt under them. So he stayed silent, and she bent down and drew the chamber-pot from under the bed and asked him gently: 'Did you flood, agraw, or will you?'

'I want no flood,' he said, dropping his trousers, and suddenly feeling sweaty and hot. 'I have my prayers said too,' he added, and got into bed. She pulled the blankets up under his chin, and then he saw her kneel at the bed and begin: 'Matthew, Mark, Luke and John, God bless this bed that I lie on . . .' And then it seemed the room was see-sawing, and something inside his head began to spin round in a slow and awful way.

'Mother! mother!' he cried.

'Wait yet,' she said, 'wait yet,' and she slipped the pot out again. Then she took his head and held it firmly, one palm pressed against the forehead, and he began to retch, vomit and cry. 'Put your finger back into your throat,' she said soothingly. 'That's a good ladeen,' she said, resting him back on the pillow. Sweat was pouring out all over him, it seemed. 'There's a pain in my head, mother,' he said. Then he saw his brother Willie come into the room.

'Have I to sleep next to that one?' said Willie.

The mother clicked him to silence, and then went off with the chamber-pot. 'It's just the price of you,' said Willie.

'Oh none of your ould guff,' he said.

The mother came back. 'Ease up now,' she said. He smelt vinegar and then felt a damp cloth press coldly against his hot forehead. At once there came relief. Only she could fix it for me, he thought. I'll be good for the future. 'It's a wonder the nuns wouldn't teach him better,' he heard Willie say. Tomorrow night the father'll be gone, he thought. He'll be on the high sea. Then he slept. He dreamt about a little cat that kept mewing, 'Mama! *Mama*!' every time he touched it, 'Mama!' And tinker lads were after him to beat him.

He woke up to find full morning light in the room and Willie gone from the bed. The house was silent. He tried to think out what was behind the lump of expectation in his mind.

England—he's going off to England! He got out of bed at once, put on his trousers—I'll say my prayers later—and tying the belt round him he hurried out of the room. He ran into the shop and saw Bid Grogan, seated on a barrel of apples, smoking her pipe.

'Are you up then, my scholareen?' she asked.

'I am, ma'am,' he said.

'You must be a great sleeper altogether,' she said, 'when all the commotion didn't rouse you. They're all gone off to the station.'

He went out and began to run down the road. In the distance he saw the train coming from the west, and he ran harder to reach the bridge over the road, before the train should cross it. He was too late, and he stopped, his hands to his ears as the train rolled heavily over. Then he felt someone running past him, and he saw Jamesey. He was coatless, and gasping loudly as he ran, and the boy followed him up the station road. The train had drawn to a halt at the platform, and as Jamesey ran uphill he began to bleat: 'Hould on there! Don't go yet! Hy, don't go!'

The breathless cries excited the boy, who found himself running harder and calling out: 'Stop! stop! don't go yet.' He caught up with the man, but wouldn't go ahead of him, and together they ran through the open platform gate. The station-master was striding along the platform, and he turned at the sight of the running figures. 'You just made it, Jamesey,' he said.

'Where's he?' he said.

'There before your two eyes, man.'

The boy saw his father at once, standing at the open window of a compartment, looking pale and uncomfortable, and wiping his forehead with a handkerchief. The mother was standing amongst a few shawled figures, talking to the father, who kept jerking his head up and down. The boy held back and then a whistle blew.

'Morcheen!' cried Jamesey, forcing his way through the people. 'Morcheen, is it to England you're goin', my love?'

'Better late than never, Jamesey,' said the father. 'Wag o' the paw.'

'Arra why did no one waken me, Morcheen?' said Jamesey. 'Glory be to God, I could have you missed altogether. You could be gone without me havin' a sight at all of you.'

The whistle blew again. The boy saw his Aunt Kate stand forward and thrust Jamesey aside: 'Godspeed, Morcheen,' she cried. 'Let the woman say farewell to her man'—she scolded Jamesey. The mother raised her hand as the train jerked slowly forward. The father wiped his eyes and there was a loud wail of 'Godspeed!' from women and men.

'Musha, ma'am,' he said, turning to look along the track, 'this is God's own pure truth I'm tellin' you—that man an' myself had great times in Ireland. We had the greatest of times in Ireland, himself an' myself, the likes was never known elsewhere in God's world. Oh an' all we drank, the Lord protect us, all we drank, ma'am, but never the wrong word, never drunk or sober had myself an' that man, the Lord protect him, the wrong or cool word.'

'You had not surely,' said the mother, 'nor would you in a hundred years.'

The boy slipped across to his aunt, who was talking to Willie. 'Hello, Aunt Kate,' he said softly. She gave him a hug by the shoulder and a kiss on the cheek. His greeting over, he went beside Jamesey.

'I saw nine go from me, Delia,' said Janey O'Malley to the mother, 'nine I saw go in the dark mornin'—an' but the one ever I saw return.'

'Ah, you did indeed, Janey,' said the mother 'an' that was hard surely.'

'I cried many the tear, God knows, ma'am, many the long tear, but all that was nothin' to seein' himself go. When that

13

day came, as come it had to, I tell you I shed the black tears that mornin'.'

'That man, God love him,' said Jamesey, looking back again, ' wherever he goes an' whoever he sees, will have luck. He'll have work too, he'll always have work, God give him the health, but no matter what luck he has an' what work he has, he'll never have times again like himself an' myself had in Ireland. Did I ever tell ye of the time we were shop-boys in Richard O'Hagan's? We brought out to the stables the bucket near full to the brim with the purest seven-year-old whisky, covered over with a handful of oats, makin' out we were goin' feedin' the mare—an' we drank the full o' the bucket of whisky between us. Oh Morcheen my love, all we drank an' all we saw will never be known again this world.' Wiping his thick hand across his face he laughed and cried.

' Bad cess to you, Jameseyeen,' said Aunt Kate, ' what have ye out of it at all at the heel of the hunt?'

' Ah the purest of memories, ma'am,' he answered, ' that will be with me to my dyin' day, no matter when that should be.'

' Will ye all come into the house now? ' said the mother.

' Indeed we won't,' said Janey, ' for haven't you enough to do now.'

' Musha England isn't too bad at all,' said Mary Doyle; ' it's when you see one off to America you'd know it was as bad as one dyin' on you.'

''Twould split my heart to see the house without him,' said Jamesey, ' if that's not the short answer, ma'am. An sure enough it will yours, this many a bright day.'

' I'll miss him surely,' said the mother quietly.

Near the shop the neighbours left the party. ' You're killed with the hunger, Kate,' said the mother. ' Is it a fry an' tea you'll have—or would we wait till the big meal? '

' Anythin' you say will do me,' said Aunt Kate, ' though maybe a fry would be the handier.'

They all went into the house together, the mother pausing to give one look to the east.

14

CHAPTER TWO

The Holy Mountain

AFTER THE MEAL she drew him into the bedroom and he helped her make the bed. 'Aunt Kate was just askin' me,' she said, 'if you'd go down to Cloonahalta with her this evenin' —just for a couple of days.'

His heart turned against the thought. 'No, no, no, mother,' he whispered, shaking his head violently. 'You know how I hate goin' anywhere. I'd go with Aunt Kate, but I hate goin' away, mother, I hate it.'

'Take care would she hear you,' said the mother, 'an' you her favourite of favourites.'

'Mother, I don't want to go from you,' he said, and his voice broke and the tears came to his eyes.

'If you don't want to go, my son,' said the mother, 'then you don't have to. I didn't want to say no to her, for she had her heart set on it.'

'Why did she ask?' he said. 'Why did you let her ask? I'm goin' off away till she's gone.'

'Take care would you ever do the dishonourable thing to a one under our roof,' said the mother, 'an' she my only sister.'

'I hate you,' he said. 'You knew—I hate you'—and he gave her a shove, sending her stumbling backwards on to the bed. Suddenly he felt himself swung round by the shoulder, and saw Willie's flushed face.

'You eejit,' cried Willie. 'Have you no sense at all— doin' that to mother?'

'Arra what's on you?' said the mother. 'We were only playin.'

'You flamer,' he shouted at Willie. And he burst out cry- ing at the unexpectedness of his brother's anger.

'Come here, agraw,' said the mother, 'come here now.'

'No, no, no I won't,' he sobbed. 'I hate you all. You're all against me.'

'Musha, don't upset yourself, my child,' she said, coming over to him. 'Willie, bring water from the well, there's a good boy.'

When his brother had gone he let his face be pressed into her warm breast. 'Wisha you had the hard day,' she said, 'an' everything went against you. He was mad to strike you, an' us only havin' fun. Sure he's no sense, God forgive him. I'll give you a grand washeen the minute he's back.'

'Don't let Aunt Kate know I was cryin',' he said.

'I'll let no one know,' she said. 'Stay here an' I'll bring the water up.'

'Don't tell her what I said about not wantin' to go down,' he said. 'Pretend you haven't asked me yet.'

'There'll not be a budge out of me,' she said, going off. She'll tell her, he thought, but so long as she doesn't know I know she was told it'll be right. The mother came back with the water and a flannel and towel.

'Don't hurt me goin' into my ears,' he said.

'Erra how would I hurt you?' she said.

'You always say that same thing,' he said, 'an' you always hurt me. Don't spit on the cloth.'

'When did you see me spit on the cloth?'

'I never saw you do anythin' else,' he said. 'Now willya go easy in my ears?'

'Musha, if the people of Cloonahalta saw dirt in your ears,' she said as she washed him, 'the word might go round in a minute. The likes of that happened old James Caulfield, God rest him, an' he never showed his face outside the door in twenty-nine years. He heard someone cast a slight on one of his two daughters, sayin' she never washed or didn't wash right or something of the sort, an' do you know what that poor man did?'

'Never stuck his nose outside the door for twenty-nine years. Suff!—that's another of your lies,' he said.

'What did you ever hear me tell a lie?' she said, her finger moving into his ear.

'I never knew you tell anything else,' he said. 'Willya go easy in my ear?' I'll stay down there two days, but not another minute. Don't spit on the cloth, I'm watchin' you.'

'Musha, aren't you a great man altogether?' she said. 'I wonder what we'll put you to.'

'That's enough,' he said, drawing away. 'You'd play in my ears all day.'

'Wait yet till I see have I you a clean shirt,' she said.

'Is it the one stuck out on the bush dryin?' he asked.

'Wait yet,' she said, 'till I see.'

She came back with a clean shirt. 'I hate that one,' he said, 'it's too small. An' it's straight from the bush without an iron goin' near it.'

'Where would you see a shirt better ironed than that?' she said. 'The fairies did it in the night.'

She took off his shirt and pulled the other over his head. 'Do you believe in the fairies, mother?'

'Arra the one who'd believe in fairies would believe in holy water,' she said.

'That's a mortal sin you're after committing,' he said, 'sayin' a thing like that. If you was to die this minute nothin' could save you from hell for all eternity.'

'Nothin' but the love of God, agraw,' she said.

'Do you know one thing,' he said, 'you make me mad goin' on with your wild jokes?'

'Wait till I bring the glass,' she said. 'There—look into that. Isn't it the fine handsome man you are, the Lord save you.' He looked intently at himself in the looking-glass. It seemed to him he was a good-looking lad. 'Come down an' let Aunt Kate see you,' said the mother.

'Two days an' no more,' he whispered. 'Will I wear shoes goin' down?'

'Sure don't they only cripple your feet?' said the mother. 'We must get you a pair one day, you're well grown out of them. Have you money in your pocket?'

'I think so,' he said.

'A right man should always carry money,' she said, 'so he can always stand his turn.' She led him into the other

17

room where his aunt was. 'Now here's your man,' she said.

'Well above all ever I saw,' said Aunt Kate, 'he beats the band, God bless him.'

'Do you think he looks like me?' said the mother.

'Divil a look,' said Aunt Kate, 'but the spit of his ould rogue of a father.'

'He'll be up at Athlone by this,' said the mother.

'He will, an' past it,' said Aunt Kate. 'An' don't be lettin' the crack into your voice, woman, for that man will know half the train by this.'

'He's a very shy man amongst strangers,' said the mother, 'though you'd hardly know it. An' he'd hate to drink a sup or eat a bite outside our own roof.'

'Well, Mickyeen,' said Aunt Kate, 'get the ass into the shafts an' we'll be gettin' ready for off. We've the seven long Irish miles before us.'

When they were ready, Willie came over to him. 'You'd be as well take the ould mouth-organ with you,' he said.

'Ah no, thanks,' he said.

'Here, man,' he said, 'I know you like a puff on it.'

Big Grogan came round the corner. 'Arra, Kate Madden, are you takin' Michaeleen off with you—my own scholar? Your soul to the divil, who'll read an' write my letters for me when he's gone? Oh my own scholareen!'

He had to lower his head, and he was glad when his aunt gave a clack of her tongue and the ass went off. He heard all their cries, but raised his head only when they were near the bend of the road. He could see his mother waving her white apron. Ashamed of himself he raised his hand and waved back. Then they went jogging down the road and into Ballyboun.

'There's T. L. Henehan comin' out of school,' she said.

At the sound of the name he buried his head down again, taking one glance at the schoolmaster, with his hook nose and bushy eyebrows.

'Good day to you, sir,' called his aunt.

'Good day, ma'am,' said the man.

How could she speak to the schoolmaster from above on an ass-cart? 'That man had the finest brain in all Europe,' she said, 'until the drink had him ruined. Is it true what Willie told me of him going into Cassidy's bar last Friday? He was that stothered that the sight had left his eyes, an' he went round the wrong side of the bar altogether—behind the counter itself. Then he rapped and asked for a glass of whisky, and turned to Cassidy at the sight of the men in the bar: "You've a power of shopboys in here today," he said.'

'It would be what he'd do,' he said.

Beyond the town the country was flat and desolate, with vast stretches of brown bogland on either side of the road, and long distances between houses. The sweet bog air made him drowsy, and he was glad when at last they reached the long hill and they got down from the cart. At the top of the hill, which they had walked in silence, the woman took him by the sleeve of his jersey.

'D'you see across there?' she asked, pointing westward and then blessing herself. He looked across the plain of Mayo towards the Atlantic, seeing the landscape of green and brown, and everywhere the grey lines of stone fences, and then away in the distance a great cone of a mountain, rising darkly to the sky.

'Is that Reek Patrick?' he asked.

'It is,' she said, 'the Holy Mountain. Praise be to God.'

'To God who giveth joy to my youth.' She put her hand on his head. 'Look well now,' she said, 'it's not every day you'd see that from here.'

They gazed in silence, and then she turned. 'Come on, Mickyeen,' she said, springing on to the ass-cart, 'it's a clear run home from here.'

He sat beside her as they went jogging downhill, the breeze in their faces. 'We are the people, Mickyeen,' she called out. 'I tell you, man, we from the west are the people. We're the people.' The breeze set her dark hair back against the thick wool shawl, and as the ass went spanking along he felt a longing inside himself to lift back his own head, and call out with her, but something inside always stopped him from doing anything free and gay, and he lowered his head and sang to himself.

19

CHAPTER THREE

Aunt Kate

THAT'S A WEEK I'm here now, he thought, and no mention of going home. I must ask her when I have the courage. The cottage was a fat, comfortable place, limewashed inside and out, with walls over two feet thick, and a low black ceiling. Set back into the far wall from the door, and close up against the fire, was the hag. This was a low-roofed recess the bed fitted into, with a curtain across the front. Every night he slept there next to his aunt, and it was always then, with the wind whirring in the chimney, that he would think of his mother and home. Then it would be revealed to him that any happiness of the day had been somehow false, that every bright moment had been a pretence, and that his true self was contained alone in the grey sadness of heart that came on him at night. He would swallow each gulp as it rose in his throat, for fear she would hear or suspect, and when the tears ran down his face in the darkness he didn't wipe them, knowing that all trace of them would be gone by morning. He wondered how his mother could get on without him, and he longed for the day when she would send for him, and often at this time he thought of his father away in England, and even felt sorry for him.

In the evenings Aunt Kate liked to build up the fire with turf and sit down for a chat. ' Close the door, avic,' she'd often say, ' an' put the hasp on it at that, for the wind's blowin' over from Ned Lyons' place, God rest his soul an' the souls of the dead, an' heaven pity the poor one that would be out in it.' Sometimes the wet wind would blow hard, forcing the thin tough bushes over, and blowing far away any washing left out to dry on them, but up near the fire he would hear little of it, except for an occasional whistle or the taste of fine turf-ash on his tongue. Though again, he felt, it was only an excuse for Aunt Kate not to be caught by a visitor with her little clay pipe going.

One day out at the bog they were footing up the grogeens —making stacks of eight or nine wet sods of turf, to allow the wind to flow through and dry them—when she called out: 'Yerra what kind of man are you at all, Mickyeen, up an' down like a jack-in-the-box?' The divil melt you, you coarse lump of a woman, he thought, my mother wouldn't say a hard thing like that to a tinker by the side of the road, not in a hundred years, let alone to one of her own. And to spite her he worked on for the next hour without once lifting up until, when he did, he could hardly straighten at all.

One early evening he was out at the bog, loading up the two big baskets straddled across the ass's back, when a storm blew up. The rain came down in torrents and he was soon soaking wet—since he had gone off without the old sack for his shoulders. This feels lovely now, he thought, the rain rolling down under his shirt, and the wind blowing hard. It was over an hour's journey home, and after a time he began to feel weary and wretched. Along the way he passed a family of tinkers camped by the roadside, a crowd of them it seemed, packed into a tent made up of sacking strung over four pieces of stick. Smoke was pouring out of the opening of the tent, and a man stuck his head out and shouted: 'Throw us a few sods of the turf down here, there's a grand lad you are.' He threw a couple down, and then one of the tinker lads came out and tried to take more. He got very angry and shoved the tinker off, and the next thing the little tinker gave him a thump in the stomach. It took his breath for the moment, but he grabbed the big sod of turf out of the other's hand. 'You bloody thievin' tinker,' called the tinker lad, running back to the tent.

Further along the road he was passing the home of the two old Dooagh sisters, and one was looking out the door. 'Urra the Lord save us,' she cried, 'come in outa the storm a minute.' He turned to her and said: 'Thank you, ma'am, but I've only a piece of a way to go—as far as Kate Madden's.' At that the elder sister came to the door, a woman with white hair parted down the middle, and a brown wrinkled face. 'Then you're Delia's lad,' she said, 'from up in Ballyboun? Come in, willya, come in outa that.'

He stopped the ass and went across to the door. 'Musha, you're dreebin' wet,' said the older one, 'dreebin'. Come in, the Lord save us.'

It was a small dark room with an uneven earth floor, bare and clean. 'I'll put the kettle on the hook,' said the younger sister, 'an' there'll be a hot supeen of tea for you, agraw.'

'Ah don't trouble yourself, ma'am,' he said.

'Is it trouble?' said the elder one. 'Urra listen to me—if that table you see there was loaded with the richest an' rarest of foods that the four legs of it would be crackin', 'twould be little enough to give to a son of *your* mother.' She looked at him keenly with her old eyes: 'Little enough, I'm tellin' you, to give to the son of Delia Madden.'

'I think the ass is goin', ma'am,' he blurted out. 'Thank you, ma'am. I must be goin'.'

He ran out to the ass that was standing unbudging in the rain, and he gave it a smack and hurried it along the road. He couldn't stop the tears running down his cheeks. 'Little enough to give to the son of your mother,' he kept thinking. My mother is thought greatly of in places. Isn't that a strange thing now? And he hurried on through the rain, gulping and wondering. The noble little ass, most holy of all beasts. The son of your mother, little enough, I'm tellin' you.

Aunt Kate was watching for him from the door, and she ran out and left the ass standing there whilst she made him take off his clothes before the fire. 'Rub yourself with the towel,' she said, 'whilst I empty the turf.' He stood before the big fire, rubbing his head with the towel. Then the woman came back. 'Of with every stitch,' she said, 'the Lord save us, you'll be killed with the cold.' He felt uneasy as she stripped him naked and began to rub his body all over with the towel. The towel made him tingle, and then he grew alarmed and ashamed as he felt his thing in front rising up.

'Where's something to put on, Aunt Kate?' he asked, bending in the middle.

'Stick the blanket round you,' she said. 'I have a feed of cally ready for you. God save us, how did you ever get back at all? Look at the night.'

After he had eaten the pile of mashed potato, peppered with raw onion and topped with butter, he began to feel drowsy.

'Now stoop your head over the table,' she said, 'while I run the fine rack through your hair. Now's just the chance.' She put a sheet of newspaper on the table, and as he rested forward, his forehead down on the table, she began to run the fine-tooth comb up the back of his head. It brought a nice tingling feeling to the scalp, except when she tugged at a matted piece of hair.

'Troth an' isn't that a wondrous thing now,' she said when she had finished, 'not a single bowdy, Mickyeen. Wisha your mother told me often an' on that others could be creeping with them, an' there wouldn't be a one next or near you. I never believed her, but now I do. In you go into the hag, an' keep the blanket round you.'

He fell asleep, and then woke up. She was not yet in bed beside him. The curtain was only partly drawn, and he peeped out without moving. By the soft light of the lamp he watched the woman comb her hair.

She was standing in her nightgown with her back to him, and he listened to the humming of her voice as she split the hair for her two nightly plaits. She half turned, and his eyes watched intently as her two plump hands combed the dark glossy hair, pulled it and stroked it, and slipped it into a plait, folding one bright rope of hair over another. She tossed the two black plaits over her shoulders, and then carefully cleaned the comb, bringing the loose hairs together into a ball and dropping them on the fire. The sniff of burning hair felt strange. He watched as she got down on her knees against a chair and began to say her night prayers. His naked body within the wool blanket felt hot and itchy. The lamp shone on the firm white nape of her neck, and he saw one curly wisp of hair that had escaped the plaits. In his fingers he felt a desire to creep out and stroke it.

23

Warning touches of conscience made him look away and whisper, 'Hail, Holy Queen, Mother of Mercy, hail, our life, our sweetness and our hope . . .' but where's the sin? he asked, and again he looked across to the kneeling woman. He took a full look at the round shoulders stooped over the chair, and there was the nape of white neck with the curl of black hair on it. At the most, all I'm committing is a venial sin. Are you sure? *Why is it called mortal sin? It is called mortal sin because it kills the soul and deserves hell.* But I'm only looking. You're trying to play with God. God will not be played with. I'm not. I have no badness in me. The woman's voice rose above the whisper, 'To thee do we cry, poor banished children of Eve,' to a loud sigh, 'to thee do we send up our sighs, mournin' an' weepin' in this vale of tears . . .' and then her voice fell again, and thrice she struck her stomach. The feeling's gone, he thought.

He heard her lock the door, then blow out the lamp, and come soft-footedly in the darkness to the bed. As he felt her come in beside him the feelings danced up in him again. And through the fear darted thoughts and desires: just the two of us here in the bed in the hag with the door locked an' the curtains across an' no one in the wide world ever to know what might go on between us. I'm sellin' my soul to the devil, I know I am an' I can't help it, for I'd love to lie up against her now an' rest up close naked to her, an' her so soft. Can she see the thoughts goin' on in my head? Is she always so silent as this, in bed beside me at night? I'd have to be certain to make one good act of contrition before I died.

'Are y'awake?' she asked quickly.

'Y—yes, Aunt Kate.'

'Whisht, d'you hear anythin'; is that the horse-trap?' she asked, opening the curtain of the hag.

He listened closely and heard hooves and wheels. All the hot feeling left him. The sounds came nearer and louder. The woman sat up and blessed herself. Louder came the sounds, and she jumped out of bed. 'Whoa back there!' called a voice. 'Whoa!'

'It's Willie!' he cried, 'Willie!'

'Oh the Lord between us an' all harm,' she prayed. 'Jesus, Mary an' Joseph, guide, guard an' help us.' She struck a match and lit the lamp. She looked her old self now, his own Aunt Kate, and not the woman he had seen earlier. She began to whisper prayers in Irish as she went to the door. The light of the lamp filled the room slowly, and he watched from the hag as she prepared to open the door. There was a soft knock. 'Aunt Kate,' said a voice, ''tis me, Willie.' She opened the door and in he came: 'God bless all here,' he said.

'Musha, what has you out at this hour of the night?' she asked in a loud cross voice, 'you divil outa hell.' And before he could speak her voice turned to a whimper: 'Oh Lord Jesus Christ, tell me is she well, Willie'een? Is she well? Is she well?'

'Arra of course she's well,' he said.

'Oh thanks be to God,' she whispered and dropped down on her knees. 'Are you sure?' she asked. 'Oh amn't I the oinseach. Arra musha you're perished with the cold, agraw. An' the awful night.'

'Hello Willie,' he called from the bed.

'Begob, yourself has the cosy spot,' said Willie, 'a night like this.'

'Is herself well?' asked Aunt Kate.

'Amn't I after tellin' you she is?' said Willie. 'But there's some kind of a Fair Day in Ballyboun tomorrow, an' she'll need your help. Could you go up tonight?'

'Indeed I could. Whose horse have you? Come—' She went to the door with Willie in her nightdress. He got out of bed and grabbed his trousers. He could hear them whispering. It was as though God had sent him. What was in me at all? They came in the door. 'I must dress,' she said. 'Get yourself soda-bread an' milk, Willie.'

She looked pale when she was ready to go. 'Don't forget the cow, agraw,' she said. 'Be careful with the fire an' the lamp. Don't throw oil from the can on the fire. Can ye look after yeerselves?'

'Why wouldn't we?' said Willie. 'But go easy with the horse—that's not the old ass, but Cavan's mare.'

They went to the door together. 'If anyone asks for me,' she said, 'say your mother had a fall, God save us, an' cracked her ankle.' She pulled her shawl close over her face and got up in the car. 'Easy now with her,' said Willie.

'Godspeed, Aunt Kate,' he whispered.

'God an' his holy Mother watch over ye till I'm back,' she said.

'Good luck, Kate,' said Willie.

She gave a jerk of the reins and went off into the darkness. They watched till all sound of her had gone. 'I'll be in in a minute, Willie,' he said. He walked to the side of the house, and was glad of the coldness of the ground under his warm feet. He began to make water, looking up at the vast silent sky as he did so. His body was eased and he went in.

'Mother sent you sweets,' said Willie, putting a bag of sugar candy on the table.

'Thanks,' he said, going over to the low fire and putting some small pieces of dry turf on it. Willie took a packet of cigarettes from his pocket and lit one. 'Now don't ever breathe a word of what I'm goin' to tell you,' he said. 'D'you remember the day you came down here—when I was mad at you? It was because mother was goin' to have a child, an' I was afraid you'd hurt her. Well, this mornin' mother had the child, above in the room with Maney Shawn O'Halloran. God's will, but the innocent babe lived but the one hour. A girl it was, God rest her soul. Jamesey baptised her.' Willie knelt before the turf and began to blow into it, until a flame appeared. 'It would have been a power of expense to have sent for the priest, because that would have meant a grave to be opened and a funeral take place. So never breathe a word I'm tellin' now—but Jamesey made the little coffin from a box. An' that's why I came for Aunt Kate, because tonight they'll bury her.'

He didn't speak. 'On the hill of Cloongarl,' said Willie, 'is where they'll bury her—on the top there where the stones are, that they call the Fort of the Innocents. It was there long ago they buried nearly all young children that died, but now it's against the law. So don't ever say a word. Nor would

26

mother like to know I'd told you. Jamesey will say the last words, God rest the soul of the child—an' no mention of it will ever be made again, an' no sign of it known, but that a piece of a rock will be put there amongst the others.'

Willie went over to the bucket with a mug and took water from it. 'Take one good draw out of that cigarette, m'boy,' he said, 'an' you'll feel the better of it. Maybe if the fire burns we could make ourselves tea.'

'You don't know, Willie,' he said, 'when I'd be goin' home to mother?'

'Please God,' said he, ''twill be tomorrow. After milkin' the cow we'll go up home in the ass-cart. An' let me tell you another thing whilst I'm at it—we'll soon be off to England. Uncle John an' the old man have a house for us. Mother hates to go, I know, but maybe this day week we'd be off. Of course it's a great secret altogether. Do you think if I put a taste of water in the saucepan it might boil? We'll be here till Christmas waiting for that kettle.'

For a long time that night he lay awake in the hag besides Willie. Everyone belonging him had had innocence in them—the mother, the child, Willie, Jamesey, Aunt Kate an' even the father across in England—but in his heart and soul had been evil. Now the funeral party would be climbing dark Cloongarl secretly, on Jamesey's shoulder the coffin made by his own one hand and inside it the small white unbreathing body. The souls of many others might be there to meet her, the souls of the only pure and sinless ones of this world, it was said, the ones that died in infancy, fortified by Holy Baptism. Better his own sinful body were being laid down into the hole now dug, than that his soul should perish eternally in mortal sin.

Turning down the little finger of his right hand be began the rosary—maybe after that I can make a good act of contrition—'Our Father Who art in heaven . . .'

CHAPTER FOUR

Going over to England

THAT LAST LOOK of Aunt Kate there on the platform had been upsetting and he wiped his eyes, and gave back a smile to a man in a brown Franciscan robe who sat in the corner of the compartment. All I said and did up to that last look had been false, he thought, but the forsaken look of her there at the end of the platform caught me unawares. He turned to the window. A woman milking a cow out in a field gave him a nod of her head. Two old men were talking by the side of the road, and a young lad was going off with the ass to the bog. Already that life seemed gone for ever. Travel enlarges a man's mind, Cavan had said. Travel leaves a man without a steam of sense, old Duffy had said, for I never knew a right man yet that wasn't his entire life in the one place.

That's curious now, how each little town presents itself and its name at the station : BALLYMOE, DONAMON. Always someone saying goodbye and always someone with tears. He looked at his mother, sitting upright, her hands on her lap and her head down a little, and the red eyes. Willie looking out the far window. He was ashamed of them both in some way before the Franciscan. That man is sure of heaven, that's a great thing to have in this life. At Athlone a man and woman left the compartment, and the mother took out buttered soda-cake from a bag. He was ashamed to see the familiar look of her cake in the strange place, and he felt very uncomfortable when she offered a piece to the holy man. To his surprise the man took it and ate it in three large bites, and took another piece after it, as though he were sitting down at his own table. Then he dipped into the folds of his habit and brought out a cigarette : ' Many a one, ma'am,' he said, ' would think I was an awful bad man to smoke. But

28

it was only after that bite of food that I'd do it. I was at home for a month an' now I'm goin' back to Dublin.'

He helped them out with their cases at Westland Row Station, and the mother refused every offer from porters until she found an elderly one with a white moustache. 'Did you ever hear of Patrick Waldron from Ballyboun,' said Willie, 'let a Dublin jackeen take up his two cases when he was over from America on a visit, an' that was the last he ever saw of man or cases?'

Amidst all the bustle and shouting of the city, he got one clear picture that stuck in his mind. It was when looking down on to the street below from the station he saw a horse. It was an old horse, standing in a pair of long shafts of a horse-car, with a tattered harness on it that had straw sticking round the collar. Its bones stuck out in sore humps on its back, and its head was sunk before it. Of all the starved and beaten horses he had seen in Mayo, never had he seen one with such utter resignation, waiting haggardly for death. Unexpectedly it raised its head, and from behind the blinkers sent him one naked look from its old large eye. *But it has the look of Jesus Christ*! came the frightened thought to him. At that moment a dirty little man jumped up on his seat, gave a fierce shout and raised his whip. Then he turned away from the window and saw no more of the street.

They were near the last on the boat at Kingstown, for the mother wouldn't join in the scramble. They were standing round their luggage in the crowded steerage, when an English soldier came forward. 'Lady,' he said, 'you ken hev me seat.'

'Thank you very much, sir,' she said, 'but I wouldn't want to take the seat from you.'

'Lady, you ken hev it with the greatest of pleasure,' he said. 'I'd hardly be usin' it myself in any case.' He was a short man with a tight belt round his middle. 'I'll give you a hand with them cases too. Come on, lads, up an' doin'.' He made a place for them and insisted on putting his topcoat against the back of the seat for the mother. 'You're favourite there, lady,' he said, ' for once we get movin' it's my bet there'll be no peace against the rail.' He opened a large packet of cigarettes and took out a silk-faced cigarette card. 'Which of you lads collects them ones?' he asked.

'Him,' said Willie.

'Thank you, sir,' he said.

'What's on you?' said the mother. 'Is something hurtin' you?'

'No, no, no,' he said, 'nothin' at all.'

'Did you do anythin' since we left home?' she whispered.

'I'm right,' he said.

'Lady,' said the soldier, 'I'll take him. Cemmon, son.'

The soldier took his hand in a fatherly way and led him off to the urinal. He stood for a minute or two with knees bent before the grey stall.

'Finished, son?' asked the soldier.

'Yes, sir,' he said, fastening his trousers.

'Can't you straighten up properly?' asked the soldier.

He's one of our enemies, he thought, but he's a nice man. 'I have a pain,' he confessed. 'I don't think I did anythin'. It's a long time since I did anything'.' If only I could stand beside a bush at home by the road!

'Hev another try,' said the soldier, 'an' I'll whistle.'

The soldier whistled and he tried to pee again but couldn't. An old man was fastening his trousers and he said to the soldier: 'What's up with the lad?'

'He's bin holdin' it that long,' said the soldier, 'till now it won't come at all. Whistlin' usually works with army horses.'

'Very dangerous,' said the old man,' 'very dangerous. He ought to see the ship's doctor.'

At that he burst out crying with fear, and in a few seconds the slow jerky stream of urine began. The soldier grinned, and as more came the boy thought the old man rather foolish. Then he heard his mother calling from outside: 'Are you well, agraw?' He felt ashamed of the sound of her voice.

'Don't go out yet,' said the soldier. 'You have a right good 'un. I'll go an' tell your ma.' All trouble gone, he thought when it was over. It's queer how all about there causes me so much worry, front and back.

When he went outside his mother was waiting. 'Is there anythin' wrong?' she asked.

'No, no,' he said, 'an' don't be makin' a holy show of yourself in front of everybody.'

'I'll look after him, lady,' said the soldier. 'We're just sailin'.' He went off with the soldier who turned to him as soon as the mother was gone. 'I'll tell you one thing, son,' he said, 'you ought to show more respect to your mother. If I'd talked like that to my mother, why, she'd have knocked me dahn with a swipe. Serve me right too.'

'I'm sorry,' he said. It was odd to think the soldier had a mother.

'Let's look back at old Ireland,' said the soldier, 'as we leave.'

That's a strange thing for an Englishman to say, he thought. 'I'll call my brother,' he said. 'Willie!' But Willie and the mother were already coming over near the rail. She looked tall and strange in her Galway shawl. The land slipped away, with many people waving from the harbour. He held the mother's hand as he saw tears on her cheeks. He looked down at the sea, its grey-green depth murmuring and sighing as the ship grunted its way through it. If I were to fling myself into it now it would suck me down into its stomach, and the most important man aboard would be powerless against the sea, once it puts its claim on a body. The soul itself would go to heaven, for even the sea must move at God's bidding, and it cannot hold the soul, that at the full touch of death must fly at once to the judgment seat of God. Well, there you are. And that's a queer hard salty breeze you get, too.

The soldier looked after them during the crossing, and took charge of their luggage at Holyhead. 'I'm afraid you've got to take the Manchester train, an' mine's the London, lady,' he said. He shook hands with her and the two boys. Then they watched him walk stiffly off along the platform.

'I never met such pure decency in all my life,' said the

31

mother. Then she paused: 'But maybe ye'd be as well not to mention him at all to your father.' They both nodded without asking any question. In his pocket he felt the edge of the cigarette card, and the thought crossed his mind that this would be the only memory of the decent English soldier.

It was dawn when he woke up in the railway carriage. He looked out and saw a mass of rows of dark houses, and high factory buildings with brightly-lit windows.

'Did you see all the houses, Willie?' he asked.

'I did. Sure the place must be paved-out with people. We've only another few minutes now, the next stop is ours.'

'Try will you both look your best now,' said the mother, wiping her face with a handkerchief and patting her hair and smiling. 'Have yeer shoulders back, an' speak up if anyone says anything to you.'

His heart was beating fast as the train slowed down and a big sign appeared on the platform: TOWLTON. 'The luggage—see that we'd get all our luggage,' said the mother. 'Careful now, wait till it stops.' They got out quickly. 'Go an' get the trunk at the van.'

He and Willie ran back to the van. 'The green one, sir, that's ours.'

'Aw reet, me old cocksparrows,' said the man, 'more haste less speed. It's Tow't'n yu' want, eh?' They nodded and dragged the trunk along the platform. The mother was watching the wide steps that led down to the platform.

'Here they are now!' she exclaimed. 'Smarten up.'

He saw two men hurrying down the steps, one wearing a new cap. He couldn't make out who was the man with the new cap, but there was something familiar about him. 'Kiss him an' greet him,' whispered the mother, 'an' take care would ye be cool.' As the man came striding along the platform he knew by the swing of the arms that it must be his father, for they stuck out almost level with his shoulders. But the red face was now pale and had a mildly stupefied look on it. He ran straight to the mother and grasped her hand and spoke in an excited voice:

'Oh welcome to England, ma'am.'

He looked ashamed as she lent forward and gave him a kiss on the cheek. He didn't let go of her hand, but kept shaking it, and tears were in his eyes. Then the other man, a taller man with a moustache, slowly came round.

'Arra John!' cried the woman, putting her arms round his neck. He gave her a hugging, and the father seemed relieved, and turned to the two boys.

'Willie'een,' he said, holding out his hand, 'how are ye, Willie'een?' Then to the younger one: 'Mickyeen, ye have a new pair of shoes. What did yeer mother pay for them?' They each kissed the father.

'Well God save us,' said the father, as they stood round looking at each other, 'the train was in great time. None better. A quarter past seven it was to be in an' damn me but a quarter past seven it was in. Isn't that a great thing now—a train comin' all the way here from Holyhead. A thing like that could never happen in Ireland in a hundred years. But the fool of a ticket-collector sent us to the wrong platform—we was here twenty minutes ago.'

'Well, Delia,' said Uncle John, 'that beats all ever I knew —younger every time I see you. Tell me, could this be Willie? Well, Willie, I've nothin' to say—you're a man altogether. A man altogether. An' this Mickyeen, well God help me but I wouldn't know you—an' you this high the last time I had you on my knee. Well, well, well, that beats all ever I went through.'

'The train was in great time,' said the father. 'Isn't this a wonderful station now! Did ye ever see the likes of it?'

'An' what do you say to himself?' said Uncle John. 'Didn't England make a man of him?'

'I never saw him better, thanks be to God,' said the mother, 'but maybe a taste thinner in the face.'

'Och, sure like a fat young bonner he was when he came,' said Uncle John, 'but the pit took the paunch off him. Down at the coalface.'

'The divil roast the coalface,' said the father. 'Urra why are we standin' here? Did ye have a good crossin', Willie'een?'

'Middlin' good,' said Willie.

He felt the cigarette card in his pocket. I mustn't mention him. They walked up the steps and out of the station, carrying the luggage amongst them. 'Tell me,' said the father, 'how's Jamesey?' All the fresh-skinned roundness had left his face and there was this paler, stronger look on it.

'He's distracted altogether since you went,' said the mother. 'He'd hardly take a drink.'

'Is it Jamesey, the poor ould creature,' said the father softly, 'wouldn't take a drink? Musha the changes comin' over the world. That train was on exact time, John. He had to take a playday to come an' meet you—he should be at his work.'

'Troth an' I'd expect no less from him,' said the mother.

'Indeed no,' said John, 'for my own sister I hadn't seen this five years.'

'Woman, this is not Ireland,' said the father. 'If all ever belongin' you was comin' at the one go they'd expect you at work. If that man drivin' the engine went to school with you he wouldn't have time to shake your hand when that whistle blew—not like Ireland where he'd leave the train go to pot an' go off an' get drunk with you.'

They went out of the station and came to the town before them. He gave a shiver as the hard breeze struck his legs, and he wondered at the solid pavement under his feet. That would never know the touch of any foot going over it. People were thronging the streets in the grey light, men and women, young boys and girls, moving with a determination he'd never seen before, and with a speed that astonished him. A constant clatter of hard sounds went with all this ordered activity, and after it puzzling him for a moment he saw it came from the clogs they wore. The party crossed a wide street, and as they did so a tram clanged round the corner. People jumped off it before it halted, and they raced along the street to catch another tram. He saw three men lift something off the tram and put it down on the pavement. As he drew near he saw it was a legless man, perched on a wooden trolley with four small iron wheels.

34

'Run for it, chaps,' he shouted as they put him down. And he put a hand to the pavement and pushed himself off, moving rapidly amongst the stream of people, and propelling himself off. He watched the man speed along, going after the tram that had set off downhill. Seeing the tram was going too fast the man stopped. Then the tram stopped and the men from the platform called out: 'Come on, Leslie, he's waitin'.' At once the crippled man went after the tram, and was lifted aboard with good-natured greetings.

'Mickyeen!' shouted the father. 'Where the hell are you? Don't get lost amongst the crowds.' He led the way to a tram. 'This is ours now.'

'Stick your luggage up front,' said the conductor, 'we're off in a couple of minutes.

'Every damn thing goes to time here,' said the father.

They were putting the luggage on the front platform when the driver came. 'It's not a blinkin' flittin' van,' he said.

'Arra what's on you?' said the father. 'You've not a finger to lay on it, an' it's keepin' you warm.'

'Aye, but it goes on at my discretion,' said the driver, 'an' don't you forget it.'

'Every flamin' gloggera you meet in this country,' said the father, 'is some kind of a boss. On the verth of me oath, if he spoke to me like that in Ireland I'd have felled the rogue with a blow of me fist.'

The conductor came for the fares. 'Tak' no notice of my mate,' he said, 'his wife's just left him. Gone back to her husband.'

As the tram went on the father pointed out shops. 'Did you ever see such glorious meat in all your life? An' the butcher shops so clean over here you could eat your dinner off the floor. I'm tellin' ye no lie. It isn't the kind of beef ye'd get at Ned Carney's.'

'Och, the poor ould beast Ned would be killin',' said Uncle John, 'could hardly stand up on its four legs, an' would need only the sharp word to end it.'

It was a short ride on the tram, and then the driver helped them down with the luggage. 'You needn't have bothered,' he said, accepting coppers from Uncle John, 'but ta all the same.'

They made their way through narrow streets until they came to two long rows of cottages, facing each other across a sloping street. 'This is our street now,' said the father, 'an' number thirty-two is the house.'

'Aren't them great two-storied houses,' said Willie.

They stopped and the father took a key from his pocket and began to turn. 'Go easy,' said Uncle John, 'for fear you'd break it in the lock.'

'If that cross-eyed scut of a landlord gave me the wrong key—' began the father. 'Ah there we are, I was wrongin' the poor decent man.'

When the door was opened he smiled at the mother. 'Go in first yourself,' he said.

'Thank you, sir,' said the woman, blessing herself as she crossed the threshold.

'In ye go,' he said to the boys, 'an' take care have ye clauber on yeer shoes.'

He followed his brother Willie and looked shyly round the new house. The first thing he felt was the evenness of the floor, a thing unknown to him. Also, there was a smooth covering of floorcloth on it. He heard his mother say: 'Musha this is a palace altogether!' and it seemed so to him. 'Wait yet a minute till I show you,' said the father, striking a match and lighting a thumb-like mantle hanging on a brass holder from the ceiling. There was a *pop*, and at once a very bright light burst on the room. He looked around and saw a large oval looking-glass over the fireplace, and opposite on a chest of drawers was another, and the white gaslight in the centre of the room reflected in the mirrors, so that it seemed there was not one but many rooms, with people in each. On the table was a yellow cloth with a peacock fashioned in the middle. There were six new wooden varnished chairs, and a sofa made of black sheeny stuff. Even the wall had paper on it, with green stripes and red roses all over. There were six holy pictures about the room.

He heard the cork being drawn from a bottle, and the

next thing Uncle John was handing out glasses of whisky. The impact of all the splendour in one room had dazed him, and when he came to take a sip from the mother's glass it set him off coughing.

'Is it whisky yeer givin' the children?' said the father.

'Sure hadn't they to drink the blessin' of the house,' said the mother, 'no more than ourselves?'

'Hadn't yourself many the glass at their age,' said Uncle John.

'I never touched a drop till I was thirteen years of age,' said the father. He looked up at his glass: 'Musha, if that's a ghost, may it appear often!' And he let out a hoarse loud laugh, his mouth wide open.

'That was old Matty Lucas's word, God rest his soul in heaven this mornin'. "If that's a ghost," he'd say, "may it appear often." Poor old Matty, the only one ever he was bad to was himself.'

Then he removed the new cap for the first time, rubbed his head and said: 'Shovin' the tubs down pit has the hair flattened on me.' The boy could have laughed to see the way his father's hair was no longer wild and bushy.

'Then it did more than oil an' brush would,' said the mother affectionately.

'I want a drink of water,' said the boy.

'Here then, I'll show you,' said the father, leading him into the kitchen. He turned the tap and a spout of water shot out.

'Where's the well, father?'

'A hundred an' fifty miles from here,' said the father, 'that's where the well is. Everythin' here comes in pipes.'

He had a drink.

'Could I wash?' he asked.

'Wash away,' said the father. 'There's the bowl.'

He turned the tap carefully. They'd go mad at home if they saw the likes of this. He washed and dried himself on the towel behind the door. Then he picked up the bowl of water and went running through the house and flung it out on to the street. As the water left the bowl he caught sight of a woman. She gave a cry and darted backwards—the water missed her but wet a dog.

' I beg your pardon, ma'am,' he said.

The woman smiled and he found the father dragging him back into the house. 'Have you no sense at all?' cried the man. 'What did you do that for?'

'To clean the bowl,' he said.

'That goes down the slopstone,' said the man, 'an' is carried away in a pipe.'

'Musha, the sight of that's worth a shilling,' said Uncle John, dipping into his pocket.

The boy began to cry. 'I hate the ugly ould house,' he said, 'an' the ugly ould pipes everywhere.' Then the mother took him by the hand and he went with her upstairs. He felt ashamed of his mistake. I'll never be able to show my face in the street, he thought.

CHAPTER FIVE

A Lancashire Lad

FALLING IN AMONGST HIS DREAMS were strange sounds, loud and yet distant, held off by a coating of sleep, but growing louder it seemed, until he woke up and felt them seemingly thudding within the room. Awake, with closed eyes, he waited for the clanging din to cease, and when it didn't he prayed hard and opened his eyes. Before him was a large square of light and a high black cross set within it, and behind it in the sky there was a bright red glow, and the incessant heavy hammering sounding all the time. I'm dead an' where am I? Am I drownded on the sea? Oh let it be purgatory, sweet blessed Virgin Mary.

A shape was next to him in bed: Willie!—the journey—the soldier—the new house—the water in the street. He looked again at the black cross. There was no outline of Christ on it. Was it some kind of window? What was the red fire in the sky? What was the din? 'Willie!' he whispered.

'Eh? hah? what's on you?'

'Willie, what's all the noises?'

'Is it only now you're after hearin' them? They come from some foundry, so Uncle John said, that does be workin' day an' night, hammerin' out bridges to send all over the world.'

'An the flame in the sky?'

'Is from the furnace.'

God cures all fears if you wait. Hail Mary fullagrace.

'What time would it be?'

'Long after midnight, man.'

'Why didn't someone wake me?'

'Wake you, is it? You was asleep since eight this mornin,' an' such a gatherin' in the house, but divil a wake.'

'I know one thing, I'm splittin' with the hunger.'

'Isn't it quick you're tune changed?' Willie struck a match and lit a candle. 'I'll have to take a few draws now to calm me down,' he said, 'now you have me wakened.'

There was a soft tap at the door and in came the mother in her nightdress: 'Is it awake you are finally?' she asked.

'I'm hungry,' he said.

She came over and kissed him and he couldn't resist the warm smell. 'I'll be up in a minute,' she said.

That's odd how a woman can be so kind, he thought as he heard her soft footsteps on the stairs. It must be their nature.

'D'you hear the ould fella snorin'?' said Willie. 'Musn't it be an awful penance altogether for anyone to listen to that all the nights of their life?'

The door opened. 'Did you see a ghost?' asked Willie.

'Seventy-nine thousand,' said the mother, handing the younger son a hunk of bread and cup of milk. 'I hadn't time to butter it. Cockroaches, the floor was thick with them, but I couldn't make it out till I heard all the crackling under me. They was like an army across the floor.'

'Is that so?' asked Willie.

'Sure I'm only goin' on,' she said.

'I hate you,' he said, 'you have me put off my food.'

'Musha, what's on your nightgown?' asked Willie.

'Oh God save us!' she cried.

'Amn't I only goin' on?' he said.

'The divil shoot you,' she said, 'for knockin' that start out of me.'

They all laughed.

'Urra what's goin' on there this hour of the night?' came the fierce whisper from the next room. 'Is it savages ye are that never saw anything?'

She winked at the boys. 'Mickyeen felt sick,' she said, 'an' I went down for water.' She kissed them both, he drank his milk off, then she blew out the candle and went off. He lay there beside his brother in the darkness, chewing the dry bread and looking out at the red sky.

He stood in the privy closet, holding the door open with his foot. The large wooden seat was before him, and he looked with distaste at the hole in the middle. The hundreds of them that must have sat on that. Well, nothing for it but sit on it sometime or other—this is the third day I've dodged it. I'll kill myself if I'm not careful. If I laid a piece of newspaper across the front of the seat it might not be too bad. At least it would be better. It's a rotten life this. All the miles of bushes back home where you could get down and enjoy it. He unfastened his new braces and sat on the edge of the seat, holding the door with his hand, for he couldn't bear the dark, confined smell. No use. Maybe I could if I squatted on the seat. I hope no one comes. He looked down into the round hole and saw in the darkness the two-handled pail. An awful job the men have emptying those. I suppose if it came to it those are the men would go to heaven. They make greater penance than any saint. Ah thank God. I feel better anyway. I hate all the smells round that house. That awful smell of the gas would make a horse sick to its stomach. I hate the smell of the oilcloth too. There's no nice turf smell anywhere. And no smell of limewash. The walls have a queer smell here. I hate strange smells. I did a bit. I hate the thought of going out in the street. The Irish clothes look so queer on us, an' our voices so different from theirs. Willie doesn't seem to mind anything. I'm sensitive. I often heard mother say that about me, an' it's true, I'm very sensitive. He wiped himself, fastened his braces, removed the paper from the seat, and went out into the backyard.

The mother was at the backdoor. 'Come an' help me make the beds, like a good man,' she said. He hurried upstairs after her. She stripped the bed in the back room and every time she flung the sheet he made a grab and missed. 'Erra is it a man or monkey ye are?' she cried. 'Grab the sheet now.' And again he missed and laughed out loud. Then she had a wrestle with him and put him back on the bed. 'You're an awful strong woman, yu' know, mother,' he said.

She put her hands on her hips and smiled. 'A finer looking woman never left Ireland than myself at eighteen,' she said.

'An' wasn't I twice as good when I returned a Yank nine years later.'

'An' you married an ould snitchahaun like himself below,' he said.

'Och, sure I must have been out of my mind altogether,' she said, 'though he was a handsome man himself in them days. Look out at the tinker.'

A man was shoving a handcart loaded with old rags and rubbing stones along the back street, wailing: 'Ee, ragabone, ee, ragabone.' He passed under a lineful of washing that was hanging across the back street, turned and gave his long cry, and quickly grabbed a shirt that was fluttering, and stuck it under the rags. 'Ee, ragabone,' he moaned, 'ee, ragabone.'

'That flamer has someone's shirt stolen,' said the mother.

Then a boy of twelve or so, small and wizened, wearing long trousers, hurried out from a nearby back yard into the back street, carrying an enamel bowl heaped with washing, and holding in his mouth a number of wooden pegs. He moved very quickly, hurrying across the back street with a piece of rope, and hanging out another line. Then he noticed the vacant place where the shirt had been. For a moment he looked mystified. Then he looked at the ragman. The mother lifted the window. 'Sonny,' she called, 'he took your blue shirt from the line.'

'Ta, missis, ta,' he said, and at once he went running after the man. 'Wut about that shirt?' he yelled.

'Wut shirt?' called the man.

'That 'un tha pinched off my line,' said the lad.

'I'll punce thee in ribbons if tha dares say I've pinched thy shirt,' said the man.

'You did,' called the mother, 'I saw you.'

'I'm havin' that shirt back,' said the lad, 'if I've to follow thee to the ends of the earth.'

The man flung the shirt on to the ground. 'It were on t'floor when I picked it up,' he said, wheeling off. The lad picked it up. 'Thanks, missis,' he called. 'I'll hatta rinse it again, the dirty tyke.'

'The Lord give strength to your limbs, agraw,' said the mother, putting down the window. 'Did you see that one, Mickyeen, with the line of clothes out, an' him not twelve years of age? Musha it does the heart good to see that spirit —you wouldn't see that in a hundred years at home, for all their goin' on.'

'Will it take ye all day to make a couple of beds?' came the father's shout up the stairs. 'I'm killed with the thirst— come down an' make tea.'

He remained upstairs until the father had gone out, and then the mother gave him a call. He went down and stood with his back to the fire until he got the seat of his trousers very warm, and then he sat down quickly on a chair. Willie came in with a steaming paperful of sliced potatoes. 'Chips, they're lovely, taste,' he said.

'The smell's enough for me,' he said. When they were nearly all gone he tried one and it was delicious. 'Come on,' said Willie, 'I'll show you where you can buy them. You get a paperful for tuppence.'

The next morning when all the workers were in the factories and the older children at school, he went for the first time alone into the street. The gable-end wall at the street corner had a friendly shiny look to it, and he stood there. The boy he had seen hanging out the washing came along with a basket.

'How're you likin' it over here?' he asked.

'Oh well, well, thanks.'

'Best country in the world,' said the boy, 'bar none.'

A woman stopped. 'How's your mam, Herbert?' she asked.

'Comin' on like a house afire,' he said, 'barrin' her varicose veins. They were up like knots of bandin' on her legs last night, but they've gone down a bit this mornin'. Han' you seen the babby?'

'Aye, he's a little gem,' said the woman.

'He sleeps through the night without a scrike,' said the boy.

'Tell your mam I was askin' about her, cock.'

'Aye, I will, Missis Hurst.' He turned and said: 'I'm goin'
to Daddy Enty's for some spuds. Comin'?'

He nodded and hurried off beside him. 'We've just had a
babby,' said the boy, 'four days old. My name's Herbert,
what's thine?'

'Mick or Michael,' he said.

'Michael,' said the other, 'allus stick to the name tha was
christened by.' Herbert led the way along a back street. 'I
daren't go up front streets,' he said, 'or else I might bang
into the school board. Aspinall, an ugly blighter in a billycock an' black overcoat. Keep thy eyes skinned for him,
Michael. He needs more watchin' than a bag o' fleas. Says
me mam should keep our Maggie off her work an' send me to
schoo'—aye, an' lose fifteen bob a week in the bargain.'

On one side of the back street was a low building. Herbert stopped at a window protected by a close grating.
'Ropewalk,' he said, 'look in.' At first he could make out
only a dark atmosphere and a whirring sound. Then he saw
lengths of string and rope, and the figures of youths and
girls, running up and down and calling out in shrill voices.
'The stink's the tallow,' said Herbert. 'They're greasin'
ropes an' bandin' so they'll last longer. Anybody who works
there tha can smell a mile away.'

At the greengrocer's Herbert bought two and a half pounds
of potatoes. 'Can you let me have two ha'penny carrots?' he
asked. He gave one to him. 'I luv a carrot I do,' said Herbert.
'They say there's all the good in the world in a carrot.'

Again they went down a back street. 'Let's have a game
of footer,' said Herbert. His sharp-toed clog kicked open a
fastener on one of the wooden ashpit doors, revealing a
square tub overflowing with ashes. He rummaged amongst
them. 'Keep clear,' he said, 'tha might catch fever. I've had
it. No can there.' He carefully closed the door again. 'Allus
leave things as tha finds 'um. " I shall pass this way but once,
any good turn I shall do let me do it, for I will not get a
second chance ".'. He looked at him with his two large serious
eyes, standing out oddly on his bony face: 'That's in the
Bible, Michael,' he added.

44

He opened another ashpit door and found a can. 'Look in folk's middens,' he said, 'an' tha can tell if they're gradely fed. They don't go short of tinned salmon here. Very nice too, a bit of John West's silverside.' He carefully closed the door. Then he darted forward, throwing the can into the air, and neatly trapping it with his toe as it fell. Then he began to dribble round the other boy. The serious look vanished, and Herbert danced around, his face flushed and happy, and his light thin legs hopping round with sprightly lightness.

'I wish I'd a ha'penny to spare, Michael,' he said. 'I'd buy a pig's bladder an' we could have a good game.'

'I have money,' he said eagerly.

'Tha never knows when tha'll need it,' said Herbert. But seeing the coppers and a sixpence he agreed to allow the other buy a pig's bladder. 'We'll dribble our way along to the slaughterhouse,' he said. He led the way through a maze of back streets, swinging the basket and kicking the empty can, until they came to the slaughterhouse. It had one gate that opened on wheels, and the pavement outside was stained with greasy blood. As they reached it a cow came galloping round the back street corner, followed by a man and boy with sticks.

'Get clear o' them bloody gates,' shouted the man. Herbert caught his sleeve and pulled him against the wall. The cow was in a sweat, and as the man and boy struck their sticks against the wall and yelled out it raced away in terror. Then the gate opened and the animal made for the far end of the back street.

'Poor thing,' said Herbert, 'it can smell the blood.' A third figure now appeared at the far end of the back street, and a stick was waved and the cow turned again. Before it were the man and boy, it turned and there was the wide gate, and it spun round, but there was a single figure rushing at it with a stick. The two boys pressed back against the wall as it went lunging past—some curious smell of fear about it that seemed to frighten them. It hesitated and the three of them fell upon it with sticks and cries, and finally

45

it was driven through the gate. There was a grating of wheels and the gate closed.

'I've a good mind to report 'um,' said Herbert, 'there's no need for all that cloutin'.' He wiped his nose. 'Anyway, I'll go an' see can we get us a bladder.'

He came back with a bladder, a mottled slippery skin, flecked with blood and slime. Herbert spat on the vent, pulled it between his fingers to clean it, put it to his lips and blew it up. 'Yu' sometimes get 'um punctured,' he said, 'but this 'un is champion.' He got a piece of string from his pocket and tied the bladder. 'Come on, Michael,' he called, kicking it into the air, 'one for Wigan.' Herbert played with extraordinary skill, and could handle the oval-shaped bladder with ease. Suddenly, in the midst of the play, there sounded a buzzer.

'Holy Moses!' cried Herbert, 'don't say that's the twelve o'clock buzzer.' He asked the time at once from a passer-by. 'I'll get laid out,' he said. 'Come on, Michael, I've kids' dinner to get.' Now his boyish delight was gone, and he ran along swiftly, his head down and his shoulders hunched, muttering: 'I don't know what came o'er me.'

'I'll see you again, Herbert,' he said at the street corner.

'Come in wi' me,' said Herbert, 'an' it won't look so bad.'

He went along with Herbert, up the back street and in the back gate. As they entered the kitchen a woman's voice called out: 'Is that thee?'

'Aye, mam,' said Herbert, 'An' I've got one of the Irish lads wi' me. He wanted to see our babby.'

'Aahe, lad,' the voice sighed, 'tha's been a long time.'

Herbert put his thumbs up as they went through the kitchen and into the living-room. He smelt the family smell in full, and there was also a smell of woman and child. A woman was sitting up in a brass-railed bed, with her thick yellow-grey hair hanging down, and she was wearing a man's flannel shirt.

'Where the heck han' you been?' she said. Then she seemed to smother her temper and she smiled at the visitor. 'His name's Michael,' said Herbert.

A small boy who had been standing at the bottom of the bed gazing through the rails came round. 'I want a sugar butty, Herber',' he said.

'All right, love, all right,' said Herbert. 'I'll give our George a butty, mam, an' I'll make some scollops for dinner.'

'They'll be in fru' schoo' now any minute,' said the mother. 'Ee, you do worrit me.'

'Now what about your allowance, mam?'

'We can't afford it,' she said.

'You're havin' your allowance,' said Herbert, 'or else your milk'll go back an' you winnot be able to feed him. It'll cost more in the long run.' He beckoned Michael, pulled back the sheet and cooed down at a small baby: 'Isn' he pratty!'

'He is, God bless him,' he said.

'I want a sugar butty,' said the boy.

'Hearken our George!'

'Blast thee an' thy sugar butties,' said the mother. 'He's eternal askin' for sugar butties.'

'Michael, cut him a sugar butty,' said Herbert, 'there's a lad. Bread, maggyann an' sugar are all on t'table.' He reached up to the mantelpiece and took some coppers from under a fringed curtain. 'I'm off,' he said. 'Be peelin' a spud or two, Michael, whilst I'm away, there's a good lad.' When Herbert had gone he stood there feeling helpless, and then he felt the small boy's hand in his, tugging him towards the table: 'I want a sugar butty,' said the boy.

He picked up the bread and the knife, and holding the loaf against him he cut off a thick piece. He opened the margarine paper and scraped some off and put it on the bread. 'Sugar,' said George, watching him. He dipped a spoon into the blue bag of sugar and shook it over the bread. 'Ta,' said George. Taking the bread with one hand, George then took his hand with the other, and clung to it as he ate, looking up and smiling now and again. The mother was lying back on her pillow staring up at the ceiling. The front door opened and two small girls came in. They stared at him and then edged towards the bed. Then in came Herbert carrying a jug.

'Is dinner not ready?' the girls asked him.

'A bare gill,' said Herbert, pouring stout from the jug into a mug. 'Skinny beggar.' He handed the mug to his mother and held the jug up, letting the froth fall to his own lips. The mother took a sup of the stout, put down the mug, and picked up the child. She opened the flannel shirt at the front and he felt a shock at the sudden appearance of a large pap. The infant gasped, and with a fierce intake of breath searched for the big well-sucked nipple. At once his panic ceased and all that was heard was a sucking, muffled and ravenous. The mother sighed and rested back. 'Is our dinner not ready yet?' asked the girls, glaring at the mother and child, and then looking at Herbert.

'I'm doin' yu' some Scotch collops,' said Herbert. 'Sum'dy put a penny in the gas. Michael, hast' peeled spuds yet?' He hurried into the kitchen with Herbert, his mind full of the sight of the woman's big breast. Herbert put a frying-pan on the gas ring and handed him a potato to peel. He took up a knife and began to peel. Herbert touched him on the shoulder. 'Lay the table afresh, Michael,' he said, 'there'll be no spud left by the time tha's peeled it.'

He went into the living-room and was in time to see her move the baby from one breast to the other. For a moment she held the infant and grinned at him, ignoring the open flannel shirt and the loose sucked pap. He stared at it, and flushed as he found she was looking at him. Temptation everywhere. 'Where are the cups an' saucers, ma'am?' he asked.

'In t'cupboard, love,' she said.

It was hard to turn away and get them. From the kitchen came the smoky smell of burning fat. 'It'll soon be ready,' shouted Herbert. 'There's some for thee, Michael.' The two girls stared at him. 'I think I'll be goin',' he said.

'Nay, stay,' said the mother.

Eyes round the table watched every move as Herbert served the meal. A slice of jelly-like meat was given to each child, and with it three fritters of potato. Each odour touched him, from hot fat to stewed tea, and the sickly sweet odour of Nestlé's tinned milk as he raised the cup to his mouth. He strove to overcome a sickness of disgust at the strange smells and flavours, the grease-blobbed fritters, burnt and swollen, the gristle and jelly on the potted meat, the bread and margarine, and all the unfamiliar mixture of the Duckworth home and family, and he gulped the hot tea to quench the nausea rising in him. He sat on a broken-backed chair, the two girls shared a chair opposite, and the boy George stood beside him, offering his hand to be held between bites. No knives or forks were used, for the food was lifted neatly from the plates and placed on a slice of bread which was then folded in the middle and eaten from the hand. Herbert moved about and ate at the same time. 'Gas is goin'! Who did I tell to put a penny in t'meter? Where is it? Anybody seen t'matches?' He darted into the kitchen and back.

'Talkin' about matches,' he said, 'did yu'ever hear that tale, Michael, about the chap as were actin' as Moses on t'stage?'

He shook his head: 'No, Herbert, I didn't.'

'You're off again,' said the mother from the bed.

'Oh tell us, Herbert,' said one of the girls.

'For his act this chap had to have a young lad hidden up in t'loft over top of t'stage. He gave this lad a bob a week to set fire to a bundle of straw every night, so that when this chap as were Moses called out: "And God sent fire from heaven," this lad would drop the burnin' straw, just like it were a miracle. An' it worked champion all week till the second house Sat'day night, an' this chap as were Moses struck his wand an' shouted: "An' God sent fire down from heaven." He waited, nowt happened. He yelled it again, louder, nowt happened. So then he struck his wand third time, an' yelled at the top of his voice, "An' God sent fire down from heaven." An' the next thing the lad stuck his head through the hole in the loft an' said: "He can't. Cat's pissed on t'matches." '

He joined in the laugh, eager to cover up his uneasiness at the irreverence, and the shock of hearing Herbert use the bad word in the home. Then he laughed a little at the joke, thinking, it's a pity God comes into it that way, for I'll never dare tell it myself.

'Talkin' of houses,' said Herbert, 'I'll be goin' to the first house pictures tomorrow, all bein' well.'

'Tha's said it,' said his mother, '—all bein' well.'

'Aye, all bein' well,' said Herbert, 'I go every Thursday. Ask thy mam, Michael, can tha come wi' me. Tell her that Herbert Duckworth will look after thee—we'll be goin' to the Premier. It's William Farnum, an' I can guarantee a good night.'

'Herber',' said George, 'sing Pancake.'

Herbert lifted his head back, clasped his nose between thumb and forefinger, and began to strum his Adam's apple with the fingers of his other hand, singing at the same time:

> 'Yu' know last night, the night before,
> Two little nigger boys knocked on m'door,
> One with a drumstick, one with a drum,
> An' one with a pancake tied to his bum.'

George laughed and danced on his toes, repeating the last line. Then Herbert began to grab the cups and saucers and plates. 'Come on, our Victoria, come on, our Nellie,' he said, 'you're goin' to be late for schoo'. Help me side up the pots first, there's a couple of good girls.'

As he stood up with Herbert and the girls he looked across to the bed, half hoping he might get another sight of the woman's breast, but the child was asleep, the shirt fastened, and the mother staring up at the cracked ceiling.

CHAPTER SIX

Mrs Duckworth's Birthday Party

'I'VE A MIND,' said Willie, 'to go along with yourself an' Herbert to the pictures.'

'Musha, I'd feel easier in my mind if you did,' said the mother.

He felt uneasy at the thought of his brother seeing the inside of the Duckworth home. 'That 'ud be nice,' he said. 'Do come.'

'I will then,' said Willie. Isn't he thick somehow, that he wouldn't see from my manner I don't want him.

'Be back here before he goes off to work,' said the mother, 'since it's his first night.'

'We'll be here at half past eight,' he said.

'Go quietly out the door,' she whispered, 'for fear you'd waken him. Have you enough rhino?'

'Another few coppers would do no harm,' said Willie.

'You'll kill yourself smokin',' said the mother, 'God save us.'

They went out the back door, blessing themselves as they left the house. The mother saw them to the back gate. As they neared Duckworth's gate he whispered: 'Maybe you'd find it a queer kind of home they have, Willie.' That should be warning enough for him not to say anything out of place.

' " Isn't each one of us queer to the other? " as old Paddy Feeney used to say,' said Willie, 'dressing himself standin' up in the hag, him not more than four feet in height.'

Please God he won't have much of the Irish talk in there, he thought, tucking a finger through the tiny hole in the gate and lifting the latch. As they went up the yard a hammering was heard in the back kitchen, and as he knocked on the door a man's voice called from within: 'Come in, lads.' They went into the dark kitchen.

'How do, lads,' called the same voice. The figure of a tall man could be seen in the shaft of gaslight that came from the living-room into the kitchen. He was standing over a cobbler's last, and he gave a couple of final strikes to a nail and then said: 'Our Herbert's waitin'.'

'Hello, sir,' they said. Then Willie added: 'You've a great sight, sir, hammerin' that hard in this light.'

'Bless thee, lad,' said the man, 'folk say I've no sight at all—bein' as I'm blind.' And he turned to them a boyish bony face, with a thick lock of hair falling on to his forehead, and in the shaft of light he held up two sightless eyes.

'I beg your pardon, sir——' said Willie.

'Ah, nowt of the sort, lad,' said the man, 'but I like to hear that bit o' brogue tha's got. In yu' go.'

They went into the front kitchen. 'How do,' said Herbert. He was pouring out a mug of tea for a girl of fifteen or so, who was at the table eating and reading a magazine propped up against a sugar bag as she did so. She was wearing a blue oil-stained pinafore, her hair had a film of cotton dust over it, and her pale unwashed face looked tired. 'Enough,' she said to Herbert. She didn't look up at the two boys.

'I've brought my brother Willie,' he said.

'How do, mate,' said Herbert.

'How do, mate,' said Willie.

'I'll be ready within five minutes,' said Herbert.

'You're not blasted well goin',' said the girl at the table, 'till you've washed the pots.'

'Hy, mam,' said Herbert, 'hearken our Maggie.'

'Now you watch that tongue of yours, young lady,' said the mother from the bed, 'whilst we've company.' She was sitting up, and on her lap was a burnt cake on which stood three thin unlit candles. George and the two girls were resting with their elbows on the bed, watching the mother.

'Shall we put gas out while we light candles?' said Herbert.

'You will heck,' said the girl at the table. 'Can't you see I'm readin'?'

'It's me mam's birthday,' said Herbert. '*I* did her that cake, Michael. Honest.'

'Aye, that's why you're suckholin' round her to let you go to pictures without washin' pots,' said the girl at the table.

'Enough of that, Maggie Duckworth,' said the mother. 'Our Herbert's been at it all day, I'll have you know.'

'An' what the bloomin' heck do you think I've been doin' in the cardroom,' called out Maggie, 'sittin' on me bloomin' behind?'

'Now shut up, our Maggie,' said Herbert gently. 'Sit down near the fire, willya,' he said to the two boys.

'One of these fine days,' said the mother, 'I'm goin' to paste your flamin' lug for you, lady.'

'Now, mam,' said Herbert, 'let's light your candles.' He tore a strip from the newspaper on the table, darted over to the fire, lit it, and quickly lit the three candles from it. 'Let's turn the gas down, Maggie,' he said.

'Not soddin' likely,' said Maggie.

'We aren't put all the candles on for every year of her birthday,' said Herbert, 'or else we'd need about thirty-five.'

'Aye, an' the rest,' said Maggie.

'You'll go too bloody far, Miss, one of these fine days,' said the mother.

'It don't look as good,' said Herbert looking at the cake and candles, 'with the gas on.'

'Ever since you started bringin' home your miserable fifteen-an'-fourpence of a Friday,' said the mother, 'you think you've bought the bloody 'ouse an' everythin' in it. Aye, you think you're keepin' the lot of us.'

'I'm keepin' mysel',' said Maggie, not lifting her head.

'Keepin' yoursel'! Keepin' yoursel'!' cried the mother, 'you're keepin' your bloody miserable self, are you? Wot kept you for thirteen bloody year, eh? Answer me that! Wot kept you for thirteen bloody year afore ever you earn't a penny? If you don't know—I'll tell you.' She gave a jerk forward and the children grabbed the cake: 'Them!' she cried, holding her two hands in the air, 'them kept you. An' kept you bloody well at that.'

'Aye,' said the girl, 'an' they clouted me too—an' more than once.'

'You'll go out that bloody door,' screeched the mother, 'you dirty little doffer.'

At that moment the father came in from the kitchen. He gave the girl at the table a quick squeeze on the shoulder as he passed, and he went across to the bed, and put his arm round the woman's shoulders, now shaking with a burst of crying. The baby began to cry.

'Now then, mother, now then,' he crooned softly, 'you're gettin' yourself all upset again, an' it'll do you no good, yu' know. It'll turn your milk back, lass, aye, it will that an' all, turn your milk back, an' our little Henry will be frettin' his e'en out if you have no suck for him. He will that an' all, frettin' his little e'en out an' nowt for him.'

I must keep these tears down. They'll think me mad in the strange house. It's the woman's crying and the man's voice.

'It's every time alike,' said the woman, 'every time alike when she sees me in bed, she's got to get agate of me.'

Victoria got up from the bed and went across to the table and stood behind Maggie and began to thump her hard and fast on the back. 'It's you, our Maggie, you're allus agate of my mam. I could kill you.' Maggie did not raise her head from the book, and when Victoria was pulled away by Herbert it was she who was crying.

'If there's any killin' to be done around here,' said Herbert, 'I'll do it.' Then he stooped over Maggie and whispered: 'Bit more tea, love?' She didn't look up, but allowed him to half fill her pint mug. The sobbing all died away. He looked to the table and saw a large single tear fall from Maggie's half-closed eye.

'What about cuttin' your cake, mother?' said the man.

'How many are we?' she said.

'Nine,' said Herbert, 'not countin' babby.'

The mother began to cut the cake.

'Me! me!' cried George.

'Wait your hurry,' she said. 'Here, them two pieces for Michael an' his brother. That piece for your dad. Herbert, give that piece to our Maggie.'

54

There was a pause as Herbert placed the piece of cake beside Maggie. 'Ta,' said Maggie. Then everybody began eating.

'Yu' think there's cherry in,' said Herbert. 'It's not—it's beetroot. It favvers cherry, it tastes like cherry, but it's beetroot. Flappin' Nora, look at the time! We've gotta hurry for the first house.' He bent over Maggie and whispered something, then he took his jacket off the back of a chair, and the three went out into the street.

As they went round the street corner Herbert gave a jerk of his thumb back to the house. 'It's our Maggie's week,' he said quietly, 'that's why her were so funny. Best not to upset 'um at times like that. Ah ha, there's old Grandma Arkwright,' ahead was the figure of an old woman wearing a shawl and a cloth cap, 'we're safe—old Tuppy Brown won't start the pictures till her's in her seat.'

A man wearing a fancy waistcoat and swinging a short cane was watching from the entrance of the Premier Picture Palace. He came out to meet the old woman with the shawl. 'Where the heck have you been?' he asked. 'I'm five minutes late starting. Where's Sarah Jane?'

'Her's bad,' said the old woman. 'Her leg. It's warchin'.'

'I wish her'd dash well let me know in time,' said the man, stroking his glossy hair, 'I've gone an' kept her seat. There's been thousands after it. Come on, hurry up.'

'Tak' your time,' she said.

'It's all right for you,' he said, 'but they've been clampin' their feet.'

'That's Tuppy Brown the owner,' said Herbert, as they paid their threepence admission. 'Used only be tuppence.'

He pulled open a door, they handed their tickets over to be torn, and then a heavy velvet curtain was pulled aside and in they went. A haze of tobacco smoke hung over a packed waiting audience. 'Three's are in front,' said Herbert, 'follow me.' He made his way down the centre sloping gangway, waving in answer to numerous greetings. The seats were made up of backless benches, filled with young people. There were many schoolboys yelling and arguing,

55

groups of pale-faced lads flecked with cotton from the mill, wearing scarves and sharing cigarette-ends, and huddles of working girls in their early teens. His heart thumped at the babble of talk, the animation and laughter, the sense of excitement, and the smell—the smell of tobacco, of mint sweets, and the tang of oranges, and the deep, hot, sweaty, human smells rising up amongst it all.

Herbert went past the front seats, and began to inspect those farther back. 'No room! no room!' cried boys and girls from each row. Herbert ignored these shouts. 'There's plenty of room round here,' he said, stopping at one seat. 'I can feel it. Hy, hutch up there you two.' 'This is sum'dy's seat—gone for a slance.' 'What a tail our cat has!' said Herbert. 'Get in there, Willie. I'll find a place for us two amongst the wenches.'

'No room, no room,' called out three girls. Herbert hesitated, and then along came Tuppy Brown. He prodded one of the girls with his stick: 'Move o'er, Liza Ann,' he said, 'go on, over with you. Get in there, lads,' he said. Herbert forced his way in. 'Only two little 'uns,' he said. Groans rose up from the far end of the seat. 'Hy, Tuppy,' called a lad, 'you're goin' to have us out on our harses, by the hearty Christ are you!'

He found himself squeezed in between Herbert and a big working girl. He could feel the plump warmth of her flowing into him, and the hot oily cotton odour from her clothes seemed to go to his head. 'Art all right?' asked Herbert. He nodded: 'I'm fine,' he whispered.

Then he heard a thundering of feet all around and raised voices. 'What about it? Get started, Tuppy!' Herbert turned to him. 'Sit down, Michael, or else bloomin' seat will be gone from under thee.' Even as he attempted to get down again he could feel the girl's thick strong thigh spreading warmly under him. 'Wriggle thyself in,' said Herbert, helping him back on to the seat. 'When it gets squashed in here,' he added, 'tha can lift a cheek of thy bum for an instant, an' tha'll never get it down again on the seat.'

A huge canvas curtain, covered with painted advertisements, began a jerky roll up. At this there were cheers. Then the lights were lowered and a single stationary picture appeared. A fat boy was biting the corner off a loaf: *Children devour Devine's bread*. A series of single pictures followed, the last one was of an old woman, drunk, clinging to a large bottle high on the crest of a wave in the ocean: *Sharman's Stout. One bottle saved her life*. Now that's very good—I must remember it. He whispered to Herbert: 'This is very good.' Herbert said: 'Ee, lad, these are only the adverts. The proper films don't start till the little white dot comes on. Here it is.'

There was a whirring sound from the back of the hall, and then a tiny white circle began to flicker about the centre of the screen. 'Down a bit, Edgar,' called someone. 'Over to the left.' 'Up. Up a bit more.' 'Shut your trap.' The din of talk stopped, and the lights went out. A film began: *Our Troops on the Rhine*. Herbert nudged him: 'This is only the *Path' Gazette*. Wait till the top picture starts, it'll grip thee like death.'

The next film was a Charlie Chaplin comedy. 'I've seen it,' said Herbert, 'at least half a dozen times.' He couldn't understand why the audience began to laugh as soon as the little man with the cane appeared. Then the actors began kicking each other on the behind, and this went on very fast, and soon he was laughing away.

'Get ready,' said Herbert, 'the top picture's next.' It had become very hot in the picture palace, and he was aware of Herbert's bony pressure on one side, and the fat girl on the other, and Willie's head in front, and he was longing to get out, for his eyes were irritated by the flickering. Then the top film began and it seemed he forgot everything around him. The experience became too intense near the end, where William Farnum stalked down the villain in a cabin. 'That gun's no use to thee,' whispered Herbert, 'he'll throttle thee.' And the hands of William Farnum went round the other man's throat, and as his struggles ceased the face of William Farnum, with dilated nostrils, filled the screen and underneath appeared the words: *Revenge is sweet*.

' And so are lemons!' yelled a lad. Then the picture of the King and Queen appeared. He stood up amongst the others. His face was flushed and he felt feverish, his eyes hurt him, there was a crick in his neck, a pain in his buttocks, and his feet were cramped. It seemed unbelievable that people could go out into the ordinary street after it all. ' He were a bad 'un were yon villain,' said an old woman, ' an' he got what were comin' to him.'

' Well, Willie, how did yu' like it? ' asked Herbert.

' Middlin',' said Willie, 'middlin' good. But it's only actin'.'

' Actin'? What do you mean? ' he asked Willie.

' There's a camera takin' it all down,' said Willie.

Herbert shook his head. ' I'll admit there's a lot of actin' in it,' he said, ' but not all. A lot of it's real.'

' Do you mean to say he actually strangled a man? ' said Willie.

' I'll not go as far as that,' said Herbert, ' but I will bet yon chap's bloomin' neck were sore after Bill Farnum had had his fingers round it. Another thing I've heard they do,' went on Herbert, ' is to look for folk who're in that position in real life, folk whose fathers have been hung in the wrong, an' they take pictures of 'um an' work it into the film.'

' We'd better run for it,' said Willie, ' or we'll miss Dad.'

When they reached home the father was getting ready for pit. He spoke to them in an oddly quiet tone. He took his bundle of pit clothes from where they had been warming over the oven, and went into the kitchen to dress. The mother filled a bottle with tea, cold and milkless, and then made cold bacon sandwiches. When the father came back into the front kitchen he was wearing the dark pit clothes, an old grey shirt, and a pair of big clogs. There was a clean new patch on the knee of his trousers, and he went shyly across to the fireplace, put a hand up the chimney and then rubbed his sooty palm over the patch. ' They'd never stop jokin' me about that patch if they saw it,' he said. He put the bottle of tea into his pocket. ' Oh woman,' he said, ' sure won't a quarter of all that bread be enough for me!'

' Then have the meat itself,' said the mother.

'Go aisy,' he said, 'you'll have me killed with the thirst.'

'Will you take two bottles?' she asked.

'It's one they all take,' he said, 'there's no goin' against the custom.' He put the bottle into his pocket and hooked the snap-can to his belt. The mother watched him in silence, and then she broke out: 'That's the poor bite indeed, to give you strength the long night before you.'

'Any more would have me destroyed at the coal face,' he said. 'Musha, amn't I goin' an' not knowin' would I be sent back as it is, after the nights off? This isn't Ireland.' He drank a last cup of tea without anyone speaking and he looked at the clock, glanced at the patch on his knee, and twice lifted the grimed neb of his cap higher up on his forehead. 'I think maybe I ought to be goin',' he said.

'Do you *have* to go?' asked the mother.

'I have to go, an' well have to go,' he said, 'or ye'll go hungry, the Lord save us.'

'If we go hungry,' said the mother, 'then hungry we go. There's things worse than hunger.'

'I must go,' said the father, moving towards the door.

Willie said: 'Godspeed, father.'

The mother whispered, 'Mickyeen,' and he felt her hand touch his back, so he went quickly across to kiss the father. The man's lips were softly greasy from bacon as he touched them with his own, and the stubble about the mouth tingled his skin. The Irish cattle-smell was gone, and on him now was an earthy deep smell of the mine, tinged with a mineral odour, warm and strange yet in no way upsetting. 'Goodnight, father,' he said.

The man and woman looked at each other.

'God an' His mother protect you,' she said.

He nodded and clumsily blessed himself. 'Goodnight all,' he said, going out the door and into the dark street. The woman and the two boys stood in the lighted doorway and listened to the slow clomping of his feet across the narrow cobbled street. He couldn't be seen in the darkness, but the clogs were heard halting, and at that the woman raised her hand and waved, calling out: 'Godspeed, Godspeed.'

CHAPTER SEVEN

St Stephen's School

'COME ON, AGRAW, you must get up,' said the mother. 'This is the day you go to school.'

He had a glimpse of the end of his dream: a black cloud had been sinking down to earth from the sky as he was on his way to school, and an old woman with clogs on had said to him, 'these are the flying cockroaches they keep talking about,' and as the edge of the cloud lowered to the street near him, big black cockroaches began to fall to the street and run about, and he had stepped into a shop door-way, thinking the old woman was going in there, but she slipped in next door, and he went to her, trying to kill one of the big cockroaches that was on her doorstep so as to get into her good books, but somehow she hadn't warmed to him, and the cockroach itself hadn't been ground under his shoe, but had forced up its back in resistance, time after time, pressing its shape into the sole of his shoe and the feeling of its arched back rising up again and again had gone through to the sole of his foot, and feeling unsure he hadn't stamped down hard enough and the cockroach he could have killed only for his weakness escaped and ran up the step into the house.

How awful unpleasant is everything when you wake up. He got out of bed and went downstairs in his shirt. Feeling sick to the stomach, he sat on the edge of a chair before the fire, the father not having yet returned from pit. The mother gave him a bowl of tea, with bread dipped in hot bacon fat and peppered. Clogs clattered fiercely along the street. God send I become a priest and don't have to go off to a factory at this hour in the darkness! I must pray hard for that wish.

'I think I hear him,' said the mother, 'take care would you be there without trousers.'

He picked up his trousers from where she had left them warming on the fender before the fire and pulled them on. Suddenly he felt a cold crawling thing on his stomach. He let out a cry and struck his hand wildly at the spot. 'A cockroach! A cockroach!' he cried. The mother's foot, wearing an old shoe of the father, crackled it sickeningly on the floor.

'I hate this ugly dirty house,' he said. 'I hate it, hate it.'

'You must shake everythin', agraw,' she said.

He flung the trousers on the floor. 'I won't put them on,' he said, and he ran upstairs. She came up after him and coaxed him into them. When he came down the father was home from the pit. His face was black, and the mouth looked pink and white when he spoke. The mother went to the press and took out a pint of beer that was in a large whisky bottle. He held the bottle to his lips and took a long drink, then he said, 'Is it to school they're goin'?'

'It is,' said the mother. 'Sit there now,' she said, 'an' I'll take those off you.' He sat down and let her take off the pit clogs. 'Mickyeen, put them under the dresser in the kitchen,' she said. He picked them up, one in each hand, and found they were too heavy to carry that way. When he put them down in the kitchen he tilted one and from it poured a heap of coal dust and almost a matchboxful of coal bits.

'I must wash,' said the man.

'Wait till you have a mug of tea taken,' said the woman.

'If I sit here another flamin' minute,' said the man angrily, 'I'll never rise out of the chair at all.'

'God save us,' she said, 'but what harm if you rest?'

'I've no bloody comfort sittin' here in my bloody filthy dirt,' said the man.

'That's the truth for you surely,' she said, 'you'd have no comfort till you're changed.'

'I had a hard night,' he said quietly.

'I'll prepare a place for you to wash,' she said, hurrying into the kitchen. 'Arra what's all the washin' you're doin', Mickyeen?' she asked softly.

'Washin' away the track of the flamin' cockroach,' he said.

'Make haste, my son,' she said, 'for the big cockroach is comin' in to wash. I'm bringin' in the water for him.' A moment later she came hurrying in carrying the pan of water which had been heating at the fire. 'Take care, take care,' called the man. The woman whispered, 'Clear out whilst he washes.'

Later, in the front kitchen, Willie said: 'He sounds like an ould seal out there—or a whale,' and the three of them made signs and laughed secretly at the sounds the father blew out over washing. The woman went in to dry his back and give him the shirt that had been warming over the oven door. He looked pale when he came in, with the dark rims of coal dust round his eyes. He sat at the table and began to eat his porridge, lifting his spoon daintily, and eating in a neat quiet manner.

'I must dress now,' said the mother, going into the kitchen, with a piece of buttered bread in her hand. When she came in she was ready. 'Give them a penny apiece from me,' said the father, 'an' let ye be good scholars now.'

He felt ashamed walking through the streets with Willie and the mother—they looked so Irish. It was ten minutes' walk to Sparrow Street, a narrow cobbled roadway, thick with old and unswept horse droppings, in which was St. Stephen's School. They entered the school gate and went into a small dark yard. From an entry facing came the din of boys' voices, rising in a mass of yells, screams, whistles and the clatter of sharp clogged feet.

A long piercing whistle was heard and instantly there was silence, broken by a piteous boyish yell. 'Gerroff me arm, tha'rt breakin' it.' The silence was then sustained for a few seconds, until a short whistle sounded. At once there was a scuttering of feet, and the party of three stood aside as a rush of boys came through the gate and made for the entry. Standing like a guard beside the entry was a hefty schoolboy, and as the boys ran by he cuffed them along with friendly encouragement. A third whistle now sounded, and as soon as it did the right leg of the guarding schoolboy rose across the entry and blocked it. Two boys who were running wildly to reach the entry ran into the leg. It stayed across. None could pass.

'Let's through! let's through!' exclaimed one boy. 'Oh Cumberland, please let's through!'

The boy on guard gave a mild shake of the head. Another whistle sounded, and at this marching feet could be heard. The boy cried out again: 'Let's through, oh please, Cumberland—' and he bent in the middle, 'afore I pee in m'pants.' The boy on guard shook his head.

Standing beside his mother and Willie he felt a bit sick at the sight of the fear-struck boy, who was now hopping from one foot to another, entreating Cumberland to let him through. Other boys had now joined the throng of late-comers held back at the entry, and they stood there, indifferent to the fear of the boy nearest the entry. One boy sidled up to Cumberland and offered him a sweet. He glanced at the boy and the sweet and turned away with a sniff. Three older boys, wearing cotton-grimed clothes, went up to him and said: 'Right, Cumby, make way there.'

He looked at them and said: 'Some 'opes!'

'Right, Cumby,' said one, 'we'll lay in wait and rattle thy ribs for thee this dinner time.'

He took no notice. Then the mother went forward. 'Ah, come on here,' she said, 'let these gents through.'

'Let 'um through?' he said. 'Ee, Missis, it's my duty to *stop* 'um from gettin' through. Any lad arriving after that third whistle is a latecomer, an' he's got to be punished.'

At the word 'punished' the boy up in front placed both hands on his genitals, pressed them in, stooped forward and winced, rocked himself up and down, lifted one leg and then the other, and said: 'Oh let me go an' wet, Cumberland—I'll come back!'

He shook his head.

'Then move aside, young man,' said the mother, 'and allow us through.'

'Yes, Missis,' said Cumberland, dropping his leg.

Like a shot four boys were through, and before the mother and two boys could get through the leg was up again. 'Feeney, Flanagan, Cartwright, Phipps—' he called after them, 'I know you! I'll get you!' Then he gave the mother a look and he kept his leg up. One of the older boys said: 'How Horatio saved the bridge.' Then Cumberland dropped his leg, but this time there was no rush, but a whisper of, 'Here he is!' and the next moment a man appeared down the entry.

He was a tall man, grey-haired, wearing a smart grey suit, pressed and brushed, a stiff white collar and a neat tie, and glossy black shoes. He had a gentle look, with soft dog-like brown eyes and silky light-brown moustache. At his side he carried a long cane. The ragged huddle of boys stopped at his approach, some bit their lips, others scraped the ground with their clog soles.

'Good morning, sir,' said the mother, going forward. 'I believe you'll be Mr Victor. My name is M'Cloud, and these are my two sons—I was hoping you could accept them into your school.'

'Certainly, madam,' he said. 'Cumberland, take this lady and her boys to the playground and wait there for me.' He gave a bow. 'I won't be more than a minute or two.'

At the end of the alleyway was the playground, a T-shaped area of uneven ground, surrounded by the school buildings. As they stood there the clear high voices of boys at prayers came through the open windows. A woman called out: '*Act of Faith.*' A loud speedy response was heard. '*O my God, I believe in Thee and all Thy Church doth teach, because Thou hast said it, and Thy word is true.*'

'*Act of Hope.*'

'*My God, I hope in Thee, for grace and for glory, because of Thy promises, Thy mercy and Thy power.*'

'*Act of Charity.*'

'*My God, because Thou art so good, I love Thee with all my heart, and for Thy sake, I love my neighbour as myself.*'

'*Sign of the Cross. In the Name of the Father, and of the Son, and of the Holy Ghost, Amen.*'

64

Mr Victor's soft voice, now slightly raised, was heard from the far end of the alleyway. 'Mullen, you were late last Friday. What's your excuse this morning? '

' Please, sir, please, sir, our clock was slow. It loses.'

' Don't depend on it then. Hold out your hand.'

Swish. A sharp cry.

'The other one.'

' But, please, sir, please, sir—!'

' Mullen!'

' I've got a sore on it, sir.'

' Same one again.'

Swish. A howl of pain.

'Shaw. You're late. What excuse?'

'We've got no clock, sir.'

' No excuse, Shaw. Tell your mother to buy one.'

Swish.

' Binks?'

' No excuse, sir.'

Swish.

' Taylor?'

' My clog-iron came off, sir, just as I was leaving the house. I'd to go in an' have it fettled on again.'

' Inspect your clogs the evening before.'

Swish. A groan.

' Makinson?'

' Yes, sir.'

' What's your excuse?'

' None, sir—'

' Please, sir, their Harry's got scarlet fever.'

' What's that, Smith?'

'Their Harry's got scarlet fever, sir.'

' Has your brother got scarlet fever, Makinson?'

' No, sir, It's my half-brother, sir.'

' Where is he?'

' They came for him in the ambulance an' took him to the fever hospital sir, last night about seven o'clock.'

' Stand over there, Makinson. Do you realise you shouldn't come to school if there is fever in the home?'

'I've nobody to look after me, sir.'

'Where's your mother?'

'She's workin', sir, at the tannery.'

'Your father?'

'Got killed in the war, sir.'

'Oh yes. But surely you've got neighbours?'

'My mother doesn't like to be beholden to them, sir. We've not been in this street long—we only flitted there last July.'

'Just a moment, Makinson, don't go. You others there! In you go this morning. I'm not letting you off—I'll give you double if you're late again this week. Right, off you go. I want a word with you, Makinson.'

The group of latecomers went through the yard, some smirking and some hugging their hands. The mother gave a sigh. Willie said: 'See the clock is made right.'

'An' him seeming to be such a nice man,' said the mother.

'Will you both be quiet—he'll be along.'

They heard a class register being swiftly called. Then a woman's voice was heard at catechism.

'Morrison,' her voice came clearly through the window, 'which are the six sins against the Holy Ghost?'

'The six sins against the Holy Ghost, Miss, the six sins are, Presumption, Despair, Resisting the known truth, Envy of another's spiritual good, Obstinacy in sin, and, and—'

'Final Impenitence. Which are the Four Sins crying to Heaven for Vengeance?'

'Please, Miss, the Four Sins crying to Heaven for Vengeance are Pride, Covetousness, Lust—— '

'Dolt!—the seven capital sins.'

'Oh please, Miss, the sins crying to heaven for revenge—'

'Idiot—for vengeance. Kneel in front of the class. Healey, which are the four sins crying—'

'The Four Sins crying to Heaven for Vengeance, Miss,' chanted a high clear voice, 'are, Wilful Murder, the Sin of Sodomy, Oppression of the Poor, and Defrauding Labourers of Their Wages.'

'And what are the Four Last Things ever to be Remembered?'

66

'The Four Last Things ever to be Remembered, Miss, are Death, Judgement, Hell, and Heaven.'

'I'm learnin' here,' said the mother.

'*Sh*! here he comes.'

'I'm so sorry to have kept you waiting,' said Mr Victor.

'Not at all, sir,' she said.

He looked at her, stroked his moustache, and smiled. Along the yard came Cumberland leading a group of boys. 'The sore eyes, sir,' he said. 'I'm taking them to the clinic.' Mr Victor nodded, and led the party into the school.

The place had a musty smell, floors and stairs were worn down, and there were dark turnings lit by gaslamps. Outside a room marked *Headmaster*, on the first floor, two boys stood palely to attention.

'Yes?' Mr Victor spoke softly to them.

'Miss Skegham sent us to you, sir,' said the smaller one, raising his hand aloft as he spoke.

'What for?'

'Fighting, sir.'

'I'll attend to you both later,' he said. 'Wait there.'

He led the way into the room, gave the mother a chair, and he sat at a table. He took their names and ages. 'You've both made your First Communion of course?' he said.

'No, sir,' he said, 'I haven't.'

'You haven't, Michael, well well! We make First Communion here at the age of seven.'

'It's later in Ireland,' said the mother.

'We feel that if a boy hasn't come to the age of reason at seven,' remarked Mr Victor, 'he'll never come to it.'

A wise man, he thought, my soul has been cluttered with sin ever since I can remember.

'William, you'll go to Mr Denning's class, and you, Michael, until you make your First Communion, had better remain with Miss Twining. The boys in her class are younger than you, but you'll move up later.'

He was leading them up to the classroom on the next floor when a shouting and running was heard on the landing above. Then a boy came rushing down the stairs, his hand

67

on the wooden rail, and moving so fast that he was like a bird in flight as he went past. There was a glimpse of two small eyes and a head of short black hair, and an apology as he disappeared. 'Please may I pass, sir!' Heavier footsteps sounded, and a middle-aged man, wearing thick spectacles, came down the stairs.

'Oh, sir,' he cried on seeing Mr Victor, 'Criddle's escaped!'

'*Escaped*, Mr Wimpole?' said Mr Victor.

'He ate the apple, sir, I mean the one I had provided for drawing lesson. He got away, sir.'

'I'm afraid you won't catch him now,' said Mr Victor.

CHAPTER EIGHT

Miss Twining's Class

He gave a light nervous knock on the classroom door, lifted the latch and entered. A woman with an oval face turned from the class of boys.

'I was sent here to you, Miss,' he said huskily. 'I'm new and my name is Michael M'Cloud. I'll be older than the other boys here, but I haven't my First Communion made.'

'Very well, Michael,' she said. 'Go and sit next to James Higley.'

James, a cross-eyed boy, gave him a smile. At once he smelt the body odour from the boy and it made him gulp.

'*Corpus Christi*, which means Body of Christ,' said Miss Twining, 'is a famous feast day. I want you each one to look forward to that morning, for he can be sure it will be the happiest day of his life. Why? Because he will have made his First Confession the day before, and all the sins and guilt of his previous years will, by the secret words of Absolution spoken by the priest, have been removed from his soul, so that his soul is cleansed and white as snow. Now I do not mean the snow you see in the streets on your way to school sometimes, but the snow that descends by night on a mountain. If you were to see that snow some morning, it would be a sight never to be forgotten, for the snow which falls through the purest air is of purest white. And after your First Confession—that is if you make a good one—each one of you here now will have a soul as white as snow on a mountain side. Every tiny trace of sin will be utterly vanished. The soul will be pure and white.'

'Please, Miss, will it be whiter than it is after making a good Act of Contrition?' asked a boy.

'Infinitely, Ernest, because the *grace* of the Sacrament is there to whiten it.'

'Please, Miss, is the soul after a good Act of Contrition like snow in our street, an' after the Sacrament of Penance like that snow on that mountain?'

'Yes, John, I think that's right.'

'Please, Miss, is the soul whiter then than the minute you was born?

'Please, Miss,' called a number of voices, 'he's forgotten about the stain of Original Sin.'

'Of course he has. Baptism removes that. Penance removes later stains. Yet, even after a perfect Confession, the soul is not as white and beautiful as it can be. True, it is like a mountain covered with the whitest snow, but to make it supremely white, whiter than all else on earth, that special grace of God, given only in Holy Eucharist, is required. Oh, if only each one of you could imagine the glorious beauty of his soul on that morning! Picture the high mountain covered with the whitest snow—that is the soul after Confession. Now imagine that mountain—when heaven opens wide and God's sunshine comes pouring down, every particle of snow gleaming white, the entire mountain shining in the glory of the sun. That is the nearest picture I can give each one of you of his soul on the morning of his First Communion.'

The class was silent for a moment, and then James Higley put his hand up. 'Please, Miss, won't all the snow melt with the sun on it?'

'No, James. God's snow can only melt because of sin.' A bell sounded in the corridor. 'Now boys, take out your books for sums.' James took out his book, holding his head on one side, and said: 'I still think that snow would melt. What do you say, Michael.'

'It might, James,' he said.

Miss Twining gave him a new sum book, blotting paper and a pen, and he shared an inkwell with James. Multiplication sums were chalked on the board. 'Now you may start,' said Miss Twining. The sums on the board were very easy, but he had used a slate before and the pen and ink felt complicated to him. 'Put your name on your book for a start,'

70

said James. He nodded and took up the pen in his thick fingers. Please God I don't ruin all this nice feeling amongst all of us by doing the wrong thing.

'Try to keep your knuckle down, Michael,' he heard her say, and then he felt her stooping down over him, the white-bloused arm coming round him from the side, and the fragrant smell of her skin close to him. Her delicate hand took firm hold of his fist. As a fine hair from her touched lightly on his eartip, he longed that he might be less mean and unworthy than he was, and then he felt the easing down of the soft breast on his shoulder, and the steady hand began to guide his own shaky one along the paper. Blood fizzed up his ears, and the heart of him thudded that loudly that he felt sure it must be heard all over the classroom. Then an unexpected cool calm took him. He heard her speaking intimately into his ear: 'M-i-c-h-a-e-l . . .' and for a moment he thought, if only I'd a great long name like an emperor, and she could go writing on, pressing this way on my shoulder, and her woman's hand clasping mine that way.

At the play-time bell the boys stood and marched in orderly manner from the room. On the stairs the different classes met, and yelling and screaming broke out, when boys bent their heads and let out a cry or screech, or grabbed the caps of those in front and flung them down, to be trodden under the rushing mass of clogs. James kept at his side. 'I'll show you the peestone, Michael,' he said.

He made his way nervously along with James through the schoolyard that was packed with boys running and fighting, laughing and arguing, bumping and crashing, and filling the air with a din of voices at a constant level. They walked round the urinal wall and went inside. There was a mass of jostling boys there, all peeing, and those in front standing on their tiptoes in their clogs, competing for the highest jet. He saw a boy beside him who was standing well behind, unfasten his trousers hurriedly and take out his little white thing, and then hold tight to the end of it until it swelled up like a balloon. 'Just watch this!' said the boy, and releasing

71

his grip a little he let out a swift squirt which went over the ones just in front and fell on to the heads of those near the slate wall. There were shouts of disgust. 'Highest yet!' cried the boy. 'Licked lot of you! Highest yet!'

He was glad to get out of the place, and he fastened himself up without having let go a drop. 'Let's go an' stand in the corner,' said James, 'or else I'll get my specs broke. I'll get coppit from my mam—she has to pay so much towards them at the clinic.' They went to the corner, beside half a dozen boys who looked older and oddly out of place. They were chatting together and passing a cigarette-end from one to the other, and watching out for a teacher all the time.

'They're called "half-timers",' said James, 'they're all turned twelve, an' they come to school at mornin' an go an' work in the mill at the afternoon. It's a shame, my mam says, that the gover'ment is stopping all half-time work. They're bringin' it in that they have to go to school till they're thirteen, an' then start work full time, or fourteen— I don't know which. It's not right.'

He was very interested in the antics of the half-timers, who looked like little old men there in the schoolyard. 'The posh ones don't go half-time,' went on James, 'They go on till they're thirteen, an' some stay in Mr Victor's Cambridge Class until they're fourteen. Cumberland there—he's thirteen. Look at the size of him.'

He looked and saw Cumberland and a group of lads dragging someone along, and it gave him a shock to see it was his brother Willie. He was struggling against a mob of them, who were pulling him along by arms, sleeves, jacket and hair. He hesitated—maybe he's not being hurt—and then ran across to Cumberland. 'Will you let him go, please?' he said, 'he's my brother.'

'Nay, lad, he's gotta face the Inquisition,' said Cumberland, 'even if he's thy grandfather. We'll not hurt him if he'll stop his bally struggling. Right, lads, get him up against the wall.' Willie was put up against the outside wall of the urinal, his arms held, and clogs held down on his feet to prevent him moving. Then Cumberland stood before him.

'Prisoner before the court,' he said. 'have you anything to say before the penalty of death by water is pronounced upon you—' as he looked at his brother tears of fear burst up in his eyes and ran down his cheeks, '—which will be executed, after due warnin', by the regimental goat, on the pronunciation of—' He made a wild dash forward to push them out of the way, and at that moment a jet of urine came quivering over the wall from the inside and fell on Cumberland. He darted out of the way and it seemed to follow him. 'Stop! stop!' he cried out. Then a red-haired boy came running round the urinal, fastening up his trousers. 'You great bally fool, Neddy,' shouted Cumberland, wiping his face and hair,' tha pissed on the Grand Inquisitor—'

'Serves thee flappin' well right,' said the other, 'tha were that long-winded declaring sentence that I bally near bust me bladder. Ain't that so, Harry?'

Just then Willie broke free. He charged head down into Cumberland, and sent the big boy to the ground with a grunt. The others didn't move. 'Cumby's winded,' said the red-haired boy, 'make room.' Cumberland looked white, lying on the ground. Then the whistle blew. All went silent. At the second whistle Willie gave the big boy a hand up. Cumberland winked. 'Ta, mate,' he said. James Higley called out: 'Quick, Michael, into line—afore you're caught.' He ran beside James and got into line. Further orders sounded on the whistle, and the lines of boys marched into school.

CHAPTER NINE

A Firm Purpose of Amendment

'JOHN KAY, what is Penance?'

'Please, Miss, Penance is a Sacrament, whereby the sins, whether mortal or venial, committed after Baptism, are forgiven.'

'When did our Lord institute the Sacrament of Penance, Peter Curry?'

'Please, Miss, Our Lord instituted the Sacrament of Penance when he breathed on His Apostles and gave them power to forgive sins, saying, "*Whose sins you shall forgive they are forgiven.*"'

'Michael M'Cloud, what is a firm purpose of amendment?'

It was when you were in the clogger's shop with your father's pit clogs having irons put on them and the clogger had the clog fastened over the last that looked like an anvil, and it was as though that were the soul, and a firm purpose of amendment was when he'd put in the last nails and he had the irons almost done, and then he lifted his hammer and started striking all along the irons and there was a loud clear bell-like clanging—that was a firm purpose of amendment. But if the clog gave a groan and he had to take the nails out again, then it wasn't a firm purpose of amendment.'

'A firm purpose of amendment, please Miss, is a—a——'

'Resolution to avoid——'

'A resolution to avoid, by the grace of God, not only sin, but also the dangerous occasions of sin.'

The door opened and Canon Hulme entered, carrying his tall hat and smoking a cigar.

'Oh, good morning, Canon,' the class chanted.

'Good morning, children,' he gave them his round-faced smile. 'Good morning, Miss Twining. Now are they all ready for their First Confession?'

'Yes, Canon,' they answered.

The Canon dabbed his forehead with a big handkerchief. 'Now for goodness sake, don't be frightened of telling the priest *all* your sins today. You won't shock him, because he's been listening to sins for many years. But please don't add any sins. I once knew a boy called Tommy, and every time Tommy went to Confession he always told a few extra sins, because he felt the priest might be annoyed if he had to forgive only a few. It doesn't matter how many or how few—the priest is there to forgive them. By making a good Confession each one of you ensures his soul being in a state of grace to receive Holy Communion tomorrow morning at nine o'clock Mass. I wonder does any boy know what it means to be in a state of grace?'

'To be in a state of grace,' they answered as one. 'is to be free from mortal sin and pleasing to God.'

'Is it a sin, boys, to receive Holy Communion in mortal sin?'

Again they chanted: 'It is a great sin to receive Holy Communion in mortal sin, *for he that eateth and drinketh unworthily, eateth and drinketh judgement to himself.*'

'Very, very good. Now I wonder, Miss Twining, does any boy know what is meant by " *eateth and drinketh judgement to himself* "?'

No one answered. Then James Higley lifted his hand. 'Please, Canon, it means you can't boss our Lord by eatin' Him.'

'That's a very good answer,' said the Canon. 'Yes, it means that the person who takes Holy Communion in mortal sin has God's anger within him instead of God's blessing. I know that that will not happen to any of you. Good morning, boys, and God bless you all.'

Shortly before noon Miss Twining marched the class out of school and into church. They tiptoed down the far aisle to the narrow pews outside the confessional doors, went in and knelt four in a row. Miss Twining stood over each row and whispered: 'Make one final examination of consciences, in case there are any sins you've forgotten. Then pray earnestly to God to help you make a Good Confession.'

He put his head down obediently, covered his eyes with his palms, and pretended he was thinking of his sins. I've thought of them so much and so often these last week, reckoning them up and down, till not a one of them looks like a sin any more. Ol' King Cole was a merry ol' soul an' a merry ol' soul was he, He called for a light in the middle of the night, To go to the w.c., The moon shone on the petty wall, The candle took a fit, An' ol' King Cole fell down the petty hole, up to the neck in—God forgive me, I'll make an awful Confession if I go on this way, thank God I'm not the first to go in or the second, O my God, because Thou art so good, will I tell him that sin that night at Aunt Kate's? —it'll come under bad thoughts just, the daft songs the lads at the corner are always singing an' they have a way of sticking in the mind. O the moon shines bright on Charlie Chaplin, an' Billy Ritchie, an' little Tichy—an' Pimple too. What could Miss Twining be praying for down there? It must be lovely to have her pray to You. You're gettin' near sin again an' ready to make your First Confession. Your whole life is lived on the very verge of sin. So is everybody else's. But you're making your First Confession. The poor Protestants never even think of sin, saying bad words just when the mood strikes them, but then they've got to pay for it all at the Final Day of Judgement.

A light appeared in the Confessional window. Miss Twining touched Ernest Keating on the shoulder. 'Don't forget to speak up,' she said, 'so that the priest can hear you.' He nodded eagerly. 'And when you're coming out,' she said, 'close the door for the boy going in, and then it doesn't waste the priest's time. All of you remember that.' Ernest said: 'Yes, Miss,' in a loud voice, opened the door and entered the Confessional with brisk confidence. In a moment his bright high voice was heard outside as clearly as though he were amongst them.

'Bless me, Father, I have sinned. This is my First Confession. I confess to Almighty God, to Blessed Mary ever a Virgin, to Blessed Michael the Archangel, to Blessed John the Baptist,' his voice lowered and he took a breath and went on, ' to the holy Apostles Peter an' Paul, an' to all the Saints, that I have sinned exceedingly in thought, word an' deed.'

Miss Twining looked round anxiously, as though considering some way to engage the boys' attention outside, but each one appeared to be gazing straight forward, deaf to the penitent within.

' Against the First Commandment I accuse myself of havin' missed my prayers about fifty-three times, an' my mornin' prayers twenty-one times. I also accuse myself of having worshipped the false image of a cat.' The priest inside made an inaudible interruption, and then Ernest went on. ' It was a cat called Ben I took to bed with me every night, Father. Folk said, ' He worships yon cat.' An' I worship it, Father. It's dead now, Father, sum'dy poisoned it.' Again a murmur from the priest. Then Ernest went on.

' Against the Second Commandment I accuse myself of having used God's name in vain *frequently*. I've *frequently* said, " Oh good God ", "God blast it", an' less *frequently* "Christ melt it". I've also sung a dirty song called, " There was a Scotch Highlander who fought in Waterloo. The wind blew up his petticoats an' showed his dolly blue." O my God, help me to make a Good Confession. My soul will be doomed to eternal damnation. Hail Mary fullagrace. Hail Mary fullagrace.

' Against the Fourth Commandment I accuse myself of having disobeyed my mother three hundred an' sixty-five times an' my father twice, of answering back an' cheekin' my mother a hundred an' fifty times an' my father twice. Also, of kicking my mother frequently—an' my father once. Of throwin' a wet mop at my mother—but missin' her. And of having had bad thoughts against my father *frequently*.' A boy called Drinkwater suddenly gave a loud sneeze of laughter, and stuck his head down out of the way, but sneezes and sobs of laughter could be heard clearly as he rocked and gulped. Miss Twining came round, and looked at the boys but said nothing.

'. . . Of havin' fought with other boys *frequently*.' He stopped over the word every time. 'I've busted boys' noses an' blacked their eyes. I once gave a boy a thick lip an' he fetched his big brother an' I gave him a thick lip.' Is that mild Ernest inside?

'Against the Sixth Commandment I accuse myself of having had evil thoughts an' desires twenty-seven times. An' some dinner-times I've peeped through a hole in the girls' petties with some other lads, an' watched them fastenin' up their bloomers—though not *frequently*.'

Miss Twining whispered to the front row: 'Don't speak too loud. The priest will tell you if you're whispering. You could even whisper loudly.'

I'm half laughing at him but he's saved an' I'm lost. I can't remember a word of the Confiteor. He's telling all his sins, but I've a lump of them hidden. I know I must have. I must change several to frequently; it sounds better. Ernest was heard reciting the second part of the Confiteor, and then followed the low drone of the priest. Then there was a movement of feet inside, the next boy stood to go in, the door opened and Ernest appeared. He looked elated, and beamed on the others, kneeling before him, and smiled at Miss Twining, and went across to say his penance.

Then came his turn, when he stood up to enter, his heart pounding and his mind whispering the opening of the Confiteor. He had seen the door closed after the other boy, and now it was closed on him. It was a cubicle of a room. He saw the kneeling board, hurried down to it, put his chin over the ledge, looked at the dark-green curtained grille, and allowed the rhythm of the Confiteor to fall from his tongue, not thinking of the meaning but only that he should say it right, and whispering lowly. Then he spoke his sins to the unseen priestly presence behind the curtain.

He had missed his prayers and had said them badly, he had used bad words, missed Mass, disobeyed his mother, lost his temper, had bad thoughts, fought, told lies, found money and told no one about it. These sins don't belong to me, he thought, they sound like another's. Near the end he began to feel a curious satisfaction, and he began to regret not having told things more fully, and he wondered how they were being received behind the curtain. It all seemed strange and yet natural. 'For these and all my other sins,' he ended, 'I humbly ask pardon of you, my Father.'

A low muttering drone came from behind the curtain. The excitement slipped away from him in his silence and he felt empty. A bad Confession. Yet no one will know. That's all that matters. He looked at the grille. Then suddenly it seemed that the hammer began to strike the last, to clang loudly and clearly: *firm purpose of amendment*! The whisper of the priest: 'For your penance, my son, say five Our Fathers and five Hail Marys. You may go now, and may God bless you.'

He said, 'Thank you, Father,' and rose to his feet, his mind swirling with happiness. He turned to feel for the door handle and found it opened for him, and the smile of James Higley greeting him. He took the door handle and closed it after James.

Everything was different, everything, the faces and the floor and the altar and the wooden seats and the marble pillars and every single thing seemed full of newness as he tiptoed down the aisle to a long empty pew to kneel and say his penance. There in the tabernacle is Our Lord, and I'd love to pray to him for ever like this, and if I was to die this minute I'd go straight up to Him and the Blessed Virgin. After a time the feeling went and he began to feel the itch of the wool undervest on his back.

CHAPTER TEN

The Coal Strike

HE SAT HIMSELF DOWN on the back doorstep and began to prepare to clean his boots for Mass next morning. He took a piece of a broken clothes-peg and scraped the soles clean, and next he removed the laces from the boots and untwisted them. I'd need a new pair of laces, but if I ask and she hasn't a pair I'd only get mad and maybe commit a sin and that would smudge my soul for my First Communion tomorrow, so I won't ask, but just the same, for the sake of the penny they cost, you'd think you could have a new pair of laces at a time like this. He took up the brush, looked to see it wasn't the polish end, and began to brush away at the right boot. He brushed all the surface and the seams and weltings, and then he did the same with the other, after which he turned the brush round, took the lid off the *Brytenup* tin of polish, and began to apply it. When he had put polish on every part of the outside upper boot, he began to clean the four pairs of eyelet holes, and also underneath the three pairs of upraised hooks above the eyelets, round which he wound the laces. Then he began a brisk polishing of the boots, dancing the brush over the leather with zest. I'd do the soles too, only folk 'ud laugh at me.

He felt the soft step of the mother in the kitchen, and her black skirt came up beside him. 'Wait yet till I'd look has he a new pair hidden away,' she said, 'before you'd put the old laces back.' He turned and watched her going into the front room, open the father's drawer—second from the top on the right—and feel carefully under his clean shirts. It's a comfort to have him out of the way for an hour, for it's an awful thing the way he's round the house since the start of the Coal Strike. Ten weeks of it now. He was right cocky when it started, but now with his watch and chain pawned, and no work and no money, he's gone quieter. He's bad enough when he shouts, but I don't like to see him quiet. She closed the door of the drawer and came back to him. 'Take care would he see you puttin' them in,' she said. He took them eagerly. 'Thanks, mother, those are lovely,' he said. She said: 'You gave a great shine to your boots, the Lord save us.' He stood up and gave her a kiss.

'Could I have a wash?' he said, 'or will he be back?'

'Urra why shouldn't you have a wash?' she said. 'It'll freshen you—it's an awful close evenin'. Musha, back home now 'twould be nice to sit by the door and have the taste of a breeze comin' in to you—you'd get it comin' down the long hill, don't you know, comin' fresh to your face.'

She brings Ireland into everything, he thought. 'Folk are on the door-steps as it is, mother,' he said. 'I'm havin' a shirt-off wash, mother.' He took his shirt off and tied his braces round his middle, filled the big bowl under the tap, dropped the soap into it, and thought how inviting it looked. Then he began to wash. He ducked his head into the cold water, rubbed himself with the bar of soap, and then began to scrub himself with the stiff brush.

'Arra will someone stop this one—before he has the entire bloody skin scrubbed clean off him!'

He turned and there was the father. At the sound of the sharp word pleasure left him and he felt in his throat at once the tear swell.

'Isn't he only preparin' himself for goin' to the altar to-morrow?' said the mother, hurrying in to his defence. I wish she'd said nothing, for I'd that lump swallowed and now here's another.

'Musha, wasn't I only sayin' it for his good?' said the father, a half-joking tone in his voice. I hate him that way, when he says things and draws them back as though he was only going on. 'But I'm tellin' you one thing, an' it's not two, the soda in the English soap would skin the hide of a flamin' elephant.'

He began to rinse himself off and edged over to the roller

81

towel behind the door. 'Isn't it well now,' said the mother, 'that you couldn't open your mouth without a curse of some kind?'

'Urra Jesus, Mary an' Joseph, is it *bloody* the curse? Indeed I wish I had a fine half-crown for every time I heard Father John Joe say that over in Ireland. I even heard a Redemptionist Father himself say it above in the pulpit at St Stephen's when I was there with John at a mission once. "*I went as white as a bloody sheet,*" he said he heard one man say to another. "*That's no swear or curse,*" he told us from the pulpit, "*for only an eejit would think a bloody sheet was white. A bloody sheet's red.*" That's what the missioner said above in the pulpit.'

He's always soft and cajoling in the evenings, and it do get on my nerves more than when he's mad at mornings. It's been the same ever since the Strike began, he's always going on soft like when it comes to the hour he'd be going off to the pit—an' then she's often short and quick with him, but he never loses his temper. But then he's always cranky at mornings, an' that's when she's trying to pacify him. Why couldn't they be both nice to each other at the same time? You'd think *she'd* have more sense anyway.

'There's a terrible heat all over the town,' said the man. 'Even the bloody weather's gone against us,' that's what he said back there in April when the Strike began and the weather suddenly went hot. 'We'll defy the hell's flamers of owners to starve us, an' if we can't get a livin' wage we'll strike. There's no justice in the world if the rogues of owners can take away at one stroke forty-eight per cent of a man's wages. We'll fight an' we'll win. Curse an' roast the railwaymen an' that arch-traitor Jimmy Thomas, an' curse an' roast the transport men too that turned cowards. We'll fight an' we'll win.' That day I offered to go for some free peasoup from the 'Weaver's Arms'. He said: 'I'd cut the tongue out of your head before I'd allow anyone belongin' me take a drop of their filthy poison.'

'Yes, a powerful heat everywhere,' said the man.

'I'll go to bed early, mother,' he said.

' Arra go out an' enjoy yourself, man,' said the father, ' so seldom you're young.'

' Didn't I tell you he was receivin' the Sacrament tomorrow morning? ' said the mother.

' Arra let him do what he wants,' said the father, picking up a newspaper, ' let him do what he wants.' He suddenly put down the newspaper again. ' I have that bloody thing read forty-nine times,' he said. ' Let him do what he wants. Let him go to bed or let him stay up. Let him do either— whatever suits him.'

' Will you stop makin' a Mulligan's monkey of yourself,' said the mother, ' goin' on talkin' without a steam of sense in what you say? '

' I know one thing, Mickyeen,' said the father, ' whatever I say is wrong. I don't know much, but I know that bloody much, that whatever I say is wrong.' He picked up the paper, began to read, rolled it up and started tapping himself on the head with it.

' Would you ever think to take your cap off comin' into the house? ' said the mother. ' You're like one who never saw anythin'.'

' Didn't I tell you, Mickyeen? ' said the man, ' whatever I do is wrong.'

' He's like a man who'd have drink taken,' said the mother, as though talking to herself, ' only I wouldn't know where he'd get it.'

' I'm drunk for the bloody want of it,' said the father. He gave a loud cough. ' I met Johnny Stewart an' he took me into the " Wheatsheaf " an' stood me a pint. A decent bloody fellow that, Johnny Stewart, an' his father an Orangeman. He took me in an' stood me a pint.'

' Well I'm glad to hear you had that itself,' said the mother, turning to good humour, ' for I'd hate to think you'd gone soft altogether.'

' D'you hear that now, Mickyeen? ' said the father. ' D'you hear how your mother talks to me? '

' It was only because you was repeatin' yourself,' he said to the father.

83

'Musha, repeatin' myself was I? Small wonder I would. Small bloody wonder surely.'

He and the mother went into the kitchen and left the father talking to himself. She gave him a cup of cocoa and two slices of bread and margarine. Then he said goodnight to the father and kissed her goodnight and went upstairs to bed. From the back room he could hear the shouts of the lads and girls playing in the street, and excited cries and laughter. He tried to ignore the loneliness the sounds brought to him. There was a tap on the bedroom door and the mother looked in. 'Here's an apple I had put on one side,' she said. 'It'll have your mouth freshened for the mornin' for receivin'. Just any raw thing now is great for freshenin' the mouth goin' to bed.'

Just what I wanted, she'd always have it. 'Is everythin' all right, mother?' he said. A smile came quickly to her worried face. 'Yerra why shouldn't it be?' she said. 'Kiss goodnight now.'

'Whatever I ask in the mornin',' he said, 'if I'm struck mad with thirst, don't give me a drink of any kind at all —or else I couldn't receive Communion.'

'Please God you won't be,' she said, going off.

He pulled off his thick ribbed stockings. The pale sweaty feet, sore and unwashed, seemed not to belong to the same person as the cool clean hands and face. It wouldn't be right to pick them this evening. He had to rub an itch away, but he kept his fingers from delving between the toes.

It'll be safer to turn to my prayers at once before bad thoughts take hold—let me no wrong or idle word, un-thinkin' say, set Thou a seal upon my lips, just for today. Hymns always bring tears to my eyes, I'm emotional. He knelt before the silver-gilt Crucifix standing on the low iron mantelpiece over the fireplace. He said his one Our Father, three Hail Marys, one Glory be, and then he recited his 'Virgin Mary, meek and mild, Watch o'er me thy little child'.

He got up and was pulling down his shirt under his buttocks to get into bed when he heard the high greeting tone of the mother, and then a man's voice, 'God bless all here!'

Uncle John! His feeling within went nice at the sound. Isn't life strange how you warm to one voice and not to another. I'll go down and say Hello. He went to take his trousers off the bedrail, and stood listening at the open door, waiting for the right moment to go down.

'Well, isn't that great to see you now,' said the mother, 'and I never saw you lookin' better, God spare you the health.'

'Musha, I'm middlin' enough, thanks be to God,' said Uncle John. 'How are you, M'Cloud?'

'Never bloody worse, John,' said the father.

'Arra bad cess to you,' put in the mother, 'haven't we a great, great deal to be thankful for?'

'D'you hear that one now, John?' said the father. 'Wouldn't she madden a saint—always thankful?'

'Sure that woman isn't the same as yourself an' myself, M'Cloud, depending on the pocket for her wealth,' said Uncle John. 'She has her gold in her heart.'

'Then indeed it's low enough there at times,' laughed the mother.

'It's like old Thatcher Tigue used to say of Una Cafferty. God rest their two souls and the souls of all the dead,' said Uncle John, 'though 'twas in the Irish he'd say it. "*I'll never believe you are poor,*" he used to say, "*till they bring me the word that death itself has struck you.*"'

No one spoke after that for nearly a minute in the room below, and then Uncle John said: 'It was the poet in Ireland long ago said that of someone. He meant the heart in them was so rich they could never be poor.'

'Musha, God rest you, Thatcher Tigue,' said the mother, 'for the soft and generous word was ever with you.'

'I tell you that's a great sayin', John,' said the father loudly, 'an' a damn good sayin', an' a bloody true sayin' at that, for the woman there, your sister——'

'Arra stop goin' on till I wet the tea,' said the mother lightly. He heard her quick step cross the kitchen floor, and imagined her shining smiling face waiting at the tap for the kettle to fill.

85

Maybe I'd be as well not go down. I'd like to but somehow I feel shy of how nice he is. He'd give me a shilling I'm sure, knowing what day it is tomorrow. Maybe I should stay here where I'm safe, with my prayers said. He put his trousers back on the bedrail and got into bed. It seemed that the voices at play in the street and the bright evening summer light kept him awake for a long time. He began to sing, ' Brave Robert Emmet, the darlin' of Ireland, Brave Robert Emmet, he died with a smile.' The evening was hot.

He woke up in the darkness from a choking nightmare, and felt himself suffocating. ' Willie! Willie!' he tried to call. There was something round his neck and he couldn't get his breath. ' Willie, I'm chokin'. Quick!' He felt Willie pulling something over his head and then his breath came back. ' You had your head through a hole in the blanket,' said Willie.

He got up the moment he heard the mother call him next morning. The room was clean and tidy when he went down, and this pleased him, for he found it easier to think and be calm amongst tidiness. She had clean stockings and a clean shirt for him, his Sunday suit of dark tweed was there, his white stiff celluloid collar was sponged clean, and his boots with the new laces were perfect. After washing the feeling of fasting felt pure and pleasant, and his head felt clear and calm, and there was a complete absence of the sense of temper rising in him. I can believe this is going to be the happiest day in my life, he thought, even though I have no money in my pocket. I couldn't have believed it.

The father got up at half past eight, and went round the house, wearing a pair of serge trousers, his wool singlet, and an old pair of lowdown shoes. He hurried straight to the door the moment the paper was dropped in, and he picked it up, went across to his chair, took his mug of tea, and sat down comfortably and opened the paper. On the front the boy could see a large bright picture of men in tall hats and ladies wearing bright dresses. Suddenly the father jumped to his feet. ' The divil roast that flamer of a paper-seller,' he cried, '—he's left me the wrong paper.' He looked for someone in the house to offer to go after the man, and when they didn't he put on an old jacket and went to the door and looked up the street.

'The Lord choke, strangle an' suffocate that hell's flamer who put that picture into the paper of them bone-lazy Ascot bastards,' he said, coming in.

'Do you hear that now,' sighed the mother, blessing herself, 'an' the child goin' out to his First Receivin'!'

'Well wouldn't it sicken a saint,' said the man mildly, 'with the Strike in its third month an' half the country starvin' an' they go exhibitin' a flamin' monstrosity like that fernenst the public. Sure isn't it only griggin' the people they are! Musha, if I'd that flamin' fool responsible for that paper here I'd take him by the throat an' choke the life out of him.'

'You'd better be goin', agraw,' said the mother, 'this is a terrible house surely. An' if I'm not killed dead with talk of the Strike no one ever was.'

'What else would I talk of but the Strike?' the father shouted.

'But surely there's a sane way of talkin',' said the mother.

'Goodbye, mother,' he said, kissing her. 'Goodbye, father.'

'So long, there's a good boy,' said the father, 'don't be mindin' me. But if you see that fool of a paper-seller tell him I'll black his bloody cross-eye for him.'

'Goodbye, agraw,' said the mother. 'I'll be watchin' for you at Mass. I'll be behind.'

CHAPTER ELEVEN

First Communion

THIS IS NICE walking along beside Willie, he thought. Sometimes he's very nice the way he walks along quiet-like. 'You don't think I'll drop the Sacred Host or anythin', Willie?'

'Ah no, not at all,' said Willie. 'Keep your head well back, then be sure you close your mouth the minute the priest puts the Host down on your tongue.'

They parted near the church, for he had to go into school to have his sash fitted on. He looked round and saw Willie watching him, and they waved to each other. It's nice to live in peace and good nature. I'd like if we had a nice clean newspaper shop, and everyone nice and friendly coming and going, and each doing his share with the nice clean newspapers and comics, and no crossness or dirt or cockroaches, but a nice simple life. He went into the school hall and there was Ernest Keating. I know about you peeping into the girls' doings, watching them pull up their bloomers. Lord save me or I perish!

'Grab a sash quick, Michael,' said Ernest. 'There aren't enough proper 'uns to go round, an' tha'll have to have one hangin' o'er thy ankles.'

He made a dash for the pile of sashes and began to sort them out. 'Not that,' said Ernest, 'try this. Aye, this 'un, Michael, it's exactly thy fit. Go an' ask Miss Twining to pin it on. Harry, grab a sash quick afore all the good 'uns go.'

He went over to Miss Twining. She was wearing a silky coat and a straw hat with a wide brim and a blue ribbon on it, and when she stooped over him to fasten the sash and he felt her hand on his shoulder and the way she pressed the pin into his jacket and the clasp of her hand on him, he thought, if she were my mother!—and then there came the sight of his mother going round the house at home and he felt a disloyal stab and was sorry.

'You haven't broken your fast, Michael?' she asked.

'N-no, Miss, oh no, Miss,' he said.

'There, there,' she said, putting the sash straight down his back. She's nearly crying, he thought, moving away and feeling a heart pain from the moment's closeness. He watched her move among the forty boys. How nice rich folk smell!

'I think we're all here,' she said. 'Now get in line.'

'Please, Miss, please, Miss,' called Ernest Keating, 'James Higley isn't here yet.'

'Oh dear! Stand in line, will you please. All of you. Has anyone seen James Higley? Will you stand in line there.'

They were almost ready to leave when James Higley came in. He was shining of face from washing, and he wore a large suit, and his shoes were polished but worn down at the heels. Miss Twining hurriedly pinned a sash on him and pushed him into place.

'Please, Miss,' he heard James whisper, 'I've broke me fast.'

On James's eyelid he could see the big tear blobs.

'James, James, James,' she whispered, 'how could you? How did you? Tell me, tell me, when did it happen?'

'Please, Miss,' whispered James, 'I was comin' to school with a lad called Ben Frost who goes to Clitterden Street School—they've no holiday—an' he suddenly gave me an Atty's mint ball an' I stuck it in my mouth without thinkin'.'

'Oh, how could you forget the day?'

'I spitted it out at once, Miss.'

'You spat it out, James! You didn't swallow any? Then of course you haven't broken your fast, you silly boy. Here's your sash. You're positive you didn't swallow any? Oh, James, you're all right. Now when you kneel down in church I want you to say one good Act of Contrition. Just that. Don't tell anyone but God, and you'll be perfectly safe.'

James let out a long smile. 'How do, Michael,' he said.

'How do, James.' The line of figures began to move across the school yard towards the church, bobbing and waggling. Have they each got a snow mountain inside or are James and I the only two? It won't melt, Jamesey love.

Through the grey cool porch into church, everybody stepping aside for the First Communicants, hand down in the font up to the palm, all wet with cold holy water, ' In the Name of the Father, and of the Son, and of the Holy . . . ' and down the aisle, stumbling over one another leaving the font. They knelt in the six front empty rows on the Gospel side, facing and looking up at the altar heaped with flowers. On the Epistle side were six rows of girl First Communicants, dressed in white. Behind was a feeling of a great crowded church.

He was about to get off his knees and sit down when the vestry door opened. A bell tinkled, followed by a weary scraping of massed feet as the congregation stood. He glanced sideways and saw the server, Winterbottom, emerge from the vestry. A boy of thirteen, tall, of solemn face and bearing, thin hair that seemed to be going bald at the sides, he now moved with slow tread, looking like an old silent acolyte in his cassock and cotta, whilst behind him Father O'Leary appeared to roll along, smiling sideways at the communicants, the silk chasuble aslant his round fat shoulders, and the alb trailing along the floor. I'm glad it's these two— Mass is never the same if you don't like the priest or server. At the foot of the altar the accustomed hand of Winterbottom received the priest's biretta, they genuflected together, then they mounted the altar. When the chalice had been placed they descended the steps. They knelt, the congregation with them.

'In nomine Patris, et Filii, et Spiritus Sancti. Amen. Introibo ad Altare Dei.'

' Ad Deum qui laetificat juventutem meam.'

To God who giveth joy to my youth. Winterbottom— they call him Coldarse. The world is ever quick to mock and make fun of one. I love the noble look of this pale fine face. At this first bit of the Mass you feel fresh. That vestment is

90

much brighter than usual, that old pale gold look, with all the tiny flowers and touches of purple and red, though it doesn't look right somehow without the cross. '*Confiteor Deo omnipotenti . . .*' I suppose the two there have their sins as well as anybody else. Does he have bad thoughts? The candle flames are bright there, but soon they'll have spots gathering round them—I can feel it coming. He's very swift is Father O'Leary. Everybody's waiting for the standing up part. Sometimes it comes quickly and sometimes you'd think it would never come. It's near now. Mumble, mumble, mumble. Catholics have great patience surely. Ah, at last. Hear them all sigh. '*Dominus vobiscum.*' '*Et cum spiritu tuo.*' Rising and sighing. Thumb crosses on forehead, lips and heart for Gospel, stretch legs and quickly scratch behind whilst nobody's watching.

All said and done, get down again on knees. Organ grunts: '*O Sacred Heart, what shall I render Thee . . .*' The English are great the way they always know the right tune it's playing. I'll pretend singing a line now and again. Why is it I have a voice that sticks silent in my throat? He'll turn in a minute after all that whispering to himself—'*per omnia saecula saeculorum.*' World without end. Amen. Straw women. Peed i' bed an' started swimmin'. There goes the organ again. How must nicer if they all had fiddles! *Trrlink*! *trrlink*! *trrlink*! God forgive my daft thoughts. First Communion Day. Help me. Spots in front of candles. *Trrlink*. Clothes sigh all round as bodies bend. The hand of Winterbottom reaching for the bell. Bow, bow, bow.

I wonder how a church can stand just the pillars holding it. There's sweat running down under my armpits. If this moment God was to take the life out of the stone the entire place would fall down. I mustn't faint. 'Soul of My saviour, sanctify my breast.' Let 'um sing, I'll rest. I can sing in my mind as good as the next. Thank God for that bell. Winterbottom never raises his eyes as he draws the snow-white Communion cloth over the marble rail. All that cloth's got to be burnt if you let the Host slip from your mouth on to it. Thank God the girls are getting moving. James leant and

91

whispered: 'They would have to be first.' All their gar-
landed heads bowed as they kneel and wait.

> O Mary, dearest Mother,
> Of heaven's immortal bowers,
> Will you gather for a little child
> A bouquet of sweet flowers?

I'll have a go at the next line. *I wish my little*—what a stuck
voice I've got. *A cradle fair and gay.* It's coming better now.
*Where my blessed Jesus may repose, On my First Com-
munion Day.* I'm beginning to feel happy like everybody
else. Father O'Leary holding the Host: '*Domine, non sum
dignus . . .*' Lord I am not worthy that Thou shouldst enter
under my roof: Say but the word and my soul shall be
healed. Swift steps down the altar. Communion starts.

He looked up as Miss Twining stooped over them, her
face pale beneath the straw hat. At last. Knees stiff and legs
aching. Church is packed. My mother'll be watching. Is my
hair straight for the procession? He waited with other boys
until girls had all had their Communion. Then forward he
went to kneel at Communion Rail. Ee, what a high step.
Marble's nice and cold. Ee, that linen's stiff. Tuck it under
chin. Host has been transubstantiated. Body, blood, soul and
divinity of Jesus Christ our Lord. He'll come into me. He
made all the factories, schools, pits, houses, rivers, seas,
ships, and is the boss of all teachers, kings and queens and
other bosses, and He will come right into me. Please God I
don't drop Him or else I'll get into trouble. Little lad at St.
Stephens dropped Host and they had to burn cloth. Nearer,
nearer, nearer. Heart striking in temple. Get ready to lift
head. Throat feels empty, dry. His voice chanting.

'*Corpus Domini nostri Jesu Christ custodiat*—' head
lifted and cool safe hand of priest presses gently against
cheek and tasteless flat flake touches tongue, '*animam tuam
in vitam aeternam. Amen.*' Close mouth quick. I didn't drop
it. It's stuck to top of mouth. Can't pull it off roof—only
priest can touch. Tongue's gone stiff. What'll I do? They're
all going, leaving me. I'd better join in and quick. Neck's

itchy. Oh if folk see flea! I can't swallow You yet. Nobody knows. Got a right good shine on shoes. We're getting round back of church—it's cooler. Spud in James's stocking. Pity. Happen I've one in my own. Strike your neck quick and get shut of flea. Funny, felt nothing. I'm not looking devout enough. What'll folk think? We're on the last stretch. I feel daft being so big. Back into seats. Kneel. Stoop head and shut eyes and cover face with hands. Oh, the particle of the Host still on the roof of mouth!

Swallow! God, God, forgive me. Making holy show of myself and You within me. Help me, God and Blessed Virgin. Joy. Joy. Joy. God in me. Soul white. O God I thank You. That's enough. I'll lift head. Will not forget you, my Lord inside me. That feels nice now. Sickness gone. Read prayer-book.

' *Would that I might obtain this favour, Lord, to find Thee alone and by Thyself, to open unto Thee my whole heart, and enjoy Thee even as my soul desireth: and that henceforth none may look upon me, nor any creature move me, but that Thou alone mayest speak to me, and I to Thee, as beloved is wont to speak to his beloved, and friend to feast with friend.*' Someone nudged him, and there was James whispering : ' I hope they give us a good breakfast, Michael. I'm right clemmed with hunger.'

When Mass was over the rest of the school drifted off, and the First Communicants were taken to a free breakfast in the school basement. Long tables were laid with sandwiches of canned salmon, cheese, and tomatoes, and there were plates of rock buns, and tea was served from an urn. The tea was watery and the food seemed tasteless to him. He thought of a thick hot sandwich of bread dipped in bacon fat at home, and of the mug of sweet strong tea. The better-off boys seemed to have got together playing games, and they were darting about and stealing hair-ties from the better-off girls. The poor boys, such as James, seemed to be very quiet. He longed for the moment he could get away, for the shouting and running about depressed him. At the end of breakfast each boy was presented with an inscribed

93

book by Miss Twining. He was watching for a chance to slip away when suddenly she came upon him and drew him aside.

' I've something special for you, Michael,' she said, handing him another book. ' That's for *you*,' she said.

' Oh, Miss, thank you, Miss,' he said. She stooped and he expected she would kiss him, but suddenly she patted his back. I think she loves me.

He kept the book hidden until he got away from the others. Then walking along towards the brewery he took it out. It was a stiff-backed book, with a green glossy cover, and on the outside was written : ' *Moore's Irish Melodies* '. He opened it and read the first verse he saw :

> *O breathe not his name*
> *Let it sleep in the shade,*
> *Where cold and unhonoured*
> *His relics are laid.*

That's well put together. I'd like to memorise that. If I was to go this minute with the white soul on me it 'ud be up to heaven like a shot. It seems an odd kind of thing, but that's the way it is. Straight into Paradise. And I'm going to keep it this way at that. O breathe not his name.

CHAPTER TWELVE

Factory and Churchyard

As he reached the street corner he came upon Herbert Duckworth wheeling the baby.

'How do, Michael,' Herbert said, bringing the baby-carriage to a halt.

'How do, Herbert.'

'Not goin' to school, Michael?'

'It's the feast of *Corpus Christi*,' he said.

'Who'd have thought it,' said Herbert. 'But honestly, I'll send *all* my kids to Cath'lic school. It's a better eddication an' more holidays.' He saw the books. 'Ee, where's tha got them from?'

'They're First Communion presents,' he said. Herbert held his hand out for the big one. 'I promise thee I'll not dirty it,' he said. It was a book of stories about animals, Mr Rabbit, Mr Fox and Mr Frog, dressed up as human beings, and having lots of tea parties. At a first glance he had known he could never like it.

'Would you like to have it, Herbert?' he asked. He felt he wanted to give something away.

'What—not *keep* it?'

'Yes.'

'For good?'

'Yes.'

'For nothing?'

'Yes.'

Herbert shook his head and remarked: 'Ee, nay, but it's thine.'

'I don't want it,' he said. 'I've got this other.'

'Then I *can* have it,' said Herbert. He looked at him and said intensely: 'Ta, ta very much. I'll see thee right for this.' Then he carefully put the book under a blanket in the

95

pram. 'I've got to be goin',' he said, 'I'm takin' our Henry to be fed. Art comin', Michael?'

He wanted to go in home and have some breakfast and be greeted by his mother, but he said: 'I'll just dash in the back way an' leave this other book. I'll be out in a tick.'

'I'll be goin' to'rds the "Wild Goose",' said Herbert. 'Her feeds him in the little churchyard.'

He hurried up the back street and slipped into their own back gate, which was open. He stopped in the narrow back-yard on hearing the sound of an unexpected voice in the house. It was that of the one-legged shopkeeper, Mr Durham.

'I've got to pay my way, Missis, just the same as any-body else,' he heard him say. 'You've run up a strap bill of nearly twenty quid these last months—that's more than I credit my old customers with.'

'But you know you'll get your money, sir,' he caught the quavery touch in his mother's voice, '—once the men go back to the pits.'

'Aye, but when is that goin' to be, eh? The way they're goin' on they'll never go back. Railway chaps wur goin' to come out wi' 'em, but they'd more sense. So had the trans-port. It's no use them askin' for this, that, an' t'other—they've got to accept that cut in wages. I'm not blamin' you, Missis, but I've got to get money in to pay my bills. I can't let you have any more till you've wiped summat off that bill.'

'Very well, sir,' his mother's voice cut in, 'I won't trouble you for any more food.'

'Now don't get on your high horse, Missis,' said the man. 'You Irish are all the same—down one minute an' up the next.' Then he heard the man laughing coarsely, and his mother's voice. 'Now, sir, remember you're a gentleman—and whose home you're in.'

He hurried into the closet out of the way. His face was flushed with shame. But he was glad no one had heard or seen. He wrapped the green book of Moore's melodies in a piece of newspaper and searched round for a place to hide it. My soul is still white, he thought, or nearly white. He couldn't find a place, and he was about to look for a spot

96

in the backyard when he heard the back door creaking open and the sound of Mr Durham's voice: 'Lovely day, I must say.' He shut the door softly and tight as he heard the man clomp across the yard and out of the back gate. After a few moments he hurried in. His mother had a broom in her hand and was muttering '"Hail, holy Queen, Mother of mercy, hail our lives our sweetness and our hope..."' as she quickly swept the floor. She turned at once at the sound of his entering the kitchen, and the worried look went from her face.

'Come an' give me the pure saint's kiss on this holy morning,' she said.

He went over and gave her a kiss. I love the soft grey-blue look of her eyes and the smell of her.

'Is he out?'

'He is.'

'Did you see me in the procession?'

'Indeed I did. There was no one to compare with you, my love.'

'I thought I had a flea on my neck.'

'Arra what flea would touch your lovely skin.'

'Sure I must chase off after Herbert Duckworth,' he said, 'I promised I'd go off with him to the "Wild Goose" factory where his mother works.'

'Did you have anything to eat, agraw?'

'Oh a great breakfast of everything they gave us,' he said.

'Have a supeen of milk,' she said, going to the cupboard and getting the jug.

She knows, he thought, she knows exactly what I ate. How does she always know everything? 'Here,' she said, 'have this morseleen of yesterday's bread.' She gave him a piece of her own soda bread, thick with butter and a sup of milk.

'Look at the lovely book I got,' he said, 'from Miss Twining. I must run off now an' catch Herbert.' He turned back and gave her another kiss.

'Oh what a wonderful morning, praise be to God,' she said. 'Look the sun comin' down even here between house an' factory.'

O.S.B.—D

He kissed her again and went running off after Herbert. He caught him as he was wheeling the pram into the little churchyard of St James the Less. The poor misfortunate souls in their graves, he thought, who tried to live right and had the wrong beliefs. They didn't know the signs of the true Church: *It is One, It is Holy, It is Catholic, It is Apostolic*. ' In Loving Memory of ' in place of ' *Requiescat in Pace*.'

'They reckon there's a gravestone in here,' said Herbert, ' which says, " Where e'er thou be let the wind go free, For holding it were the death of me." I've looked but I've never seen it. But they do say it's true. It were a toff as were at a society party an' were burstin' to let off but hadn't the sense to because he thought it were bad manners, an' at last he dropped dead. Serves him dash well right if he'd no more sense.'

The churchyard was empty. ' Keep a look-out for the school board,' said Herbert, ' in a black billycock an' a long black overcoat. He's the bane of my life, yon chap. If he catches me I'll get summonsed. Tha'd think a grown chap 'ud have summat better to do.'

It was pleasant sitting in the shade, with the nice clean paths, flower borders and all the graves so neat and tidy, and the little church in the middle. Behind them, across a short street, was the ' Wild Goose ' factory. It was six storeys high, with hundreds of windows.

'See that window up there,' pointed Herbert, ' second from the end on the fourth floor—that's where my mam works. Somebody'll ha' spotted us an' told her. The women allus send summat down for me. Apples, toshies, an' a piece of cake for certain.'

The baby in the pram began to cry and Herbert took him out. ' Hungry, love, eh? Well, don't worry, she'll be here in a minute.' He felt a pain at the first cry of the child. ' Here,' said Herbert, ' like to nurse him for a minute whilst I make his pram?'

As he took the child his heart tapped away with anxiety. Will I drop him? I hope he doesn't suffocate. He might die because nobody has told him how to live. He doesn't know

98

the difference. Oh, if he dies in my arms! Oh, he might die at any second—he doesn't know the difference between death and life. The child stopped crying, gazed hard at the boy, then opened his mouth wide and smiled, his eyes bright with joy.

'Ee, smilin' for little Michael are you?' cooed Herbert.

'Do you bring him every day, Herbert?'

'Twice a day. Once at mornings once at afternoons. Old Paddy Bryce said he hadn't to be put on milk powder stuff just yet awhile. Anyway you can't beat mother's milk. Stands to reason—it's put there for the job, eh? Here's my mam now.'

Mrs Duckworth came clacking along the stone path in her clogs. She slid a hand inside the top of her dark blue pinafore as she approached and was unfastening buttons underneath, and she took the baby from him with a swift absent-minded movement, gave an accustomed twist of the shoulder to swing her breast free, and the child at once fastened himself upon it with a fit of excited grunting. Then she sat down.

'Everything all right, luv?' she asked Herbert.

He nodded, 'Aye, mam.' Then she smiled, and he realised it was the first time she had become aware of his presence. Her pinafore was greasy, her black ribbed stockings were covered with cotton dust, and her clogs were cut open at the sides. She blinked in the sunshine. Her face was oily pale, and that first mother look had gone, that look had been rich and warm, that had been large, soft and living with mother-hood. He recalled how he had once wanted to press himself to her breast and now he could hardly believe it. She had an odd odour of hot oil and cotton. But the child had not turned against her. Oh Blessed Virgin Mary, is this a sin? His arms now felt empty without the child. I never knew a baby was so lovely to hold.

'Hetty an' Alice sent these down for you,' said the woman taking two oranges and a paper bag out of her pocket. Herbert handed him an orange, and then opened the bag. 'Why they've sent two pieces,' he said.

'Aye,' said the mother, 'they must ha' seen Michael.'

Herbert gave him a large piece of Nelson cake and said: 'We'll give them a wave.' The boys looked up to the windows, waited, and then waved to two women who were looking down. The women smiled and waved. 'Oh my God, because Thou art so good, I am very sorry that I have sinned against Thee, and I will not sin again.' If that thought about the breast was a sin, then I am free once more, because I am sorry. Soul a white snowy mountain.

'Gas chap called,' said Herbert.

'Did he take much out?'

'He'd a whacking big capful of coppers.'

'How much discount did he give thee back?'

'Fourpence.'

'He's frauded thee,' she said. 'Wait till I see him. It shoulda been at least a shilling.'

'That's what I said to him.'

He looked at the woman's face. He had never seen sweat dribble out before. She didn't trouble to wipe it, and it rolled down her forehead, gathered on her eyebrows, and then trickled through on to her eyelids. 'By gow, it's hot in there this mornin',' she remarked.

'There's a heat wave comin' from America,' said Herbert. 'I saw it in t'papers in t'papershop. Hy, mam, just look what Michael's given me—' he carefully took out the book and showed it to her.

She blinked. 'Ee that is nice,' she said. 'Where did you get it, luv?'

'It was given me as a present,' he said. He paused: 'It's my First Communion Day.'

'Oh, that's why you're dressed up,' she said, swinging the child across to the other breast. 'What did you do?'

'You have Communion,' he said.

'Aye,' said Herbert, 'you have a swig of wine, don't you?'

'The priest has wine,' he said, 'but we have unleavened bread. I mean it looks like bread, but it's been consecrated, and at the moment of—of transubstantiation it's miraculously turned into Jesus Christ Our Lord, his body, blood, soul and divinity—' he stopped himself, ashamed, showing off again. He could hear only the child's *suck, suck, suck,* in the graveyard.

'Order two ounces of roast heart for thy dad's tea,' said the woman.

'Aye, I will, mam,' said Herbert. 'Dun't go back yet, mam, Hetty an' Alice will keep your cards runnin'.'

'Never put on good nature,' said the woman, putting the child back in the pram. 'Anyway, we'll be closin' down at week-end as it is, if this damn strike's not settled.'

He flushed.

'I reckon it's all right me going to the Chantbent coal tip?' said Herbert. 'I'll be back about five or six.'

'Aye, we could do wi' a bit o' coal,' she said.

'I'll leave our Henry with Mrs Beardson.'

'Here y'are, Michael luv,' she said abruptly, handing him twopence out of her purse.

'Oh no, thanks, ma'am,' he said.

'Tak' it,' she said. 'It's for your Communion.'

'Go on,' said Herbert, 'tak' it afore she changes her mind.'

He took the two warm pennies. Then the woman hurried off. He watched her slip out of the churchyard into the factory. She didn't turn round. She gave no kiss to Herbert or the child. Herbert put back his shoulders. He sensed Herbert was proud of the fact of his mother having given away twopence.

'Tha's got thy tram fare,' said Herbert. 'What about comin' to the tip pickin' coal?'

'Yes, I'll come.' he said.

'Tha'll need a bag,' said Herbert. 'Never mind, I think I've got a kitbag as should just do thee. Tha'd better slip on an' tell thy mam first. There'll be a few of us going, but tell her I'll look after thee.'

'I'll run in an' change my clothes, Herbert.'

'Aye, but don't be too long about it. We'll wait for thee at the corner. Tha'll want a few butties wi' thee too, tell thy mam.'

He went in home. 'Oh mother,' he said, 'I'm going off picking coal with Herbert and some others.'

'Musha, won't it kill you on a day like this?'

'Will you give me some bread and butter?'

'I haven't a scrap, agraw, till I bake. Change your clothes quickly before he comes down.'

'Will you go up and get my old ones, mother, off the side of the bed? He might hear me.'

The mother got the old trousers and jersey. He changed, put on his clogs, and was ready to go, when she went and lifted the dresser cover and gave him threepence. 'Buy yourself something,' she said. 'I'm sorry there's no bread in the house, agraw.'

'It doesn't matter, mother,' he said.

Willie came in. 'Where are you off, Mickyeen?'

'Getting coal from the tip.'

'Take care would you let the old fella hear you,' said Willie.

'Why?'

'He'd say you were a blackleg breaking the strike.'

'Take care of yourself, agraw, take care,' said the mother.

'Herbert Duckworth's looking after me. I must run.' He hurried out of the house fearing less something would happen to stop him from going. *Blackleg*, a dark word. Down at the bottom of the street they were ready for leaving.

CHAPTER THIRTEEN

Picking Coal in the Sun

'I've got thee a kitbag for thy coal, Michael,' said Herbert. He went in amongst the party of five, and a boy called Spadger Chadwick turned to him and said: 'Keep thy eyes skinned for the school board, mate. You Cath'lics have got a proper holiday, but we're liable.'

As they walked up Back Greenley Street he felt the air about him thickly hot and unstirring, and the unshadowed spots in the open had a heat like that from a baking oven. Flies buzzed everywhere, stinks rose up from sewers, hot cobbles glistened in the roadway, and along by the low cottages were dark airless alleys and the low humming of heat crooned in the ear.

'Our old chap reckons it's worse nor Mesopotamia,' said Spadger Chadwick.

'It'll go hotter yet, unless I'm mistaken,' said Herbert. 'It's the heat wave from America.'

'I wish they'd bloomin' well keep it,' said Ben Shilliton.

'There was a picture in th' paper this mornin',' said Ernie Haddock, 'of a chap frying an egg on the sideset at Piccadilly Circus in London.'

'Oh aye,' said Jimmy Taylor. 'An' who had it?'

'Had it? Had what?'

'Bloody egg, you chump.'

'How the hell does he know?' said Spadger Chadwick. 'He were only sayin' that there were a picture of a chap fryin' one in the street at Piccadilly Circus.'

'Well the next time tha comes with a tale come with a proper 'un,' said Jimmy. 'An' all I can say is that a chap who ruins a good egg an' takes a photo of it, just to tell folk it's hot when the flamin' sun is all but settin' 'um afire deserves geldin'.'

'M'mouth fair runs, Jimmy,' said Ben Shilliton, rubbing his groin with a hand in his trouser pocket, 'when I hear a guggy egg sizzlin' in the pan.'

'Shut up, Ben,' said Spadger, 'tha can see old Jimmy's got that egg on the brain. Why, the lad's gone green in the dial from suppin' the strikers' free pea soup from the "Weaver's Arms".'

'We've had our share,' said Jimmy, his face flushing, 'our share an' no more.' He turned on Ernie Haddock: 'Thy mam's allus the first in the queue of a dinner-time.'

'Aye,' said Ernie, 'but she gets it in a jug.'

Jimmy stopped. 'Art tha hintin', Haddock,' he said, 'about my mam supposed have taken the chamberpot for soup?'

'I never said so,' said Ernie; 'I only said my mam gets ours in a jug.'

'That's a lie been spread about my mother,' said Jimmy. 'An' I only wish I could lay hands on him as started it.'

'Talkin' about poes,' said Tommy Roberts, 'did you hear about that lad at school as had to spell "potato" an' he spelt it "tato", so the teacher says—'

Spadger cut in: '"Where's your *po*, Willie?" she says, an' Willie says, 'Po, Miss?—we aren't got one, we use a four-pound jam jar."'

'Why does tha allus have to chirp in, Spadger?' said Tommy. 'Anyway, there's no such things as a *four*-pound jam jar,' said Herbert. 'Jam jumps up from two-pound to seven-pound.'

'Tha'rt thinkin' of pickles,' said Spadger. ''Course I wouldn't know for certain. We allus have our jam delivered in fourteen-pound jars of Shiver's best blackcurrant.'

'Thy mam, Spadger,' said Tommy, 'buys twopenn'orth of loose jam in a saucer, plum an' apple, when you're lucky.'

Jimmy turned on Ernie Haddock: 'I know one thing my mam never has done,' he said, '—stitched old stocking-legs on my jersey for sleeves.'

Herbert said to Jimmy: 'don't thee be personal, lad. We're none of us perfect. Neither in looks nor clothes.'

Ernie said: 'I'll let thee 'ave it one of these fine days, Taylor.'

'Insult my mother!' exclaimed Jimmy, rising on his toes and putting up his fists,'—why, I'll lay thee out on this bloody spot I will!'

Herbert stopped. 'If you two want a scrap,' he said, 'you can 'ave one. But if you do, you don't come pickin' coal with me. I've enough on my plate as it is. Especially as neither one of you could knock a fly off a custard.'

'He started it,' said Jimmy.

'I never did,' said Ernie.

'Tha brought up that rumour about my mother an' the pea soup,' said Jimmy. 'Nothing but a blasted lie.'

'An' what did tha try to say about my mother an' sewin' stocking-sleeves on my jersey? You damn liar.'

'Hush!' said Herbert. 'You're in danger of death for twenty-four hours when you call somebody a liar. It's in the Bible. Now look here, lads, what right 'as either of you to say things about another chap's mother? They've brought you into the world, 'aven't they? Then it's only right an' proper to think the best of 'um. Dash it all, a mother feeds you, clothes you, looks after you—what more do you want? Say what you want about a chap to his face, but keep mothers out of it.'

They were all silent for a moment, then Spadger added: 'His fathers too!'

'So shake hands now, said Herbert. The two boys held back. 'Come on, come on,' said Herbert, 'act like Britishers, can't you?'

'Aye, even though the Gatling's jammed an' the jolly old colonel dead,' said Spadger, 'an' the regiment blind with dust an' smoke, the least you two can do is play the game.'

Jimmy and Ernie looked at each other and each put out a hand. 'Good lads,' said Herbert as they shook hands, 'you'll not go far wrong if you're British.'

Spadger began to whistle *Rule Britannia* and the party moved happily along. At the top of Back Greenley Street some small children were playing beside a grid in the gutter.

One boy had a broken clog-iron with which he was scraping away the earth from between the cobblestones, whilst another beside him piddled on the earth. Two little girls were pressing the damp earth into tin lids, and laying out the moulds on the pavement.

'Hot pies,' called out one of the girls.

'You'll be catching fever from that grid,' said Herbert. 'Now come on, play over there, away from it.' He coaxed them away, although they didn't like to be disturbed. 'What's up, Michael?' said Herbert, 'tha looks as though tha wants to play with 'em.'

He felt himself flushing and shook his head. Suddenly he realised that he had wanted to join in and scrape away at the black bits of earth, for the endless pavement of the street was like some hot stone field, that made him want to dig like fury at times into the bits of earth between the cobblestones.

'Did you get your butties, Michael?' asked Herbert.

'I forgot,' he lied. 'But I've got some coppers.'

'Tha can have some of mine,' said Herbert.

'I'll buy some sweets,' he said.

'Tha means toffees,' said Herbert. 'Let's get 'em from Daddy Addison's.'

He bought a pennyworth of toffee and shared it. They all seemed impressed with this, and felt them warm to him. They were running for the tram when Ernie Haddock cried out: 'Oh look, our Bess!'

A rough-coated mongrel dog came up uneasily, wagging its tail. 'I'll murder you,' said Ernie. 'How have you got out?'

'Send her back,' said Spadger.

'She's on heat,' said Ernie. 'My mam doesn't want Jack Brown to get at her. He's allus round the door.'

'Tak' her back then.'

'I aren't time.' He turned to Herbert. 'Can I fetch her, Herbert?'

'Aye, tha might as well,' said Herbert, 'bein' as the poor thing's here.'

Ernie hugged the dog and she wagged her tail with delight at the change in greeting.

'On top,' said Herbert, 'on top up in front.'

They hurried up the steps of the tram and ran along to the open front, where there was a round seat. They rushed for places, but Herbert stood, facing the breeze. The tram swayed along the road, with the boys talking excitedly and eating toffee, whilst Herbert remained silent and standing. Then the tram began to climb until it clanged along into open spaces, where there were green fields, and the heat was purified by the rush of cool air. Tommy Roberts began to sing '*There's an old mill by the stream, Nellie Dean*,' in a high boyish voice, and they all joined in, even Herbert, '*Sweet Nellie Dean, O my sweet Nellie Dean*,' and Tommy waited and then poured his voice along into the lead, '*Where we used to sit and dream*,' and the others caught it up and sank their voices into the song, 'Sweet Nellie Dean' and Tommy bright-faced, '*And the waters as they flow, Seem to murmur soft an' low*,' and he looked round at their faces so lifted and shining, and there went through him a long, '*You are my heart's desire, I love you*,' all their faces in the breeze, '*Nellie Dean*.'

The tram shuddered and stopped and a voice called out: 'All change. Coal Lane End.'

'Hy, we're here. An' he never collected the fares.'

'Shut your mouth,' said Spadger, 'an' give your behind a chance.'

Herbert led the way off the car, and as he was going down the steps the conductor looked up and said: 'Hy, did I collect your fares?' and Herbert said: 'No, you didn't.' And the conductor said: 'Tha'rt a damn liar, lad, I know very well I did. Quick, I'm not looking.'

It was nearly two miles to Chantbent pit coal tip. Herbert kept a steady pace in front, and he kept it up with him, whilst the others made frequent stops to burst the tar bubbles along the road.

'There'll be a couple of coppers guarding the pit road,' said Herbert, 'so we'll cut across the fields.'

He had never felt as happy in England as he did at that moment. The fields and hedges were full of sweet summer smells, and he kept drawing in deep breaths until his head spun with dancing spots. Herbert turned. 'Go quiet, lads, along by this wall—the tip's just at the other side. Right, here we are.'

A sulphurous tang stung his nostrils as he looked up at the great slag heaps. He had expected to see stacks of coal dirt as high as houses, but these were like dark steaming mountains in the midday heat. They excited him. And the sharpness of the air cut clean into the lungs as he breathed, cleansing and scouring away the old dust, it seemed.

'There's the pit where thy dad works,' said Herbert.

'That—' he asked, 'where the two wheels are?'

'That's it,' said Herbert. 'Them's the windin' wheels. Cage is under 'um. It goes down into the earth.'

'I've heard it said, that if tha takes milk to pit with thee,' put in Spadger, 'it's bloody butter by the time tha gets down.'

'What, with the heat?' asked Tommy Roberts.

'No, you mawp, with the damn shaking.'

'It all depends on the chap as is winding the cage,' said Herbert.

He looked at the two big wheels at the top of what seemed a frail and rakish wooden structure. Now he realised why his father hated going to pit at night. What strange people they are that would get coal in place of cutting a nice bit of turf at the bog!

'Right,' said Herbert, 'let's get started.'

'Or shall we have our jackbit first?' asked Jimmy Taylor.

'Nay, by gow,' Herbert gave a laugh, 'we're never going to start eating *afore* work. Nay, it aren't come to that yet.'

'I only thought it 'ud save time,' said Jimmy.

'Jimmy,' remarked Spadger, 'why dussent tell the truth —just for once? Just to give it an airing?'

'Shut up,' said Jimmy, bending down to the job.

He was pleased at how simple picking coal appeared to be. He bent down and saw the others putting small pieces into their sacks, and he did the same. In a short time his back began to ache, but he didn't mind, for already his bag was quarter full. Then Herbert chanced to come near him.

'Nay, nay,' said Herbert, as he picked up a piece and dropped it in his bag, 'that's not coal, lad, that's brass.' Then he peeped inside the bag. 'So's that, an' that—' he went on. Finally he turned the bag upside down. 'Michael,' he said, 'tha's not a gradely piece of coal in all the lot. Look, see that—that has only a surface of coal on it, that underneath is stone or brass. If tha took one of them home an' thy mam put it on the fire it 'ud blow up an' smash your glass-backed dresser. Feel the weight—it's like lead. Now then, feel that piece—that's a luv'ly nut that is. Just the right weight. Feel it. This is not a heap o' coal, lad, it's a heap o' stuff spread out. Tha's got to pick an' scrape for a black diamond. Keep thy eyes skinned. Here, I'll give thee that piece just for luck.'

He was near tears at making such a fool of himself. Bess came near and began to lick his hands. She looked hot and tired. It was a strain to examine the black dull mass for the shiny pieces. Soon his back was aching intensely, his eyes pained him, and his head reeled a little. But when the sweat began to pour out all over he felt better.

A number of men and youths who had been picking at the far side now moved over near the boys. 'Hy, you lot,' said one of the youths, 'eff off.'

'Who?' asked Herbert.

'Who?—You, an' your bloody mates. We don't want the coppers round.'

'Language,' said Herbert. 'Anyway, we're not going. We were here first. An' it's a free country.'

'Yu' cheeky little monkey,' said the youth, coming across. Herbert stood beside his sack, unbudging.

'Art gettin' thyself off,' asked the youth, 'afore I lay thee out?'

'If tha puts a finger on me,' said Herbert, 'I'll par thy shins in. An' I'll raise such a din as'll bring every bobby for miles around.'

'Aye,' put in Ernie, encouraged by Herbert's front, 'an' I'll turn our dog on thee an' it'll chew thy cods off.'

The youth didn't know what to do. Herbert was small and wizened, yet had an odd air of determination about him. One of the men laughed. 'Pick away, lads,' he said, 'but don't make so much noise.' Herbert looked at the youth, and the latter walked away. Then they all bent down to picking once more. He looked and saw Ben picking. His thin face was bright red, and from under the neb of the big dirty cap on his little head a constant stream of sweat seemed to be pouring. Ben's eyes searched the great steaming pile, and every time he saw a piece of coal the long slender fingers moved quickly. His arms, protruding from the baggy adult shirt, were like thin white sticks, and as he drew nearer he heard the rhythmic adenoidal breathing. O sweet Jesus, help us and the poor souls in purgatory!

'Look, Ben,' whispered Spadger, 'a butter'!'

'Where? where?'

Spadger pointed to a fluttering whiteness in the bright air, moving with weary persistence across the slag heap. At once Ben grabbed his coat and went running after it. Spadger tapped his forehead. 'He's got a brick loose up here has old Ben. He'd sooner have a butterfly than a gold watch. But I've never known him to catch one yet. He's allus frickened of striking.'

He's innocent, as they say at home. If this mountain was to open now and swallow us all up he's the only one that would go straight to heaven. I might go with him, because my soul's still white, but I might have to suffer purgatory. But that poor one, with his nose running and he can't swallow a breath of air—he's God's chosen. He's innocent, can't sin, and would be whisked at once to glory by the angels of heaven.

'I vote,' groaned Jimmy Taylor, 'we eat.'

'For once,' said Spadger Chadwick, 'I'm with thee, Jimmy.'

'By rights,' said Herbert, straightening up, and looking at the slag heap, 'we should break its back afore we eat. I've

110

nobbut quarter of a bag—little more. Anyhow, perhaps a break would do us good. I wonder is there anywhere we could get a bit o' shade?'

'We'd have to go across to yon trees o'er the field,' said Tommy.

'Aye, an' leave our bags,' said Herbert, 'an' when we got back they'd be empty. Not likely.'

'It's a bloody swealin', roastin', burnin', parchin' hot day,' remarked Spadger, 'in other words "warm".' They sat down at the foot of a slag heap. 'Ooh, I've sizzled mi arse,' he cried, jumping up. They all laughed as he kept fingering his buttocks. 'Hole in mi trousers,' he said. 'I musta sat with that spot on a piece of hot slate. Who said they could smell pork? Fry an egg i' the street i' London?—what rot! I could roast a leg o' lamb in that sun. Ha, taste at your water, chaps! Mine's on the simmer. Two-three grains o' tea an' I could make a good brewin' up outa this. Ooh, my backside!—can you smell it? Who said "no more than usual"?' Spadger let out a screech of laughter. 'I'm a right bloody comic I am—an' don't bloody know it, Micky, don't know it.' He looked at Spadger's face, streaked with grime and sweat, with its two shining laughing eyes, and suddenly he burst out laughing at the sight and fell on his back on the coal.

Herbert nudged him when he sat up. 'Here, Michael,' he said, passing him a squashed sandwich, 'banana. It'll cool thi' down.'

'Thanks very much,' he said, 'but I'm not hungry.'

'Get it down thee,' said Herbert firmly.

'What—no tommy, Micky?' said Spadger. 'Here, have a bit o' mine——' he handed him a sandwich, 'it's lovely stuff, pig's dick an' lettuce.'

'If tha wants another,' said Tommy Roberts, 'tha can have one of mine.'

He ate greedily, to force down the lump rising in his throat. I've kept myself back from them, he thought, and didn't let myself think they could have decency in them. I'm guilty of Lucifer's sin of pride. The way their faces and voices were so lovely when they sang on the tramcar!—I can never look like that. They're really the innocent ones —and I'm the bad one. I never have been innocent. He looked upward at the towering dark mountain. The soul in mortal sin. The great white mountain of radiant snow was the soul in a state of grace.

'I—I just missed it,' panted Ben. He stood before them, his face purple, and the sweat rolling off.

'Tha'rt out of wind,' said Herbert.

'Nay, he's not,' said Spadger, 'it's just that he's got more than he can get shut of in time.'

'Now, Ben,' said Ernie, 'did tha strike?'

'Aye, 'course I did!' said Ben. 'Well, I did an' I didn't.'

'Now how the flappin' heck does tha expect to catch a butterfly 'bout strikin'?'

'I were just about to strike when I could see I might crush it,' said Ben, 'an' I had it cornered a bit later but I were worried about battin' all the pollen off its wings. They say a butter' dies if tha bats pollen off its wings.'

'Sit down an' curl up in thy hole, Ben,' said Spadger, 'tha'rt sendin' spasms of cold shivers through me.'

'There's one thing about Ben,' said Tommy Roberts, '——he can lick any runner I've ever seen.'

'He were dropped out of th' Olympic Games,' said Spadger, 'on account there wasn't enough room to pin a medal across his chest.'

'Cut it out, Spadger,' said Herbert. 'Ben old boy, sit thee down an' have thy nourishment.'

'Bloody punishment,' said Spadger, 'if he sits where I sat. Honest, I'm not coddin' you, lads, I've a blister on my backside, Micky, holds a quart an' a bit o' water.'

He giggled at the solemn look on Spadger's face. We're going through the same world at the same time, him and me.

'I woulda copped it,' said Ben slowly, 'I would—only I were frickened of hurtin' it.'

'Tha means tha were frickened of it turnin' on thee,' said Spadger. 'Not as I blame thee, Ben, for a butter' can be very

nasty when it turns. I once got attacked by a Red Admiral
—Christ, what a din they make when they bat their wings!'

'It feels like a bloody blowlamp on the top of my nut,'
said Ernie, rubbing the top of his head. 'Can you feel it,
chaps, the heat?'

'What d'you think we are—bloody mummies?' said
Spadger.

'I'd give owt for a little knob o' ice what they put under
fish,' said Ben.

'I could put a half-gallon jar of Pott's herb beer to my
kisser this minute,' said Tommy, 'an' I'll bet all the money
in the world I wouldn't put it down till I necked the lot.
What does tha say, Spadger?'

'I'll tell thee what I do fancy,' said Spadger.

'What?'

'Bein' stuck under t'blankets at home. I'd like to be stuck
in my mam's feather bed——'

'Some feather bed,' put in Ernie, 'more like cotton an'
waste flocks, an' old shavings.'

'I said "*feather* bed,"' went on Spadger, 'I'd like to be
stuck down in it wi' my head under the clothes, an' about
a dozen blankets on top, an' my dad's army topcoat for
good measure——'

'Tha'd be nowt but a blob o' grease——'

'Then I'd like sum'dy to wakken me up,' went on Spadger, 'with a big plateful of boilin' hot potato hash, loaded
wi' pepper, an' the oven plate in bed aside of me to keep
me warm——'

'Sum'dy examine that chap's nut,' said Herbert. 'I reckon
he musta got a touch of the sun.'

'It's not that,' said Spadger, 'it's just that I'm a proper
little bleeder for agony.'

'Spadger,' said Ernie, 'has tha just blown off?'

''Course I have,' said Spadger. 'Tha doesn't think I allus
smell like this! An' I'm not like these women toffs who
never make a smell.'

'It's a human failin' is breakin' wind,' said Herbert, 'rich
an' poor alike.'

'Aye, but I've heard these society women have powder puffs fastened with elastic to their behinds,' said Spadger. 'Honest, I'm not coddin'. An' when they blow off it sprays all the powder around an' you get the scent of Araby.'

'You've got wind on the brain, Spadger,' said Herbert. 'Change the bloomin' subject.'

He was sorry Herbert had spoken, for he would have liked Spadger to tell more of the ways of rich folk. For a moment he had the image of a woman wearing one. Bad thoughts—a sin. Jesus, Mary an' Joseph, guide, guard and save me.

CHAPTER FOURTEEN

Spadger and his Mates

A LEAN GREYHOUND appeared and began to sniff and prance around Bess. 'Get off with thee,' shouted Ernie. 'Bess, love, come here.'

'A pup of yon should be a flier,' said Spadger.

'My mam's goin' to have her crossed with a black re-triever from Astley Bridge,' said Ernie. 'Get off, you whelp, before I par you away.'

'Hy, laddie,' called a man. 'don't talk to him like that—he's the Pride o' the Pollie.'

'I don't care what he is, mister,' said Ernie, 'he's not to interfere with our Bess.'

'That 'ud cost you a fiver,' said the man.

'It 'ud be cheap at twice the price,' said Spadger.

The man went off with his dog, and it turned its head a few times. Spadger found a cigarette-end on the ground and Herbert gave him a match. They each had a draw at the butt and passed it from one mouth to another. The tobacco smoke smelled nice in the sunshine.

'It's gettin' right hot,' said Ben.

'It's news we want,' said Spadger, 'not history.'

'If sum'dy were to offer thee five bob for all thy coal, Herbert,' said Jimmy, 'would tha take it?'

'Not likely,' said Herbert, 'I'm takin' it home. I wouldn't sell it for ten bob.'

'For two bob an' a sup of cold water,' said Spadger, 'I'd sell my coal, myself, an' all our soddin' family.'

'Let's get started pickin' again,' said Herbert.

They turned to the slag heap once more and bent their backs. The sun was white and dominant in the sky, and its heat drew acrid fumes from the coal dirt. It frightened him to feel how hot the sun could be. He had always imagined sunshine as a warm friendly thing, but now it was pouring down as though with hatred. His head burned and pained him, and he longed to go away and find a cool sheltered spot. He prayed hard for strength, and he wondered how the others kept going without prayers. Can the English be stronger than the Irish?

'This is slow murder, Micky,' said Jimmy Taylor.

'Bloody quick murder I call it,' he heard himself say. He saw Herbert look at him. I don't care for him, he thought, and I don't care for my soul. I'm fed up with this life.

'Look out!' yelled Ernie Haddock. 'Snigs!'

At once alarm struck the party.

'Where? Where?'

'Look—two of 'um!'

He looked across the tip and saw two policemen. His heart seemed paralysed with fear at sight of them. Disgrace! He tried to pray but couldn't get back his hold on God's help.

'Gimme a lift!'

'Give me one!'

'Hy, just a hand, Micky!'

All the boys except Herbert were wildly attempting to get their bags up and carry them away. Ben Shilliton, with furious fear, was the only one to get the bag on his back.

'Leave 'um,' yelled Tommy Roberts. 'Let's make a dash for it. Come on, Micky.'

He made to run off with Tommy, but then he turned and saw Herbert, standing beside his bag. He stopped; he was ashamed to run and afraid to stay.

'Are you comin', Herbert?' he called out.

'No, Michael, I'm not,' said Herbert loudly. 'I'm not seein' good work go to waste.'

Spadger and Jimmy Taylor had left their bags and were running away, with Ben following, stumbling as he carried his bag. Tommy Roberts stopped and looked back at Herbert and him. The two policemen came up on the three boys.

'What game, eh?' said the younger one.

'We've been pickin' coal,' said Herbert, 'to take home for the fire.'

116

'Fire—this weather?' It was the young policeman who spoke again; the other had a troubled face.

'You can't do a gradely week's washin' without a boiler fire,' said Herbert.

'You know you're liable for trespassin',' said the same policeman. 'An' also for stealin'. So you'd better empty your sacks.'

Herbert didn't budge.

'Come on, Harry,' said the older man.

'By gum,' said the younger one, 'this is a stubborn little monkey. Do you smoke, lad?'

'When I have any,' said Herbert.

'Here y'are,' said the younger one, taking a packet out of his pocket and giving Herbert a cigarette. 'Your two mates haven't much to say for themselves.'

'They're like me,' said Herbert, 'they've got too much on their minds for gabbin'.'

The policeman laughed. 'Let's give you a light,' he said. 'But do get off afore the inspector comes.'

'Aye we will, Officer,' put in Tommy Roberts.

Herbert said, 'Thanks,' and waved as the two went off Spadger, Ben and Jimmy came back.

'Hy, what did they say?' asked Jimmy.

'They said you were a bunch of windybags,' said Herbert, taking a puff at the cigarette.

'Spadger,' said Spadger, 'you're a cowardly caitiff. Salute your officer at once.' He saluted Herbert. 'Now I must answer a call of nature. Yu' can all come, chaps, I'll pay for this round.'

'Has nob'dy no paper?' said Tommy Roberts.

Spadger put both hands over his heart and recited: 'In days of old when knights were bold, and paper wasn't invented, you'd wipe your hass with broken glass an' go away contented.'

Three of them went off to a hollow. Herbert said: 'Yon Spadger's not a bad sort, Michael, but don't take him as a sample of Towlton.'

'He's a bit comical, Herbert,' he said.

'He'll grow out of it,' said Herbert lightly. 'Now I'll show thee how to carry thy coal. First give us a lift with it on to this tree trunk. Now when tha takes it up, take it all but on the nape of thy neck, an' then the weight will ride on thy shoulders. An' keep a good grip on the ears of the sack. Tha'll find them very handy tips all thy days, lad.'

Spadger and the others returned and the party got ready to move off. 'In the absence of a mule,' said Spadger, taking up his bag, 'the senior N.C.O. must take the shafts. Army orders one-eight-o-four. Come on, Micky, death or glory.'

He was surprised to find that the bag felt light when carried high up. He found he was last in the line of figures, and with his head down he could just see the legs and bodies of the boys in front. The legs were thin, some bow-legged and others knock-kneed, and their raggedly-clothed bodies looked weak and bony under their burdens. For a moment the sight made him almost laugh, but as they struggled along, humming and whistling now and again, recovering from the odd stumble along the way, he felt some strange brotherly love for them almost overcome him, so that he felt like running up and hugging each one. These are my own true mates, he thought; and he found it a nice feeling.

They turned into a lane and Ernie Haddock gave a cry.

'Holy Moses! Look at our Bess wi' yon greyhound. An' I daren't let my bag down, else I'll never get it up again. I'll get murdered if my mam finds out.'

'We'd better *all* let our bags down,' said Herbert, 'we'll get 'em up again somehow.'

The boys let the bags slide off their backs. 'Yaa!' yelled Tommy, 'you dirty things.'

'Don't blame the dogs,' said Herbert, 'it's only nature.'

'How're we goin' to separate 'um, Herbert?'

The greyhound's owner came running up. 'Don't lay a hand on them dogs, lad,' he said. 'They'll separate in good time. As it is, it's a fiver down the drain for me—that's his mating fee.'

'D'you think she does it for nothin'?' said Spadger.

After a time the two dogs were separated. Ernie got hold

of Bess by the ear. 'You've got me in trouble again, lass,' he said. The dog had its head down and looked deeply repentant: now that looks like a firm purpose of amendment, he thought.

With the help of the man they got their bags up again, and they made their way to the main road. With every step his bag seemed to slip a little, and his grip to loosen, so that now it felt very heavy and hurt his back. His arms ached until all sensation left them.

'Up, up, my lad,' said Herbert, '—go on, give it a jerk. Drop it an' you're done. We'll stop at that wall ahead there.'

Encouraged by Herbert he felt the blood move quicker, and he got the bag up a little. When they stopped to rest he was astonished at the beautiful ease that flowed through him. I didn't know toil could hurt so much, he thought.

'Right, chaps,' said Herbert, 'take up your loads. Ready, Michael?'

He nodded and took hold of his bag. The pains began at once. The dog Bess kept beside him along the way. It was a comfort to him.

'I keep fancyin' I can see a big factory lodge,' said Jimmy Taylor, 'bubblin' o'er with lemonade.'

'Don't forget we're not broke yet,' said Spadger. 'We've got the pennies he didn't take for our fares. I vote we stop at that little shop along the road here an' see what we can get. Pew, how I brought the good news to Ghent!'

'Are you all right, Michael?' asked Herbert.

He flushed and answered: 'Oh I'm great, Herbert.'

'I'll tell thee summat,' said Herbert, 'tha'rt doing damn well.'

'Aye, he is,' said Spadger. 'Even his tea-an'-sugar's coming out.'

'What's that?' he asked.

'Don't feel now,' said Spadger, 'but thy shirt's hangin' out of thy britches arse halfway down thy leg.'

At their next stop they rested their bags on a wall outside a small shop. He put a hand behind him and was ashamed to find that his shirt was hanging out from a rent in his trousers, and that part of his buttocks must have been showing.

'I believe I've a safety-pin somewhere,' said Herbert. 'Aye, here it is. Bend thee down, lad, an' I'll see what I can do. Go on, get down.' He bent, and Herbert fastened his trousers with the safety-pin. 'How's that?' he asked. 'Oh that's great, thanks, Herbert,' he said. His own voice sounded fluted and high beside theirs, and he often flushed at hearing it.

'Right,' said Herbert, 'let's go an' have a look what they've got.'

'Ee, American cream-soda,' said Spadger, looking in the window. 'I once had a bottle of that. Ah ha, the old original Dr Thompson's throat pastilles—fu' coughs an' colds, kiddies, an' inflammation of the boles.'

'Don't forget we've gotta save a penny apiece for our return fare,' said Herbert.

'They won't let us on t'tram with the coal,' said Ernie.

'I know,' said Herbert, 'unless we see Mester Aspy. If he's on this shift he'll let us put it up front.'

'Ee, wouldn't that be luv'ly!' sighed Ben.

'Now what are we goin' to get?' asked Jimmy.

'Let's count up first.'

He had fourpence, and the others had a penny each to spare, except Ben, who had lost his twopence when chasing the butterfly.

'It's not fair Michael putting all that to,' said Herbert.

'Ah go on,' he said.

'We'll put a penny aside for Ben's tram fare,' said Herbert, 'so that leaves us sevenpence. Come on in, lads.'

The shop was cool and dark. An old woman was waiting behind the counter, watching them closely. 'What do you want?' she asked.

'Summat to sup, Missis, please,' said Herbert.

'Summat you got a lot of,' said Spadger.

'You've come at a bad time,' she said.

'Han you any Pott's herb beer,' asked Herbert.

'Delivery's not till Sat'day.'

'A half-gallon stone jar o' that,' said Herbert, 'would go down well.'

'What han you got, Missis?' asked Spadger.

'American cream-soda,' she said.

'How much?'

'Threepence ha'penny a bottle,' she said, 'fourpence ha'penny if you take it away.'

'We'll tak' it away in our bellies,' said Spadger. 'What about two bottles, Herbert, an' whack it amongst us?'

'Han you no home-made herb beer, Missis?'

'No, I haven't.'

'What about summat to eat?' asked Jimmy.

'Aye, a pound of dry dog biscuits without water,' said Spadger, 'an' I'll bet you'd eat the lot. Now what about the jolly old cream-soda?'

'I say cream-soda,' he said, 'if you do.'

'It seems a poor bargain to me,' said Herbert with a shake of his head. 'Posh bottles but naught much inside 'em. We'll have two.'

She took the money and said: 'Drink them outside.'

'It's the same the world over,' said Ernie, 'once they've got hold of your money they want to see the back of you. That's what my mam allus says.'

'She should know,' remarked Spadger. 'Ee, don' it look good!'

'She never took her eyes off me,' said Tommy.

'No wonder,' said Spadger. 'Now how do we whack it?'

'You three have one,' said Herbert, 'an' us three t'other.'

He stood with dry swollen tongue watching Herbert opening the bottle. A glass marble served as a cork, and had to be pressed downwards into an opening in the neck of the bottle to allow the liquid out. Herbert pressed with his thumb but failed to release it.

'Here,' said Ben, 'try my knife.'

'Wipe thy nose, Ben,' said Herbert.

Ben flushed and grinned and turned away to blow his nose between his fingers. There was a sharp click as the marble was forced free, and instantly there was a violent fizzing, the cream-soda pouring out of the bottle. 'Quick, get under it!' shouted Herbert. Ben made a dive and got his face under, but Herbert failed to catch any in his hands. In a second or two it was over, and on the ground frothing patches of cream-soda were disappearing.

'Oh suffering Nora,' sighed Herbert, 'look at that!' He held up the bottle to show less than an inch of liquid was left. They all looked on aghast, except Spadger, who let out a screech of laughter and hugged the other bottle to his heart. 'Threepence soddin' ha'penny,' Herbert burst out, 'an for a tanner-meg we could have had a full half-gallon stone jar of Pott's herb beer.'

'How're we going to whack it?' asked Ben.

'You two can have it,' said Herbert.

'Old Ben's had his share,' said Spadger. 'His bloody head were down under the bottle like a whippet at a rat hole.'

'A bit,' said Ben to Herbert, 'is better than none.'

'It is,' said Spadger, 'if *tha* doesn't get the first sup.'

'Why don't you borrow a spoon?' said Ernie.

'If tha supped a pint of ale in spoonfuls,' said Spadger, 'it 'ud make thi' drunk.'

Herbert took a quick tilt of the bottle at his lips. 'Here y'are, Michael,' he said, and passed it to him. He did the same. Just the cool bubbly touch on his tongue. Temptation. Down with it. He passed the bottle to Ben.

'Ta,' smiled Ben, 'I aren't done too bad.'

'I'll show you a trick,' said Spadger, 'of opening one of these against a wall without sheddin' a drop. I want you to keep it in mind for . . .' He let out a cry as the bottle slipped from his grasp. He made a grab but just missed. The bottle struck a large round stone and burst with a loud crack. The woman came running out of the shop. 'That's a penny you owe me on the bottle,' she said.

'Is that all the sympathy a chap gets when he loses his life's savings?' said Spadger.

Bess was licking the frothy spots, and Spadger gave her a gentle push in the behind. 'You're havin' *all* the bloody fun,' he said. 'Missis, we'll pay you next time we're round.'

'When will that be?' she asked.

'Sunday. I'll be coming round in my dad's car for a breath of air.'

'You'll be sure to know it,' said Ernie, 'it's a Rolls-Ford.'

They went to take up their bags.

'I don't know what you think,' said Herbert, 'but I rue the minute I went up to yon shop. I felt it in my bones I did. Remember I didn't want to buy anything?'

'I said as we should have had summat to eat,' said Jimmy.

'I vote we stop an' ask for a drink of water,' said Tommy.

'Aye, happen they'll give us summat to eat,' said Jimmy.

'Aye, let's call at that big house on the left,' suggested Ernie.

'Nay, not there,' said Herbert, 'that's Squire Kershaw's house.'

'Herbert's windy o' callin' on the squire,' said Spadger.

'I'm not windy,' said Herbert, 'an' I'm not bladder-headed. Yu' can all go against me again, an' I'll call wi' yu', an' yu'll see what yu' get.'

They found a low wall to rest their bags on. He always found the act of balancing a bag difficult, and he had to push and hug and press to make it stand up. He had felt its presence so intensely on his back, and in his grip, that the bag now seemed to have a life of its own, and had become like a living thing. And the coal inside, though he had hated it at first, was now beginning to mean something to him. Spadger led the way down the drive to the house. Suddenly it was there before them, a red brick house, a lawn, flowers, coolness and freshness, lace curtains. They slowed down.

'Let's go back,' said Tommy.

'Aye, we'd better,' said Ben.

Spadger looked at Herbert. Herbert said: 'We've come so far we might as well go the whole way.'

He was walking towards the door when a window opened. 'What do you want?' called a voice. It was a woman with white curly hair and a red face.

'Well, lady,' said Herbert, 'we wanted a drink of water, if it's all right with you.'

'Get out! Off with you! Away!' she called, '—you filthy rascals.'

They all hurried away, except Herbert. He stood there, pale, and called back: 'There's no need to be rude, Missis. A civil question deserves a civil answer. We're human, you know, same as you an' yours.'

The window shut with a slam. When Herbert came back the others looked at him. He looked at them and said: 'That's no squire's wife, I'll warrant.'

'Ignorant,' said Spadger, 'as pig muck.'

He looked at him with surprise, for it was the first time he had heard that common Irish word 'ignorant' on English lips.

CHAPTER FIFTEEN

The Long Carry Home

'WHAT ABOUT THAT LITTLE COTTAGE across there?' said Jimmy, when they reached the road.

'It's nobbut four hundred yards to Coal Lane End,' said Herbert. 'A mouthful of water there an' we'd make it.'

It was a small dark cottage, with a cool old fragrance. The woman looked at them: 'Sit you down in the shade, lads,' she said, 'an' I'll bring you some tea out. That's what you want.'

She came out with a large plate of cake and a jug of tea. He felt he would have preferred a cold drink, but he was astonished at the good feeling the tea brought. He felt the sweat pour out of him. About him the others looked very happy.

'We might do as much for you one day,' said Herbert solemnly.

'Aye, you never know your luck in this world,' said Ernie.

'Here, Ben,' said Herbert, 'get a handful of coal out of each bag an' bring it in thy cap.'

'If they were all like her,' said Herbert, 'this 'ud be a happier world.'

'Same as my mam says,' said Ernie, 'it's the poor as helps the poor.'

'Poor?' said Spadger. 'Talk for thyself.'

'Taking it all round,' said Ernie, 'tha couldn't call us rich.'

'Aye, an' we're not poor,' said the others warmly.

'We,' said Herbert, 'are what you call the *middle class*.'

'Middle o' what?'

'We're in the middle between the top an' bottom,' explained Herbert. 'You've got the royalty an' aristocracy right at the top, an' at their tails all them wi' money. Down at the bottom you've got the poor. We're what they call the middle class.'

'Am I middle class?' asked Ben.

'Thee,' put in Spadger, 'tha'rt in a class of thy own. Tha'rt a bloody ape as has lost its way.'

'Suits me,' said Ben.

'An' who do you call the poor?' asked Ernie.

'Them as are poor,' said Herbert. He added: 'Folk as never know where the next meal's coming from. Folk as can't keep body an' soul together.'

'Abroad,' said Tommy, 'my father reckons there's millions live on a handful o' rice a day.'

'What—between the lot of 'em—or one apiece?'

'One apiece.'

'I like rice pudding I do,' said Jimmy.

'Pudding!—they never see a drop of milk from one year's end to another,' said Herbert. 'They die like flies. An' in this country,' he added with a dark look, 'there's slums where poor little kids crawl about covered with sores cryin' their hearts out for a jam butty.'

They were all silent for a minute.

'We're living in a fool's paradise,' said Tommy, 'an' we don't know it.'

'We're livin' in a fool's summat,' said Ernie.

'Fancy him trying to put us in t'lower class,' said Spadger, 'an' we've got a concertina.'

'We've got a lot to be thankful for,' said Herbert, raising his eyes to the sky and tightening his belt. 'Now lads, can we do Coal Lane End in one go?' As they set off with the bags on their backs Tommy began to sing: *Are We Downhearted?* and they all joined in: 'No!'

A continuous procession of coal pickers was seen as they reached the junction of Coal Lane End. Men, women and children, hundreds of them, all of the poorer kind, were coming from the Tatherton and Brickley pits, moving on in one wide stream towards Towlton. Here and there, a man or a woman could be seen carrying a bag, but the majority had some means of conveyance. Handcarts, barrows, prams, bicycles, and trolleys all loaded up with bags, were being pushed or pulled along. One boy was pulling a bag along on a roller skate. Another had a piece of a gate on which were two bags, which he dragged along on rollers, his mate pushing one under every yard or two. The party stopped and dropped their bags to the ground.

He watched the ever-moving flow of people and coal: *Wheels, wheels, wheels,* he thought, everything moves on wheels.

Many of the pickers who were carrying their bags attempted to board the trams with them, but they were turned away. Some, however, did force their way on and couldn't be got off. One cheery driver called out: 'Room for a bag or two here in front,' and there was such a rush that he couldn't get to the controls to drive away, for an enormous pile of bags suddenly rose up in front. Herbert learnt that Mr Aspy wasn't working that shift so the chance of a tram ride was gone. There were horse lorries and donkey carts with owners offering to carry bags to Towlton for a shilling each. The boys stood watching all the bustle for a time.

' I vote we spend our pennies,' said Jimmy, ' and then chance our luck.' Herbert nodded: ' We might as well get a bit of extra nourishment, and then get going on shanks' pony.' He sat on the ground beside Bess and his bag of coal. He had no interest in anything. The wheels and the legs moved by. The feeling of rest was beautiful. It all felt nice and light and floating, and he didn't want to be disturbed. The thick coarse hair of the dog and its moving warmth next to him felt good. When a thought of his mother and home came up he had to shut it out because it made him feel like crying. Someone gave him a lime drop.

Herbert led the way back. It was difficult to find a resting place along the road, for the suitable ones were taken up by other carriers. Sometimes they would rest against a window-sill, and usually that brought out an irate householder. Herbert watched for a place, and then he would rest his bag first and help the others. One could drop a bag to the ground, but that meant asking a man for help in the lifting of it again. He moved in a dreamy silence through the heavy summer heat, aware occasionally of the weight on his back and the ache of his bones, and the dog Bess that kept near his feet. Suddenly he saw Spadger, giving an impression of a bowlegged man carrying a bag of coal. The caricature itself did not mean much, but a thought struck him that under his head queer things went on in Spadger's mind. He let out a laugh, and dropped to the pavement, still laughing, with the coal scattered about him. Herbert helped him up with his bag and they all had a laugh. 'We aren't got much money,' said Herbert, 'but we do see life.'

When they reached Hill Green Road, about a mile from home, it was after six o'clock. He had become aware of a beggarly air about the party that had not been apparent an hour before. Then there had been an atmosphere of workers going home, unwashed but respectable; now this had changed. The atmosphere of toil had vanished, and that of leisure had taken its place. People were going out dressed up. He heard occasional sighs of pity: 'Aahe what a shame to see them poor lads carrying them heavy bags!' It was painful to him to be thought poor or unfortunate. But the others seemed to enjoy it at times, and would even catch an eye to invite it. 'I wish they wouldn't feel sorry for us,' Spadger would say, 'but give us a copper instead.'

He had his head down, looking to the ground, when passing along by a row of villas with small gardens, when something made him look up. He saw a woman in a blue summer dress just leaving a door and walking down the short garden path. The first sight of her gave him a shock, though for a moment he didn't realise who it was. Then she turned and looked straight at him—*Miss Twining*!

At once a panic was let loose inside his stomach. He stooped his head instantly. Had she seen him? Did she know who it was? What could he do to escape? Shame, shame, shame. Oh, Miss Twining, Miss Twining, she would never kiss him again. Oh I love her. He wanted to stop before he should draw level, yet he was afraid to do so fearing lest his

128

mates would draw attention to him or call out his name. She was standing a yard or two ahead, standing by a gate. She hasn't seen me. There was a car, an open two-seater, and he heard a man's voice call out: 'I say, you'd better put a coat on—it's going to rain, dear.'

He moved up against Spadger. 'Reindeer? I reckon tha'd be better keepin' rabbits,' said Spadger. He could sense the blue dress and his whole body was aware of her presence. Oh had he been seen? He heard her voice: '*I hardly think so.*' Oh her lovely voice. No mistake. Only a yard away. Nobody knows I know. The man: 'The glass is dropping.' Spadger: 'Pick it up.' A stab of hatred came to him passing the man, as he looked and saw the male presence of him with a short red moustache. Her voice again: 'It'll blow over.' She doesn't love him. Hot—hotter—hottest—burning hottest . . . passed!

Spadger began to whistle *Colonel Bogey* and then began a husky singing: '*I met the Colonel's daughter, she was dressed in blue, an' shouted Rollocks, you made a mess of me.*' The car engine roared up and he looked to the road as it went by, and she was looking at the boys as she tied a silk scarf over her head, and he looked boldly back at her with the bag on his back, as she sped by, I love you and you love me, '. . . *you made a mess of me.*'

Near Dankhill Station they came to a garden wall outside a pastry shop, and there they rested their bags. A relief at having escaped being seen by Miss Twining gave him a turn of affection for his companions. More God is in each of these than in you, a thought told him, because they are not so secretive, cunning and full of hidden thought for themselves, and there is more empty space in them that has to be filled by God. There's too much of you in you for Him to get in.

'Another half a mile to go,' said Herbert. 'I guarantee we'll be home by seven.'

'Aye, an' we'll be wet through in the bargain,' said Spadger, looking upwards.

Ben nodded brightly. 'Tha'rt right, Spadger,' he said, 'I can feel it in this knee.'

'It's the same wi' anybody who's had rheumatic fever,' said Herbert, 'they can tell when it's goin' to rain. Our Elsie's the same—her leg starts warching.'

'Look at them pies,' said Ernie. 'I like pies well done. I won't half have a feed when I get home.'

'I'll eat till I bloody burst,' said Tommy. 'I'll have a good feed of pratie pie, wi' plenty of meat in it.'

'Tha'll have pea soup,' said Spadger, 'same as us all. An' what soup!—one pea to a quart o' water, an' he takes it out halfway through so it won't be too strong.'

'Speak for thyself, Spadger,' said Jimmy.

'Aye, if you're clemmed we're not,' protested Ben.

'It's none o' thy business anyway, Spadger,' said Herbert, 'what folk have. A chap can enjoy a crust of bread if it's paid for.'

'Aye, Herbert,' said Jimmy, 'yu' can't eat in peace unless you can keep the house-door open.'

'I can,' said Spadger. 'An' give me a nice juicy bit o' roast pork on the strap than all your bloody crusts as were paid for. An' I don't care whether the bloody door's open, shut or missin'.'

'Tha must be inhuman, Spadger,' said Herbert sorrowfully.

'Goin' far?' asked a voice. It was the woman standing at the door of the shop.

'Not too far.'

'I could do wi' a bit of coal for my oven,' she said. 'Are you sellin'?'

'Sorry, Missis,' said Herbert, 'we're taking it home.'

'Ee, Missis,' said Spadger, 'you can have mine.'

'Is it good stuff?'

'Best trencherbone nuts,' said Spadger. 'It'll do your pies in half the time.'

'How much do you want for that bag?'

'Two-an-a-tanner, Missis,' said Spadger. 'An' I've humped it all the way from Chantbent Colliery.'

'Say two bob,' she said.

'You're on,' said Spadger. 'Shall I carry it in the front?'

'Nay, nay, Spadger,' said Herbert, 'tha can't sell up. What will thy mam think?'

'What do I care? She'll be satisfied if I give her a bob out of it.'

'But if tha wants to sell thy coal tha can sell it to Granny Heyes. She's short o' coal.'

'An' do you think she'll thank me for carryin' it that extra half-mile? Out of the way, Herbert, I'm sellin' now whilst I've got a buyer.'

They looked at each other wonderingly as Spadger went into the shop. In that moment the spirit of the day seemed suddenly taken away.

'Not for a measly two bob,' said Herbert, looking at his bag.

'It's all right for thee,' said Jimmy, 'you've regular money comin' in.'

'Aye, I suppose there's that to it,' agreed Herbert.

Spadger appeared at the door with a pie in one hand and a bottle of lemonade in the other. 'Come on, lads,' he said, taking a bite, 'she'll have yours too.'

'Not mine,' said Herbert.

Jimmy Taylor gave a look at the juicy middle of the meat pie in Spadger's hand and hurriedly got the bag on his back and went in. Tommy Roberts picked up his: 'Come on, Herbert, let's have summat to eat.'

'Aye, you'll get no credit for it when you do get home,' said Spadger. 'Get what you can when you can, is my motto.'

He heard the satisfied gurgling from Spadger as he raised the bottle to his lips, and he saw the lovely pale green liquid descend with *glug-gluggings* from the bottle to the mouth, and the Adam's apple quiver. At that moment nothing would have given him more pleasure than to empty the contents of his bag, and take a bottle to his own lips, but he gave one glance at Herbert's face, and that was enough. When Spadger offered him a drink and a bite, Herbert said: 'It 'ud poison me.' Then he gripped his bag and got his back under it. He also refused Spadger's offer, with a thankful

131

wink. Ben took a quick swig and a bite, and picked his bag up. And as the party of three went off Spadger called out: 'You feel like you're floatin' on air. Honest, the minute you get rid of that coal you feel like you're floatin' on air.' As he drew near Herbert he could hear him muttering: '*It's a long way to Tipperary . . .*'

Back Greenley Street looked unfamiliar to him. Was it this morning he passed here where the children were making dirt pies? Did he pass along the bottom and there on his way to his First Holy Communion this morning? Is it still the feast of *Corpus Christi*? Ben's short fat mother with the hairy chin was at the door, and Ben went loping self-consciously past her into the dark room, with a short grunt of farewell to the two boys. Then Herbert's father came along with his white stick and after a word the two went off together up the front street. Alone, he felt a keen humiliation at the waif he was. He hurried up the back street to avoid being seen. Suddenly he became aware of his father standing at the gate in the silent back street.

'Hello, father,' he mumbled.

'Eh? Is that you, Mickyeen?' He paused: 'A bloody holy show you are with filth and dirt. Where was you?'

He couldn't lift up because the bag was heavy: 'I brought coal home for mother,' he said.

'Coal? Coal? From where?'

'From Chantbent pit.'

'What you picked it? Took coal from the bloody swines of pit owners?' He let out a roar that set the boy trembling: 'You'd break the strike! You—you bloody renegade——' and he snatched the bag and with one furious swing he sent all the black shining pieces scattering about the back street: 'Get in! Get in outa that!'

He dodged past the man and up the yard. Uncle John was standing at the back door, but he stooped his face avoiding the man's smile, and ran past him and up the dark stairs to the bedroom, shutting the door behind him. A dry sob came out. He put out his hand and clung to the old black rail of the bed. Across the room on the mantelpiece reeled the blue

Virgin and the gold Christ on the Crucifix. He felt sick.

'That was no right thing to do, M'Cloud,' he heard Uncle John say scoldingly, 'no, not to the poor innocent ladeen. Strike or no strike, you had no cause to hurt his feelings an' him bringing home the few biteens of coal to his mother.' Filming up against his eyes were the tears he didn't want, and through the window out there in the back street he saw an old woman with a basket gathering in his coal, and he heard his mother's voice speaking sharply to the father, and he felt sorry for the man, and then he heard her footsteps coming up the stairs, and all in the room was reeling about, Crucifix, bed, fireplace, walls, floor and every single thing reeling and reeling and he felt himself falling face downwards to the floor.

He felt the mother's arms snatch him up and put him down on to the bed. 'The doctor!—will someone of ye go for the doctor? Salt! give me a taste of salt for my child, God between us an' harm.' He was peacefully outside it all, until the salt was forced between his lips and the fluid rolled from his tongue. He heard her voice sobbing out the old Irish prayers against evil, then she was kneeling by the bed, and Uncle John speaking softly to her. For a moment he felt himself back home in Ireland. Then he heard the rain outside, spattering from the house-ledging into the tin bath in the yard. It was my home, he thought, and now I'm lost from it for ever. This made him feel a quick sorrow for himself, and brought tears to his white face.

BOOK TWO

CHAPTER ONE

Back Street Holiday Game

―――

THE SICKNESS was almost over. He was out of bed and seated by the bedroom window.

'How do you feel, agraw?' said his mother, coming into the room.

'I'd like to go out, mother,' he said.

'Good,' said his mother, 'but try not to go tiring yourself.'

She helped him dress and he went out. A few children were squatting about a grid in the gutter, playing with broken bits of pottery and mud, and apart from them the street was empty. It was the annual holiday week in Towlton, and an atmosphere of desertion was everywhere—no movement, no workers hurrying along the streets, and no buzzers moaning. He went to the bottom gable-end instead of the top street corner, for there were fewer windows there to be looked at through. Mrs Chadwick turned the street corner swiftly, shawled and stooped with the beer jug hidden, and looked with neighbourly curiosity.

'Ee, you have been poorly, luv,' she said. 'But it's brought you out. Watch you don't o'ergrow your strength. Happen they'll send you to Southport Sanatorium—if you can get sum'dy to speak for you.'

'Thank you, ma'am,' he said.

He sat down against the gable-end privy closet, facing Back Greenley Street. Up from his open shirt front came the peculiar sweaty smell of his bodily weakness, about him was the smell of the warm stone pavement, and the smell of Back Greenley Street and sewers hung about in the air. It was nice to be out again.

A few yards away, just inside the turning of the back street, three girls and some younger children were getting ready to play a game. One of the girls, Rosie Beardson, stared at him, and he tried to outstare her back in a casual way, for she belonged to a very poor family, but his eyes didn't feel very strong in the light, and she had some kind of a look that was not easy to stand up to, so he had to drop his gaze before hers. He listened to the girls squabbling over the site of the mock hospital. A girl called Ella Sharley wanted it at the gable-end, but Rosie insisted it should be just in the back street.

'You mawp,' shouted Rosie, 'that were my finger. Ee, some folk have mawpin' kids.' He heard a call: 'Hy! Hy, I say, you——' and turning he saw Rosie, her small eyes looking keenly at him: 'Will you hit whilst I hold?' she asked. She spoke to him in a way that made refusal hard. He had a look round first, to make sure there was no boy in sight, and then he went to Rosie round the corner of the back street.

Two old brooms with long handles were being used for the supports of the hospital. They were inverted, with the handles dug down between the cobble-stones just off the narrow back street pavement. Ella Sharley, younger than Rosie, was holding a brick, with which she had been attempting to drive a broom handle into the ground.

'Will you hit whilst I hold?' Rosie asked.

'Hy, give it 'im,' she said to Ella.

The girl said: 'I'll 'it it.'

'Don't be daft, it wants some strength. Give it 'im,' shouted Rosie.

Eyeing him sullenly, Ella quickly handed him the brick, letting go before he could take hold of it. A fat girl called Phyllis gave a cry: 'Me toe! Oh me toe!' and burst into tears.

'See what you've done, you mawp,' shouted Rosie. 'She'll take her blanket 'ome now.'

Ella said: 'Never mind, Phyllis, you can be our first casualty. After all, we want a proper one.' She coaxed Phyllis to stay.

Rosie picked up the brick, handed it to him, looked closely at him and said: 'Go on, give it a clout.' She had very knowing brown eyes that seemed to look right into him. He took the piece of brick and raised it up. He struck the broom in the middle.

'Good shot!' said Rosie. She was very close to him. 'Give it another,' she said. He did. Ella came up. 'Let me knock t'other in,' she said.

'Don't be daft,' said Rosie, 'it needs a man on t'job.'

'A man or a sample?' asked Ella, looking at him.

'Don't you be so cheeky, madam,' said Rosie.

He felt good after knocking both broom handles into the ground. 'Don't go yet,' said Rosie, 'we need nails knocking into the wall.' The end of a nail was pierced through string and then he hammered it into the mortar. The strings were fastened to the poles, and across them was draped the blanket. Pieces of torn blanket were put over the ends, and an army topcoat was placed on the ground inside the tent. It was all neatly arranged. A corrugated zinc washing-board was the stretcher. Phyllis and Ella, with white cloths fastened over their foreheads, carried a child in on the stretcher, and Rosie, who was the doctor, examined the patient and prescribed treatment. He went off and sat down.

After a time Ella came round to him and said: 'Rosie wants to know will you play?' He shook his head. 'No,' he said, 'Sorry.' She went back and then came again. Most of the children had drifted away. 'She says it's only for once. We haven't had an officer yet.' He shook his head, yet, feeling he was being unobliging, got to his feet to go and tell Rosie himself. He was uneasy for fear any of his pals should come along.

'A wounded officer!' exclaimed Rosie. 'Here, lay him down here on this bed. We'd better take his tempa'ture.' He allowed himself to be led inside the tent and laid down on the army coat. It was very comfortable and strangely exciting. 'Only this once,' he said. He had never played such games before.

'That's a nasty wound in the forehead,' said Rosie, 'we'd better get that bandaged. Sister, answer the telephone.' She began to bandage his forehead with a piece of an old shirt-lap. 'Hy, you're coverin' me eyes,' he said. 'Quiet, please, Captain,' she said, 'you're nearly blind. Any further wounds?' she asked. Ella felt at his knees and listened to his heart. 'No legs broken,' she said. 'Heart beating faintly.' The three girls' legs were around him as he lay there on the ground, and when Rosie turned her back he could squint through the bandages up her legs as far as her torn bloomers. He was in a panic, in case his mates should come, but he couldn't get himself to stir. 'I think I've had enough,' he said weakly.

'Oh but we can't discharge you out in this state, Captain,' said Rosie. 'You've been at death's door, if you only knew it.' She was oddly like a nurse or doctor and he was a little afraid of going against her. She turned to her assistants: 'Any more wounded on the battlefield?' she asked. 'I can't see any,' said Phyllis. 'Then go out an' look,' said Rosie. 'You too,' she added to Ella, 'don't you dare leave any soldiers to die of neglect.' They both went out. Through the roof of the blanket he could see the glimmer of the afternoon sun. Inside it was cool. 'I think I have to be going,' he said.

'Yay, Yay,' said Rosie, 'but first the lady doctor has to make sure you've no broken bones.' She stooped over him and coolly felt with her fingers about his head, his ears, and down the back of the neck. 'Don't move, please,' she said. Then her hands went lightly along his chest and heart, felt at his stomach, went swiftly down his legs to his ankles. 'I think everything is sound,' she said, bringing her light touch slowly up his legs, lightly over his knees, and then very secretly and gently up under his trousers' leg. He felt hoarse in the throat. He had a panic of thoughts and he kept still and quiet, for fear she didn't know what she was doing. Her small fingers crept up, and nimbly felt round his cold paralysed thing. He lay motionless, his heart pounding. For a second her fingers moved ticklingly over the skin, and then her hand took hold of his thing in her palm, and gave it an affectionate squeeze, and she smiled. 'Herb beer sold here,' she whispered, 'sausage round the corner.'

'I saw you, Rosie Beardson!' cried a voice.

'Eh? You saw what?' asked Rosie jumping up.

He looked up, pulling the bandage off and saw Ella Sharley looking into the tent. 'Where you had your hand,' she said.

'What are you hinting at, Ella Sharley, you dirty cat?' cried Rosie. 'I tell you I never did. I never did. And if you say I was feeling up clothes I'll thump your flamin' lug for you.'

'I saw,' said Ella, going away.

He got to his feet. 'Did you hear that dirty little cat Ella Sharley?' said Rosie. 'I'll tell me mother of her if she goes on like that.'

He went out of the tent. There wasn't a soul in sight, except Ella, who was chalking on the wall, and the fat girl, Phyllis, who was staring at him. 'Oh look what that hussy's done!' said Rosie, 'just look'. Along the wall in large letters was chalked '*R.B. feels up clothes with M.M.*' He looked at it and said: 'What's that mean?' Rosie said: 'R.B. stands for me, and M.M. stands for you.'

The sight of the big chalk letters revealing his sin to the world made him feel sick. 'Don't you worry,' said Rosie, 'I'll wipe it out.'

'I'm not worrying,' he said weakly.

'Why should you?' said Rosie, 'it's not as though we'd done anything to be ashamed of.'

He felt he dare not go in home, for his mother would surely spot that he was upset. He went up Back Greenley Street, forcing himself to walk fast so that the trembling of his limbs would cease. Oh why did I ever leave my safe and cosy bed? he thought.

After a short time he began to feel weak and the sweat came out on his forehead, so he made for home. As he came to the street corner he gave a glance at the wall, just to make sure the chalked-up words had been wiped off. There was still a line of writing there, and when he got close he read: *E.S. feels up clothes with M.M.* For a moment he couldn't grasp what he saw. E.S.?—it must mean Ella Shar-ley. Who could have written this new terrible thing? He suddenly realised that Rosie Beardson had rubbed out her own initials and put different ones in their place. The shock of this trick made him feel sick, and the thought that people had passed by and possibly read it filled him with panic. He went up to the wall and spat on his own initials and rubbed them out first with his jacket sleeve, and then he rubbed out the entire line.

When he got in home the mother said: 'Musha you tired yourself out, agraw, I can see it on your pale face.' He cried when she said that, and he let her help him up the stairs to bed. But he slipped off his trousers quickly and hurried in between the sheets, for fear the trace of Rosie's hand might show on him. And now I have that sin to tell in Confession, he thought.

The next day he went out again, but avoided the bottom corner and went up to the top. He was standing alone there when a man called Farmer Akky thrust a can of milk into his hand. 'Tak' it along to number seventeen, lad,' he said. When he got there with the can he saw it was the Sharley home, and when he knocked the door was opened by the girl Ella. She had a jug in her hand, and without saying a word she held it out. He took up the can and tried to pour the milk out. 'Hy, you're sheedin' it all,' she said. He felt his face go red and he stopped pouring. Her manner changed and she asked gently: 'Shall I do it for you?' She took the can in her small firm hand, and with one sure movement she tossed the milk into the jug. 'Oh thanks!' he said. She smiled at him and he ran back to the milk float.

'Stand properly on the step, lad,' said Farmer Akky, 'or else tha'll fall off. Right, put can in its proper place, lad, an' I'll tak' thee round with me.'

For three hours he went round with Farmer Akky, and when the delivery was over Farmer Akky said: 'Go in an'

tell thy mother tha'rt havin' a run out to the farm with me.'
He ran in home and told her and then dashed off. 'Sit down
properly, lad,' said Farmer Akky, 'don't half sit an' half
stand.'

In half an hour they were out in the country. In the fields
the men were making hay, and he felt a sickening excitement at the smell. And the sight of the green thicknesses of
the English hedges made him feel very happy. I'm so happy,
he thought, I wonder why? When they drove into the farm-
yard it reminded him of Ireland, even though it was so different. I didn't think there was any green country in
England, he thought.

'I want thee to go an' hand the tea out to the men,' said
Farmer Akky, 'an' if tha'rt a good lad tha'll get a cheese
butty an' a cup of tea thyself.'

He tramped out across the stubble to the men making hay.
Down by the far hedge a short man—an Irishman surely—
was swinging a scythe. He went up behind him and thought:
I know what my mother would like me to say and he
called out: 'God bless the work, sir!' The man turned with
a start and stared at the boy, and his eyes shone as though
tears were in them. 'God bless you, son," he said; 'you're
not long over here, are you?' 'No, sir,' he said, 'only these
few months. From Mayo. My name's M'Cloud.' 'I'm from
Sligo there beside you,' said the man, holding out his hand.
Then the man took the tea and sandwiches. He didn't rest
himself, but half stood and half sat, in what seemed an
uncomfortable way, and the tea slopped over the side of the
jug when he put it down, and he ate the bread in a careless
way. I'm at home with this man now, he thought, and it's
nice to be with your own. He told the man their address
and said his mother and father would like him to call. 'Indeed and I will,' said the man, 'I'll call round surely.' And
he knew from the way the man said it that he'd never call
at all.

It was evening when he left the farm, having been given
sixpence by Farmer Akky and told where to catch the tram
home. He ran down the clean country roadway, delighting

at all the lovely smells of evening. The hedgerows looked even denser, with the thick grasses growing up into them. He could see the soft distant moorlands beyond, and the hay-sweet air seemed to make him dizzy. At one high point he stopped and gazed down at Towlton. He could see the town hall and countless factory chimneys, set peacefully in a hollow, it seemed. I live there, he thought. Then he ran down to the tram and sat up in front on top. As the soft breeze blew into his eyes and flushed face, he thought over the happy day, and said a prayer of thanksgiving for it. Oh what a pity this lovely feeling will be going, he thought, and by tomorrow nearly all trace of it will be gone. But it's strange how misery lasts longer, and gets down under the heart's skin, in a way that you'd think its pale mark must be left there for ever.

CHAPTER TWO

The North Wind doth Blow

ON THE MONDAY MORNING he had to go back to school he got up with a sick dry feeling in his stomach. His mind had been full of thoughts of Miss Twining, but now he was uneasy for fear she had changed. A nice clean shirt and handkerchief were ready for him, but they had been washed hurriedly and left airing by the mantelpiece, and this had left a smoky odour on them. The father had repaired his clogs, but in place of clog-irons he had hammered on thick chunks of scrap leather. They felt very uneven under his feet. He was late home from the pit, and the mother was listening anxiously for him. 'That's his step now, thanks be to God,' she said, as the slow clomp of a clog sounded across the cobbled street. 'It's greatly changed, God save us, it's slower than before.'

'He's a quieter man altogether since the strike,' said Willie. 'He never talks about the conveyors any more.'

'I'm glad I got the gill of beer for him,' she said. 'Move out till he comes in.'

The two boys went into the back kitchen as the man's step sounded outside the door. 'Musha you're late,' said the mother softly as he entered.

The man answered in a tired voice: 'There was a fall of dirt,' he said. 'We had to stay to clear up after for the day shift.'

'You can go in now, Mickyeen,' whispered Willie.

He went into the front kitchen. 'Good mornin', Father,' he said quietly. He looked at the black face with the two eyes looking out solemnly. 'Is that you, Mickyeen?' said the father. 'Is it goin' back to school you are?'

'Would you be washin' now or later?' the mother asked.

'Later, I think,' he said, 'I'll rinse my hands now.'

When he came into the front place again she had taken the bottle with the draught beer in it from the cupboard. ' I thought after the weekend you'd like the wettin' of your lips,' she said.

' The divil roast the beer,' he said angrily. ' Didn't I tell you never to get me a drop again comin' in from the pit? Poison I should be drinkin' after the night's work, crawling down on my stomach for coal an' the rogues of owners payin' me a cursed eight shillings an' ninepence.' She said nothing, but put a clean sheet of newspaper at his place at the table and placed the large shining porridge plate there and the silver spoon. ' I haven't a stitch of strength left,' he added, ' workin' for the bloody ould Duke of Ellesmere, the divil shoot him.' The house was quiet for a minute, and then the man said : ' Give me the bottle then, woman, so long as you got it.' The atmosphere relaxed.

' Oh sure I had a great dream of home last night,' said the mother. 'Kate an' myself were down by the river of Mannon, an' who else was it now was with us? Was it Paddy Caulfield? Och, sure an' it was, my bould Paddy no less. Oh a great dream it was, an' I feel it comin' back to me now.'

' Home! will you never have done dreamin' of home, woman? ' said the father.

' Never,' she said, ' never in this life. An' it was the same when I was across in America—I'd never put my head to the pillow in that house in Hoboken but I'd be back home in the instant.'

' Well it's far from that way with me,' said the father. ' The only bloody dream ever comes into my head is the pit —the pit an' the tubs an' the sweat an' the bloody work. That's the dream, woman, an' it's the flamin' reality too.'

' Then God help you,' she sighed, and into the back kitchen she went. ' Mickyeen,' she whispered, ' are you ready for school? ' Willie turned and said : ' There's plenty of time yet.' She gave him a prod of her finger: ' He won't eat whilst you're around,' she said. Willie cocked a hand to his nose and pointed to the front kitchen : ' Then let him do t'other,' he said.

When they were ready the two boys left the house together. 'Go easy now, Mickyeen,' said the mother anxiously.

'I'm fine, mother,' he said. He turned quickly for her face looked as though it might be near tears. 'Goodbye.'

'Toodle'oo,' said Willie.

They walked quietly along together, separating at the school-yard. 'Take it easy now, man,' whispered Willie, and went off. Ernest Keating came running up: 'Ee, hello Michael!' he said. 'Whose class are you goin' into?'

'Miss Twining's,' he said.

'Ee, you can't,' said Ernest, 'she's got wed. She got wed on Holiday Saturday an' won't be comin' back.'

I don't believe it, he thought. She married without telling me! How could she? The whistle blew and he took up his place in the old lines. But the new teacher sent him to see Mr Victor. He couldn't find the headmaster, and then he hurriedly followed the classes into Mass. After Mass he went to the headmaster's room. He began to feel frightened.

'What is it, M'Cloud?' asked Mr Victor.

'I've no class to go to, sir,' he said. 'The teacher said I'm too big for her class.'

'Then go to Miss Skegham's class. Tell her I've sent you.'

He went off to find Miss Skegham's class. He tapped lightly on the door when he found it, and then went in. A woman with a large bosom and tight grey hair looked at him from her desk. He prayed she'd be nice to him the moment he saw her eyes.

'Please, Miss,' he said, raising his hand high in salute, 'Mr Victor says can you find me a place in your class?'

'Go and sit in the fourth row next to Radford,' she said.

A thin-faced boy beckoned him eagerly and he went and sat next to him. The class was sitting up in silence, and it felt strange to him to be amongst older boys. She married without telling me—yet maybe on this morning she's as unhappy as I am.

'Sheed,' called Miss Skegham, 'if I catch you yawning once more I'll put your head under the cold water tap.'

'Please, Miss, Miss, please I wasn't yawning, Miss,' protested the boy. 'I was feeling where I've got toothache, Miss.'

'Sheed, if you attempt to tell me any more of your absurd lies I'll deal severely with you.'

He glanced at the boy called Sheed. He had a face that seemed large at one side and small at the other. His forehead looked wide and fresh at one side and narrowed to a wrinkly piece at the other side, so that one eye opened wide and the other watched from a half-closed lid. As he sat down after being addressed by Miss Skegham the wide side of his mouth murmured, 'Sorry, Miss,' and this was instantly followed by a low audible hiss from the other side of his mouth, 'Fat arse.'

'You will all draw from memory this morning,' said Miss Skegham. 'And remember, I shall make an example of any boy I catch using a rubber. Above all, no talking and no copying.'

She had a pale fine skin and a large shapely nose, and her eyes were pale blue. He looked at her full bosom, and felt that though it was round it somehow hadn't that real warmth of a proper mother's breast.

Most boys started drawing at once, whilst a few gazed at the backs of other boys' hands, and others looked down at their drawing books with faces screwed up, and others bit their lips as they thought. He looked down at the greyish naked sheet before him. He felt a stoppage somewhere in the throat. His imaginative life was buried within him, always hidden out of sight, and now there was no way of getting in touch with it. A drawing from memory—he didn't know what it meant. All about him could be heard the adenoidal grunts of boys at work. He had to do something, and slowly he began to draw the profile of a man. That was soon done, for he was skilled at it. He decided to give the man a moustache. As he was doing this he felt a violent jabbing at his elbow, and he looked to see the boy next to him, with face stooped over his drawing, shaking his head. He stopped, not knowing what to do. Then he heard Miss Skegham move, stand up, and he peeped and saw her going out of the classroom. For two or three seconds after she left not a boy lifted a head, then at once a buzzing of talk began.

'Tha'll get murdered,' said Radford. 'Tha'll get laid out.'

'What's the matter?' he asked.

'Hy, look what this chap's done,' said Radford, picking up the drawing and showing it round. 'He's drawn a mon's face.' Some boys laughed and others shook their heads in pity. Radford felt down in his pocket and brought out a tiny red rubber. 'Here, quick, rub it out,' he said, 'afore she rubs thee out.' He began to rub it out, but Radford said: 'Flappin' Nora, what a mess! Here, let me do it for thee.' His thin fingers began to rub out the drawing, removing at the same time all traces of the use of a rubber.

'But what have I to draw?' he asked.

'A tulip,' said Radford.

'What's that like?'

'One of them flowers toffs have in long vases. Practically all stalk—that's the beauty of 'em. At the top they're like an egg-cup.'

'Isn't there something else?'

'No, nothing,' said Radford.

'Aye, if tha wants to keep in fat Ada's good books,' said Radford. 'She's infatuated wi' flowers, an' we all have to draw 'em. Look, Smithy's done a tulip, so 'as him, an' him, an'——' there was a sharp click of the door-latch, and the buzzing chatter stopped instantly.

Then there was a loud snigger from the door, and cries of 'False alarm!' 'You miserable rotter, Froggy.' 'Drop that latch again an' I'll spill your heart's blood.' A boy seated near the door had crept forward and touched the latch. The buzz of talk had now risen to what seemed an uncontrollable pitch, and he was in a panic in case Miss Skegham would return. 'The only ones that draw other things,' explained Radford, 'are good drawers like Amberson, he can even do roses, daffodils an' hyacinths. He does 'em for anybody for a toffee. Only takes him half a minute. But we have to draw tulips. If tha'rt in her bad books or tha wants to show spite, then tha can draw a trilby hat or a burning candle. That makes her mad, but she can't say owt if tha does 'em well. Look, Sheed's doing a candle.'

The boy Sheed, who was talking to a boy called Johnson, turned round, and the left side of his mouth said: 'Aye, I know what I'd like to do with it.' Then suddenly the latch clicked, there was instant silence, and Miss Skegham entered. He found he was the only boy in the class whose head was not down to his work. Her eye caught his and he flushed guiltily, then he bent to his drawing.

Some minutes later the bell sounded in the corridor, and the boys put down their pencils. A monitor came round to collect the papers, and when he took his he said: 'What's that—a cabbage?' And at his words he suddenly became aware of the fact that when drawing the tulip the image that had been in his mind was a cabbage.

He stood with Eddie Radford during playtime. 'I used to be a Protestant' said Eddie. 'My father were a Cath'lic when he an' my mam got wed an' she were a Protestant. He didn't turn for her, but he let his own religion drop. I went to a Proddy school, Pink Lane, but my dad were a bomb-thrower in the Loyal North Lancs, an' he kept havin' visions an' things in the trenches, so he wrote to my mam for her to send me to the Cath'lic school, an' she didn't want to go against him, with him bein' in the trenches an' it might be his dying wish. So she sent me here. But when he came back all right after the war she were sorry. It costs a lot more being a Cath'lic, what wi' raffles for the church, collections, money at the church door, keeping the priests an' all that, an' then a new suit every year for Walking Day. You've got to pay two-an'-threepence for a new school cap once a year, an' my mam reckons you can get the same thing from the shop-with-the-man-at-the-door for ninepence. Here, feel at the top of my skull. Put thy hand on flat and press. Feel owt? Hollow, see. It's like a soup plate on the top of my head. Our Albert's responsible for that—he kept clouting me on the nut when I were a baby. It takes a full twelvemonth for the crust of a child's head to set, an' he kept smackin' me, an' it were a bit doughy, so when it set it set with this hollow in it. They say that if I were to head a football I could drop dead. I'll never forgive our Albert for that I won't. My mam still thinks Cath'lics worship statues. She'll not be told that they're only there to remind us. They have many a row, her an' my dad, about it.'

Marching back into school the boys of Miss Skegham's class were more orderly in file than had been Miss Twining's, but the moment they turned a bend in the stairs, or came to a spot out of her sight, they would begin a turbulent stamping of feet, kick their clogs against the wall, and, if they got the chance, they would thump a boy in the back. He saw Johnson give a kick to a piece of skirting board, and then turn on him with an accusing glare. No matter what a boy was accused of he denied it instantly, and then seemed to enjoy the brief perplexity of the teacher, as well as the moment's excitement of which he was the centre.

The first two days in Miss Skegham's class were not as bad as he had feared. The pleasant ease of Miss Twining's class was gone for ever, he knew that, but in its place had come a taut and tingling sensation that held a certain interest for him, that made work simpler, and gave to home-time a deep sense of relief. When he looked into the big mirror during the dinnertime of the third day he was surprised to see the change in his face. The holiday freedom had gone, and there was an intent, quiet look there. And it was the same with the other boys, they looked a less unruly crowd than on the first day. After three o'clock playtime on the Wednesday, Miss Skegham began poetry lesson. The class was divided into four seasons, and each one had to chant a verse suitable to the season.

' Sheed, let me hear you give Spring,' said Miss Skegham. ' The rest of the class silence.'

Sheed faced her, giving a whisper first, ' I'll spring you——,' and then opening the right side of his mouth: ' " Summer is a-comin' in," ' he piped, ' " loudly sing cackoo." '

' Cuckoo,' she corrected.

' Cookoo, Cookoo,' he trilled.

He admired the boy's coolness. If she asks me, he thought, I'll drop dead. 'M'Cloud,' she called, 'let's hear "The North Wind" from you.'

He stood facing her and the circle of faces, his heart shaking, and praying mentally for help from the Virgin, he forced his dry voice out:

> ' "The North wind doth blow,
>   And we shall have snow,
>   And what will the robin do then, poor ting?
>   He'll———" '

'*Ting?*' she repeated. 'Poor *ting?* Say "thing". Start from the beginning again. No need for you others to titter.'

Ting, thing, ting, thing? He cleared his throat but couldn't remember the opening. She said: ' "The North wind doth blow . . ." ' He coughed. The blood felt up to his eyes. Ting? thing? He'd have to watch for that. 'Right,' she said. He began: ' "The North wind doth blow. And we shall have snow, And what . . ." ' 'Not so fast,' she said. 'Go on. "And what . . ." ' ' "And what, and what will the robin do then . . ." ' it was somewhere near and he'd have to watch out for it, they were all listening and watching him. 'Go on,' she said. He went on: ' "And what, what will the robin do then, poor t'ting . . ." '

'Ting! ting!' she said and he heard them all snigger. 'Don't you know the king's English yet, M'Cloud?'

King's English—I'm Irish. She's saying that against the Irish. The flush died down and his face went cool. '*Thing*!' she called out, '*thing, thing, thing*. Class, say "poor thing".' They let out one loud, 'Poor thing.' 'Right, M'Cloud,' she said, in a rather kindly voice: 'Yes, "The North Wind . . ." ' The nice touch in her voice almost started him, but not quite. 'M'Cloud,' she shouted, 'come on, "The North Wind . . ." '

He stood unbudging. He saw her eyes bulge and the redness swarm up her throat as she came up to him and gave him a swinging slap on the side of the head. It made things spin for a moment, but he didn't feel any pain, and he stood

149

as erect as he could, feeling that half the side of his face was missing: 'Now will you say it?' she asked. He didn't speak. He could only half see her, for the spots were still jumping. 'Right,' she said, going for her cane. 'Hold out your hand.' He put his right hand out and she held up the cane. It came down clean across the palm. 'The other,' she said. He held the left hand out. The cane came down with a sharper rush. It made him tremble with pain. She waited a second: 'Now,' she said, 'we'll have "The North Wind doth blow."'

He stood there trying to stop all his body from shaking. The pain was simple to bear, but he longed for a calm moment to come to him. He didn't speak. She thrust her cane under his right armpit and nudged his arm out. She gave him a rap on it. Then she gave him a rap on the other hand. He hoped the tears wouldn't start. He found running through his mind the words, 'Brave Robert Emmet, the darling of Erin, Brave Robert Emmet he died with a smile,' in answer to the king's English. The class had gone very silent. She said: 'Right, M'Cloud. Now we'll have "The North Wind doth blow . . ."' He felt the turn of heart inside him, and something in his mind said, you won't! It was all right now, that calm thing had come, and she could crucify him and he wouldn't cry, nor would he ever say 'The North Wind.'

He felt himself caught by the ear, and pulled up to the front of the class, just below her desk where she forced him down on his knees: 'Kneel there,' she said, 'and kneel up straight. Keep your hands behind your back. And tell me when you're ready to say "The North Wind . . ."' I'll stay here happily, he thought, till there's a hole in the ground.

It was a relief to kneel with face unseen by the other boys. Outside the bell in the corridor rang for afternoon catechism. Now that he was over his punishment he felt he wouldn't have been without it. He had to avoid thinking of his mother's face, because when he did the tears would come to his eyes in spite of himself. So he imagined himself taking long leaping strides all the way from home to school, and he counted them as he went along. And when his mother's face came he thought of Robert Emmet.

Miss Skegham spoke about Rome. He was kneeling down there in front of her high desk, and her words went over his head, and behind him all the class was listening, but he didn't have to listen if he didn't want. He had forgotten all about " The North Wind." She told of her visit to St. Peter's during the holidays, of the splendid ancient glory of the architecture, the magnificent paintings, and the Vatican, the shrines and bones of famous saints. As he listened he hoped that one day he would have enough money to afford a visit to Rome, and then he'd pass by without visiting the place at all.

The bell rang and then the class knelt on their seats for prayers. They chanted the Our Father, Hail Mary and the I believe. 'And now,' said Miss Skegham, ' I want you all to say a good Hail Mary for a private intention.' It struck him as an unclean expression, " private intention ", and it pictured itself in his mind as the warm surface somewhere on the inside of Miss Skegham's legs. ' Pray for us sinners, now and at the hour of our death, Amen. In the name of the Father, Son, Holy Ghost . . . Amen.' The clogs and shoes went tramping past him. He felt a touch on the shoulder and saw Sheed's narrow mouth whisper ' Begger off home, Mickey,' and the small eye wink, and as he looked up he saw Eddie Radford's distressed glance, and in half a minute they were all gone. He was alone with Miss Skegham in the classroom. She went to the cupboard and brought out a pile of exercise books, placing them carefully on her desk. She sat down at the desk, but before starting he felt her pause, and he hoped she wouldn't speak nicely to him, for then he couldn't keep himself in his grudging mood against her.

' M'Cloud,' she said, calmly—with quick relief he felt the absence of tenderness—' I have a large number of exercise books to mark, and I shall be here for a long time. Would you like to say " The North Wind " and then go home?' He couldn't sustain his impoliteness any longer, and he just managed to say, throatily: ' No, Miss, thanks.' That was the hardest thing of the incident, being bold and defiant in that way. He felt a bit ashamed of it. His mother wouldn't have liked it at all. 'Very well,' she said. 'Kneel up. I can wait until you change your mind.'

Outside in the street he could hear the loud voices of boys, and it struck him that they sounded very foolish. He hoped Willie had gone home, and that no one had told him. Then it went very quiet suddenly. There was the soft breathing of the woman above him there on her high chair, and the soft stroke of her pencil on the paper. He felt at peace now alone with her in the room. The afternoon sun was slanting through the window on to the wooden floor. Could a small boy go with a woman? He felt that at any minute she might kiss him or something. The feeling went and the pain began to come to his head. It was an ache and made him feel dizzy. He was a bit frightened, because it felt so very late. He wished she'd let him go. It was strange how he didn't feel the stings of the cane or the smack across the ear, except for a moment, but now he could feel everything coming back. He tried to keep straight up. Cold drops of sweat came from under his armpits and trickled icily down the skin of his body. He was glad she couldn't see them. He felt a bit sick in his mouth. Slowly things began to twirl. Then he fell face forward, and with a painless bump struck the floorboards.

When he came round it felt as though he had been asleep. He had been dreaming vividly, and then he saw her face above him. It frightened him a bit, because now it had lines across it, and the eyes looked worried. 'I'm sorry, Miss,' he said. She said: 'Rest for a moment. I'll bring you a drink.' He felt at his forehead and found a lump there. He heard her footsteps. She leant over him. He could see the dark tunnel between her breasts down her blouse, but it meant nothing to him just then. He drank the water. He didn't want to get up, but she helped him. He felt very sweaty and was ashamed of it. The water had spilt down his shirt. Her eyes looked queerly at him. She helped him across the room. He said, 'I feel all right, Miss.' She said:

'Are you sure?' He said: 'Yes, Miss.' He wondered did she want him to go or had he to kneel again. He didn't like going without being sure, and he was ashamed of all the trouble he had caused.

At the door she said to him: 'Now, Michael, would you like to say "The North Wind" for me?' He felt he would have liked very much, but he couldn't. It wasn't stubbornness, it was as though everything was somehow blocked up in his throat, and he had forgotten the poem. Her asking him upset him, and he shook his head, and she let him out of the classroom. His clogs sounded very loud as he tiptoed down the corridor and outside into the street.

He slipped to the left by the infants' school and walked alone up to the church. The moment he entered the cool darkness of the porch a peaceful calm took hold of him. He tiptoed down the aisle of the empty church, genuflected and knelt. As his bare knees touched the kneeling-board his heart and everything within him went right. About him he felt the safe high hush of the silent church, and joining his hands he looked toward the tabernacle away on the high altar and began to whisper the Hail Mary. I wonder will that faraway light come right out here to me and touch me inside? He felt a warm easing of the spirit. He's heard me. He prayed and the feeling stuck to him for almost a minute. Then as it slowly left him he let his eyes gaze round, at the blue of the Blessed Virgin's statue, St Patrick with the snake beneath his foot, St Anthony, and then 'Veronica wipes the Face of Jesus' where the Son of God was beneath His cross. Before rising he turned again to the altar, and thought lovingly and with thanks of the relief that had come, and how he sensed the smell of candles burning for the Holy Souls, and a faint fragrance of flowers clinging lightly to the silent air. The Father, Son and Holy Ghost are always waiting for me here, and the Mother of God herself, all present and waiting here for me, always waiting for me to come to them.

CHAPTER THREE

Charlie Criddle has a Mishap

———

'MOTHER, COULD I HAVE BROKE-DOWN for breakfast,' he whispered to her, in the back kitchen, 'in place of dip butties?'

'Erra why wouldn't you, my treasure?' she said 'I'll make you a tightener of broke-down that'll burst the trousers on you.'

'Not too much, mother,' he said, 'I'm not so hungry.'

He watched her shortfingered hands break the thick bread into the cracked basin. She took up a large spoon, scooped it into the sugar, and poured it over the bread, then with a wink at him she added more. He turned to the kitchen tap and began washing himself under it. It's a nasty feeling, he thought, comes on one going back to school after holidays. Yesterday morning it began to creep into me, and now it's taken the full hold on me. *Come O holy Spirit, fill the hearts of Thy faithful, and kindle in them the fire of Thy love. Send forth Thy spirit and they shall be created, and Thou shalt renew the face of the earth.*

He went into the living-room, treading softly with his clogs, and sat at the table. His father, freshly washed after his night at the pit, was reading the paper with a tired, sane look upon his face. His mother brought the brown earthenware teapot from above the oven and poured the bright tea over the bread in the basin. Tea leaves clung to the bread. She poured milk over the mixture, allowed it to stand, and then began to break it up with a big spoon.

'Thanks, mother,' he said, picking up the spoon. His courage began to rise as he ate, but when he stood up, seeing the clock at twenty-five minutes to nine, he could feel the broke-down lying cold and alone in his stomach. I was never as bad as this before, he thought. And yet I've nothing to worry me because I'll be moving up from Miss Skegham's class to Mr. Wimpole's. He went across and stood by his father's chair: 'I think I'll be goin',' he said. He kissed the man on the unsmooth face, and went towards the door. The mother came beside him and kissed him warmly just before he opened the door, slipping a penny into his palm.

'Godspeed you, agraw,' she whispered.

'Goodbye, mother,' he said.

He went swinging down the street so as not to give away his feelings to any neighbour by door or window. At the corner he turned and waved to his mother, and then walked down by the lower part of Back Greenley Street. The street was quiet: lucky Protestants, don't get caned for being late. He stopped outside Ma Clarkson's shop and looked into the window. I'll buy sweets, he thought, and the pleasure of them might drive away the uneasy feeling.

He watched the tall figure of the old lady as she came out of her living-room and walked with a sigh behind the counter. 'Well, sonny,' she asked, 'what would you like?' 'A penn'orth of Bartlett's lime juice drops, if you please, ma'am,' he said. I wonder should I have said 'an ounce'—they are a penny an ounce. It would have shown her that I know how much to expect for my money, though it might have looked a bit forward of me. Taking the glass jar from the shelf she shook it to loosen the sweets. I wonder does she eat many herself? She poured a heap out on to the bright brass scale scoop. Her son had been an actor in London and had shot himself in his bedroom. He was the only boy who knew that, for the woman had told his mother. She was from good people; that he knew by the way her natural teeth protruded and the fact that she called him 'sonny'. He looked at the generous heap of sweets: there's more than a penn'orth. I hope nobody else comes in whilst she's serving me. I suppose it's because she knows my mother. She was about to scoop them into a bag when she looked at the penny on the counter: 'Oh dear, I'm givin' you two ounces instead of one.' She replaced the two-ounce weight by a smaller one, and gently tilted half the sweets back into the jar. 'Thank you, ma'am,' he said, you mean old rap.

The bag felt very small. It would have made no difference to her and so much to me, he thought. My mother would never do a thing like that. She would never go back on a mistake—knowing it was God done it. He put a sweet into his mouth and tucked the bag carefully away in his pocket. For a time as he walked by the big factory he felt content, with the uneasiness overcome by a sensation of pleasure.

Farther along he felt a desire to bite into the sweet, but resisted for a time, then his will suddenly gave way, and after the first splitting bite he crunched the hard sweet to bits in his mouth, feeling the delicious pungency rise up to his nostrils. When he put the second sweet into his mouth it seemed tasteless. Quickly he added another to it, and then another. It's sinful to give way to desire, he thought, crushing the sweets between his teeth and feeling a delicious taste in his mouth and the rich lime-juicy saliva swimming about his tongue and gums.

He turned into Derbyshire Street. Round by the corner of the salt shop came Sheed. The sight of him washed away all taste in the mouth, and the foreboding twinge took hold again. The power of the sweets had gone, and now he felt worse than before. Sheed turned and saw him. 'Howgo,' Mick,' he said.

'Howgo,' he answered. He's seen the track of sweets on me or he wouldn't have said my name. He took the bag out and between his fingers gave Sheed a sweet, feeling ashamed at the sense of sucking up to him.

'Ta, mate, ta,' said Sheed. 'Hy, hast heard the news? I mean about Fat Ada. Her's got wed.' The lump inside him jumped up and down at the sound of her name. Sheed rubbed his hands like an old man and scratched his chin with his shoulder. 'Pity 'elp the poor sod she's got hold of—I'll bet she rattles his lug for him.'

Further along the street they met Johnson. 'Giss a toshy, Sheedy,' he said. Sheed said: 'I got it from M'Cloud here.'

'You rotten liar,' said Johnson. 'Giss one, M'Cloud.' He hated being asked for anything and he didn't like refusing.

He felt in his pocket and handed Johnson the last one in the bag. 'I wouldn't take thy last, M'Cloud,' he said, 'only I need it badly.'

'Hast heard about Fat Ada gettin' wed? asked Sheed.

'Who'd wed her?' asked Johnson.

'I tell thee she's got wed,' said Sheed. 'I heard it on good authority. Hast another toshy, Micky?'

'I gave him the last,' he said.

'You daft foo', said Sheed, 'Tha should have saved it for me.'

'Hy, Leach,' called Johnson, 'hast heard about Fat Ada gettin' wed?'

'I don't believe it—I've heard the rumour times out of number.'

'I'll gamble my life on it,' said Sheed. 'Tha'll never see Fat Ada again.'

They had turned down the street to the school. 'Then who's that,' said Leach, 'goin' round by the caretaker's midden?'

He looked. The lump began to tremble and swell. It was Miss Skegham.

'Holy bloody Nora!' whispered Sheed. 'Ah, happen she's only come for her farewell present. I know I heard on very good authority.'

'Sheed, tha'rt a pillock,' said Johnson.

'What's up?' said Leach. 'We'll all have moved up, won't we?'

'I allus feel that with her out of the road,' said Sheed, 'I could start breathin'. I feel as though her'll dog me to the end of m'days.'

The boys went into the playground. Unlike the normal morning it was quiet, and boys were standing around talking, and very few were playing games. The whistle went and the classes assembled. 'Look,' whispered Sheed, 'her's natterin' to old Victor. I'll bet her has only come back to say goodbye.' Miss Skegham walked smartly across and faced her old class. She looked them up and down, and then her eyes went along the line of faces.

'You're standard five now,' she said. 'Quick march.'

'Jumpin' Jesus,' whispered Sheed, 'we've got her for another bloody year! Sum'dy hold on to me quick—I'm bloody goin' at the knees.'

The boys glanced at each other and went marching into school. I'll not stick it out, he thought, I'll kill myself first. *Come Holy Ghost, Creator come*! What a rotten life! Up the dark stairways, kicking and shoving. Into the classroom. Same places. She began to shuffle them about. He was put alone on a double-seat near the back of the class. I like this. Prayers; call the register; catechism.

'Leach, "Is it a sacrilege to contract marriage in mortal sin, or in disobedience to the laws of the Church?"'

'It is a sin—please, Miss, I mean it is a sacrilege to marry outside the church—'

'You fool, Leach, "to contract marriage"—'

'Please, Miss, "It is a sacrilege to contract marriage in mortal sin, or in disobedience to the laws of the Church, for the anger of God—"'

'Carterham, say it for this idiot Leach.'

'"It is a sacrilege to contract marriage in mortal sin, or in disobedience to the laws of the Church, and, instead of a blessing, the guilty parties draw down upon themselves the anger of God."'

She was working her way round to him.

'M'Cloud—' he stood at once, 'which are the seven gifts of the Holy Ghost?'

'"The seven gifts of the Holy Ghost are Wisdom, Understanding, Counsel, Fortitude, Knowledge, Piety, and The Fear of the Lord."'

He sat down and the door opened after a knock. A boy was pushed in by the hands of two other boys, and the door was closed. It was the palefaced boy he had seen speeding down the stairs on his first day at St Stephen's.

'I'm Criddle, Miss,' he said, 'Charles Criddle. Please, Miss, I've been sent to your class, if you can find a place for me.'

'Go and sit there—next to M'Cloud.'

'Thank you very much, Miss.'

He moved over to make room for the newcomer. The bright face grinned at him. A bell in the corridor rang. 'Get your sum books out,' said Miss Skegham. He saw the stubby hands of the boy next to him dig inside his cloth schoolbag. He had never seen such fingers; the nails were eaten away down to narrow strips nestling beside the cuticle, and each finger looked like a short stump.

During sums the boy Charlie began to nibble at the fragments of nail. First he bit them with his upper teeth, but as he became more immersed in the long division sum he began to gnaw them with the lower incisors, going frenziedly from one finger to another in search of a morsel of nail. I'd offer him mine if it 'ud help, he thought.

'Oh heaven help you, Criddle,' said Johnson, when Miss Skegham was out. 'Wait till hygiene inspection this afternoon—old Fat Ada will murder thee. Her's death on nail-biters.'

After lunch the boys were lined up with outstretched hands, and Miss Skegham went round with the cane. Four boys had been punished, and then she came to Charlie Criddle. For some moments she gazed at the quivering fingers, and then she spoke in a quiet voice: 'Criddle, you may go on biting yours.'

He took a liking to Charlie Criddle and his peculiarities. One of these was the hair on his head just above his ears, which grew upwards, giving one an impression that he might suddenly fly into the air. Another feeling he got from sitting next to Charlie was that the Holy Ghost was at his side. Charlie had lapses of mind. Once he was asked, 'What is God?' and he answered at once, 'God is a supreme creamy caramel.' Miss Skegham was astonished, and without caning allowed him to correct the description to, 'God is a supreme spirit.'

One Wednesday morning Miss Skegham was looking at her Dutch bulbs in the cupboard and the class were reading history books. Next to him Charlie was half turned, fumbling under the desk. He didn't look, because it was a strain to

159

worry about Charlie as well as himself. When Miss Skegham's voice cut across the sleepy classroom:

'Criddle, what are you tinkering with under your desk?'

'Oh, please Miss, nothin', Miss,' he heard Charlie's alarmed reply, 'nothin', please Miss.'

'Stand up, Criddle, when I speak to you,' she said.

'Uh, Miss, please Miss—' beside him he heard the panic in Charlie's voice and he began to pray for him and for himself.

'Criddle!—come out here at once—'

Charlie's feet began to scrape, but he didn't go out. He could sense him crouched over the desk, but he didn't dare look.

'Criddle!'

He saw her flushed face as she strode down between the line of desks, her black apron swinging. She put out her hand and caught Charlie by the ear, and dragged him from the desk. As her back turned he gave a sideways glance. For a moment he couldn't make out what it was he saw, and then it struck him: Charlie Criddle had an inkwell stuck to the front of his trousers.

'Well, Criddle, what's all this nonsense—' Miss Skegham swung him round to face the class. For an instant she looked at his face, but then her eyes saw his lower person. He was standing obediently before her, and the white pot inkwell was dangling on his trousers.

'You filthy beast—' she whispered, giving him a swinging slap on the ear that toppled him over and caused the inkwell to free itself and bounce along the floor. She gave him a look of disgust and walked out of the classroom, slamming the door behind her.

For a second no one moved. Charlie looked white and helpless, and that touched something in him, so that he got up from his place at the back and hurried to the front of the class. Johnson and Parkinson followed. The three boys stood round as Charlie got to his feet. There was a red splotch on his face where she had hit him.

'Button up thy pants, Charlie,' he said.

'Aye, quick, afore she comes back,' said Parkinson.

'Were it fast on thy old man?' asked Johnson, picking up the inkwell. Sheed came out beside him and they both gazed at the small hole in the top.

'Thy pants are full of ink, Charlie,' said Leach.

'How he got it into that hole I never will understand,' said Sheed.

'Whatever wert' thinkin' of, Charlie?'

'I dunno,' said Charlie, blinking about him. 'I done it outa sudden curiosity. Then it got stuck.'

'I thought I'd started seein' things, Chey,' said Johnson. 'I thought he must have tied it on.'

'I seem to have gone deaf,' said Charlie.

'Hy, no wonder his pages are full of blots,' said Leach, 'if he does all his writing with that.'

'Charlie, sling thy hook afore she comes back—'

'I'll never forget Fat Ada's face when she saw it,' said Sheed.

'Sh, they're here!'

The boys darted back to their places, and Charlie Criddle dodged down behind the boy nearest the door. The door opened and Mr Victor and Miss Skegham entered, and the next moment there was a patter of feet and Charlie had gone. Then the bell sounded for playtime.

Out in the yard the inkwell incident was talked about by groups about the place. 'Tha must have seen it happenin', M'Cloud—what exactly took place?'

'I wasn't looking,' he said.

'Hy, is it right about Criddle?' said one of the boys of Mr Denning's class. 'I've heard Miss Skegham opened the cupboard to look at her bulbs an' there was Criddle with a gladioli or summat stickin' out of his pants. Then she flung an inkwell at him an' it stuck on to his doings.'

Sheed came up with Johnson and began talking out of side of his mouth:

'We've been havin' tests in the petties,' he said, producing an inkwell, 'an' not one of us has managed it.'

Charlie came back to school a week later, and there was

no mention of the incident. When Sheed tried to question him, Charlie said: 'I've got to report to old Victor anybody who talks about it—but I'll let thee off this once, Sheedy.' Later he whispered: 'I'll tell thee, Mike, an' thee alone. I had to go afore old Victor, an' I told him straight it was because she'd refused to let me leave the room. I said I were burstin', an' it were either a matter of leakin' some in the inkwell or wettin' me pants. He gave me two soft 'uns on either hand. But that ink didn't half take some washin' off, mate.' 'What—off thy pants, Chey?' 'No, off my pinkler. It were blue-black for days after.'

CHAPTER FOUR

At the Swimming Baths

THE BOYS marched into the classroom after the Monday
morning Mass, and stood at their desks until Miss Skegham
called: ' Sit.' She called the register and they answered with
their faintly uneasy Monday voices. Beside her desk there
stood on a table a tall brown parcel. During the silence that
followed the taking of the register, Sheed whispered: ' Another of her flappin' blasted plants. Her must have botany
on the brain. I wish I were a cactus—I'd prick her bum.'
He sniggered behind his hand, but the others remained
silent, watching Miss Skegham as she began to remove the
paper from the plant.

Her manner was bright and gentle as she surveyed the
plant, and the class, led by Carterham, gave a low exclamation of pleasure as they looked upon it. She turned to them,
smiling, and said: ' Now I wonder if any boy can tell me
what plant that is?'

' Please, Miss—' ' Please, Miss—' ' Miss, please—' a number of hands rose in response. Sheed whispered: ' Keep her
in her " plant an' bulb " mood, lads, an' we can all settle
down to a nice happy day.' And at once he raised his hand,
and cried out eagerly, drowning the echoes of his whisper:
' Please, Miss, I know, Miss, I know.' Miss Skegham ignored
him and looked at Carterham.

' Please, Miss, a hydrangea.'

She shook her head. More boys raised their hands, enjoying the calling out, ' Plissmiss! plissmiss!' and the movement
of their hands, and the chance to speak aloud without getting into trouble. She looked at Charnley. He called out:
' Please, Miss, a laurel.'

' No, it isn't a laurel. Yes, Johnson?'

' A common privet, Miss.'

'A common privy?' whispered Sheed.

'It's very like the privet,' said Skegham, 'but it certainly isn't one. Anyone else?'

'A fuchsia, Miss.'

'Common hawthorn, Miss.'

Sheed cried out: 'Miss, please, Miss—a banana tree.'

There was a titter, at which Sheed looked indignant. Miss Skegham smiled: 'Sheed isn't so far out,' she said. 'It is an exotic tree.'

Charlie Criddle called out: 'Orange tree, Miss.'

'Yes, that's right,' she said, 'it is an orange tree. What made you say orange tree?'

'They've one in their backyard,' whispered Sheed.

'Please, Miss, I once saw one at Belle Vue,' said Charlie.

'Tha'rt a bigger liar than me, Criddle,' whispered Johnson.

'Yes,' said Miss Skegham, 'this is a myrtle-leafed orange tree. *Citrus Aurantium*—' and she wrote it on the blackboard. 'Of the variety *myrtifoliat*.'

The class stared at it unbelievingly for a moment, until Leach had the presence of mind to call out: 'Please, Miss will it grow oranges?'

'Yes, it will certainly grow oranges,' she replied. 'Not large oranges, but oranges nevertheless.'

'Call that an orange tree?' sighed Sheed. 'Someone ain't half been pullin' her leg. Crikey bon, if that ever grows an orange I'll show her my arse.' Then he stood up with arm raised: 'Please, Miss, will you be able to eat the oranges?'

'We'll see, Sheed,' she said, carefully carrying it to the window.

The class watched her, knowing that at such a moment they could turn in their seats, thump one another, whisper and pull faces, without being punished. After a time she turned to them, warm and smiling. How can she love a plant in a pot, he thought, and not me?

Every morning when Miss Skegham entered the classroom her first glance went to the Orange Tree. She had a habit of marking its growth with a pencil on the window, and the sign of any new shoots was something very gladdening to her. The class followed up this interest closely, and they would hum with apparent excitement as she approached the Tree. This was especially so on Monday mornings, when the weekend had produced a larger growth. Then boys would raise their hands and cry out eagerly: 'Please, Miss, how much has it grown?' And Miss Skegham would answer softly, and in this way the relation between teacher and class was often more happy than it otherwise might have been.

One day Miss Skegham gave a cry of pleasure as she was looking at the tree: 'Look—they're forming! the oranges:'

At dinnertime the boys had a look at it: 'If you ask me,' said Charlie Criddle, 'them buds will never see oranges. It's a bloody potato plant off its beat.'

But slowly the oranges formed, seven small yellow spheres. Sheed said one day: 'Went in the class today with my gols on—an' there was Fat Ada whispering to her Orange Tree. I'm not coddin', she were up against it, with one of the oranges all but in her kisser, an' she was whisperin' away, an' know what—the blessed tree were answerin' her back.'

'Gerroff, Sheedy,' said Johnson.

'He's right, chaps,' said Charlie Criddle, 'It tells her every thing we say. I've watched her when she's been out of the room—she goes to her little pen an' after that she knows everything that's happened.'

'It's positively indecent,' sniffed Sheed.

He listened to their talk in silence, thinking how he always avoided looking at the tree, for whenever his glance met it he felt uneasy.

Mr Victor came round to the class one morning and said: 'Can any of you boys swim?'

I knew it, I knew I'd get found out. He recalled one winter playtime in the schoolyard some months before when the topic had been swimming. 'The Irish are said to be good swimmers,' said someone, 'I suppose tha can belt along, Mike?' 'I suppose I wouldn't drown,' he'd said. 'How many lengths can tha do, Mike?' 'Half a dozen perhaps,' he said. For days it had preyed on his mind, whether he'd ever get found out, and he'd resolved to learn to swim at the first chance. But now he was caught.

'I can swim about five lengths, sir,' said Peak.

'I can do almost a length, sir,' said Charlie Criddle.

'Anyone else?' asked Mr Victor.

'M'Cloud, sir,' said Peak.

He stood up. Miss Skegham was watching and so was the Orange Tree, and Mr Victor said: 'Can you swim, M'Cloud?'

'Yes, sir,' he said.

I don't know, I've never tried. Perhaps I can.

'Right, I'll put your three names down,' said Mr Victor. 'We're going to have classes going weekly to the swimming baths, and you boys will be helpers in training the learners. Any boy wishing to go must ask his parents first. No boy with sore eyes will be allowed to go. The class begins two weeks on Wednesday.'

At playtime crowds of boys gathered round Peak, Charlie Criddle and himself to talk of swimming, and to demonstrate various strokes. He felt a bit sick. But there was a fortnight in which to learn. Men were often unable to swim until it happened they were drowning, and then suddenly the power came to them. In India they flung all newborn babies into the Ganges, and if they didn't swim they were let drown. But he'd never heard of one actually drowning. Dogs could swim without being taught. The Irish good swimmers! His father and mother who'd never been in a bath their entire lives, let alone swim. In fact I've never been in one myself. I've never even been in one, except in a plumber's shop. Make me do but one stroke right, Blessed Virgin, and I promise I'll swim a mile.

On his way home from school he got two library books that taught swimming. The printed word assured him at once. It was easy. That evening he practised on a chair in the back bedroom. He satisfied himself on all strokes, and did an amount of life-saving. He wrote down instructions in a notebook in block capitals. Next morning he beckoned his mother into the kitchen, and nervously asked: 'Could you let me have my Friday fourpence today, mother?'

'Erra I'm not sure, agraw,' she said. 'Would tuppence do?'

'I needed fourpence,' he said, 'but don't bother.'

She looked worried, then her face cleared: 'Wait till I'd look is there coppers for the gas in the silver mug.' She got twopence from the mug, a penny from the cornice and a penny from her pinafore pocket. 'Thanks, mother,' he said. She looked at him, hoping, it seemed, he would tell her his trouble. If I did, he thought, it 'ud make more worry.

At quarter-past four when he went out of school he dodged the other boys and went off to Tall Street swimming baths. It was in another district, so there was no danger of meeting any of his school pals there. He put down his fourpence at the window and picked up the towel and slips.

The turnstile wouldn't go round. 'Shove,' said the man. He shoved hard and it spun round.

The moment he entered the door the smell of soapy steam, bodies and water made his heart go pounding nervously. The place had a big empty look. There were about thirty boys and a few men. Every shout echoed and re-echoed, making him more nervous. A few skinny small boys were chasing each other with wet towels. The mad English. The pool was rectangular, seventy-five feet long and twenty-five wide. The depth increased from four feet six inches in the shallow end to six feet six inches in the deep. There were four black lines running along the bottom. The water had a clear greenish appearance. Along either side of the pool were dressing cabins, but youngsters had to go on the gallery to undress, leaving their clothes piled on a bench.

He made his way carefully up the iron staircase, for it was slippery to his clogs. Then he walked along the gallery and found a quiet spot. Slowly he began to undress, putting on the slips under his shirt. He put his clothes in a tidy heap, hoping no one would steal them. He was surprised to see how thick his pubic bush had grown. The hairs were dark brown and curly. He was afraid they might show outside the slips. It was the first time he had been so naked and he felt uneasy. But he tried to appear casual as he strolled along to the staircase. It was cold to his feet, and draughts swept into the warm humid atmosphere when anyone opened the door. He went along to the wash bath.

As he was walking towards it a number of boys ran ahead. When he got there the wash bath was full, and newcomers had to crouch around it waiting for an empty place. It was a four-foot square, about eighteen inches deep, set in a dark recess opposite the cold shower. Four squat youths, miners, with faces and bodies coal-grimed, were in it, scrubbing each others' backs and laughing and singing. Two small boys were huddled up in the far corner, trying to keep warm. The sweaty male smell caused a retching in his stomach which he had to force down. The boys who had chased ahead were all crowding round the bath trying to get a foot in.

'Here,' said one of the miners, 'it's time you two young beggars were out,' and he good-naturedly kneed the two boys out of the corner. 'Hy, you've been in once,' cried the other boys, and they chased the two off. The scrubbing brushes were almost a foot long, with hard fibre bristles, and the miners scrubbed so loud and hard that he wondered how they could have any skin on their bodies. When they were nearly ready they began to play, shoving each other around in the footbath. One kept trying to make enough room to sit down and rest back, and finally he managed to. Then a little muscular one shouted: 'Turn the shower, that's a good lad. Full tilt.'

He went across to the shower and turned the tap at the side. The water shot down: 'Harder!' called the miner. 'Turn it on full.'

He did so, drawing back at the same time, because the cold spray splashed him. Then the miner leapt out of the hot bath and taking one deep breath, ran under the shower.

He stood beneath the torrent, looking upward, rubbing his head and face furiously with his hands, and then his hairy chest, bending to let the shooting shower fall on his back, and then opening the front of his slips to let it rinse away all the soap from his genitals. At the same time the

168

other miners were yelling out: 'Stop splashing, you bloody foo'! Stop it!' and hiding behind each other to protect themselves from the cold spray. He was almost breathless from the cold drops that bounced from the man's body on to him. He watched wondering how anyone could have strength enough to stand the force of the spray.

A man came along who had a thick rusty grime all over his face, hair and neck, and he thrust his way cheerfully into the bath. 'Mind yourself,' he said, 'and let a mon come.' He and another boy were pushed out.

'Good Christ,' exclaimed the man, 'this watter's cold. Hy, laddie,' he said, 'go an' tell Harold we want some fresh watter.'

'I've just been,' the boy answered, 'an' he's havin' his tea.'

'He's bloody lucky,' said the man, 'I'll be fain if I see mine for another hour. Tea or no tea, we've gotta have some hot watter in here.' He got up and went off, and came back a minute later with Harold.

'I don't care a toss what the watter's like,' said Harold, 'I filled it fresh twenty minutes ago. I'm not made o' steam. I'll give you a bit to hot it up, but no more.' He felt in his trousers pocket and took out a box-spanner, with which he turned a tap.

'Ah that's better,' said the boys in the bath. 'It's gettin' nice an' warm now.' 'Ee, aye, doesn't it feel nice!' 'I think that'll do nicely, Harold, ta.' Harold said: 'You bloody asked for hot watter and you'll bloody get hot watter.'

'Crimes, go easy, Harold, tha'rt scaldin' us.' The boys jumped up out of the bath and danced along the tiled edge. Then the man with the grimy hair got into the water, sat down with a sigh, and said: 'Just a bit hotter, Harold.'

When Harold heard that he shut it off and went away. 'I thought that 'ud get him,' said the man. He thought: This is my chance. The boys were all hopping around, just putting their toes in. He put his foot in and pulled it out at once. The water was scalding hot. The dirt and scum were swirling round. As the man washed his head the water took on a reddish hue. 'Shag this for a comic song,' said one of the lads. 'Here, let's fill this bucket under the shower.' They filled the bucket with cold water and carried it across, but the man wouldn't let them put it in until he'd finished his bath. 'By the beard of the prophet,' said one of the lads, when he stood up, 'he looks like a bloody overdone lobster. What sayest thou, brother?'

Steaming the man staggered out and under the shower.

Finally all the boys were able to get into the bath, he with them. This time he got soap and a scrubbing brush, but the very touch of the hard bristle edges on his skin was extremely painful. As the water had become very thick he decided to use extra soap and give himself a good bath, since it was the first in his life. 'Ah sure the Irish have such lovely soft skins,' his mother had once said, 'they wouldn't need a bath in a lifetime. Sure how could you get dirty anyway in Ireland the air so soft would bathe you night and day?'

'Thee scrub my back, mate, an' I'll scrub thine.' He took the soap and rubbed it on the scrubbing brush and began to scrub the strange back, thin and white and boyish. 'Go on, lay on a bit harder.' He did, though still gentle. 'Right, now I'll do thine.' 'Wow! that'll do.' 'I ain't bloody started yet, mate. Tha'll soon get used.'

Harold came along. 'It's about time you lot were out of there. Come on, let's be having you. Get under that shower.' He supervised each boy's shower, sending any one back who had the least speck of soapsuds on him. It came his turn. He slopped across, half blinded with the carbolic soap. The next thing he felt the cold biting needles of the shower, hundreds of them, at the same time his breath left him. He tried to get out, but found himself forced back by a big bristly broom which Harold was holding. He couldn't see a thing, and turned in circles, breathless. Then at last he was let scramble out. He made for the gallery to get his towel and wipe his eyes. Then he found he had walked into the iron steps and hurt his nose. He stumbled up the steps and got his towel, instantly covering his face for relief.

When he took it away he heard an exclamation: 'Ooh, God help thee!' He looked and saw blood on his body, running down from his nose. 'It'll wipe off,' he said. The boy said: 'It's a Corporation towel! Harold'l lay thee out if he sees it.'

He looked over the gallery rails down at the pool, and felt that perhaps he had had enough for one day, and he would put the swimming lesson off. He was worried about the towel, and decided to leave it wrapped round himself, and steal it out under his shirt, fear less Harold should discover it with the blood on. When he was nearly dressed he found his socks were missing. He didn't know what to do then, and was relieved to find them a few yards away, where it seemed they had been put for a joke. When he was going out he glanced at his face in the big mirror and he was pleased to see how clean and well he looked, except that he was a bit swollen round the nose. The towel under his shirt felt bulky, but he got out safely with it.

He was walking along Tall Street, feeling clean and distinguished, when a girl came along. He felt himself flush as she looked at him, a nice quiet-looking girl of thirteen or so. He smiled when he saw her smile.

'Hello, Michael,' she said.

'Oh hello, Ella,' he said. He flushed again, recalling the time she had come unexpectedly into the tent when that cheeky Beardson girl was there. He noticed what a pretty neck she had. Her voice seemed different. It was hard to believe the change in her.

'Have you been swimming?' she asked.

'Yes. Well, just a little splash round.' She spoke her words nicely, so he spoke his very nicely in return.

'I could tell by your skin,' she said. 'I always think swimming makes your skin nice. Your eyes too.'

That was a nice thing of her to say. He tried hard to think of something appropriate to say in return and went dry. What a nice name 'Ella' is! It never struck me before. It's like her—different.

'Are you going home now?' he asked.

'Yes,' she said. 'Yes, I am.'

'So'm I,' he said.

They walked on without talking for a while. He felt very happy one moment, and apprehensive the next. The towel was slipping. He couldn't be sure, but he thought he could see out of the corner of his eye a white fluttering just below his trousers. It frightened him and sent his bowels stirring. He prayed savagely to the Blessed Virgin to keep it up, at the same time he put one hand in his trousers pocket. Ella didn't say anything but she gave him a look, a gentle look. If it fell down in the middle of the street he'd be disgraced, and perhaps run in for stealing.

'Are you in a hurry, Michael?'

'No, Ella.'

'Could you wait whilst I go into Veal's for some manifold for my dad's tea?'

'Yes. Of course I could.'

'Do you want to come in with me?'

'No thanks, Ella, I'll wait here.'

'Are you sure, Michael, you don't want to be going on?'

'No. I mean yes, I don't want to be going on.'

He watched her go into the shop and began to think about the towel. He recalled that nearby was a corporation lavatory. If he went in to have a pee he might be able to fasten it or do something. He hurried round the corner and down the steps. Men were standing up against the stalls. He looked to the row of w.c.s and then realised one had to have a penny to get inside. A door opened, and a man coming out caught his eye. 'Get in,' he winked, 'save thyself a penny.'

He went in and locked the door. Usually the smell upset his stomach, but now it didn't. He unfastened his trousers and tugged out the towel. It shocked him to see all the blood on it. He looked upward to see that no one was peeping, and then searched about for a place to hide it. There was only one place: yes, down the hole and pull the chain. That would be a good idea. He stuck the towel down the hole and gave the chain a pull. The water flushed and circled in the bowl. The towel was stuck in the hole and the water was tumbling in so fast that it must surely overflow and run all about the floor and then the man would come in and catch him. Then just as the water reached the top of the bowl it stopped. What had he to do now? He couldn't leave it. He took his jacket off silently. He lifted the towel and then pressed it against the round discoloured enamel edge of the w.c. bowl. He decided to roll it up and put it on the floor against the back of the bowl and leave the place as soon as he could. He did this, then noisily flushed the cistern and went out, slamming the door after him.

'Hy! Hy, you, young fellow me lad!'

He turned and there was the attendant calling him. You were never safe in this world, even behind the closed door of the unwindowed closet. 'Hy, you. Do you know there's a charge for using the sit-you-down? You went in there without payin' your penny, didn't you? I spotted you.'

'I'm sorry, sir.'

'All right, me laddo, I'll let you off this time. I just wanted you to know that you can't get away with it.'

'Thanks, sir,' he said. 'I'm sorry.'

'All right, laddie, toodle'oo.'

He hurried off as fast as he could. There was just a chance that if he ran up Derbyshire Street he might catch her and explain. He ran out and turned up the street, when suddenly he heard her voice: 'Michael!' He turned and there she was standing waiting for him in the spot he should have been.

'Oh I'm so sorry, Ella,' he said, 'but I couldn't help it. You see, what happened was——'

'That's all right, Michael,' she said calmly. 'I knew you wouldn't go.'

Her remark brought a lightness to his heart, and he felt that the weight of the world had just been taken off him. The only thing to do now was to get away from the corporation lavatory attendant. He hurried along the street beside her, delighted at the wonderful difference. She looked so noble. His mind struggled to think of something to say, something to let her see he was no fool, and when he saw the small spare ground at Knife Street, where young kids were playing with bits of old brick, he said to her: 'They should build houses on that spare ground instead of having it go to waste.'

They scarcely spoke again except when they were nearing home, and she said: 'My auntie lives near Tall Street swimming baths. I leave there about this time every Tuesday.' When he left her it seemed that in all his life he had never known such a curious breathless tingling making him so light that he felt if he fell off a house he would only float lightly along the air down to the ground. He tried to shut from himself the thought of a fortnight Wednesday when he had to help teach boys to swim.

The hours of day and night went by, loaded with prayer and worry about swimming day. Then one dinnertime he became aware of himself walking back to school with a towel under his arm and a penny in his pocket for the use of slips. God, God, God, he whispered as he went down the back streets to dodge his mates, what are You going to do? What way out is there? Save me from disgrace. Suddenly he saw the boy Norman in the back street beside him.

'Hello, Michael,' said Norman quietly.

'Hello, Norman,' he said. He looked at the pale podgy cheeks and the blue eyes so mild, and the faded hair that stood stiff and dry. 'Lookin' forward to the baths, eh?'

'No, Michael, I'm not going.'

You lucky lad, with your legs like sticks and your thin neck like a clay pipe with skin on, God loves you. 'Why not, Nor'?'

'On account of my ears, Michael,' said Norman.

'Why, what's the matter with 'em?'

'They run,' said Norman. This is my chance now. 'When they get in water they run, so I've not to go in.'

He looked at Norman's pale patient face, and felt he could kiss the little half-smiling mouth. 'See you later, Nor',' he said. 'I've got to make a dash for it.'

'Yes, Michael,' said Norman, smiling.

He ran on, hurried down side streets and went into church. He knelt and, pretending praying, had a look round,

174

'Tha'll fun four raps with her stick if tha doesn't change it. *Found*, you daft nut.'

'Oh holy mackerel, so it is, Mike. Quick, is there owt else?'

'Put an " e " on came. Chey, what's " unconcon "? '

'I'm blowed if I know what tha'rt talkin' about!'

'Tha'll be blowed if tha doesn't. Should it be " unconscious "? '

'Holy Moses, I were goin' at it that fast I didn't have time to cudgitate. Go over it, Mike.'

'That sounds a bit odd to me, Chey—" He had thick golden hair growing down the back of his chest." '

'What's odd about it?'

'The *back* of his chest, Chey.'

'Holy Mother, that would mean down his lungs, wouldn't it? He couldn't have hair growing down his lungs, could he?'

'He could, perhaps—but it's not likely tha'd have heard about it, Chey.'

'An' me thinkin' I'd written the best composition of all time,' said Charlie, 'that 'ud have been framed in letters of gold in the school hall, whereas I'd ha' got my bum smacked. Comes from not cudgitatin', Mike. I'll remember thee in my will.'

The door-latch clicked and the class went silent as Miss Skegham entered. He went on with his own composition. The classroom felt very warm, and the desk where he'd been sitting was very warm, and for over an hour he hadn't stood up, and it all felt warm about his trousers. He felt a fluttering of fear and secret excitement as his thing seemed slowly to uncurl from its warm spot against the inner part of his left thigh and suddenly give one stiff upward jerk. It was so violent that he was afraid someone might have seen it. He tried to go on with his composition and screw up his face as though concentrating. It'll do it again—six or seven times. It always does. I wish I could get hold of some pure thoughts to drive it away. Up it goes again. I hope to heaven she doesn't call me out now—my trousers must be bulging something awful. Oh my God, it makes me feel full of bad sin—and all these lads have innocent faces. If I could only slip my hand inside my pocket and force it up against my stomach it would begin to sag, and it wouldn't show as much. I mustn't think of paps or things. *Groin*: the curved portion between belly and thigh. He must have been a dirty man who put that into the dictionary. *Teat*: pap of woman. How can educated men put such things in print? I don't know what the world's coming to. I'm getting stuck in sin. It'll rip my pants next. Lord save me or I perish.

Suddenly a sharp ringing explosion burst against his right ear, followed by a stinging daze down the side of his head. After a moment he realised vaguely that Miss Skegham was standing behind and that she had struck him across the ear with her hand. He let his head droop forward a little. He overcame an urge to rush away.

'M'Cloud, you dolt!' he heard her voice coming closer. 'How dare you end your "d's" with a downward stroke? How dare you bring a word to an end in that slipshod manner? Don't you realise, you confounded idiot, that writing must flow? How can you break off every word from its fellow in that way? You write like a barbarian. Watch this——' and snatching the pen from his fingers she demonstrated with swift strokes how the letter *d* should end.

'Mike,' whispered Charlie when she had moved on, 'there a bit of blood on thy ear. Her's done it. Tell her.'

'Shut it,' he said.

At playtime Charlie insisted on inspecting his ear. 'Tha's a dint near thy ear, Mike,' he said.

'It's from her ring,' said Peak, 'turns stone inside an' wams thee with it.'

He slipped into church on his way home. He had a toothache and he whispered: The pain is me. I've got to make friends with all my miseries. He knelt at the back of the church and looked at the tabernacle away on the altar. Then he closed his eyes and began to say the Our Father. But the line of Light did not come out and reach to his heart. Sometimes it was like that. Bad thoughts came in-

178

stead, and he tried to pray to the Blessed Virgin to put them out of his mind. Women's legs. Women's paps. He tried to pray to her but the thoughts got into the prayer. He put his hand down to straighten up his thing against his stomach. The very touch of his hand upon it seemed tingling with temptation, making him feel sick from guilt. It's a sin for others but not for me, he tried to think, looking at the statue of the Blessed Virgin, but the thought didn't convince him and he left the church in misery.

Along the street the tooth began to ache more keenly. It was a back tooth on the lower jaw, and to ease the pain he began to suck and draw at it. There was a sharp pain and a taste of blood. I shouldn't suck it. It'll go worse. But I can't stop. He sucked and sucked, drawing hard at the hollow of the tooth. Suddenly a fierce pain ran up his jaw and his mouth filled with the thick black taste of blood. He walked along with the blood thickening and warming in his mouth, and looked for a quiet spot where he could spit out unnoticed. He went up a back street and stopped at a grid. He opened his mouth and watched the thick steaming slime of blood slip slowly through the air to fall dark and red upon the gutter beside the grid. It stinks. It's my own blood, bad blood. Blessed Virgin Mary, don't let me be lost.

The class was getting ready to go off to the baths. He watched them, longing to go with them. Miss Skegham came round inspecting ears. He felt her hands on his shoulders, her face close to his, her eyes peering into his ears. He trembled. She passed on to Charlie. He waited.

'Criddle,' she said, 'how often have I told you about those ears.'

'Please, Miss,' said Charlie, 'I'll give them a good scrub at the baths.'

'You will not,' said Miss Skegham. 'You'll stay behind. I'll attend personally to them.'

'But, Miss! Please Miss! I'm doing so well——' began Charlie.

'Criddle, you're staying behind,' she said, 'to have your filthy ears scoured.'

There was a silence in the class. Charlie looked for a moment as though he might defy her, and then he flushed up. The next moment footsteps were heard in the corridor, and Mr Denning called in: 'Ready, Miss Skegham? Right, boys, fall in.' And the swimmers went marching out of the classroom.

'Francis,' said Miss Skegham, 'go and see if Mr Dwyer has the hot water ready.'

Miss Skegham placed a stool in front of the class. Carterham returned carrying an enamel bowl of steaming water. 'Place it on here, Francis,' she said. He placed the bowl on the stool, his manner detached and a faint worried grimace on his face. An odd silence was on the entire class as Miss Skegham called out: 'Criddle, come here.'

Charlie went out. She gripped him by the shirt at the back of the neck, forced him down over the bowl, picked up a cloth, and began to wash his neck and ears. Then she took up a small nailbrush and scrubbed, raising a rich lather. Charlie allowed her to twist and turn him at will. She put his head down into the bowl, and she scrubbed it all over. Then she sent Carterham for cold water. Charlie had his head ducked into the cold water and rinsed. He made no sound, except once or twice to give a jerking sob. The class was still and silent.

The washing of Charlie Criddle seemed more upsetting than any caning. And Miss Skegham herself appeared glad to get it over, for there was something peculiar about the silence of the class; and also, an odd intimacy began to creep into her washing of the boy. She had begun it in a cold temper, and was finishing off almost tenderly. She dried his head and ears. When he stood before the class he looked very different. 'Well,' she said, 'does he look any better?' Nobody spoke a word. 'Very well,' she said, 'we'll go on with our handiwork. You, Charles Criddle, go and sit next to M'Cloud, and note the useful articles we make while you're taken up with ducking each other in the water.'

180

He didn't speak when Charlie sat next to him. He got the purse he was working on, and began to sew. Charlie sat silent for a long time, and then he gave a snigger.

'What's up?' he asked.

'Call that summat useful?' said Charlie.

'It's a purse, isn't it?'

'Aye, but it won't hold nowt. A penny won't fit in, an' a tanner'll slip through the stitches.'

Charlie smelt very nice from the soap Miss Skegham had used. 'You look right bonny, Chey.' Charlie said, quietly: 'I'll get even with her.'

He was relieved that Miss Skegham did not inspect the handicraft articles that day. But the next day she picked up the purse and held it before the class. 'M'Cloud,' she said, 'out of my own pocket I bought leather, needle and gut for you to work on. And then you perpetrate such a monstrosity. Keats said: "A thing of beauty is a joy for ever," and that may well be applied to Edward Radford's wallet, on which care and attention have so obviously been lavished. But this—this ugly thing, a child of three could certainly have done better. Take that!' and she let him have a sudden swing of her hand that caught him unexpectedly, and sent his head against the pillar. 'Get back to your place, you oaf. And if you dare put a finger to a piece of leather in my presence again I won't be responsible for my actions.'

He went back to his place and sat down. His head was full of spinning dots and he knew it would soon begin to ache for the rest of the day. Turk her and her leather. He noticed Charlie was biting his nails ferociously, and he heard a whisper: 'I've got something very secret to see thee about, Mike. Say nowt to nob'dy, but don't dash off at dinnertime, hang about till I tap thee.'

The dinner-time bell went and Miss Skegham had them say prayers, inserting at the end of them: 'And now I want you to put your hearts into one special "Hail Mary" for a private intention of mine.' With closed eyes he prayed, his thoughts to God touched by some dark uneasy image of her private intention. Then the class bundled out quickly, taking

181

advantage of the temporary leniency that appeared after a prayer had been said on her behalf.

'She don't get no buckshee appeals out of me,' said Charlie. 'What—working my innocent little soul on her behalf? Not likely! You've got to say the prayer, I'll admit, because she has her lamps on you and you've got yours shut, but she can't see inside here, mate, an' that's where the proper workings of a prayer is. Know what I do Mike?—I always imagine God sitting there stiffly on his throne, with the Blessed Virgin, Saint Michael the Archangel, Saint John the Baptist, an' perhaps a few little saints looking on, an' the angels floating about seeing as everything's in its place. And one thing—I'm not keen on angels. The saints are all right, because they've had to suffer an' labour their way through this life the same as we have to, but these angels seemed to have walked in, or flown in, tha might say, to some right cushy jobs. And I can't say I hold with it. But same as I were sayin' about God, there He is, sitting on the old throne, an' I say to Him: "Listen, God, I'm not prayin' *for* this private intention, I'm praying *against* it. What she has in mind, I want You to make the opposite come true. If she wants somebody to live, You make 'em snuff it. If she wants somebody to snuff it, You make 'em live." I'll tell thee summat, Mike, it's always such a shock to me,' he added, 'when she gets us to say a prayer of thanksgiving for a petition granted. The only way I've been able to work it out is that she's got some heavy artillery on her side—Masses, Rosaries, an' money in the Holy Souls' box. Under them circs I can see how a little prayer of mine wouldn't come out on top every time.'

The two boys were separated by the dash of bodies scrambling through the school gate. Then Charlie whispered: 'Art game for a desperate measure?'

'About what?' he asked.

'Keep thy head away from mine,' said Charlie, 'it looks as if we're plotting. Would tha like to get thy own back on Fat Ada?' I don't want to get my own back on anybody, he thought, I only want to be left in peace. 'Follow me then,' said Charlie—'into church.' Weakly he followed Charlie, dipped his fingers in the holy water just after him, and slipped into a seat in the corner after him. They scanned the rows of long pews for a head. 'We can see,' said Charlie, 'but can't be seen. There's an old woman down there near the altar.' 'She's there every day,' he said. They both knelt and prayed, but he knew his prayer was no good, because he had never been able to pray in church when he had gone in with a companion. He always had to be alone to get the Light from the altar into his heart.

'What's in thy mind, Chey?' he said.

'Let's do her Orange Tree in,' said Charlie.

The suggestion made him almost sick with fear. 'Do it in?' he said.

'Well, geld it, at least,' said Charlie. 'Swipe the oranges off. She'd go mad.'

'But what good would it do us?' he said.

Charlie looked annoyed. 'Tha doesn't look life square in the face, Micky,' he said. 'Tha's not got to think of thy own good—justice has to be done. Leave it to me—I'll plan it all out for tomorrow.'

He was ready to go when Charlie tugged him by the sleeve. 'Let's say a damn good little Hail Mary together. We'll need her on our side.'

CHAPTER SIX

The end of the Orange Tree

THE NEXT MORNING he was surprised to see Charlie Criddle looking so clean and behaving with such quiet attention in the classroom. Miss Skegham had her Friday mood on her, and it seemed to him she was like some plump kindly aunt at her desk. This is the only way life should go on, he thought, in peace and amity. Why do people live at such variance when they could so easily live like this? It looks like Charlie's called it off—and thank the Lord he has!

At playtime he tried to get a moment alone with Charlie, but every time he drew near Charlie brought others into the chatter. Back in class he attempted to broach the matter three times, but Charlie always produced a blank expression. And slowly he began to realise that this blank look was more significant than anything else. As they blessed themselves after dinner-time prayers he heard a soft whisper in his ear: 'Twelve-forty. Don't forget.' Please God we'll be seen and have to call it off.

He hurried home. There was a nice basin of chips and peas for his dinner. He shook plenty of salt and vinegar over them and began to make himself butties.

'I've got to rush off the minute I've had my dinner, Mother,' he said.

'Don't choke yourself, sir,' she said.

It's funny, they don't seem to have the proper Friday dinner-time flavour when you're in a hurry. The best meal of the week spoiled. Blast you, Charlie Criddle. He had a good wash under the kitchen tap.

'If anybody asks did I go back to school early, Mother, don't say I did.'

'There's guilt in your eye,' she said, 'if ever I saw it.'

'Don't talk daft. There's not honest, is there, Mother?'

'Guilt an' secrecy, my boy. Wait till I see would I have a penny for you.'

Derbyshire Street seemed oddly deserted. Funny how it gets overcrowded and then empty within a few minutes. He cut up a back street and entered the school-yard. There was a dog waiting for someone. Not a soul in sight. He went into the urinal and began to whistle as he pretended to pee. He looked up at the school windows. All appeared clear until he saw his own classroom window. His heart gave a turn as he saw a face watching him. It can't be! He could see the Orange Tree, just the top orange, and to the left was a face or what seemed to be a face. As he stared hard to make sure he felt the gaze of the two eyes upon him. It was so fixed from behind the window, so old and all-knowing it seemed, that his own startled feeling gave way to submissiveness, and he bowed his eyes before that look. He glanced upward once more, and then he saw the solemn beckoning of a hand, and the head gave a familiar jerk. 'Chey Criddle, curse him. Thank God just the same.' He went quietly into the school, the sudden fright having split the suspense. He went upstairs, his footsteps echoing nervously in the emptiness. He opened the classroom door softly and saw Charlie, his arms folded, watching by the window. He turned and spoke: 'The wheel is come full circle. I am here.'

'Tha nearly frickened the wits outa me.'

Charlie produced an old pair of scissors. 'We'll snip 'em off,' he said. Then he took a small wool glove from his pocket and put it carefully on to his left hand.

He had avoided looking at the Tree until that moment, but now as Charlie prepared himself he gave a timid glance at it. The golden orbs seemed to hang in curious innocence now. It seemed as though the Tree had become indifferent. And Charlie now had the air of a man about to perform an operation. 'I think we ought to cut three apiece off, Mike,' he said, 'then we're in it up to equal culpitude.'

He watched as Charlie raised the scissors. He envied Charlie's steady untrembling hand as he gently took hold of an orange, the lowest one, held by the glove, and then

185

placed the scissors against the stalk, turning to him for a moment. They looked at each other in silence. Then the fingers pressed the scissors, *krek*, and an orange came away from the Tree. His tongue felt dry. Charlie raised the scissors once more, after carefully placing the orange on the window ledge. The second orange came away. A spot of sweat came up on Charlie's nose. He put the orange down. Then he quickly cut off the third, and handed the scissors over. 'Don't forget the glove, Mike.'

He put the glove on his shaky left hand, and then picked up the scissors in his right. Everything was silent in the school. He took hold of an orange, held it unbelievingly in his hand, and then put the scissors to the stalk and cut. 'Quick,' whispered Charlie.

But at that first cut all his trembling had stopped, and very calmly he selected the second orange and cut it. 'What about the one that'll be left on, Charlie?' he asked, as he took hold of the third. 'I were thinkin' we should leave it on as a reminder of her bereavement,' said Charlie. He snipped the stalk. 'It don't seem right, Chey,' he said. A sweet calm was flowing through him.

'Christ, someone's comin'!' whispered Charlie. 'Listen!' For a second they both stood perfectly still. Footsteps could be heard coming up the stairs. 'Right, Chey, stick thy three in thy pocket. Quick. I'll hold on to these.' He stuffed the scissors into his pocket, and the glove. Then the oranges. One was left on the tree. 'Tis the last rose of summer. Charlie looked alarmed, and was about to make for the door, but he put his finger to his lips: 'Don't move,' he breathed, 'happen they'll not be comin' here. No time to get away.' He pulled Charlie down behind the benches at the back of the classroom. The footsteps came nearer, hesitated in the corridor outside, and then the door opened and closed softly again.

Through the medley of steel desk supports he saw a pair of thin legs, and he made a movement of his lips to Charlie: 'Norman Tribley.' He glanced up at the Tree above them. Its fruit was gone and it looked oddly lost. Norman went to his desk and took out his bag. He appeared to be studying one of his books for some seconds. 'The square of the hypotenuse is equal—equal to the sum of the squares, the sum of what squares? the square of the hypotenuse, is equal —oh Mammy, Mammy, I can't do it—the square——' Then he moaned like a child: 'Oh Mammy, Mammy, I can't do it, I can't do it.'

The two boys kept still. If I were to rise now, he thought, Norman would drop stone dead. 'What shall I do, Mammy?' Norman whined. I've done the deed—what shall I do with the body? There was a moment's silence, then Norman stood up. He felt Charlie prodding him and pointing. He looked sideways along the aisle between the desks. Norman Tribley had taken an inkwell out and now had it to his lips. He took short sips, putting his head back. Suddenly there was a light thud. Norman gave a frightened start and turned. The two looked up and saw that the last orange had fallen from the Tree. He caught a glimpse of Norman's face. It was white and his eyes were staring at the tree. He gave a gurgle of terror, put down the inkwell and ran from the room.

The two boys rose up stiffly. 'I don't know whether to laugh or scrike,' said Charlie. 'What can we do with this?' he asked, looking at the fallen orange. 'I'll handle it, Chey,' he said, picking it up and putting it in his pocket. He felt he had just witnessed real fear, and he was no longer afraid for himself. 'Look at bloody Tree,' said Charlie, 'it favvers naked.' 'Aye,' he said, 'it looks right daft without its oranges, I must say. Come on, Chey, let's slip off.' 'There's the one o'clock buzzer,' said Charlie. It seemed strange that it could all have happened in twenty minutes. 'Thee go by the boilers, Charlie,' he said, 'an' I'll go the other way. We'll meet near the ironmonger's.'

He went down the stairs and through the lavatories. No one in sight. Norman Tribley's fear and the drinking of ink were in his mind, and he had almost forgotten the Orange Tree. Charlie was waiting at the ironmonger's shop. 'Quick, Charlie,' he said, 'let's get on this tram. Come on.'

They hurried to the stop and boarded the tram. He pulled out a penny. 'Two ha'pennies, please,' he said to the conductor. It was a five-minute ride to Glebe Hill. They got off and he led the way to the brickfield. He knew every bit of it well. He began to throw duckstones about. 'Get delvin' at that spot there, Charlie,' he said, 'whilst I distract attention. Here, use thy scissors.' Charlie made a hole with quick movements of his hand, scooping the dry clay out. 'Look out, Mike,' he whispered, 'there's an old chap across there.' 'He's blind, Chey, I know him. Get diggin'.'

He was surprised to see how deep down Charlie had got into the earth. They felt in their pockets and took the oranges out. Charlie was about to take a bite but he knocked it out of his hand. 'I often eat an orange at dinner-time,' said Charlie. 'This is one of them days, Charlie, when tha won't. Now here, let's bury everything, thy mother's soap-scissors included.' They put everything down the hole, and made runs and throws and let off shouts, as though they were playing duckstone. Then when they had smoothed down the surface soil they flung stones around it. 'Spin round, Chey,' he said, 'so that tha'll never know where that spot is if tha lives till tha'rt ninety.' 'I'll never forget,' said Charlie, 'if I live till I'm two bloody hundred an' ten.' 'Right, let's hurry back,' he said. 'An' remember this, Charlie, nothin' ever happened. I'm not going to ask thee not to split. Nothing's ever happened. This dinner-time tha whitewashed your petty.'

'That's bloomin' funny, Mike,' said Charlie, 'but that's exactly what our old girl is doing. We're havin' some company at weekend, so she's whitewashing. That's a sign from God.' They ran and caught the tram. At half-past one they arrived separately at the school-yard. There was still ten minutes to spare before going-in time, and the yard was crowded and lively.

Eddie Radford came over to him. 'Hast been in the class-room, Mike?'

'Aye, many a hundred times.'

'I mean this dinner-time.'

'What a daft question to ask, when tha's seen me just come in the school-yard. Why?'

'Tha's not see the Orange Tree?'

''Course I haven't. Why?'

'Then for the sake of the mother that bore thee—keep out!'

'Why, what's up, Eddie?'

'Blessed oranges are gone!'

'Don't talk daft.'

'Well, I can't say I've seen it, but that's what everybody's saying. It's all round the school-yard, an' nobody'll go in. Carterham reckons he's seen it, but then he says he hasn't. Sheed's been ordered back early to finish a composition, but he won't go in.'

Charlie Criddle came up. 'Hy, have you heard? Someone reckons there's an orange missing on the Tree!'

'Orange!' exclaimed Eddie. 'I've just been telling Mike here that I've heard a rumour that there's not a bally orange left on the Tree!'

'Holy stinking cheese,' sighed Charlie, 'an' it's Friday. Still, I won't believe it till I see it.'

'I won't believe it then,' said Peak. 'If I could both feel an' see I still wouldn't believe it.'

'Look out, there goes the whistle, chaps.'

As they marched into the classroom most boys gave a quick glance at the window and then turned away. They all stood behind their places until Miss Skegham called out: 'Sit.' She was wearing a new blouse and her nose was powdered. She stood at her desk for a moment, opened the register, and looked towards the window. He saw her and looked down. He saw her get up and walk very slowly towards the window. She went past his desk. Then he heard her stop. The class was perfectly still. She spoke in a low voice:

'Boys!' He turned with the others and looked at her. Her face was ashen, and she had her hand to the Tree. 'Boys,' she said in that strange voice. 'does anyone know anything about this?'

They let out gasps of horror: 'Oo, Miss!'

'Oh, Miss!'

'No, Miss, I don't!'

'I don't, Miss.'

Johnson said: 'Have the oranges gone, Miss?'

For a moment it looked as though she might fall. She picked up the Tree in its pot and carried it to the front of the class. He felt sorry for her. The boys looked at her. He saw the white skin disappearing and a red flush rising swiftly. But she held herself in for a moment, and asked: 'Which of you did this?'

Not a boy budged. Then she let out a loud cry: 'Who did it? Who committed this outrage? Do any of you know anything about it?' And at the silence she flushed to her hair. At that moment he didn't feel sorry for her any more, but for himself and Charlie Criddle. He thought of the tremendous secret concealed behind his lips. He had only to relax for a second and it would burst out. He wondered how his mind could hold it. He wanted her to start talking again, for the silence was hard.

Again she let out an angry cry: 'Who did it?' Silence. Every boy appeared to be striving to be more silent and, by the use of accusing looks, appear more innocent than the next. But it seemed to him that they all looked guilty.

'Very well,' she said. 'No boy cares to admit. I'll cane round the classroom until the one or ones who did it confess.'

She began with Francis Carterham, since he was nearest, and gave him two raps, and then the next boy, going round the class and between desks, caning every boy. It was strange to watch the other boys being caned, for something they were guiltless of, and he felt it a relief when his turn came and she gave him two hard ones. Sheed look round with piteous eyes at the others, pleading for the culprit to confess. Charlie Criddle let out a howl at his first rap, and had to be forced to hold his hand for the second. He looked about at the faces, just as other boys did, with an expression of wonderment on his face. He found himself actually thinking: Who can it be? After caning forty-two boys Miss Skegham was very flushed.

' Now,' she said, ' did any boy see my Tree before he came into the classroom with the class? '

Norman Tribley stood up: ' I think I saw it, Miss.'

'You *think* you saw it.'

' I saw it, Miss. I saw an orange fall off. I came in to do my geometry, Miss, and an orange fell off.'

' Where is it? '

' I don't know, Miss. I couldn't recognise the tree properly, and I ran out when I saw it.'

' Did any other boy see that orange? You are sure, Tribley, there was only that one orange? Was any other boy in the classroom during dinnertime? '

She was angry yet impotent, and he thought it was odd, how she, who could catch a lad for a mistake in last month's composition, was helpless when it came to finding the one who had taken the oranges from her Tree less than an hour ago.

' I'll give the boy or boys one last chance,' she said. ' Will the boy who did it or who knows anything about it come out here? '

The silence was a temptation to him. ' Very well,' she said, ' I'm going to cane the class once more.' And as she heard the murmur of the class she said: ' Yes, I sympathise with the innocent ones. They should remember what punishment the guilty classmates have brought on them.'

She went to the front of the class, and again had to start at Carterham. He looked pale and red-eyed from the first caning, since he had never been caned by her before, and the shock seemed to have upset him. He was frightened and quite unlike his usual self. As he watched he saw that when Carterham was punished, a look came to his face of the same kind that came to the faces of Sheed and Johnson, and his entire expression changed, and all the pleasant unafraid openness disappeared. ' Out with your hand,' said Miss Skegham. ' And see you let him have it as bloody hard as you let the rest of us have it,' hissed Sheed: ' Please, Miss,' he called, ' you aren't going to cane *me* again? ' ' I'll cane every one of you,' she said.

He noticed that Norman Tribley's thin back was shaking, and then he heard him call out: ' P—p—please, M—miss! don't! I—I—I did—did— ' and the spasm of trembling stopped and Norman collapsed. He darted forward, but missed him, and when the boy's back slumped against the desk he took hold of him under the armpits.

' He's fainted, Miss,' he called. ' Sheedy, give's a lift. Shall we take him to the top of the steps, Miss? ' Sheed and Johnson, and half a dozen others crowded round Norman. They all lifted, but were tugging and pulling with relief at the interruption, and he was in danger of dropping him.

' Up on my shoulder,' he heard himself say in a high Irish voice. ' Aye, up on Mike's shoulder,' shouted Charlie, ' an' carry him firebobby's lift.' ' On mine,' Said Johnson. ' No, on M'Cloud's,' shouted Charlie. The hands went under Norman and he was lifted up and placed down on his shoulder. ' Get back,' called Charlie, ' you're blockin' his way.' ' Take him on the outside landing,' said Miss Skegham. ' One of you take this chair for him. Carterham, get some water. Mind you don't drop him, M'Cloud.'

Escorted by half a dozen boys he carried the small figure on his shoulder. The legs hung like two frail bones, and on the entire body there didn't seem to be a fingerful of flesh. He must be dead, he thought, for how can anything keep alive inside this skin and few weak bones. ' Make way there,' called Charlie. ' Gangway,' Sheed cried, ' for a naval officer with casualty.' They went along the passage and a good blast of fresh air came as someone opened the outer door. ' Here's the chair,' called a voice. ' He doesn't need a chair,' said Johnson. ' Get his head between his legs when we get him down.' ' Careful,' he called.

They lifted Norman down gently, and placed him on the broad stone step. Charlie Criddle stooped down and his queer fingers unfastened the celluloid collar at the front, and opened the shirt. There were two pale bones sticking out. On his tongue was the trace of the dark ink. His face was waxen, covered with drops of sweat. 'Give him air,' said someone. 'Shove his head between his legs.' 'Here, look out, here's the watter.' A thick cup was put to Norman's white lips, and the water was spilled over them and down his throat. And then he blinked open his large eyes, and said: 'Where am I, please?'

'Thar't in lovin' hands, me old cocksparrow,' said Charlie. 'How do you feel, Norman boy, ready for three rounds with the gloves?' Norman smiled at him. Johnson said: 'Didt' really pinch them oranges, Nor'?' They all turned on him: 'Shut thy big fat gob!' 'Shut it, Johnny, or I'll paste thy lug.' 'You flamin' pace-egg, you can see the lad's not well.' 'I were just wonderin',' said Johnson, 'for I don't believe as he did. An' it's only right an' salutary to say so.'

The boys looked at each other, and he and Charlie and passed a swift glance. There was something comforting about the certainty of guilt, compared with the perplexity of innocence all around. Carterham said: 'We'd better be gettin' back, lads.' 'I'll stay another minute with Norman,' he said. Charlie said: 'Me too.' Norman said: 'Can I get up, please, it's cold!' They helped him to his feet. He took out a handkerchief and wiped his face. 'I'm sorry,' he said. 'Shall we go back now?'

CHAPTER SEVEN

Benediction and Ella

AFTER TEA he had a sudden impulse to go to Tall Street baths. He remembered his first visit there, when the footbath had been crowded with miners, and the water had been scalding and dirty, and the soap had smarted his eyes, then the breathless time under the shower, the unpleasant figure of Harold, and then the bleeding nose and the stolen towel. Somehow he felt drawn back to it all. He got his fourpence spending money and an extra twopence, asked could he put his shoes on, and hurried off, so as to get there well before halfpast five, when the spinning mills loosed. He also felt that he'd like a bath after the sort of day it had been. Miss Skegham had ended the day with a challenge: 'One of you has taken the fruit,' she said to the class,—not Norman Tribley, but the Tree will grow bigger and stronger, and in time it will bear more fruit.' When he thought of the seven lonely oranges buried on the brickfield he found it hard to believe. Just the same I'll have to watch that spot.

He arrived at Tall Street baths during a lull. It was ten minutes past five, and schoolboys were splashing in the plunge, but the footbath was empty. He was about to go in when Harold came along. 'Ee, me lad,' he said, 'tha can't go in that—it's dirty. Just hold on a minute whilst I fill it up afresh. Here, pull that plug out for me.' The plug was a foot long and heavy. 'Hold on,' said Harold, 'an' I'll rinse it out.' The tiled bath was rinsed with hot water, the plug was put in, and the bath filled with fresh clear water.

'How's that?' asked Harold. 'Oh fine, thanks,' he said, looking at it. 'Try it,' Harold said, 'try it for heat.' He put a foot in. 'It's fine,' he said. Then he went in, and after a minute or two he laid himself down in it.

It was unbelievably clear water, and such comfort and

194

the warmth, and all the soap and brushes for himself. He suddenly began singing, ' O Salutaris Hostia '. He had a scrub from top to toe. When he came out he went straight under the shower. This time he was able to stand it much better, because the bath had so warmed him up that the cold water did not chill.

He went to the plunge and forgot all about 'Swimming Made Easy.' He stood on the side and after a minute he took a quick dive when no one was looking. It stung his stomach a little, and also his eyes, but not his head. He came to the surface, and discovered that by putting his arms forward and then pulling them sharply to his side he could stand up. The mass of water still took his breath a little. He made a jump to reach the pipes that went round the side, missed and swallowed water.

' Art' learnin' to swim? ' asked a boy. ' Then what tha wants to do is to push thyself off. Get on them steps, and I'll stand here, and thee push thyself off.' ' You won't go out of the way? ' he asked. ' Nay, nay,' said the lad, ' I'm not one of them sort. If I says a thing I does it.' He had three attempts, none of which was good. ' Tha'rt too rigid,' said the lad. ' Tha'll never swim whilst tha'rt rigid. Let all the strength go out of thy limbs. Then put thy head on the water. Then push off and float along.' He had another try. ' Aye, that's better. But keep doin' it without thinkin'. Just let thy arms flop a bit.' He pushed off again, his arms outstretched, waiting to be picked up, but the boy had moved aside. ' See—tha did it on thy own!' exclaimed the boy.

The first sensation of moving along the water without any support, merely by the movement of arms and legs, was delightful. He kept on practising, and when he left at seven o'clock he could swim twenty-five feet. He felt tired and very happy. He ran up to the gallery and began to dress, joining in singing with a boy who stood a few yards away: ' Praise God from Whom all blessings flow.' Protestant hymns had always seemed faintly sinful until then, but now he sang away in tune with the boy. And as he was putting on his shoes he sang away in tune with the boy, but before he quite realised it he was singing: 'Old Missis Oliphant she lives at number 9, Hairs on her belly like balls of twine . . .' He cut off suddenly and decided to hurry to St Stephen's, go to Benediction and Confession, so he'd be pure and sinless that same evening. He didn't feel the Orange Tree affair to be a sin. A sin was something between you and God alone.

He went out into the street and standing there at the Bath's window reading a poster about a polo match was Ella Sharley. He felt the blood leave his face at the unexpected sight of her, then he flushed, and he was afraid that when he spoke no sound would come off his tongue. She turned suddenly: 'Eh, hello, Michael,' she said. 'Fancy seeing you again!'

'Hello, Ella, hello,' he said in a thin hearty voice. 'Have you been to your aunty's?'

'Yes. Have you been swimming again?'

'Yes.'

Her face was brightly warm to him, and her forehead broad and lovely. He wondered for a second how a person so beautiful could have come from the Sharley home; her mother the silly gossip and her father a sour ugly man; a gravedigger. Perhaps it was the touch of the Holy Ghost upon her, the Paraclete who brought mysterious beauty into the world. He quickly moved on to the outside of the pavement. He felt it was as though the two of them had a secret from the world. A nice feeling. He walked a few steps beside her along the street, then she stopped suddenly.

'Where are you going?' she asked. 'Home? I'm not. I've a girl to meet.'

It was like a stab at the heart, the sudden cool change in her. He filled up in his throat: 'Goodbye then,' he said, and he turned and walked away. He would never forgive her that. The longest day he lived.

'Hy, Michael,' she called, 'where are you off?'

He didn't want to turn and answer, but he did: 'I'm going,' he said. 'I must be going.'

'Where?'

'Oh somewhere,' he said shortly, and turned and went off.

196

She came running after him: 'Just a minute, Michael,' she said, 'I want to ask you something.'

He turned to her again: 'What is it?' I can talk with a better voice than she can.

'Would you leave me, just like that?' she asked slowly. He saw feeling rising up to her eyes. He looked downwards: 'You told me you had a girl to meet.'

'I'm asking you would you have left me just like that?'

'You told me you had a girl to meet, Ella.'

'You would have left me,' she said, wiping her eye, 'and I've waited two hours for you!'

'For me? You've waited two hours for me?' He looked round for fear people were watching them. But she didn't mind.

She was crying: 'I saw you go in,' she said in a low voice, 'and I've been waiting all the time for you coming out. I was going home.'

'Then you haven't got a girl to meet?'

'Of course I haven't a girl to meet!'

'Oh Ella, I'm so sorry,' he said, 'I'm so sorry, Ella.'

'Yes, but you'd have left me, wouldn't you?'

'No, Ella, I would never leave you.' Then he remembered Confession and Benediction. 'I've *got* to go,' he said.

She said: 'Where?'

He was ashamed of telling her, but he didn't want to tell her a lie. 'To church,' he said.

'To church?—on a Friday?'

'Yes,' he said, 'we Catholics go at any time.'

'Can I walk along the way with you?' she said.

'Yes do,' he said. 'Come on, Ella, please.'

They walked along together in silence. He hated the way he had behaved, yet was glad to have seen her tears. It was as though he had known her for years now, she was so close to him, so near and close, and God forgive him if ever he'd do or say anything against her ever again. Her shoulder was level with his, a narrow nice smooth easy shoulder, and her face was so lovely, and he was ashamed of himself.

They walked along in the early greyness of the spring

evening on to the main road and down along the street where the trams ran, where people were coming and going and talking, and all the Friday evening bustle everywhere. Then up the familiar street to the church, and it feeling so strange to have Ella at his side there. 'Do you want me to go yet?' she asked. He said: 'No, not yet, Ella. There at the corner maybe. I won't go to church if you don't want me to.' 'I'd never, never stop you,' she said. He said: 'Well, here we are now, Ella. I don't like leaving you.' But the sins were pressing on his soul and he wanted to be rid of them. 'Goodbye, Michael,' she said. 'Goodbye, Ella.'

She looked at him and said: 'I couldn't come in with you, could I? I'm not allowed, am I?' It was an awful risk to take her in for fear anyone he knew should see them together. He would be made fun of for months if they did. And it didn't seem right to take her in. No, he couldn't. He didn't want her in there with him. 'Yes,' he whispered, 'come in. But what'll your mother say?' 'Sanfairyann,' said Ella. 'I'll tell her I met a girl.' 'Come in then,' he said, 'just after me. Not together. Do what I do. And come on the same seat. But not just next to me. If anybody talks to me and I have to go off you wait.' 'Michael, are you sure you want me to come?' 'Amn't I just tellin' you I want you to come in?' he said shortly.

He passed through the gloom of the porch and into the church, paused at the font and blessed himself with the holy water, Ella, beside him, did the same uncertainly, and then he walked softly round the back of the church, and she tiptoed behind him. About fifty people, mostly middle-aged women, were scattered about the vast church for the week-day Benediction. He knew he would have to miss Confession, so he led the way round to a secluded spot, genuflected, blessed himself again, and knelt. Ella went down on two knees, and put her hand to her forehead and heart, but not to the shoulders. Isn't it easy to see the one that hasn't been brought up in the Faith? he thought. Then he looked to the altar, and as he did so he could feel the stiff pride creeping into him, and he felt himself so superior. And he knew the way

198

his elbows rested and his hands joined themselves piously and he lifted back his head and gazed away at the altar with her humble gaze on him from the end of the seat that it was all jigacting and not one bit of prayer would ever enter his mind from beginning to end. They were late and had missed the Rosary, for which he was glad. It was the same pew he had knelt in with Charlie Criddle. 'We can see but can't be seen.' If the other only knew the associations a place has for us! The altar lights were switched on and Winterbottom lit the tall candles. A few seconds later the procession of six altar boys, deacon and celebrant, came from the vestry and mounted the altar. He gave a sideways glance at Ella, and saw she was gazing with awe at the high altar. The organ grunted and got on its way, and then the ' *O Salutaris* ' filled the church as the women and a man here and there sang with full voice, and soon the incense was mistily travelling everywhere, and suddenly he realised that up there on the altar the White Host had been placed for adoration and he hadn't given a single thought to it : ' Jesus, Mary an' Joseph,' he whispered, ' I offer you my heart and my soul.'

Then came the ' *Tantum Ergo* ' and he raised his voice and joined in. As he was singing he felt someone beside him, and he realised that Ella was next to him, shoulder to his shoulder, and she too was singing though not the right words. He put his hand out and touched hers and they looked at each other and then up to the altar. ' She's like a saint beside me,' he thought, ' a beautiful young saint.' The incense swirled up in their corner as the service went on, and then at last it drew to its close : ' *Blessed be God.* ' ' Blessed be God.' ' *Blessed be His Holy Name.* ' Blessed be His Holy Name.' ' *Blessed be Jesus Christ, true God and true man.* ' ' Blessed be Jesus Christ, true God and true man.' ' *Blessed be the Holy name of Jesus.* ' ' Blessed be . . .' he touched Ella ever so lightly, and whispered. ' We'll go, Ella, before the crush go out.' Ever the double mind, he thought, they cannot see us as they enter, but they can as they leave. She wanted to stay on, he felt, and he waited until the procession was leaving the altar before he pressed her to her feet.

It was already going dark. 'Will you get coppit,' he asked, 'if you're home late?' 'I don't care if I do,' she said. 'Shall we go back by Robert Murdoch Street,' he said, 'and past the Topping Lane factory?' 'Yes, Michael,' she said, 'I leave it to you.' 'We'll not see anybody that way,' he said. 'That's right,' she said. They walked side by side, though not holding hands. He was surprised how conspicuous a boy felt when he was walking with a girl. They passed the Topping Lane factory. 'Are we going round Genoa Street or through the ginnel, Michael?' 'Through the ginnel.' The ginnel was a narrow cinder path between two factories, with palings on both sides. 'Can I link you through here?' she asked as they entered the dark way. She took his arm. It was very dark and he was a bit nervous but happy. It was a happiness that made his throat feel tight. They hurried along until they came to a street corner near home. 'Hadn't we better separate now, Ella?' he asked. 'I don't want to,' she said. 'I wish you had a sister and I was her and I lived in your house.' She was always saying what he would only think. 'When will we meet again, Michael?' 'I don't know,' he said. A sadness had come over him and he didn't want to give it up. 'The nights'll be getting lighter,' she said. 'Yes they will, won't they?' he said. 'When's your birthday?' she asked. 'The twelfth of June,' he said. 'I'll be thirteen then.' 'I wish my birthday was on that day,' she said. 'When is it?' he asked. 'The first of November,' she said, 'I'll be fourteen then.' 'All Saints Day,' he said. 'You lucky thing, you'll be starting work. Ella!' 'Yes, Michael?' 'Ella, Ella, can I give you a kiss, please?' 'Yes, Michael,' she said at once, 'but suppose somebody comes?'

He saw the black entrance of the backstreet beckoning, but the street lamp was shining on her face where they stood, and he liked it, and wanted to see her face, and he wanted to be sure where her mouth was when he kissed, so he said, 'Let's chance it,' and he put lips to hers and kissed. It felt very nice. 'Goodnight, love,' he said. 'Good-

night, darling,' said Ella. He was tingling all over with joy
and he couldn't hold himself back but had to run off, dash-
ing along the street, whistling and shouting and clacking the
heels of his shoes against any vacant piece of wall as he ran
along.

CHAPTER EIGHT

The Incident on the Moors

═══

'SIT IN THERE, GENTS,' said the mother, placing two dinners upon the table. 'Come on, Mickyeen—have done looking at yourself in the glass, you're good enough for anyone, God bless you.'

He turned quickly and gave her a scowl for talking that way with the father in the room. She must be daft—making hints like that about Ella. I can feel it. Willie, home from the foundry, came in out of the back kitchen, his hands washed and his face powdered with a rust grime, and sat down and began to eat quickly. He looked down with inner distaste at his own plate, the three boiled potatoes, the piece of dark curled steak, the taste of fried onion beside it, and the gravy fat.

'You gave me too much, Mother,' he said.

'Urra how could I give you too much?' she said. Any damn thing that comes into her head she says. 'Musha, eat what you want,' she added, 'and leave the rest.' He saw father glance from his paper at the remark, but he didn't speak. He cut off a piece of steak, not easily, and lifted it to his mouth. Chew, chew, chew. I'll master it if it kills me—I won't swallow a stringy lump. Chew, chew, chew. I once tasted a piece of steak that was good and juicy, but that was when I was a kid. All the taste's gone out of it, but it's still leathery. A chap could choke swallowing that. Funny, I never do enjoy Saturday dinner. I never feel hungry. And just hearing that steak spluttering in the frying-pan is enough to put me off, the way the pan keeps setting on fire and the smell of gas about the house. I fancy a Ditchfield's hot meat pie, something you can sup tea with and eat bread-and-butter with. I'll have to swallow this lump after all.

a tip from Danny this morning for Steve Donoghue's mount
—Lady of the Rose.'

'Lady of the Rose,' said the mother, '—I like that one
better. Sure it'll beat mine.'

'It's not in the same race,' said Willie.

'I'd better put the shank on,' said the mother. 'I'm never
done cookin' from mornin' till night. There are times when
I wouldn't blame poor ould Madame Fahmy.'

I wish they'd both shut up, he thought, that music's
lovely. It gives you a lovely feeling in your back and that.
It might sound daft to some folk, but what 'ud be wrong
about buying a barrel-organ instead of a piano or fiddle and
playing yourself a few tunes any time you fancied a bit of
music? Folk never think of something that's a bit different.

' " Drift with me," ' hummed Willie, jumping up from
the table, ' " along the shores of Minnie-had-a-donkey and it
wouldn't go—gee up!" '

'Have you your dinner ate, man?' asked the mother.

'Ned'll be round,' said Willie. 'We kick off at three.'

'Wouldn't you be wiser to sit an' rest,' she said, 'if only
for five minutes?'

'I'll be resting long enough,' said Willie.

'God send it won't be this ninety long years,' said the
mother. 'Sure I don't understand how he can go kickin' a
football round a field, Mickyeen, an' the dinner not rested
within him. Leave it, my love, leave it if it's tough.'

He pushed the plate from him with relief: 'It like gets
stuck in your throat, Mother,' he said, 'the potato bein' dry
an' that.'

'I'll be makin' a sup of tea in a minute,' she said, 'an'
maybe I'd have a cake in the tin for you. Musha I'm never
done surely, either the kettle or the pan.'

'I don't want any tea then,' he said.

'Sure amn't I makin' a sup for myself?' she said. 'An'
what else would I be doin' if I wasn't on the go? After God
gave me the health? But some days now I don't seem to have
the fling I used to have. Once I could roar through the work.'

She wants a change of air, that's what she wants, but I

don't like to tell her. One day if I'm well off I'll just come in and put fifty pounds on the table and say to her: Have a change of air, mam.

A sharp knock sounded on the partly-open door. I was waiting for that—I hate being in when it happens. The mother calmly put a finger to her lips. He flushed at the thought of the organ-grinder standing at the door with his collecting-box, and the neighbours at their doors and windows, and everybody seeing they'd given him nothing. Again the sharp knock. The mother wiped her lips on her apron, struck back her shoulders and went to the door.

'Not today, sir,' she said in a high firm voice.

She came in: 'The thick impertinent monkey,' she said, 'to knock that out of me. Standin' there like a floorwalker, the box before him an' the big curled moustache at him.'

'Why wouldn't you give him a penny to quieten him,' said Willie, bouncing up before the fire in his stockinged feet, 'since you give to every beggar an' singer that ever set foot in the street? Where's my pants?'

'I'll give to no one that would try to knock it out of me,' she said. 'Sure your heart would go out to some ould fella that would be singin' with a bad head—but that one!'

'If he'd an Irish mug on him,' said Willie, 'she'd give him everything within the house.'

'Troth an' that's the true word for you, Willie'een,' she said, 'the sight of an Irish face out in that street splits open my heart, an' he could have my last farthing.'

'Where's my pants?'

'Get them from behind the middle door, Mickyeen,' she said. 'Here's Ned now.'

Willie darted into the back kitchen.

'Bill! Bill!' called a voice at the door.

He hurried across to the door. 'Come in, Ned,' he said.

'Is yon man not ready yet?' said Ned, giving a knock on the door as he came in. 'Hello, Missis M'Cloud!'

'Hello Ned, How are you?'

'Champion. Never felt better an' less thought of. Your Bill not ready yet?'

'Howgo, Ned,' called Willie. 'Two minutes.'

'Some two minutes,' said Ned. 'By gum, I'll tell you something, Missis M'Cloud, your Mike's gettin' a size.'

'Do you think so, Ned?'

'Do I think so? Why he's fairly comin' out in leaps an' bounds. He'll make two of your Bill in time to come.'

'Would you join us in a quick cup of tea, Ned?' asked the mother.

'I wouldn't refuse one if it were proffered me, Missis M'Cloud,' said Ned.

That's nice now, he thought, somebody comes in and brightens the entire home up. I like anything like that.

'I've done the Wanderers for a draw on the short list, Bill,' said Ned. 'Three draws, fifteen to one.'

'If they couldn't do more than draw with Cardiff at home last week,' said Willie, combing his hair, 'I can't see how they'll draw with the City away. Especially as old Joe Smith scored two for 'um.'

'Always a good draw, Wanderers an' the City,' said Ned. 'When do you leave school, Mike?'

'Not till next June, Ned,' he said.

'It's a cryin' shame keepin' 'um at school till their fourteen,' said Ned. 'What do you say, Missis M'Cloud?'

'Maybe a life of work is long before them, Ned,' she said.

'Aye, if you retire at seventy you'll ha' done fifty-six year. Not bad. But I allus say the most important years in a chap's life are from twelve to fourteen. Nice cup of tea, Missis M'Cloud. Thanks very much.'

'I'm ready, Ned,' said Willie.

'I'm not,' said Ned. 'By the way, don't forget tha has to come to Sunday School tomorrow, Bill. The United Methodists won't let him play unless he comes once a month, Missis M'Cloud.'

'Does it make no difference that he's a Catholic, Ned?' asked the mother.

'Not a flappin' bit,' said Ned, 'he could be a Mommadun if he wanted. An' it's a champion Sunday school—we allus have a game of cards at the back. An' you needn't worry about Bill losin' his religion, Missis M'Cloud, because the captain of the team doesn't believe there's a God at all. He reckons it's only something in your minds makes you believe. So you don't have to worry about your Bill at Sunday school—he'll be safe amongst yon lot.'

'Come on, Ned,' said Bill. 'Like to come an' watch us, Mike?'

'Uh, no thanks, Willie,' he said, 'uh, I'm goin' somewhere.'

'He doesn't say much your Mike,' said Ned. 'but he thinks a lot. Cheerio, Missis M'Cloud. Cheerio, Mike.'

'Goodbye, Ned. Goodbye, Willie. Are you not takin' the bikes?'

'What, Missis—an' have 'um pinched?' said Ned. 'Not likely.'

Willie turned back and slipped threepence into his hand: 'I nearly forgot, Mickyeen,' he whispered.

'Ta, Willie, he said, 'ta.' He put the coins into his pocket. Comes in handy I must say. And it makes him feel somebody. I wonder who I'll have to give threepence to when I start work? What a pity! I'd better get ready to go off and meet Ella.

'Will I dry the dishes for you, Mother?'

'Ah sure it won't take me a minute, my son,' she said.

'Is it all right if I wash here?'

'Wash away, my boy, wash away,' she said. 'I'll see have I a clean towel for you.'

'This roller's all right, mother,' he said.

She came in with a clean towel. 'Try would you wash all the soap off you,' she said.

'Yes, Mother,' he said, staring into the mirror. Another blasted pimple—that's about three I have. I wonder what's up with me? Happen I've caught a disease. If I scrub my face hard it'll happen burst. But I don't want it spreading. Pimples are a proper worry. He turned on the tap and began to wash himself under it. I wonder what that million and a half folk with no homes are doing. I suppose they have to lean against walls. But will there be any? God help 'um. I wonder will the king's horse win. If I were king I'd dashed well see that it did. Uncle James there, never been heard from twenty years. I hope I never get scurvy and all my teeth drop out. 'Course it 'ud be handy in the case of toothache. I hope Ella hasn't got one of her funny 'uns on her. I can clean my teeth with the end of my finger, then polish them up with the towel. I'll buy myself a toothbrush when I start working. 'Course they do say once you start using one you've got to keep it up, or else all your teeth go black. I wonder what I can pinch to take with me? A few biscuits anyway, and some carrots.

He kissed the mother goodbye. If she thinks I've something on my mind she never asks where I'm going. I like that about her. You get some mothers picking and prying into everything you do. I suppose in some ways we're what you call a happy family. The old fella's not too bad when he's in a good mood, but I never feel comfortable with him around. I've got to dodge any of the lads, so I'll go this way, down by the brewery. I don't like all that excitement you get about the streets on Saturday afternoon. Seems like when you let folk out of work with a weekend off they fairly go mad. I think it 'ud be better if they worked seven days a week. Look at all the extra money they'd have. I suppose the country couldn't stand it. Well, away to the moors for me.

He came out into a street where children were playing a game. A ring of girls with two small boys singing: *The wind, the wind, the wind blows high, The rain comes tumbling down the sky.* The high sweet voices caused a trembling somewhere within him, and he slowed down to hear more, *She is handsome, she is pretty, She is the girl of the golden city.* The feelings the song left with him felt nice, a nice gurgle and flow of emotion so pleasant in heart and body— but then he looked at his trousers and thought: time I had a new pair.

She wasn't there at the meeting place, so for a minute he had a look down at the trains from the footbridge. When he came out again he saw her. She smiled and he rubbed his nose. They didn't speak or go up to each other, but stood amongst the people waiting for trams. This is where I saw that chap without legs on the morning we came to England. I hope nobody has spotted us. A tram with a H in front swung round the corner and Ella looked at him; he gave her a nod. When it stopped she got on and went downstairs and he went on top, right up in front, where it was open.

It seemed a very long journey to him, and he kept thinking of Ella below. He was sitting there looking down at the road, the tram stopped, when he noticed a familiar figure walking up the hill. Ella! . . . why, we must be at the terminus. He was hurrying down when the conductor came up. 'Tha'd better make a dash for it, laddie,' said the man, 'thy girl will be halfway up Smithills by this.'

You're never safe anywhere in this world. He ran down after her. Sod 'um, I don't care who sees me. 'Ella!' he called. She turned smiling : 'Michael, my pet. What happened to you?' He took her hand for a moment : 'I was thinkin' of something,' he said. 'Here, your penny tram fare.'

'Don't be daft,' she said.

'I insist,' he said. 'I'm not taking a girl out and letting her pay for herself. It's against my principles.'

'I think it's a shame,' she said, taking the penny.

'Do you know how much that would be worth in Germany?' he said.

'How much?'

'Just a minute an' I'll tell you. Sixty million mark to the pound, that makes fourpence—no, threepence a million. Roughly you could say a penny is worth three hundred an' thirty-three thousand, three hundred an' thirty-three marks. We'd both be millionaires if we went there.'

'Ee, fancy.'

'I read in the paper, Ella, of a man who decorated his room with marks instead of with wallpaper.'

'I wish pound notes 'ud come that cheap,' she said.

He was about to explain that they'd be no better off, but then he thought, why disappoint her? 'What about a bit of catechism?' he said. '"How should you begin the day?"'

'"I should begin the day by making the Sign of the Cross as soon as I wake up in the morning, and by saying, *O my God I offer Thee my heart and soul*."'

'"How should you rise in the morning?"'

'"I should rise in the morning diligently, dress myself modestly, and then kneel down and say my morning prayers."'

'Champion, Ella,' he said. 'The priest is going to get a shock when we go along together and tell him you want to be a Catholic. You'll know as much as him. I mean to say, we'll have to wait a year or two yet. Happen when we start courting properly.'

They walked on, up to the moorland, and he became aware that Ella was quiet. I've said something, but what it is I do not know. Well, if she won't talk I won't. Two can play that game. I've marded her too much. They went on across the springy moorland in silence. The sweetness of the air, the clear sky and moorland stretched before them made him too happy, and he put his arm round her. 'Let's rest here, sweetheart,' he said. Then he brought out of his pocket a piece of cake, an apple, two carrots, and a bar of chocolate. She had a little bag with her and she took out two rock buns and a bottle of lemonade made from powder.

He turned to her: 'I haven't kissed you yet, Ella,' he said. He expected her to turn to be kissed, with closed eyes. Instead she turned and looked at him, said nothing, and then let her gaze fall down to the heather.

'Ella,' he said, 'do you not want me to kiss you?'

She shook her head slowly and turned to look away at Towlton, lying like a huge saucer of smoke in the hollow. Was it because I went on top of the tram instead of on the bottom with her? No, because she was nice when I met her. Was it over them there marks? No, it wouldn't be that. I can feel tears coming. I'd better be careful. He sat for a minute in silence, and then turned to her:

'Why? why? Tell me why, Ella?'

'Because . . .' she said slowly, 'because it's a sin.'

211

'A sin? A sin to kiss?' he said. 'How do you make that out?'

'Because . . .' she gave a sudden sob,' . . . you're . . . baptised . . . and . . . I'm . . . not.'

He put his arms round her shoulder and kissed her wet cheek: 'Ella, how could you say that?' he said 'It's daft.'

'It's true,' she answered. 'It's in the catechism.'

'Why, it never even mentions kissing . . .'

'No, but it mentions Baptism. It says, "Baptism is necessary for salvation, because Christ has said, *Unless a man be born again of water and the Holy Ghost, he cannot enter into the kingdom of God*."'

Water and the Holy Ghost. 'How does that make kissing a sin, Ella?'

'Because I've never been baptised and I've still got the stain of original sin on my soul,' she said. 'And when you kiss me it is like the sign of a mixed marriage, which is unlawful and pernicious.'

He let himself fall back on the earth and he looked up at the sky: 'If it had been a sin,' he said, 'wouldn't I have known about it?'

'Not if you hadn't thought about it,' she said. 'How can I be happy any more going to Benediction with you? I kneel there and know I'm not in a state of grace, and never can be until I've been born again of water and the Holy Ghost.'

I know one thing, Protestants never understand properly. They take things too seriously. 'You will be one day, Ella.'

'An' suppose we both got run over by a tramcar on the way home?' she asked. 'You'd go to heaven an' I'd go to hell.'

'It's a sin to talk like that,' he said. 'Anyway, you'd go to limbo.'

'Where's limbo?'

'Limbo is a place of rest, where the souls of the just who died before Christ were detained. Our Lord hadn't opened the gates until his death on the cross.'

'I don't want to go to limbo,' she cried out. 'I want to go where you go.'

'But Ella, darling,' he said, 'don't blame me. What can I do about you being baptised?'

She turned and looked at him with a solemn gaze and spoke in a whisper: '*You can baptise me.*'

'Eh? What? Me? Ella, Ella, what are you saying? Ella, listen, a priest has got to baptise you.'

'*Anyone* may baptise in a case of necessity.'

'Yes, but this isn't a case of necessity.'

'How do you know, Michael M'Cloud? How can you sit there an' talk so big? I might die . . . you'll be to blame. You . . . you . . . you . . . You'll answer to God for that . . .' she cried springing to her feet.

'Ella! Ella!' he called, 'come back! come back when I tell you!'

He got up and ran after her, his voice blown behind him in the breeze. She ran very fast and he had to put desperate feeling into himself before he could catch her. He leapt upon her from the side, his right arm round her neck, and he bore her to the ground: 'I could kill you, Ella Sharley,' he said.

'Why don't you?'

'Oh Ella, Ella, come back to where we were. You're spoilin' the day for us.' He looked at her closely: 'Perhaps one day I will baptise you . . .' he said.

'Truth an' honour?' she asked.

'Yes, yes, yes,' he said. Thank God she's all right again. 'But I can't baptise you today.'

'Yes, you can,' she said.

He laughed loudly: 'Not without holy water,' he said.

They walked back in silence to the spot where the food was lying on the grass. She picked up her cloth bag and drew something out. She held up a small bottle: 'From the font at St Stephen's,' she said. 'Holy water.'

He grabbed the bottle, and she didn't attempt to stop him. 'Ella, when did you get it?'

'At nine o'clock Mass this morning,' she said. She put her hands on his shoulders: 'You won't refuse to baptise me now, will you, Michael?' she asked.

'Here . . . on the moors? Oh Ella, I daren't.'

'You'd baptise a dying baby, wouldn't you? Aren't I just as fit to be baptised?' He felt her looking at him. 'Oh Michael, I want my soul to be like yours.'

The breeze was stirring the grasses. The invisible Third Person. 'Three sacraments are different from the others,' he said. 'Baptism, Confirmation and Holy Order.'

'I know,' she said. 'A *character* is given to the soul by these. It is a mark or seal that can *never* be effaced.'

'So that if I were to do it now, Ella, you'd never in all your life be able to receive Baptism again.'

'I know.'

'Not a priest, bishop, nor—nor even the Pope himself dare attempt to baptise you after I've done it this once. Do you understand?'

'What you do now lasts for ever,' she said.

'Let's kneel an' pray,' he said, 'an' see if what we're going to do is right or wrong.' They knelt together in the heathery turf and he prayed aloud. 'Remember, O most loving Virgin Mary, it is a thing unheard of that anyone ever yet had recourse to thy protection, implored thy help, sought thine intercession and was left forsaken . . .'

It calmed him. 'You kneel down there, Ella,' he said 'and I'll kneel here above you.' He looked round—the moorland was deserted. She knelt, joined her hands and closed her eyes. He looked at her closed eyes: how did she make him agree? He pressed her head backwards and brought her hair tightly back from the forehead with the palm of his hand. Make this right, God. Here is the bottle, and waiting on my tongue are the words, and in ten seconds the soul will be freed from sin and filled with the grace of God and the spirit of the Holy Ghost. 'I'm ready, Ella,' he said.

He raised the bottle and as he tilted it and saw the bright water flow on to forehead and scalp he cried out: 'I baptise thee in the Name of the Father, and of the Son, and of the Holy Ghost.' And he poured all the holy water out, and some drops were sprayed away by the breeze.

She didn't open her eyes. He watched her kneeling upright, her head back and her face turned to the sky. He felt some childish weakness come over him, and he lay face down on the earth and began to cry. She didn't speak or touch him, and soon the spasm was over. He turned then and looked at her. She was sitting erect, with her hands on her knees, and she was gazing somewhere far away. Drops of holy water, undried by the breeze, were on her forehead. He put his hand roughly on her lap to bring her thought to himself. Then she looked at him and smiled: 'I'm hungry, Mike,' she said. 'Give me a carrot.'

CHAPTER NINE

Mrs Criddle hits out

━━━

'I'LL BE WITH THEE NOW, MIKE,' called Charlie Criddle, picking up a glass marble from the gutter and flicking a halfpenny to a boy called Healey. 'I'll get my own back tomorrow, Healey,' he called.

'Dinner money gone again, Chey?' he asked.

'Aye,' said Charlie, 'but there's always tomorrow, Mike, always tomorrow. Here, next to my last Roocroft's nut-milk cube.'

'Ta, Chey. Why dussent buy summat else by the way of a change?'

'Squirtin',' said Charlie, ejecting a swift white stream from his mouth. 'Tha gets more saliva in these than in other toshies. Why not let me file thee a little opening between thy front teeth, Mike, tha'd make a damn good squirter?'

'When I buy toshies I want 'um to eat, Chey,' he said, 'not to spit away.'

'Has anybody ever told thee, Mike, tha'rt a very fussy lad?'

'Has anybody ever told thee, Chey, tha'rt a damn fool? That's the third mornin' this week to my knowledge tha's gone an' lost thy dinner money playin' marps.'

'Aye, but there's always tomorrow,' said Charlie. 'I get fourpence a day—twopence for a meat-an'-spud pie, penny for a barm cake, an' a penny for a bottle of pop to go with it. Now I allus buy a penn'orth of nut-milk cubes an' I have a good gamble with the rest. Suppose one day me luck's in —I'll buy one o' them two-an'ninepenny pork pies, an' a half-gallon bottle of herb beer. It'll be worth it, Mike. Come hither, come hither, here shall we see, no misery, but winter an' rough weather.'

'Now, Chey, if tha'd take a father's advice tha'd stop

playin' marps with Healey an' a few more as are too good for thee. Look for a few cans.'

'I luv thee, Mike, like I luv mi life,' said Charlie, grinning, 'but tha'rt too damn careful. I works on impulse. I feel things comin' like an affair in the tide of men—or t'other way about. I felt summat i' my bones this mornin', an' I thought I'd win or summat, but I didn't. Anyway, there's another day tomorrow. Tha cudgitates too much, Mike, till tha doesn't know where the hell tha art.'

'Let's hurry, Chey,' he said, 'it's nearly takin'-in-time.'

'There tha art again,' said Charlie.

At Catechism that morning Charlie allowed his eye to be caught first by Miss Skegham. 'What are the eight beatitudes, Criddle?'

'Er, pardon, Miss, the eight what, Miss?'

'Beatitudes, idiot. "Blessed are the poor in spirit . . ." Go on!'

'"Blessed are the poor in spirit,"' said Charlie, '"for they—they——"'

'Yes. They what, Criddle?'

'"For they shall be made rich in body."'

With a glance she quelled the titter from the class. 'Yes, Criddle. "Blessed are the meek"?'

'"Blessed are the meek, because, because they shall be unmeeked."'

'"Blessed are they that mourn . . ."?' she said.

Charlie looked more confident. '"Blessed are they that mourn," Miss, "for after the funeral they shall be fed."'

'"Blessed are they that hunger and thirst after justice"?' she said.

'"Blessed are they that hunger and thirst after justice," Miss, "because justice shall hunger and thirst after them."'

'The merciful?'

'"Blessed are the merciful,"' said Charlie, looking round the class, '"because they shall be let off."'

'The clean of heart?'

'"Blessed are the clean of heart," Miss, "because they shall enjoy voluntary poverty."'

'The peacemakers?'

'"Blessed are the peacemakers," Miss, "because they shall make peace."'

'They that suffer persecution for justice' sake?'

'"Blessed are they that suffer persecution for justice' sake for they know no better."'

Charlie had another look round the class and sat down. Miss Skegham said: 'Criddle, come out here.' Charlie got up and went out. She looked at him for a moment. 'What a monstrous specimen!' she said. 'In all my years of teaching at this school I've never come across anything or anybody like you, Criddle.'

'No, Miss?' said Charlie.

'What were you thinking of yesterday when the others were learning the eight beatitudes? Carterham, what is the fifth beatitude?'

'The fifth beatitude, Miss, is, "Blessed are the merciful, for they shall obtain mercy."'

'That's what I said, Miss, only I put it in my own words,' said Charlie.

'Parkinson, what is the eighth beatitude?'

'The eighth beatitude, Miss, is, "Blessed are they that suffer persecution for justice' sake, for theirs is the kingdom of heaven."'

'M'Cloud, what is the seventh beatitude?'

'The seventh beatitude, Miss, is, "Blessed are the peacemakers for they shall make peace."' He knew as soon as he heard the words come off his tongue that a ridiculous beatitude of Charlie Criddle had taken root in his mind, and what he should have said was something about the children of God.

'M'Cloud, what is this impertinence? Come out at once. You kneel there, I'll deal with you later.' He knelt down in front of the class.

'Criddle, hold out your hand,' she said. 'Hold it out.'

Charlie held his hand out, but when she raised the cane he began to curl it round in the Sheed manner. 'Bit nearer thy ear, Chey,' whispered Sheed approvingly. Miss Skegham said : ' Out, Criddle, and woe betide you if I have to tell you again.' It was a serious warning, and Charlie immediately put his hand straight out. But when she raised the cane again it seemed that a power beyond his own was twisting Charlie's hand back, up near his shoulder. As he did so Miss Skegham made a dart with the cane, in an attempt to draw out his hand, and Charlie let out a cry : ' Oh me eye! oh me eye!'

' Up!' shouted Miss Skegham, ' up, I say!' at the same time beating Charlie across the back with the cane. Charlie let out a howl. ' Oh me eye, you've hit me in my eye—you cruel woman!'

He heard it and could scarcely believe. You cruel woman! And yet Miss Skegham did not get more angry. She said : ' Remove your filthy hand from your eye, and let me see it. But first, hold your other hand out.' Charlie shook his head. ' No, Miss,' he said, ' I've had enough.' Even then she didn't strike him. ' Go to the cloakroom, Criddle,' she said, ' and bathe that eye. I'll attend to you when you come back.' Charlie went off. ' M'Cloud,' she said, ' you go and see he bathes it thoroughly. Then come back and kneel there.'

Charlie was grinning away when he caught him up along the corridor. ' I reckon I didn't come too badly out of that lot, Mike.'

' She sent me after you to see you bathed your eye, Chey. It looks a bit sore.'

' It 'urts,' said Charlie.

There was a large unwashed enamel bowl, with a big tap above it, and Charlie turned on the tap and put his eye under. ' It's bloody cold,' he said. ' Funny about them what's-his-names, Mike, it were like a little voice inside me tellin' me what to say.'

' A pity it didn't know the answers itself.'

' I don't care whether it did or not,' said Charlie, ' I allus give way when I hear that voice.'

' Tha'll give way once too often, Chey. Now bathe thy flappin' eye, because it's comin' up like a balloon.'

' It's no use hurryin',' said Charlie, ' we might as well

hang it out till playtime here, as draughty as it is. Art sure, Mike, tha doesn't want to file just a little space between thy front teeth? Tha'd make a gradely squirter.' 'I've other things on my mind, Charlie, than just squirting spit at folk.' ' Aye, lad, tha'rt changing lately. Ever since tha started growin' that little moustache on thy lip. Here, let me try an' file it off, Mike.'

'Now look here, Chey,' he said, 'I vote we get back as quick as we can, or else we'll have Fat Ada down here an' she'll bash the daylights out of us if she sees us hangin' it out.'

'Her's a damn good teacher, tha knows, Mike,' said Charlie.

'A damn good teacher! Tha calls her a good teacher, Chey?'

'Aye, an' she bloody is! Tha should ha' heard what my dad used to say about her. He were in her class, 'course she were only young then, but she clouted his lug more than once. He used to say to me when he came on leave: 'Tha'll never learn owt, lad, till old Fat Ada gets hold of thee.' He got killed in the war, tha knows, my dad. He went all through it in the trenches without gettin' so much as a scratch, an' got himself killed in t'last fortnight.'

'God rest his soul,' he said.

Charlie said: 'Thanks. My mam said it were just like him, he always would slip up at the last fence. But he allus swore by Fat Ada. An' he were right, yu' know, Mike. Why, if she didn't bash us about we'd be like a lot of cannibals.'

'Charlie, Charlie lad,' he said, 'I don't know how tha can say that after the way she poked her cane into thy eye.'

'She didn't! She never poked her cane into my eye. I did it myself. She put the cane through my elbow, like that, see, but it were me as shifted my elbow, an' it were me as sent the stick into my eye. A sharp bit stung into it—that was what made me yell.'

'But she were responsible, Chey.'

'No she weren't. Fair's fair. Now tak' these who go to Proddy schools, they get a couple of raps now an' again,

220

an' it is now an' again, but they never get a real good tanning like we do. An' look at 'em, just look at 'em—they'd think the eight beatitudes were a bloody football team. As for things like affinity, consanguinity and spiritual relationship, they wouldn't know either one of them from a blasted black pudden'. Naw, don't say owt against Fat Ada to me.'

' By the way, Charlie, what is consanguinity? '

' Consanguinity? What is consanguinity? Does tha mean to tell me tha doesn't know what consanguinity is? '

' I did know,' he said, ' but I've forgotten.'

' Come to that,' said Charlie, ' so've I. There goes the jolly old bell, let us away to the woods. Allez! Touchsweet!'

They went out into the narrow playground and took up a corner. In a minute every spot was crowded with a mass of struggling lads. Eddie Radford came up. ' Flappin' Annie, Chey, what an eye! Get thee to the infirmary.'

' Get thee to the petties,' said Charlie.

Then Sheed came along. ' Bugger me, Chey, but that eye's comin' up. Tha needs a bit of steak on it.'

' Aye, Sheed, go an' get a meat pie, an' I'll put that on.'

Johnson said : ' I've a bit of a mirror here, Chey, so tha can have a squint at it.'

Charlie took the mirror, breathed on it, and polished it up on the seat of his trousers. Then he casually held it up to glance at his eye. ' Christ awmighty!' he exclaimed, ' is that my eye? Why it's all but shut up!'

' We've been tellin' thee that for the last two hours,' said Sheed.

' But an eye like that can be very serious,' said Charlie.

' You daft thing,' said Eddie Radford, ' isn't that what I said? '

' I'm not stayin' at school with a thing like that,' said Charlie. ' Crimes, it's cripplin' me. Here, let me have another look. Holy Mary, what an eye! I'm off! One of you see me to the gate. I can't see.' They all crowded round, knocking youngsters out of the way, and then they escorted Charlie to the gate.

' Where you goin', Chey—to the infirmary? '

'Not likely. I'm goin' to the factory showin' my mam. That fat cow won't half coppit when my mam sees this.'

'Old Missis Criddle won't half bash Fat Ada about. Her's as strong as a mule, tha knows, the way she handles yon cotton bales.'

'Her doesn't lift 'em herself,' said Peak. 'Her only works the blasted hoist.'

The whistle sounded and the boys halted, ran in line, and marched into school. He was hoping Miss Skegham had forgotten he had been kneeling, and he went back to his place apprehensively.

'M'Cloud, I thought I told you to come back and kneel down after bathing Criddle's eye.' He stood up. 'Please, Miss, the bell went for playtime by the time we'd finished.'

'If it was home-time by the time you'd finished I'd still expect you to come back. Come out and kneel down at once. By the way, where is Criddle?'

'Please, Miss,' called Sheed, 'his eye came up something terrible and he had to go off.'

'Go off where?'

'He wouldn't say, Miss. Someone said he should go to the infirmary.'

'Nonsense! Take out your English books, and I'll see if I can make some of you dolts understand what an adverb is.'

Kneeling before the class he heard Miss Skegham's words as he gazed at the floor, and suddenly he became aware of what an adverb was. Every word she said was plain common sense, and there was the class, listening and not following a word of it. He began making up all kinds of adverbs, one after the other, as quick as he could. She began to ask questions, and the boys began to give her the wrong answers, and there on his knees he felt an understanding of how hard it must be to teach stupid boys. It's driving me mad to hear how numb they are, he thought. Outside in the corridor there sounded a patter of feet, then a knock and the door opened. He looked up and saw Charlie Criddle and his mother enter. Miss Skegham looked at them with disapproval.

He gave a glance at Charlie's mother, and saw the thin neck with a lump in front, thin calloused fingers, and all about her a film of oily cotton, from the top of her shawl to the tip of her clogs, and there was a smear of grease across her pale agitated face. At the sight of Miss Skegham and the class her first bold manner seemed to leave her.

'Yes?' said Miss Skegham.

'Good morning, Miss,' said Charlie's mother. 'What I had come to see you about, Miss Skegham, was our Charlie's eye.' Charlie let out a sob to help her on. 'I'm a bit worried about it——'

'Have you been to see Mr Victor?' asked Miss Skegham.

'Well, no, I haven't, because I thought it 'ud save bother——'

'Then you must,' put in Miss Skegham. 'No person is allowed to enter a classroom,' she went on briskly, 'without first having permission to do so from Mr Victor. Will you please go and see him at once.'

'Ee, but it were you as did it,' said Mrs Criddle, trying to make a stand. He stooped his head, because he was sorry for her and somehow ashamed. 'I mean to say, the poor little chap came to see me in the factory and showed me.'

'He had no right to leave the school without permission,' said Miss Skegham.

'I know he isn't all he should be,' said Charlie's mother, 'but it's bad enough havin' to leave him from six in the mornin' till six at night, without him being knocked about so much.' There was a break in her voice. He saw her oily clogs standing humbly a yard from Miss Skegham's soft-leathered shoes, and looking up he saw the greasy skirt of Mrs Criddle keeping clear of the smooth black pinafore of Miss Skegham, the old soiled shawl of the woman and Miss Skegham's white blouse, the uneasy anxious face and the solid cool face. 'I'm not one to make bother, Miss Skegham, and this is the very first time I've ever been to the school,' her voice lowered, 'but I would like to make sure as it didn't happen again.'

'You must go and see Mr Victor,' said Miss Skegham. 'I really must get on with the lesson. And after all, it was his own fault, and I feel in no way responsible.'

'In no way responsible!' exclaimed Charlie's mother. 'Well of all the brazen hussies! You haven't the common decency to say you're sorry.'

'One of you boys bring Mr Victor,' called Miss Skegham. 'You, Carterham——'

'You stay where you are,' said Charlie's mother. She turned on Miss Skegham. 'I'll give you Mester Victor—I'll give you pokin' your stick in our Charlie's eye!' Miss Skegham hurried for the door, but Charlie's mother made a nimble run and jump, and caught her by the back of her pinafore, and then grabbed at the neat bun of hair. Her small hard hand swung round and slapped Miss Skegham across the ear. The teacher let out a cry of distress and fear, which seemed to startle the class. 'I'll give you "oh! oh!"' cried Charlie's mother, swinging her round and giving her a smart slap across the cheek. He looked up and saw the white face of Miss Skegham, and he felt sorry for her.

'It's all right when you're hittin' these lads,' cried Charlie's mother, grabbing her by the wrist, 'but see what a miserable thing you are when you're gettin' it. Off with you now to your Mester Victor, an' see what he has to say.'

Miss Skegham didn't move. She leant against the radiator, trying to recover. Charlie looked at her and turned to his mother and said calmly: 'I fancy her's had enough, mam.'

Miss Skegham made her way to the door and hurried out. Charlie picked up the cane and began to swish it through the air. 'You should ha' given her one on the backside with this, mam,' he said.

Mrs Criddle turned to the class. 'I'll bet she's not as spry in layin' a hand on our Charlie again,' she said, grinning. 'Well, she drew it out of me.'

'Don't get windy now, mam,' said Charlie.

He had the image in his mind of the grey-faced frightened woman who had hurried out of the classroom. Is that the

224

person I've been frightened of all these years? It seemed the lump of her-and-him that had grown on top of his heart had shifted. He went back to his place.

'What a massacre!' whispered Sheed.

'Hy,' said Peak, 'did you see that left swing?'

'It were only right an' salutary,' said Johnson. And Charlie, one eye shut, looked at his mother and grinned. Then the door opened and Mr Victor walked in.

'Mrs Criddle,' he said, 'what's the meaning of this assault? Miss Skegham is in my room in a prostrate condition.'

'An' what condition is my lad's eye in?' asked Mrs Criddle.

'But do you realise that you can't take matters into your own hands? You should have come to me and complained.'

'You've got childer of your own, sir,' said Charlie's mother, 'would you let one of 'em have an eye poked out an' then go an' complain?'

'Well, yes.'

'Then I wouldn't! That's the difference. Once my blood's up it's up. I'm sorry if I've caused you any bother, sir, because I've always respected you. But suppose I took him across to Canon Hulme—what do you think he'd say about a teacher doin' that?'

'I think you'd better take him to a doctor, Mrs Criddle,' said Mr Victor, leading her and Charlie out.

'Uree!' cried Sheed, 'hip, pop, uree!' The boys began running about, thumping each other and shouting, flinging pens, rubbers and rulers about. He sat there. He couldn't get the strange scene out of his mind. You can think till your head nearly bursts and nothing happens but once folk start hitting out! Peak went up to the desk and sat in Miss Skegham's place. 'Ah ha, little orange tree,' he said, looking across at the window, 'has sum'dy bobbed you, my little pet?' Sheed went out and dragged him off the seat and sat there himself.

'Today, dear boys, I shall recite you a poem. "The Fart," by Vilhelm Shakespoke:

" A sigh is but a spout of wind
  Comin' frae the heart,
  But should it take the downward course
  It's often called a fart.
  To fart it is a pleasure,
  It gives the bowels ease,
  It scents and warms the bedclothes,
  And suffocates the fleas." '

The home-time bell sounded in the corridor. ' Come on, lads,'
said Sheed, ' we'll be the first out today.' Carterham looked
round and said ' What about prayers? ' ' Aye, prayers,' said
Johnson—' it's only right an' salutary.' Sheed stopped, joined
his hands and closed his eyes, and the class blessed themselves and began the Grace: ' Bless us O Lord, and these
Thy gifts, which we are about to receive, from Thy bounty,
through Christ our Lord, Amen.' ' A Hail Mary for Charlie's
eye,' said Eddie Radford. The class joined in: ' Holy Mary,
Mother of God, pray for us sinners now and at the hour of
our death. Amen.' They blessed themselves and marched out
of the class. Eddie Radford said: ' We won't be seein' Fat
Ada for a few days.'

He went home quietly after a short prayer in church. He
felt relieved but faintly lost, for all the fear of Miss Skegham
had gone. He had always imagined that if such a thing
should ever happen it would be as though a ceaseless joy
were pouring through him, but now it was not so. It seemed
that yesterday and all the days before it were dead and all
before him was new. And in some curious way there was a
stain of guilt there within him in the feeling he had that he
was not blameless in the matter. It had not to do with his
first act of defiance, but with his long submission to her.
He felt he had connived at the persecution of himself, and
that now she would be as free of him as he was of her.

She was there at the desk when they marched into school
that afternoon. The boys gave silent stares at her. She stood
there with unchanged authority fastened upon her. The
class said prayers. She looked around. ' M'Cloud,' she said

'I believe that you were kneeling out here—were you not?'

He stood. 'I was, Miss,' he said.

'Yes, and may I ask why you've taken it on yourself to go back to your place?'

'I had no wish, Miss,' he said, 'to remain there.'

'In that case,' she said, 'I have the wish that you do. Come out at once and kneel where you were this morning.'

He didn't budge. At odd moments the face before him would evoke an image of the old fear, but then he would recall that livid face he saw on her that morning, and so kill the old image.

'M'Cloud, did you hear me?'

'I did, Miss.' The Mayo flutiness crept in.

'Then come out.' He didn't answer. 'I said come up and kneel down here.'

'I'm sorry, Miss,' he said, 'but I can't.'

'Why can't you?' He didn't answer.

'M'Cloud,' she said, 'you had better go to Mr Victor. But before you go is there any other boy who intends to be disobedient?' The silence was faintly defiant, but no voice spoke out. 'Very well then, M'Cloud, go alone. Tell him that I sent you because you were disobedient.'

'Yes, Miss,' he said, bowing slightly. He walked slowly through the corridors to the headmaster's room. I am nearly free, he thought, I wonder what will take the place of that little lump of misery that had got itself stuck so tight on me? All the Hail Marys I've poured round it, and the thousands of thoughts, whispers and fears that have gone into it. It gets as it's hard to part.

Mr Victor looked worried. 'I don't like this sort of thing, M'Cloud,' he said. 'Why wouldn't you kneel down when you were told?'

Something prompted him that the best answer would be silence. Mr Victor said: 'Well, hold out your hand.'

'Yes, sir,' he put his hand out at once. Mr Victor wagged his long thin cane in the air and swung it downwards. It stung his hand and sent a swift unexpected pain shooting up under his armpits. He held his left hand out. Mr Victor hesitated, and then brought the cane down lightly. No pain at all. The man stroked his moustache with three fingers. 'Oh, M'Cloud, you'll soon be going up to Mr Denning's class, and I'd like to feel you were a sort of chap to be depended on. Er, Miss Skegham's had a very trying morning. Hum, do you understand?'

'Yes, sir,' he said.

'Very good, M'Cloud. You may go.'

'Thank you, sir.'

He felt free but somehow old, and oddly made into part of the school. Back in class he avoided the eyes of the other boys and sat down quietly at his desk. I feel made over again, he thought. He began to whisper prayers of thanksgiving.

BOOK THREE

CHAPTER ONE

'A Funny Lad is our Charlie'

I MUST put that swimming lie behind me, he thought, or I'll never lift my head. He raised his hand. 'Please, Miss!'

'Yes, M'Cloud?' Miss Skegham looked hard at him. He met her gaze fully. He kept the flush under control.

'Please, Miss, may I start goin' to the baths with the class? My ears have stopped runnin' and are all right now.'

'I'm not sure, M'Cloud—the others will be advanced in their swimming lessons.'

'Please, Miss, I *can* swim.'

'Then go and ask Mr Denning—if he'll take you, you may go.'

'Thank you, Miss.'

He went into the top classroom and the wide half-smiling mouth of Mr Denning put him at ease. 'Please, sir, would you let me join your swimming class on Wednesday? Miss Skegham says it's all right with her.' Says it's all right with her. Sounds daft.

'If it's all right with her, M'Cloud,' said Mr Denning, 'then it'll be all right with me. The only condition being that you are prepared to accept a ducking. Are you?'

'I am, sir.'

'Right, M'Cloud, that's the spirit. See you on Wednesday.'

'Thank you very much, sir.'

They marched in twos through the streets, Mr Denning at their side. They'll be watching me. Thud, thud, thud, goes my heart. I feel a bit sick. Peak's looking at me. 'Where's thy towel an' drawers, Mike?'

'Eh? Oh I didn't want to be bothered carryin' 'um about —I'll get 'um at baths. It's worth tuppence.' Toff lads always have towels an' drawers of their own. Toff houses always have toothbrushes on the back windowsill. A paper bullet pinged his ear. He turned—*Not me, Mike*! The English are always shooting or tripping. We're getting nearer. Through the turnstile. I hate the hot steamy smell and the yells of lads unclothed. Folk with nothing on their minds are fools. Look casual, look easy.

He undressed on the gallery amongst the others, but unhastily, and was almost the last to descend the iron staircase. I hope that bumping of my heart doesn't show on my skin. He walked evenly along the wet parapet, turned his back on the crowd round the footbath, and went straight under the shower. Harder, harder, harder. That should impress them—uh, uh, uh—'Look at Mike's chest!' He shut off the tap, shook his head, wiped his hands across his face, and strolled towards the big plunge. Every eye on me. Here goes—deep end. He dived in a daze of watching eyes. He rose in the water and swam and swam. Keep goin'— they're all watching. I'm done, I'm done. Get to side—bugger 'um. He pulled himself up by the rail and got out and stood up. Face 'um. Face 'um all.

He stared at his watchers. All about him were running and yelling figures, a screaming and singing in the air, a splashing and smacking of water. Not a single eye was on him. No one had been taking the slightest notice. There's something so nice about the English. He faced the water and took a dive. It's easy when you know how. What the heck was I worrying about? I'll never tell another lie the longest I live.

Being as we're off early I'll call round at Criddle's an' see if Chey's out of the infirmary yet. Old Fat Ada's worried; she doesn't give the show away much, but that's what I think. There's Charlie's mother.

' 'Ello, Missis Criddle.'

'Ee, 'ello, luv.'

'I was just comin' round to see if your Charlie had come home, Missis Criddle.'

'Ee, no, luv, he aren't. I'm just goin' t'infirmary to see him. Would you like to come with me, luv?'

No, no, no. 'Like this? Shall I go an' change, Missis Criddle?' I don't want to go.

'Ee, you're champion as you are, luv. Come on—I know our Charlie'll be glad to see you.'

'How is he, Missis Criddle?' Stop saying *Missis Criddle*.

'Ee, did you not know? It all festered up an' the eye doctor said it 'ud be best to have it out in case it got hold of t'other. He's goin' to have a glass 'un. Ee, I wouldn't let our Charlie go round with one of them shades over his eye —they look like pirates. How's that Miss Skegham goin' on?'

'She seems quieter, ma'am.'

'She best be. I'm sorry now I didn't give her a right good hammerin'. I reckon I let her off light.' She lowered her voice. 'Folk say I'm daft for not suein' her. They say it's a hundred quids' worth an eye—at least. Ee, luv, but I couldn't. Not against St Stephen's. I'd never lift my face again if I did. An' Ted 'ud never rest in his grave i' France if I did. Money's not everything, luv.' Is it not? The root of all evil—then give me a piece of a branch. That's what folk say. 'A body wants peace of mind. Anyway, it won't fetch his sight back. But yu' don't lose it all, luv, because you get twice the power in t'other eye. We'll take a tram.'

The sight of Charlie lying in bed with one side of his head swathed in bandages gave a twist to his heart. He looked so oddly calm, his face so spotless, with the turned-up ends of his hair curly beside the white cloth.

'Where've you come from, Mike?' he asked.

'Your mam said I could come—I'd just called to see how you was.'

'Has she told you they've nicked it out?'

'Yes, luv, I have,' put in his mother, 'an' that you're goin' to have an artificial eye, the best money can buy.'

231

'Artificial eye, the best money can buy,' said Charlie. 'You're a poet, mam. He is a fool an' doesn't know it, who makes himself a craphouse poet. I don't fancy owt too fancy, mam. Just an ordinary glassy. Tell him not to make it favverin' a real eye, cos it gives folk a shock when it ain't.'

'How are you feelin', luv? I've got you some grapes an' a bunch of bananas.'

'Him across in yon bed, Mike, 'as 'ad his eye out too. I were reckonin' up—I know four lads wi' only one eye, an' three grown-ups, one a woman. How many does tha know, Mike?'

'I know two lads.'

'To talk to?'

'One to talk to—one not. Three——' I'd better not count Charlie in, I'll make one up. 'Did I say two?—no, three.'

'I've been askin' you how you're gettin' on?' said Mrs Criddle.

'Gettin' on? All right. I've been wonderin' which eye you wink with, Mike, when you've a glass 'un. If you wink with your proper eye it means you go blind for a time an' you can't see who you're winkin' at. An' it don't seem like playin' the game to wink with a glass 'un. Sweet unction and true love.'

'Stop keep goin' off like that, our Charlie!' exclaimed Mrs Criddle. 'It's every time alike. Have they been good to you, luv?'

'Aye. Who?'

'Nurses.'

'Naw, they're a narky lot. All except a fat 'un. But say nowt or they might go worse.'

'I won't have 'um narkin' you, luv.'

'I know a blind chap, Chey, who can hammer in the dark. He can mend clogs in the dark.' Should I have said that?

'I were cudgitatin' last night, Mike, about dark an' that. I'll tell you what I were cudgitatin' on—*is darkness black daylight?*'

''Ow do you mean, Charlie, luv?'

'Aahe, mam, you'll never get it—but happen Mike will.

Say you get a field covered at night with darkness—is that just *black daylight*? Or come to that, is the daytime *white darkness*? '

'Whatever are you talkin' about, our Charlie? '

'Oh now shut up, mam,' said Charlie mildly, ' till I get this off my mind to Mike. I were cudgitatin' on an invention called *black* electricity or *black* gas. Instead of folk havin' to buy blinds an' curtains an' stuff, they just press a button an' there's a bulb or a mantle what comes on full blast with *black* light. Fills every corner of the room wi' darkness. Tha could have two switches, white for lightin' up an' black for darkin' up. Got me, Mike? '

' It 'ud want thinkin' out, Chey.'

'Well think it out. Han' they said prayers for me at schoo'? '

'Nob'dy knows you've had it out yet, Chey. She keeps havin' private intentions said, an' I've got an idea they're everyone for you. Anyway, we'll be goin' up into Mr Denning's class the week after next.'

' About time too,' said Mrs Criddle. ' Our Charlie was allus a lot happier when he was in Mr Wimpole's class.'

'Who—that old praty-cake? '

' I say you was allus happier in his class.'

' Happiness ain't everythin', mam,' said Charlie.

'Whatever are you talkin' about our Charlie? ' said Mrs Criddle. ' He's never been the same since he went in that woman's class. Then she goes stickin' her stick in his eye.'

' I've told you before,' said Charlie, ' an' I'll tell you again —it were my fault an' not hers.'

' Hush, luv, don't let folk hear you.'

' They can hear me as likes. She had nowt to do wi' it except she were holdin' the cane. Fair's fair. Come to think of it, Mike, chap as made cane were one of the first causes, barrin' him as planted it. That's the rotter we want to get at.'

' Aren't you goin' to eat your grapes, luv? '

' Yu' know I don't like eatin' when folk are watchin'. Best little feed I get is in the dark at night.'

O.S.B.—H*

' I fancy that's why he wants his black daylight, Missis Criddle,' he said. Why don't they laugh?

' Give some to Mike, mam.'

' I don't want any, thanks, Missis Criddle.'

' Stuff 'um down his kisser, mam. Tha looks clean, Mike.'

' Aye, we went swimmin' today.' Should I have said it? ' My ears are better.'

' Did Peak say owt? '

' Nar. Why? '

' He tried to threep me out as tha couldn't swim an inch. Anyway, he's sucked. How's the orange tree? '

' What orange tree, our Charlie? '

' How is it, Mike? '

' It'll never lift its head again.'

' I wonder will any oranges grow where we planted 'um? I'd like to see it—a right big yellow orange tree growin' on the bricky there. When the season came there'd be scods of oranges. They'd be ours an' Fat Ada's by right.'

' Is that the bell, Missis Criddle? '

' Don't go yet.'

' How is it, luv? '

' What? '

' Your eye? '

' Which eye? '

' The one you've had—yu' know, the one you've had out.'

' What a daft question, mam. How do I know? I'll bet cat's 'ad it by this.'

' Ee, luv, don't talk like that. I mean the place where your eye's come out of.'

' Socket. Feels like a factory lodge.'

' What, is it wet? '

' Is it heck as wet. It's that flappin' big.'

' That's the bell again, Missis Criddle.'

' Ee, we don't seem to have been here no time.'

' You don't have to go till it rings the third time—an' not then straight away.'

' I reckon as I needn't have come, lad, for all you've had to say to me.'

'How sharper than the serpent's tooth——'

'What's that, love?'

'Don't go yet, mam. Hang on. Never mind t'others—I'm a serious case.'

'*Time to go, please.*'

'Wait till she's shouted the third time. Am I a thankless child, mam?'

'Ee, nay! Never, love!'

'So long, Charlie.'

'So long, Mike.'

'Good luck, Charlie. It's rotten 'bout thee in class.'

'Good luck, Mike. Hang on, mam, I've summat to tell you.'

He left them and slipped out of the ward with the other visitors. Mrs Criddle followed him a minute later. They walked together in silence towards the gate, then she wiped her eyes.

'He's a funny lad is our Charlie,' she said—'just like his dad.'

CHAPTER TWO

Farewell to Miss Skegham

'PACK YOUR BAGS for moving up.'

From under his desk he brought out the home-made linen satchel and began to pack his exercise books into it. Michael M'Cloud: *Sums*. Michael M'Cloud: *English*. He put his ink-stained ruler down into the bottom and his two pens, and then he carefully fastened the twin tapes into neat bows. He looked at the desk: the impression of every grain, stain, dent and scratch on its surface seemed fastened for ever in his mind. Sitting here at this desk I've gone through the worst misery of my life, and now I've got to go and let some daft lad take my place.

'Class, rise!' He looked up. She has an all but tender look. 'Class, march in orderly file up to Mr Denning's classroom.' They began to clatter out of the room. Charlie nudged him. 'Ready, Mike?' Leisurely he tucked the bag under his arm and moved off after the tail of the class. He heard Charlie mutter aloud.

'What's that, Criddle?' asked Miss Skegham.

'I was just sayin', Miss, "Parting is such sweet sorrow!"' They stood in some obedience before her gaze. '*Romeo an' Juliet*, Miss. It came to my mind, "That I shall say good-night till it be morrow!"'

'If you're being impertinent, Criddle——'

'I'm not, Miss.'

'Very well.'

He felt Charlie hesitate beside him. 'My dad was in your class, Miss.'

'I—I taught your father, Criddle?'

'Yes, Miss. Edward Criddle.'

'Edward Criddle,' she repeated. 'Edward——'

'Edward Aloysius Criddle, Miss.'

'Oh——!'

'Got killed in action, Miss. Nineteen-seventeen in Flanders.'

'Yes, yes. Was Edward your father?'

'Yes, Miss.'

She shook her paled face. 'Strange I didn't know. I wish you had told me before, Charles,' she said. Charlie didn't answer. 'You may go,' she said, nodding them through the door. A file of new boys was moving along the corridor to her room.

Charlie turned to him as they were going upstairs: 'If tha hadn't been there, Mike, I couldn't have kept down a feeling I had—to tell her we struck her tree down in its prime.'

'She knows, Chey,' he said.

'Gerroff! Did tha tell her?'

'No.'

'Then how does she know?'

'She does, Chey,' he said. 'Don't ask me how, but I know she knows.'

He turned and made himself say what he had seen: 'Chey, thought for a second she were going to cry or summat.'

'Funny, so did I,' said Charlie. He rubbed his nose and sighed: '"That mine own tears do scald like molten lead."' Words that touch the heart. I'll burst out sobbing myself if I'm not careful. Together they entered Mr Denning's class.

A broad-faced man, with grey eyes that had wrinkled skin about them, was jingling money in his pockets as he watched the new boys pushing and scrambling for the best places. 'What about it, Mike?' whispered Charlie, beckoning to an empty desk for two at the front. He disliked the thought of being so close to the teacher, but feeling the man's eye was on him, he nodded and they sat down.

Mr Denning remarked, as he glanced at the struggling figures: 'I want to sit with Bill Brown, sir, but he wants to sit next to Jack Smith, who wants to mate with Tim White, who wants to be alone.'

'Quiet!'

'Sir! Please sir!'

'Quiet, Finch. Remember, "he who seeks private advantage loses those which are common." You sit there—and you there—and you there——' In less than a minute the class was seated before him. 'Those are your places,' he said. He walked to and fro a time, hands in pockets. 'I shall need a monitor. Hands up those boys who do not wish to be the monitor.' Four hands went up. 'Hands up those boys who wish to be the monitor.' Most of the class raised their hands.

'M'Cloud.'

'Yes, sir.' He stood quickly to attention.

'I perceive you were amongst neither group. In fact, you never raised a hand.' How did he spot me? 'Perhaps you could explain?'

'Well, sir, I had no wish at first not to be monitor.' It's odd how easy I feel talking to him. 'But then I found I had no wish to be monitor. So I didn't put my hand up.'

'Right. Fill the inkwells.'

'Yes, sir.'

There's no entanglement with him, makes you feel nice and free. Thought I'd never get used to being a monitor, but it's come natural to me. I'll never want to leave school whilst I've got him for a teacher. I feel I can say anything to him. But not quite like old Charlie can. I'm not able to pull my mask off. When I try to act like other lads I never feel I'm myself, because the weight of secrecy inside me is like a great big lump of lead. Confession eases it off, but happen it'll take that last final Confession before God to get properly shut of it.

He watched from his place by the window as Willie stood up from the tea-table, wiped his mouth and turned at once to the sofa. 'I think I'll stretch the old legs for five minutes,' he said, stooping to unlace his rust-grimed hobnailed boots and sighing comfortably as he slipped out his feet, pressed and shiny in the thick wool socks. 'How would tha like to

238

be a rivet lad, Mick m'boy? Throwing red hot rivets about all day long. I'll bet it 'ud kill you.'

' If you can do it,' he said, ' I'd do it on my head.'

' You wait an' see, boy,' Willie said, stretching out on the sofa. 'Little Danny'll keep you busy. Give me a shake, mother, just in case I drop off. Ned'll be callin'.'

The mother nodded, brought over a shawl, covered him and tucked him in. Soon a faint snoring could be heard. Lack of willpower, he thought, looking across from the window. I could never get myself to go off like that in my dirt.

' Mickyeen,' whispered the mother, softly entering from the kitchen, ' is the clock right? '

' Where are you goin'? ' he asked, seeing her with a coat on.

' Didn't I ask you was the clock right? '

' If you want to know the time,' he said, ' old Hatton's just gone by with his bell, so it's five past six.'

' Then I'll have the factory folk missed nicely,' she said, speaking in a whisper. ' I'm just off to Mrs Flann's.'

' A new money club startin'? '

She nodded : ' They're shakin' the dice for numbers, so wish me luck, willya,' she said, giving him a thump, 'that I might get an early one. I could well do with the money.'

' Where will I say you are if he wakens? ' he asked, pointing a thumb to the ceiling.

' Och, sure he won't waken unless you make a noise,' she said, ' after all the potatoes he has ate.'

What will I say if he *does* waken? he was ready to ask, but seeing the anxious look cross her face he left it unsaid. He kissed her. ' Good luck, mother. Can I take my shoes to be mended if you win? '

' A new pair for you,' she said, ' if I get number one. Sure if he should waken, you'd be as well to say I slipped out to the shop for pepper. I'll come in the back way, so he won't see me with the coat on.'

' Are you not puttin' on a hat, mother? '

' Isn't it only five minutes? ' she said. She looked into the

239

big looking-glass. 'I'm a prisoner,' she said, 'a prisoner in the home,' she went on, smoothing her hair down at the sides, 'an' signs is on my poor shrunken mouth. I can't go out for five minutes without having to lie. Arra musha I'm shrinkin' altogether, like some ould strooleen.'

'You want to do some Ross's height-increasing exercises, mother,' he said, 'they'd bring you out.'

'An' to think I was always the proud one, Mickyeen,' she said. 'I'd split with the shame if one from home was to see me.'

'You're not bad-lookin', yu' know, mam,' he said. 'You've nice hair an' a nice complexion. It's that Roman nose of yours spoils you.'

'I'll be back in half an' hour,' she said, 'an' if he's up he's up. Don't leave the house. Kiss.' She gave him a kiss and slipped off noiselessly out the back way.

He sat on the chair by the window and looked out through the curtains at the street. I mustn't forget I've got to meet Ella at seven near the brickfield. That damn' Missis Flann knows what she's doing with her money clubs. They'll all be shaking dice there trying to get an early number. Them who don't will sell their later share for cash—thirteen bob for a pound. With poundage that makes eight bob in the pound profit. Folk'll give anything for ready cash. *Sex*—his eye caught the word at the bottom of a newspaper column under his elbow, and he began to read.

'*What Every Woman Fears. A Penalty of her Sex.*' *All women realise that they can scarcely expect to escape, from time to time, suffering which men are not called upon to endure. Most often, especially when a girl is entering womanhood, the one cause of pain, low spirits and back-ache, is anaemia. In full womanhood, and again at middle age, other miseries come to some, due again to the scarcity of good blood. Every woman, at the first sign of ill-health, should take Dr Williams pink pills, for these pills are famous for their power of creating rich red blood.*

He read bits of it again : '*entering womanhood*'—sounds a bit like they were going into a convent. I know what's at

240

the back of his mind—their courses. Funny how women are always full of suffering and disease. Thank God I'm not one. Thank God a thousand times. They say Indian brandy is a good thing at times like that. I must get Ella some of those pills before she enters. It'll be no joke married to her if she's going to have low spirits an' backache most of the time. No wonder some of 'um looks so miserable. '*What every woman fears.*' Very good of Dr Williams to tell them. They must go to their graves full of fear an' trembling. I'd never fancy doing that there to any single one of them—their insides must be in a bad state. No, not even when I'm wed will I do it. Ours will be a *pure* marriage. I don't care what the Church says—it's bound to be a sin. How can it be anything else? I'll be satisfied just coming home to Ella, having a kiss, Knowles's fried sausage for tea, together with pineapple chunks. I wonder is there anything good in the kitchen?

He went softly into the back kitchen and looked around. He picked up the milk jug and took a sip: they'll never miss that drop, and it's a bit of strength for me. Bread, bacon, margarine, sugar—not much there. Happen there'll be a Chivers' jelly packet hid away somewhere—a nice bit cut off that 'ud be good. Or a banana, if there is one. No, there's nothing.

He looked up on the shelves. Two dark loaf-tins caught his eye. I once found something in one of them. He took a chair and put it near the dresser, quietly stood on it and reached up. He put his hand in one tin—empty. There'll be nothing in the other. Quickly he felt. Something cool and round met his palm. He gripped it and took it out. Why, a pear! A nice quiet pale pear. Why, it looks lovely. I wonder how long it's been there? Months, I'll bet. I think I felt another as well. He put the tips of his fingers back into the baking tin and felt another pear. Righto, I'll eat this.

Carefully he got down and lifted the chair away. He put the pear into his trousers' pocket. It only just fitted. He lifted the latch of the back-kitchen door, opened the door softly, and tiptoed down the yard to the closet. He went

241

inside and closed the door, and after some trouble managed to get the pear out of his pocket. He polished it on his shirt sleeve. Now I wonder should I put it back? I've got the willpower, I know that. I could put it back as easily as eat it. It'll do thee good, lad, eat it. Oh I could resist if I wanted. Temptation never got me—not when I had my willpower ready. It 'ud only go bad. Go on, bite.

Don't, whispered a thought as he raised it to his lips, but he overcame the whisper. The juice ran across his gums and over his lips as his teeth went into the fruit. A sensation of pleasure, rare and intense, brought a momentary touch of weakness to him. He took another bite and another, giving way to the urge for pleasure. It's lovely. He caught the juice in his palm and licked it. He ate every bit, spitting the pips down the privy hole. I feel different. He rubbed his hands together and wiped his mouth with his handkerchief. Fancy being a millionaire and eating them all day!

She'll have forgotten that other pear too. That taste is still on my tongue. Temptation's hold of me. All mixed up with the smell and the darkness of the privy. Willpower's gone. He went into the back kitchen, then into the front kitchen and glanced at Willie, then into the back kitchen. He put the chair against the dresser, reached up, took out the pear—I'm deaf an' blind an' I can't stop myself—put the chair back after he'd got down, and went back to the closet with the pear tucked under his shirt.

He took a sudden bite. The juice flushed out of it. Taste seems gone. I can't taste it like before. He took three big bites and flung the core down the hole. Guilt—that's all I can taste. Tastes dark. What came o'er me? I must have gone daft. The pleasure only lasted thirty seconds. I feel black an' miserable inside. The soul's got to stand Sammy for everything the body does. Crimes, I wish I'd never laid eyes on that baking tin. Lead us not into temptation. How rotten I'll feel if she's not forgot 'um. I won't admit it. Pears? I've seen no pears.

He went into the house again. Oh I'd better go an' cover the pips up with a piece of paper, just in case anybody looks down. The muckmisers come round tonight emptying 'um. My mam could be saying to Mester O'Haggerty, I missed a couple of pears the other day, and he could say back, Why, I remember I spotted the pips of some pears when I was emptying your closet the other night. That's how murderers get found out. He went into the front place and looked at his brother. Look at the way his face is all twisted lying there—how anybody can sleep like that is beyond me. No trouble on his mind.

A knocking on the ceiling caused him to jump. He looked at the clock and ran into the back kitchen and went to the bottom of the stairs.

'Did you knock, father?' he asked hoarsely.

'Is that you, Mickyeen?' called the father. 'Where's your mother?'

'Gone to Durham's, I think,' he said.

'What time is it?'

I could turn it back a good ten minutes without him knowing. 'Twenty-to-seven,' he said.

He waited a few seconds and then moved away. I'd better do it before I forget: he went to the clock, opened the front, and flicked the minute hand back to twenty minutes to seven. I mustn't forget to tell mother.

He went to the sofa: 'Willie, Willie,' he whispered. No stir. 'Willie!'

'Eh? what's up?'

'It's after seven. Ned'll be round any minute.'

Willie blinked and turned over. I wish I were boss in this house. They're too soft with us. I'd say one word and he'd jump up. He waited, and when he heard the father's footsteps on the room floor above he turned the figure on the sofa again: 'Willie! he's up. Yu' know what a row there'll be if Ned calls an' you're not ready.' Willie got up. He favvers a redfaced baby, yawning, rubbing, scratching an' stretching. Happen he is tired. Willpower is what he needs.

'Where's mother?'

'Durham's, I think.'

Willie went into the kitchen. A minute later the father

243

clomped down the stairs, and came into the room wearing a flannel shirt, a pair of old blue-serge trousers, and an old pair of high-up boots cut down as slippers.

'I'm killed with the sleep,' he said. 'Where's your mother?'

'I think she went to the shop, father,' he said.

'Is it Durham's—the bloody ould fraud? That one would rob an' plunder all before him. What's she doin' there this hour of the evenin'?' He took the evening paper from the sideboard.

'Will I make you a drink of tea, father?' he asked.

'Urra won't herself be in in a minute,' said the father mildly. 'That's a great evenin' now, thanks be to God.'

I'd hate to live with two men in a house. The father began to read. 'Don't drown the bloody kitchen with water,' he suddenly called out. 'Urra what the hell's keepin' your mother, Mickyeen? Go an' see would you see, for I have my bloody work to attend to. I have that an' all.'

I'll pretend going, he thought, walking into the back kitchen. 'Oh come back,' called the father, 'give her another couple of minutes.'

'I won't go, father,' he said, 'but I'll watch out.'

He went to the back gate and looked down the backstreet. I hope she hasn't got run over. What a dreadful thing that would be, to see her brought home half dead and bleeding. I don't care about the pears. Poor mother. Then he saw her come hurrying round the corner. He went running to her.

'What kept you?' he whispered. 'He's up.'

'Arra what do I care?' she said. 'I didn't get the first week but I did get a third one—you gave me luck, Mickyeen.' She opened her purse as she hurried along and fingered out some coppers. 'Fourpence would take you to the pictures?' she said.

'No, no, thanks, mam,' he said. At her soft kindness he felt the rising in his throat.

'Take it,' she said, 'before it would fall from my hands.'

'Thanks, mam.' What a magical thing is the woman's purse! 'I said you was at Durham's. Oh, before I forget, I
244

turned the clock back ten minutes. Will you fix it when he's not lookin'?'

'I will so,' she said, 'an' put another five minutes on.' She winked and slipped off her coat as they went into the back kitchen.

'Mother, have I a clean shirt?' asked Willie.

'Indeed you have, siree,' she said, 'an' two—if you'd like to wear one over the other.'

'What the divil in hell kept you?' called the man.

'Pepper,' she said. 'There wasn't a taste of pepper to be got.'

'I'm destroyed with all I slept,' he said. 'The potatoes have me blinded with sleep. Have you tea ready?'

'I have, sir,' she said. 'Just a jiff, if you please.'

'Did you know your mother was Yank, Mickyeen?' said the father.

She darted into the back kitchen. 'I'd be as well make fresh tea for you,' she said.

'Don't be all evenin' then,' said the father, 'for I have my work to go to.'

CHAPTER THREE

The Street Corner

═══

I ENVY THEM, he thought, slipping out of the house to go off and meet Ella. How happy I'd be if I hadn't sinned! He hurried secretly out of the street and along a backstreet towards the brickfield. He saw her looking into the big window of the Co-operative Society grocery shop. At the sight of her he felt the tightening in his throat that meant his voice wouldn't come out right. I'd better watch out we're not spotted.

'Ella! hello, Ella.'

'My sweetheart,' she said.

'Now which way shall we go?' he asked, putting his hands into his pockets and swaggering on a step ahead. I can't understand how other lads don't go mad on her.

'Through the ginnel,' she said. 'I've got a surprise for you.'

I've got to watch out for a chap called Pilling who lives about here, he thought, and any other lads from St Stephen's, and I don't want to bump into Herbert as he's going off to toss the pigeons. 'If I have to suddenly walk on in front,' he said, 'don't call out or anything. It's just that someone might have seen me.'

'I don't care who sees me,' she said. 'You can face the world when you're in love.'

'It's all right for girls,' he said, 'but lads feel daft if they get codded. What's the surprise, may I ask?' That was a nice brave thing she said then.

'I sometimes wonder what I like most about you, darling,' she said, 'your eyes or your voice. Yu'know you can talk nice when you want. Why don't you talk fine all the time?'

Y'ought have heard that chap in the peestone at Nelson Square that time: *I suppose that in the normal course of events that place is a drill hall?* The words came out like a long deep cough. The first aristocratic voice I ever heard.

'Er, what is the surprise, Ella?—or am I not to know?'

'Wait till we get to the ginnel,' she said, waving a small sugar bag.

There was one man in the ginnel, and after he had passed they squeezed hands and she gave him a quick kiss on the cheek. Then she took something out of the bag.

'For you, my darling,' she said, putting a large tomato under his nose.

He tried to mask his disappointment by a hurried gasp: 'Oh how nice, Ella!' What am I supposed to do with it? 'Thank you very much.'

'Don't you like tomatoes?'

I've never had one. 'Of course I do.'

'I've pinched you a bit of salt to go with it,' she said, opening a screw of paper.

The firm smooth tomato felt pleasant to the touch, and the smell was cool and unsweet. I suppose it'll taste like an apple.

'Go on,' she said, 'eat it.'

He took a bite. The pungent rawness almost sickened him, yet he forced himself to chew it. 'That's right good, Ella,' he said. 'Come on, you have a bite.'

'I'm daft on tomatoes,' she said, sprinkling the salt on. 'But I won't have any—I brought it for you.'

'Come on,' he said, 'have a bite—an' a big 'un at that.'

I could swipe you when you do daft things. She took a bite. 'Take another,' he said, 'I've just had my tea.'

'I've got to take the washin' back up Howcliff Street as soon as I get home,' she said. 'You wouldn't like to come with me?'

What—be seen carrying a basket of washing through the streets with a girl? Either she's barmy or she thinks I am. 'I'd like to, Ella,' he said, 'but folk 'ud stare, yu' know.'

'Let 'um stare. Let 'um sken if they want. We owe 'um nothin'.'

She does talk broad when she's excited. I'll have to get her out of that. I mean to say, if you was mixing in posh company. Funny how's she's always that much nicer when I think of her than when I meet her. Fancy having no more sense than fetch a chap a tomato, and then expecting him to go and carry washing through the streets with her. I hope we're a bit above that caper.

'When I start work in November,' she said, 'I won't be so beholden to folk. I won't care what they say or what they think. When you're bringing home money regular you can tell 'um all to mind their own business. My mam's on the lookout for a job in an office in town for me.'

Some office! 'Oh—!' he cried, as the tomato fell. 'Oh Ella, I'm so sorry—it slipped out of my hand.' He looked at the piece of tomato lying on the ground. But it did slip out of my hand.

'It doesn't matter,' she said. 'Don't pick it up—it's not nice eatin' things off the floor.'

'I'm so sorry, Ella. Where did you get it?'

'It were supposed to have been for my dad's tea,' she said, 'but then the kipper chap came round, so he had a kipper instead. My mam put it back int' cupboard for his tomorrow's tea.'

Oh crimes, if he only gets to know I've eaten his tea! I don't want to be mixed up in a row in the street. 'Ella, what'll your mam say when she finds out?'

'Oh I don't care. I don't really, yu'know.'

How could she have done it? As though I'm not in enough trouble as it is! He felt the fourpence in his pocket. No, I'm not giving her that. Not likely. Oh there's them pears when I get home. 'Ella, take this fourpence. You've got to buy another tomato and put it in its place.'

'Oh darling—it was a present.'

'I—don't care what the heck it was, Ella. Can you hear me——?'

''Course I can—I'm not deaf.'

'Well, here's the fourpence. An' I'll come with you to Enty's.'

'They might be shut.'

'They're open till eight.'

248

' I've got to dash back an' take the washin'—or else I'll get coppit.'

' Yes, when you've bought that tomato,' he said. ' An' ask him for one big 'un, the shape of the other.'

' I'll bet that other cost ninepence,' she said.

She came out of Enty's with a tomato. It didn't look at all like the other one. ' See you slip it back into the cupboard,' he said.

They walked on in silence. She's not half caused me some trouble, what with one thing and another. I don't think it's worthwhile, frankly, I don't. They stopped at the corner nearing home.

' Well,' she said.

' Well,' he said. Two wells make a river, you jump in an' shiver, an' I'll come out like a lump of liver.

' Goodbye—' she said.

' Goodbye,' he answered shortly. Then he looked at her. Her face looked small and pinched, and her hurt eyes had tears near them. At once he felt his heart warm swiftly: Ella, my love, and in pain! ' Town Hall steps tomorrow night,' he said quickly.

' What time? ' she said, her face brightening.

' Seven o'clock,' he said.

She gave a look of such thanks that he felt upset again, and then she turned and hurried away. He watched her. She seemed to be moving awkwardly. He caught a glimpse of naked skin at the heel of her black ribbed stocking. A hole— and she's trying to hide it. He heard the uneven clack of her clogs along the pavement: She's got an iron off as well. Her figure looked oddly shrunken and pathetic. I hurt her feelings. I'm a pig. He could feel the tears close to his own eyes. Instinctively he turned for home, but then he remembered the stolen pears. He turned at the first corner and made for St Stephen's church. I can't turn to Mother, I'll tell the Blessed Virgin.

The prayer in church brought no comfort. He walked the streets for a time and then, feeling lonely for human company, feeling an odd longing for the faces of boys he knew,

249

he went to the street corner. At one end the younger lads were playing 'Ride or kench'. He watched the caterpillar chain of their backs crouched to the wall. I wish I wasn't too old to join in, he thought. You're not. Who's not? I feel like a blooming old man.

He walked to the corner, beside The Dirt, where his old mates were gathered. They were now little piecers in the factory, and as he drew near he smelt the oily odour. He saw their thin bony figures, their shoddy cotton-grimed clothes, their pale thin necks, the loose sweaty mufflers, and the group of eager white faces, laughing and arguing. It seemed they were always doing one or the other, arguing or laughing. I'm not one of them, he thought, but I'm very drawn to them.

'There's an effin' grub here I can't get out,' said Ernie Haddock. He was seated on the pavement back to the wall, his trouser leg rolled up, squeezing blackheads out of his knees. Ben Shilliton and Tommy Roberts were also squeezing blackheads.

Spadger Chadwick caught a ball he had been throwing, and came across.

'I'll effin' show you,' said Spadger.

That terrible word that begins with f, he thought. The last thing in human abandonment when you say that. It's as though you'd given up all hope of heaven.

Spadger bent down over Ernie's white thigh. 'Tha'll never get it out without a key,' said Ernie.

'Who says?' said Spadger. They all crowded round and watched. Spadger's greasy oil-pale fingers first drew the skin tightly across Ernie's thigh, and then he placed his thumbs firmly on either side of the large blackhead. Firmly and surely he began to press. Ernie gave a wince. 'Easy, easy,' said Spadger, 'here it comes.' The ugly black spot suddenly lifted, and as Spadger pressed harder, a long wormlike excretion seemed to wriggle out. Spadger caught it on his thumb-nail and exhibited it round.

'What a beauty!' exclaimed Ben Shilliton.

Spadger bowed. 'Sir Spadger Chadwick,' he said, 'the

king's physician and pox doctor. I squeezed twenty-bloody-seven out of our side-piecer's legs today, an' didn't bust a one.'

'Like to squeeze one o' mine, Micky?' said Ben, in a kindly tone.

'I don't know,' he said.

'Might as well learn, Mick,' said Ernie Haddock, 'for if tha starts work in the spinning tha'll have hundreds after the first week. They come from wiping under.'

'Here,' said Ben, 'that's a nice un.'

He could feel their eyes on him, and he had to stifle a feeling of nausea as he placed his hands on Ben's bony thigh.

'Get a good hold with thy thumbs,' said Spadger, 'an' once it starts movin', keep on squeezing, even if he screams his bloody 'ead off.'

He began to press weakly on the thin bony thigh.

'Put some bloody weight behind it,' they called. They excited him, and he pressed hard and saw the thing come out. He let go suddenly.

'Tha's left bloody root in,' said Spadger.

'He's a gentle touch has old Micky,' said Ben.

'Not the same as them women in the cardroom, Ben,' said Spadger. 'I heard about 'em greasing thy pinkler.' Ben flushed.

'What were that?' asked Ernie Haddock.

'Some of the women got hold of Ben,' said Spadger, 'got him on the floor in the cardroom, pulled out his john henry and daubed it with grease.'

'I'd ha' kicked their rops in,' said Tommy Roberts. 'Eh, Micky?'

He nodded weakly. The image of women doing that with grease on their hands had made him dry-throated. A woman's hand touching my trouser-buttons. That rotten sex is rising in me. I can feel it. I'd better hurry off and put my trouser front right before they spot it.

He walked away. They do the talking but I do the suffering. If you can call it suffering. It's getting its grip on me.

251

Another minute and it'll have full hold of me. Lord save me or I perish. Perish, you sod! Oh good grief, there's Dad going to work! I wonder does he know about the pears? I'd better go this other way.

That got the evil thoughts out of my mind. Did it?— they're coming back. I'd better walk faster. He put a hand into his trouser pocket. Swing it over the minder's side, then it might drop. He hurried past some young factory girls. When he got by them they suddenly let out shrieks of laughter. He flushed to the eyes. I wonder did they know? What a rotten awkward life! Give way to this sex thing once and you're done for ever. No way out.

When he got home, Willie was just going to bed.

'There's a little meat an' beetroot, for you,' said the mother, ' an' here's a cup of tea.'

'Thanks, Mother,' he said.

'You're late,' she said.

' Am I? ' he said. He felt her walking about in silence as she raked the fire with coaldust, ashes and tealeaves.

'Tell me,' she said, after a time, ' did you see any pears in a tin on the kitchen shelf? '

' No, Mother,' he heard the answer leave his tongue promptly. ' Pears? I saw no pears.'

She turned to him and said quietly : ' Your father had to go out to pit tonight without a taste of fruit to take with him. I had the pears there, so he could take one to quench his thirst in the night. And I had to send him off with the bottle of cold tea alone.'

He forced down the food and got up from the table. The instant he got out into the darkness of the backyard he felt the blood flushing his face. How rotten everything is! If I could get out of this I'd never touch another pear the longest day I lived. I wish I could admit it. But I can't. He stood in the darkness. Above in the back room there was the grunting of the brother at his weightlifting exercises, and about the house the mother was moving, sighing and humming her prayers as she laid the table for morning, and prepared the porridge pot. Happen he'll be thirsty now in the hot dust-smoked pit. If I'd never touched the pears how different life would be! He opened the kitchen door.

' Good night, Mother,' he said.

' Good night, my son,' she said, kissing him.

He went up the stairs slowly. She gave me my chance then.

He wakened during the night and heard the scavengers emptying the privy pails in the backstreet. The stink filled the room, and he got up and closed the window. He heard the clatter of shovels, and the man calling to the horse, and the roll of the cartwheels on the cobblestones. The light from their lamps shone on the curtains. They're working amongst muck, but they're happier than me. I wish I were one of 'um. That comes from feeling on top of things. I'm safer when I'm kept under.

CHAPTER FOUR

Ella starts Work

ON A NOVEMBER SUNDAY EVENING they met at the tram
stop near the tripe-dresser's. She was there waiting for him
in the doorway when he arrived at half-past six. 'It's all
right, dearest one,' she whispered to him when he put on a
show of silence for a start, 'there's no one we know knocking about.' He glanced round just to make certain, before
speaking. 'What did you tell your mam?' he asked. 'I told
her I were meeting you.'

'Don't be daft, Ella,' he said sharply; 'what did you say
to her?'

'I told her I were meeting a girl from school.'

'Did she believe you?'

'No. So then I told her I were meeting you.'

'You didn't honest, did you, Ella?'

'No, not if it frightens you, I didn't.'

'I'd hate people to know,' he said.

'Everybody knows already,' she said. 'An' why shouldn't
I tell her? I'm turned fourteen an' I start work tomorrow.'

'Yes, but I don't. I've another seven month to go before
I start. Anyway, I hate people gabbing about me.'

' "Sticks an' stones may break my bones," ' she said, ' " but
calling does not hurt me. And when I'm dead and in my
grave, they'll wish they'd never called me." '

'Yes, yes,' he said impatiently, 'here's the Colton Lane
tram coming. You can catch it an' wait outside the old tram
shed. I'll come on the next.'

'Oh darling, can't we both go on this?—being as it's the
last Sunday.'

'What do you mean by "the last Sunday"?' he asked.

'I mean that next Sunday I'll have been a mucky doffer
for a week.'

254

'But you'll still be my—my girl, won't you?'

'I'll be your girl till my dying day,' she said, 'but do come on this tram with me, just for once.'

'All right,' he said, 'just for this once. But only if it's nearly empty on top.'

'It is!' she cried in a whisper as the lighted tram came along, 'it is!'

It's funny, he thought climbing the steps, that I get grumpy when I'm out with her. I'll have to be nice with her now or she'll begin to think I don't love her. Of course it's only for her own good. Folk don't always see that. He sat down beside her at the front. She hutched up against him. It was cold and he wished he had an overcoat. That was always one sure sign of being poor when you hadn't an overcoat. She hadn't a proper coat either. It was a very thin cottony one that easily creased. One day he'd buy her a lovely thick wool fawn coat like the one he had seen Miss Twining wear. And he'd have a thick blue one with broad shoulders for himself.

'My dad took us to the Royal last night,' she said. He suffered the instant pang of envy at the thought she should go to a place where he hadn't been. 'We'd been to the closed-in market lookin' at the pigeons, and as it were no good of a film at the Lully he thought it 'ud be a grand idea to cut up St George's Road to the Royal. It were "The Dangerous Age."'

'"Lewis Stone as the man who went wandering, Ruth Clifford as the girl who sent him squandering, Cleo Madison as the wife who waited,"' he put in quickly. 'I knew it 'ud be no good of a film as soon as I saw that advert.'

'It were quite a nice film,' she said warmly. 'It had a moral in it—that's what most films haven't got. And I'm mad about Lewis Stone. I always think I'd like to marry a man like that.'

How can she be so stupid as to spoil the entire evening for us both? he thought. A stroke of jealousy separated him from her.

'Of course you're really my ideal, darling,' she whispered,

255

squeezing his arm. I hate that swine of an actor, he thought. 'It's a wonderful film next week, "Monna Vanna". It's a film by Meterlink.'

'I've heard it's no good,' he said.

'It hasn't been shown in Towlton yet,' she said. 'Why, there's a cast of over thirty thousand in it.'

'I don't care if there's thirty million,' he said, 'you wouldn't get me in a shop like the Royal.'

He changed his look as he heard the conductor's footsteps on the stairs, and he felt in his pocket.

'Two, please,' he said, 'to Colton Lane.'

'Two halves?'

'No, two wholes, please.' He handed the conductor sixpence and got threepence change. He liked to pay everything in silver and get change. There was always something pinchbeck about paying just the right money.

'Ee, why didn't you get two halves, Michael?' asked Ella.

'I didn't think,' he said.

'What I like about you, Michael,' she said, 'is that you're very sensitive. You don't get many sensitive boys these days.'

He didn't answer but he was pleased. He gazed straight through the window as though he were the eyes of the driver, and had to steer the tram safely. She was having a ride and he had paid for it. He liked the feeling. That was a nice word, "sensitive", and it had surprised him to hear Ella say it. He put his shoulders back and made a delicate faraway look come into his eyes. Then when he felt her arm slip under his—shielded by the tram seat—he tensed the muscle and made it big. He felt so strong since he began doing all his exercises, especially with the corks, that he was always itching to try his strength out on anything he came across, from breaking string to attempting to shove over letterboxes in the street.

'When we're married,' he said, 'you're not going out to work.'

'Why not?' she asked. 'People are always better off when both go out to work.'

256

'You're not going out to work,' he said, 'and that's the end of that. I don't care whether they're better off or worse off, I'm not having you going out to work.' Then he looked at her and smiled.

He was very happy when they got off the tram at Colton Lane. It was higher up than Hector Clinker Street, and there were no factories, so the breeze could blow hard, and there was a smell of grass, and at once he felt free and better. The road was wide and dark and nobody could see them, so he gave her a kiss and put his arm round her. In his mind was the thought of her going to work next day, and he felt unhappy about it. I hope it doesn't make her lord it over me.

'Nobody saw the prayerbook I gave you?' he asked anxiously.

''Course not,' said Ella. 'Well, our Alfred did come into the bedroom last night when I were reading it, an' he grabbed it out of my hand. But he didn't know what it was, because I grabbed it back. He said: "Who's the owd chap with the fryin' pan on his nut?"'

'The fryin' pan on his nut? Who did he mean?'

'Well, he'd seen the picture of the priest serving Mass, with that holy thing over his head.'

'That's the halo or nimbus,' he said. 'That illumination over his head is a sign of sanctity.'

'Are all Cath'lic boys as clever as you, Michael?'

'Did he really say that about the fryin' pan?'

'Of course he did—you don't think I'd been making it up? But I think he'd had something to drink. He won't half coppit if my dad catches him drinking.'

A drunken youth of twenty who didn't know the nimbus or halo from a frying-pan! He could be thankful for his ignorance in that God would allow no sin without culpability. He had said a thing blasphemous and profane, that would have blackened another's soul, yet the justice of God was such that he would go scot free. He himself could sin by a passing thought, but God would not allow this man of twenty to sin by word. He would go through life and never know he had sinned in that way. 'Keep it from him, Ella,' he said. She said: 'Yes, Michael, I will.'

'I'm sorry you're going to work tomorrow, Ella,' he said.

'Geroff with your bother,' she said, clutching his arm; 'look at the spendings I'll get. My mam says she'll give me a penny in the shilling out of my earnings, so I'll have eighteenpence a week once I've learnt. An' on top of that there's sometimes extras, as much as two or three shillings a week—that's when another girl's off an' you do her work, or half of her work.'

'I've heard of some funny goin's-on in the factory,' he said, 'especially in the cardroom.'

'What do you mean by funny goin's-on?' she asked.

'Oh just funny goin's-on,' he said. 'I've heard them talkin' —Spadger Chadwick an' some of the others.'

'Well let me tell you there's nothing like that goes on at the Wild Goose,' she said. 'That's a respectable cardroom.'

'I didn't say the Wild Goose, did I? I just said that there were some funny goin's-on in the cardroom.'

'Well, I don't like folk as hint.'

'I never hinted. And if you don't like me you don't have to hint.'

'Darling, let's not fall out on this night.'

'I'm not falling out.'

'Dearest, I know you're not. I'm sorry.'

'It's all right, Ella sweetheart. It was my fault.'

'No, it were mine.'

'Let's kiss an' make up.' They stopped for a moment and kissed. 'We've never stopped properly like lovers do,' he said, 'you know, Ella, in a doorway.'

'What—gumsucking? I don't think it looks nice.'

'Neither do I. I only just said it.'

'They must get starved with the cold, Michael. Anyway, I've got to be home by nine o'clock at the very latest. I've got my clogs an' things to clean for tomorrow. I wonder what time it is?'

'Oh it's not near that time yet—you don't have to worry. Leave the time to me. Why, we've only just come out.'

'I've been thinking what I'm going to buy you, dearest. I'm going to buy you one of those silverplated cigarette-cases, a long shiny one.'

'I'd like it, Ella,' he said, 'but you know I don't smoke.'

'Well I was thinking mainly of you handing them round. I do think it looks nice to see a man open a case and hand cigarettes out.'

'You can't hand so many out, Ella,' he said, 'at ten for a tanner.'

'Oh people often refuse,' she said.

'Not them as I know,' he said.

'You're always goin' against me, Michael.'

'Oh I'm sorry, darling,' he said. 'I'm worried.'

'What are you worried about?'

'What's worrying me,' he said, 'is when we can meet. You can't go to your auntie's near Tall Street baths now. You won't be home till six, an' by the time you've had your tea an' washed pots it'll be nearly eight.'

'Oh I'll run out an' leave 'em.'

He didn't speak for a time. 'Don't take things to heart so, Michael,' she said. 'Ee, it's startin' rainin'.'

'Let's shelter under them trees.'

They stood under the trees holding hands. He faced her and putting his hands on her shoulders gave her a kiss.

'Darling, I'm out of breath,' she said. 'You don't know your own strength.' He looked out on the rain and filled his lungs, expanding his chest. 'Do you know what a French kiss is?' she asked.

'Yes, I do,' he answered, thinking hard.

'I think it's awful, that sort of thing,' she said. 'Rosie Beardson told some of the girls.'

He was glad of the darkness when he heard the name. 'There are different kinds,' he said. 'What was the kind you heard of?'

She shook her head. He said: 'Come on, Ella, what was it?' He had to keep asking her before she said in a low voice: 'They put tongues in each other's mouths.'

The words struck an image at once, and he felt almost

259

sick in the throat at the thought of couples kissing. He felt a thrust of envy that couples enjoyed something he had never heard of, and he was put out that an ignorant girl like Rosie should know of something denied his learned mind. The tongues, wet, thick and fleshy, put out into each other's mouths. What other things were there he didn't know of? Did they have one tongue over the top of another? Sin had such an ugly taste that it could be recognised at once by the conscience. French kissing was a sin.

'I've heard of that way of kissing,' he said 'and others beside it.'

She didn't ask what they were. 'The rain's coming through,' she said. 'Shall we be goin', sweetheart?'

'Yes, ma chérie . . .' Sweetheart. My cherry. Cherished, French—but she doesn't know it. Acushla machree, the vein of my heart. Sounds a bit sticky to me. My love, my treasure, my brightness . . . funny, they've got no love words in Towlton. Cock, chick, chucks. Close the door softly, says Mother. Shut dur! says Missis Duckworth. All boils down to the same thing in the long run.

They walked off in the rain to the tram stop.

'I've a good idea about tomorrow,' said Ella. 'Supposin' you meet me on my way home from work?'

'Where?'

'At the corner of the churchyard.'

'Suppose somebody sees me?'

'Suppose they do? They won't know who you're waiting for.'

'But you'll have to go straight home after, won't you?'

'Not straight away. It's Bonfire Plot night, so I can pretend I was looking at the fires.'

'I don' feel too happy about that. Wouldn't it be better if we met later?'

She turned and kissed him. 'It's my first day in the cardroom' she said. 'I'll want to see you before anybody else.'

'All right, Ella, then, I'll meet you. Just near the churchyard. What time?'

'About twenty-five to six. It'll be dark, yu' know, so I'll

260

watch out for you. Ee, you're gettin' soppin' wet through, Michael. Be sure to dry your head when you get in.'

The wet Sunday evening streets were dark and deserted, and they walked almost to the street corner together. They kissed good-night. 'Don't forget, dearest,' she said, 'outside the churchyard.' He watched her run down the street and into the Sharley home. He thought of her entering the house where her gossiping mother would be, the surly father, the brother who thought a nimbus was a frying-pan; she, Ella, would have to make herself at home amongst such people. The wanton unsuitability of it was almost more than he could stand, and he felt a sick taste at the idea. Then, glad of the wetness in the air, he walked slowly home himself.

'Urra what the hell's blue blazes was you doin' out in the pourin' dreebin' rain?' shouted his father. He looked coldly at the man's face, savage with sudden temper, and then went quietly into the dark kitchen and up the stairs to the back bedroom.

He heard his mother come softly up after him with a towel and matches. She lit the candle and handed him the towel. 'Is he going to work?' he asked.

'Sure I'd hardly think so,' she said, 'a night like this.'

'The divil shoot an' double shoot him,' he said.

'Dry your head, agraw,' she said. 'Look at the two cheeks on you like two apples after the rain, the Lord spare you.' She kissed him and went quietly down the stairs. He took off his clothes and began to exercise. He made up his mind to do the knees bend one hundred and fifty times without stopping. When he had it done he felt better. Then he rubbed himself harder with the towel and did some Swedish drill. Next he did trunk lifting from the ground. For every exercise he made a mental note before starting, and he never gave up until he had reached the number he had set for himself. At times he almost collapsed, but he wouldn't give in. He ended with deep-breathing exercises before the window. Then he knelt and said his night prayers: a decade of the rosary and, since it was November, the *De Profundis* for the souls in purgatory. Then he put his shirt on and went

into bed. His mother came up quietly, bringing him a mug
of tea and a plate with three mutton sandwiches.

'Is that one as nasty as when I came in?' he asked.

'Ah sure it's the nerves, agraw,' she said, 'with the work
an' the worry an' one thing and another, the Lord help us.'
She said it in a simple way that took away any bitter feeling
he might have had to speak against him. The French kiss
seemed a bit silly when he came to think of it.

At twenty minutes past five he was standing at the corner
of the churchyard looking up at the lighted windows of the
Wild Goose Mill. He could see the moving shadows of
women on the windowpanes, and of pulleys and straps, and
he thought of Ella inside, and wondered how she would be
after her day's work. He went for a walk round the churchyard, and when he heard the half-past-five buzzer blow he
went back to the corner. Already a flow of rapidly moving
figures was coming out into the street. He withdrew a pace
from the corner, so that the throng went by without notic-
ing him. He watched for Ella. There was no sign of her in
the first rush, and he was afraid something had happened,
when he saw her passing under the lamp-post thirty yards
away. He had expected to see her coming alone to him, but
she was amongst a bunch of girls, all laughing and chatting
away. He was nervous, wondering what she would do and
what he could do. He stayed there, in spite of an urge to get
out of the way. He watched her. He saw her glance in his
direction, but a girl was telling her something, and though
he was sure she had seen him, yet she made no sign. Suddenly they all burst out laughing. He flushed in the darkness.
Then he watched her, watched unbelievingly as she went
on, went on with the crowd of women workers, her slight
familiar figure gone from sight amongst them.

Did she not see me? Oh surely she did. Why did they
laugh like that? Could they have laughed at me? He
couldn't bear to stand at the corner another moment, and he
hurried off, finding himself walking in the direction of St

Stephen's church. Were they laughing at me?—he flushed to the rims of his eyes at the thought. Had she said anything about him?

His knees rested on the hard kneeling-board and the panic and fears went. God, God, God. Holy Mary, Mother of God, Holy Mary, Mother of God, Jesus, Jesus, Jesus, Sweet Heart of Jesus. It was dark except for the flicker of three candles and two small faraway lights. You always come running back to Me, my son, when the world hurts you. Why do you think I let it hurt you? Pray, pray, pray. He knelt for a long time, letting the comfort seep into him, and then he rose stiffly to his feet and went out.

The dark dampish night air was tinged everywhere with the throaty odour of new smoke, the acrid cane smoke from old skips, the sweet smoke from burning branches and old tree trunks, and the moist smoke from old smouldering straw mattresses. Almost every back street had its fire, and some had two or three fires, with the figures of men and boys in the foreground, calling out and waving fireworks, with girls screaming and laughing, and back in the shadows the women talking. He walked from fire to fire, half hoping to see Ella, feeling lonely and not belonging, yet glad that he was free and could move faithlessly from one group to another, watching the biggest rockets and hearing the loudest bangs, and then going on, giving nothing and secretly taking all there was to take.

She might be standing at the churchyard corner, he thought, and he made his way there. There was someone standing there, it seemed to him, and he hurried along, but when he got there it was nothing, nothing but some image that had come to his eyes. He felt a rising in his throat at the disappointment. He turned back towards home. Nobody loves me. Folk joke at truth when they say that and laugh. It's just how it feels inside me. Nobody. He reached the Dirt, where the lads had a fire burning. I'll keep away—it's not them I want. But for all that he drew nearer.

'Hy, Micky, Micky.' He turned and saw Ben Shilliton handing him something. 'A roasted spud. Here—here tha

263

art.' He took the hot potato and jingled it from hand to hand. The other lads were gathered about, shouting and eating. He heard Spadger Chadwick's voice: 'Our old chap used allus say, "Keep a full belly an' warm feet an' tha'll not hurt much".'

In spite of himself he felt the pain lifting, and looking round at the faces in the firelight he began to smile to himself, and it struck him that against the red glow of open fires and the raised voices, the rows of cottages looked oddly dark and subdued. Then he took a bite of the potato. The flavour of its burnt crust filled his mouth, until his teeth reached the hard middle, and then he got a full potato taste, saltless and raw, that was unpleasant for a time, until he had chewed taste into it, and began to enjoy it. Spadger's dad was right—full belly and warm feet. Sod love.

CHAPTER FIVE

Love Hurts

'Willieen! Willieen agraw! 'tis after seven.' He heard the mother's whispered call from the bottom of the stairs, and then Willie beside him stirred, 'Righto, mother, he gave a throaty answer, 'comin'.'

'Then do,' she said, 'that's the fourth time I'm after callin' you.'

'Didn't I say I was comin'!' said Willie.

The daze of sleep and dreams went from him at the sound of the voices, and at once the thought of Ella came. The image of her had been poised there every day and night for the weeks since he had last seen her—a thing put there by the mind and it seemed to soothe the heart; grey hunger. A hunger full of long pale pain. She'll be just waking now. I wonder did she dream of me? I wonder are her first thoughts of me in the way mine are of her? Her face'll be smooth and sleepy after the night and her hair untidy as she gets out of bed, takes off her nightie or happen one of her dad's old shirts and starts dressing herself modestly in the darkness and kneels and says her morning prayers before going downstairs.

He stopped his thoughts as he felt Willie move, scrape a match on the box, light the candle, and then get out of bed with a long yawn, stand up in his shirt at the side of the bed, yawn again and scratch his head noisily. With half-closed eyes turned to the wall he listened, and felt the pause as Willie put the cigarette-butt between his lips and lit it at the candle flame, taking one deep wincing drag at it and closing his throat on the lungful of tobacco smoke. He was impatient for him to go, so that he could relax his legs across the bed and think of Ella, and be free from the male presence of his brother, for of late the odour of him, of iron and smoke and manhood had become nauseous. He felt him pulling on his trousers and overalls, sitting back on the bed to put on his socks, slinging his braces over his shoulders, and even humming a tune after a second pull at the cigarette, and departing in his stockinged feet, clomping softly down the stairs, candle in hand, and leaving him alone in the morning darkness. At that he eased and stretched, stiffening his lower limbs across the bed, easing outward with a slight touch his genitals from their clammy all-night hold at his crutch, allowed a prayer to pass through his mind and then he thought of Ella.

Images of her and talk with her scurried through his mind. He heard a buzzer bugle forth, falling away to a wail as four or five other buzzers joined in the signal. Half-past seven—she'll just be going off. Perhaps I'd see her if I went to the window. He got up and tiptoed barefoot in his shirt into the empty front bedroom. A street lamp sent a piece of light into the room, and he went over to the window and peeped down from behind the curtain into the misty street. He heard clogs and voices. The street went quiet, and then he heard clogs hurrying along, and a voice called:

'Maggie! Maggie!' His heart gave a twist as he heard it —it was her voice, but it was strange.

'Be walkin' on, Ella luv, I'll catch you up.' *Ella, Ella, Ella,* he wanted to pull the window up and stick his head out and call to her—he couldn't. Was she walking slower? Did she look up? He waited and listened, his face suffused and his heart thumping heavily. The sound of the clogs went on and he listened hard to catch every echo—then the swift clatter of Maggie Duckworth's clogs burst upon him. He went back to the other room, the thought of her having risen so thick and intense that he felt faintly sick in the throat. 'Oh my God I offer Thee the prayers, works and sufferings of this day . . .' Pain, heart, pain, heart. It hurts.

It would make the father cranky if he went downstairs early, and he knew he would feel depressed later if he went back into the bed that had once been left, so he lay himself back on the top of the bed, pulled the front of his shirt down and between his legs, and began a pedalling exercise. Next he put on his trousers and took off his shirt and did some arm exercises, and then he opened the window wider to do his deep breathing. The cold damp air chilled him a little, but he continued to fill his lungs, lifting his arms at the same time. ' Art makin' thy will? ' He drew back when he heard the woman's voice in a backyard opposite. ' Other folk have business to do as well as thee.' Listening he heard a grunt, a tearing of paper and a rustling, a shuffling of clogs, and then a man's slow footsteps down a backyard. ' It's about time too,' said the woman. ' I were about to fetch you the oil-can,' and then her feet pattered up the yard. I'd hate to follow someone and have the warm seat after them, he thought, unless it was a woman.

He massaged his scalp, did some drill, ankle and wrist exercises, and then the buzzer sounded. Quarter-to-eight— I'll go down and risk it. At the bottom of the stairs he stopped as the mother came scuttering into the kitchen bearing before her the big iron saucepan of steaming water. With a swing she lifted it and flung the water into a two-handled bath-tin set on the slopstone. ' Curse it, didn't I tell you lave me carry it in? ' called the man from the living-room. ' On the verth o' me oath you wouldn't lave an inch or half-inch of skin on you if that pan slipped.' The man's loud voice made him uneasy, and he paused on the stairs and looked to the mother.

' Is he washin'? ' he whispered. She nodded. He turned to go back upstairs when she called in a surprised voice: ' Are you up, Mickyeen! Arra come in before the fire now that you are.' He followed her in. The father was standing by the table in his pit dirt, taking a drink at a mug of tea.

' Are you down, Mickyeen? ' he said.

' I am, father.'

' The water is ready, siree,' said the mother, putting the man's day shirt and undervest across the open oven door.

' I'll go in then and wash,' said the man, sighing.

' Musha, what's the hurry? ' said the woman.

' I'd be as well get it over,' he said.

267

'Sure maybe you're right,' she said, following the man as far as the middle door, and turning to wink at the boy. 'I think you have everything there,' she said. She waited a moment and then asked: 'Will you be needin' me?'

'Och, I'll manage,' said the man from inside the back kitchen.

'Give a call when you're ready,' she said, 'I'll have the towel warmin' before the fire.'

She closed the door softly and began to whistle whisperingly and jig around the room and the boy relaxed himself and sat down on the rocking-chair, but got up at once, for it was warm and the odour of the coal mine and seat was on it, and it felt unpleasant to him.

'Sit there at the table, agraw,' said the mother, 'an' I'll give you your breakfast quick.'

'I hate to eat without first washin',' he said.

'It's either eatin' now without washin',' she said, 'or waitin' for him an' eatin' under his two hawk's eyes, God forgive me.'

'All right, mother,' he said mildly, sitting at the table.

'Let me put a clean cover on for you,' she said, whisking a newspaper from the bottom of the pile on the corner table by the man's chair, and neatly arranging it over the soiled newspaper already on the table. I suppose that big slob Alfred sat down at the same table as Ella this morning. The awful way nothing fits right in the dam' world. Were Adam and Eve the real cause of it all?

'Thanks,' he said, 'mother.' The clean newspaper made a nice difference. He began to read whilst she scooped the porridge out of the iron pot on the hob, set it before him and put milk and sugar on. *Scene in colliery office. Angry crippled employee strikes foreman. Charge of assault. Foreman reprimanded him for not staying behind to clear up fall of dirt. Defendant said he thought eight hours on one leg down pit was enough. Witness told him he would have to go home for day for not doing as he had been told. Defendant said he had a wife and three children to keep and could not afford to lose a day's work. He turned to leave*

268

office and suddenly struck witness in the eye. Witness seized him and told him to go home for good. Defendant had lost a leg as the result of an accident in the pit when he was sixteen. Magistrates ordered defendant to pay costs, and hoped the colliery company would be sympathetic and take man back on his job.

'Could I have a bit more sugar, mother?' he asked.

'Take it,' she said.

He helped himself to the sugar. Fighting in the mine. Colliers who must choose other battleground. John Pocock and Peter Hutton were each fined ten shillings today for fighting in the drift at the Park mine. Mr A. Hellis who prosecuted said men must find other battleground. Defendants were ordered to pay ten shillings costs for breaking the frame of the Coal Mines Regulations Act.

She moved his plate away, took up a used cup, rinsed it with tea from the smoke-grimed teapot and flung the drops into the ashes, remarking, 'It was only the track of myself was on it.' She grabbed a piece of toast that had slipped from the fork into the fire, blew on it and put margarine on from the packet on the table.

He looked up when a light tap sounded on the door, and it was softly opened and Mrs Chadwick peeped in. The mother pointed to the closed kitchen door, making a movement of a hand upon her face, and at that the visitor entered quietly. 'I've run outa sugar,' she said, bringing out a cup from under her shawl, 'haven't a bit for his breakfast.' She followed the mother to the cupboard, and whispered: 'Can you let me have a bob till tomorrow?—I'll let you have it back afore ten.' He heard the mother dipping into the silver mug and saw her giving the neighbour a friendly thump and wink as she slipped the coin over. 'It's as well you didn't need more,' she said, 'I'm in the same boat myself.'

He caught the woman's eye for the first time as the worried look went from her face. 'Good morning, Mrs Chadwick,' he said, half rising and making a bowing nod.

'Ee, hello, luv,' she said, 'how's your knees an' things? Isn't he gettin' a size!' The worried look came back. 'Master

269

Chadwick's come home jiggered up,' she said. 'The new manager's had clocks put in every room an' he's got to punch his round every hour. It doesn't give him a minute. I've got to get him a packet of Woods an' a fresh laid egg.' She dipped into her skirt. 'Are you havin' a pinch?' she asked the mother, 'go on——' and she held out a snuff tin. 'Here, come on, Micky luv, it'll do you all the good in the world. Nay, left hand not right.' He dipped awkwardly into the tin and put the dark dust to his nostrils; I'll not sniff it up, she won't know. He gave a sneeze. 'There, get it out, luv,' she said.

She crossed beside the mother and whispered into her ear. 'Oh dear me,' said the mother. Mrs Chadwick drew away and grinned. 'What Bessie could see in little Cyril is beyond me,' she said, 'he's not the size of ninepenn'orth of copper an' skens like a basket of whelps.'

'The poor mother'll be upset.'

'Don't you believe it. Her'll be fain to have a chap round the house—an' he gets good money at yon shop. An' Bessie were no chicken.'

A shout from the kitchen sent Mrs Chadwick hurrying to the door. 'Comin',' called the mother, snatching a towel from the chair before the fire.

'I'll see you later, ma'am,' she whispered. Mrs Chadwick turned at the door and smiled at him. 'Toodle'oo, Micky,' she said. He got up from the table. Cyril, the lodger, has put Bessie Chamley in the family way. The mother came back for the undervest and shirt from the oven door. He heard the man grumbling in the kitchen.

'Frank Hall was bloody right,' he said when he came into the living-room. 'I'm twice as well since I stopped the big wash. "The hot water draws all the strength out of you," he said. The bloody man's right. All that washin' I was doin' wasn't leavin' me with a stitch of strength.'

'Well now that the word's drawn from me,' said the mother, 'I never liked to see you slotherin' away at all that steamin' water. I felt there could be no good in it.'

'Arra doesn't it stand to flamin' reason?' said the man

270

loudly, staring the boy in the eye. 'Wouldn't all that hot water take the bloody life from a horse—if you'd get a right horse near it! "Hot water will draw the nature out of a wool vest," said Frank Hall, 'so why wouldn't it draw the strength out of a man?'

I wish he'd take his two eyes off me, thought the boy. 'I must have been off my bloody nut,' said the man. The last word came oddly to the boy from the lips of his father, and caused a tickle of a grin to come to him.

'Was that Chadwick rap borrowin' again?' asked the man sharply. He saw me then, thought the boy, he's quicker than you'd think.

'Bringing back,' answered the mother calmly, 'a cup of sugar I let her have yesterday.'

'Some bloody bringin' back!' said the man.

The boy went softly into the kitchen. He went up against the slopstone, and as he made to turn the tap a stab of irritated thought rose in him, for the thin tap pressed hard into the soft palm flesh below his thumb, and didn't budge. He picked up the scrubbing brush to knock it loose. Why does that old fool always have to turn it off so hard? The water spouted out and splashed on to his shirt and trousers. How I hate this damn daft bloody daft house! If only they'd take you into the Navy at thirteen.

'Here's a taste of warm water for you, avic,' whispered the mother at his elbow.

He shook his head, the temper disappearing at the soft sound of her voice.

'I like the cold better, mother,' he said. The warm some-how took the pleasure out of the cold, and there wasn't enough of it for a real warm wash.

'Sure won't that cold cut you to the heart?' she said, withdrawing.

He put his face under the tap and rubbed away at his cheeks and forehead. The cold bitterness of the water felt good, and soon he felt his blood beating it and turning it warm, so it seemed. Then he reached out and felt for the soap. Blast it—a new block. The hard-edged half-pound

271

block of soap was difficult to hold, and it yielded no lather when he rubbed it against his palm. It annoyed him to be slowed up in his washing movements by the heavy clumsy block, and as he felt his arms going cold he began to rub the soap on to his face. Then with a quick coaxing he managed to get a lather. He could hear someone shouting and he shut the tap off and listened. 'Don't be all day there, Mickyeen,' called the father, 'that bloody ould stone floor would draw the life from a horse, the Lord save us.' He rinsed himself under the tap and felt for the roller towel on the door.

He gave a quick glance up at the windows opposite, and seeing no one he began to spar around the yard, his sleeves rolled up. He made furious swings and punches as he shadow-boxed around. That wind is lovely—seems to be coming straight from the North Pole to our backyard. I wish I went to one of those schools where you had to learn to box. Learn to drive a horse and clean it. Even to drive a car. You could be learning all day long. Even just learning to tie knots. Any lad who could tie a few knots would always have a crowd round watching him. Just think of all the time wasted, lads walking about with their hands in their pockets when they could be learning something useful. A few foreign words, say, or how to use a chisel, or the most scientific way of cleaning windows. It sounds daft, but you'd never be out of work. That's the half-past-eight buzzer —I'd better put a move on.

He was fastening the stiff winged holes of his celluloid collar over the stud when the father looked up from his paper.

'The price of bread goin' up a penny the two-poun' loaf,' he said. 'I'd drown every bloody curraghbuck of a politician, the Lord toast them in hell!' the mother gave a sighing and clicking of the tongue. 'Arra amn't I right?' said the man. 'On me oath the people here are mad—nothin' on their minds but bloody ould football.'

The price of bread is going up and ladies' underwear is coming down—now we men must examine these things. That's what a comedian said one night at the Grand. Very

272

clever when you come to think of it. I wonder who makes them all up? The old chap 'ud go mad if he knew what was on my mind. Funny how you can think something and a hundred folk with their eyes open watching you wouldn't know the least thing about it. It's a sin in a way, I suppose. Bad thoughts. 'I think I'll be off.' He's glad to get rid of me, I can see that.

The mother kissed him goodbye just inside the door and he went out into the morning street. That's a relief that I stopped kissing the old man back there; one trial over at least. His mouth was always so strange and bristly. It's very hard to change a thing once you start, or to start a thing again once you stop. He turned at the street corner and waved quickly back to the mother at the door. It's time I stopped that too. Though I'd hate to hurt her feelings and not turn. But the chaps 'ud think you a bit soft if they saw you. And I did miss her one day that something stopped her from coming. It felt a bit empty. But if you knew she wasn't coming you wouldn't miss her the same.

With a purposeful air he strode past the intimate street corners and gable-ends, on the watch for an inclination to slow up, dawdle and dream. Folk stare if you go slow, but they take no notice if you step it out. I must get hold of those corks. His right hand felt into a pocket and took hold of the two large corks. He squeezed hard at one. I've got to get one into my left hand without folk seeing me. That right arm muscle is getting too big for the left. I'll slip a cork from my right to my left hand when I'm taking the turning at Tom Street, then folk won't see me. I might as well get a couple of Hail Mary's in whilst I'm waiting. Grace always comes in useful.

Nearing the corner he began to punch his left palm with his right fist. Good idea that—I can swop the cork easier that way. Turning the corner he slipped the cork into the left palm. Done it; now I can start my exercises. Suddenly he was aware of a woman in his path coming down Tom Street. Her and me alone in the street, walls all round. The red-faced strooleen with a streese from lug to lug. From her

heavy oily clogs rose up two fat bandy legs in black ribbed
stockings, and the old open-fronted coat showed a dark blue
cotton skirt, oily and shiny, and a big belly and heavy upstairs tilting forward as she walked. Bandy Bella. Folk say
her father . . . Nay, never! It don't stand thinking about—
living in the same world. Then don't think about it. But
that's what they say. What—feyther an' douter? Hell for
certain for both of them—if it's so. What folk risk for That!
I'll stick to rum-an'-butter toffee an' comics when I'm a
chap. Say I'm earning four quid a week I could buy every
comic going on Friday night an' a couple o' pound of toffee.
Cheaper an' safer. Four ounces of blood to make one ounce
of that precious fluid.

'Ello, luv,' she said, her grin opening wider and her
weakly brown eyes smiling larger.

' 'Ello!'

I should have said ' ma'am '—or should I? She's only
twenty-eight and she's not wed. I've gone red. The corner
of his eye caught the fat figure waddling by. I wonder did
she spot me at the corks? What happened to that couple of
Hail Mary's I started? I remember getting up to *thy womb*.
It's a funny thing but I don't remember ever once in all my
life concentrating on a Hail Mary past the *thy womb, Jesus,*
without something sticking its nose in. I'll try again and
squeeze the cork at the same time. Develop body and soul
—no, soul and body—at one and the same time. Grow up
to be the Perfect Man. Tip the scales at one hundred and
eighty pounds, standing five feet eleven-and-a-half inches in
the stockinged feet, chest forty-two normal, forty-eight ex-
panded. *Mens sana in corpore sano.*

At Back Martha Street his step slowed for a moment as
he asked something in his mind, was it his turn to go the
Back Martha Street way to school. Over the years he had
accustomed himself to three different routes to and from
school, and these he varied according to the day and the
time of day, and whether he was going to school or coming
home from school. On Monday mornings he invariably went
straight down Derbyshire Street, but on Fridays he never
274

even gave a thought to going that way. The reason was that the fish shop was in full display on Fridays, with boxes of herrings and other fish right out on the pavement, with melting ice oozing through the box joints and creeping across the pavement, and the open window hung with enormous fish bodies that gave off a fish smell that could make him sick to the stomach.

When he went to school along Derbyshire Street at mornings there was a woman down on her knees mopping the dentist's doorstep, and sometimes when she was leaning forward and you glanced over the rails you got a full look of the fat white part at the back of her leg. He never went Derbyshire Street way going to school after dinner, for the street looked somehow tired after all the feet of the factory folk walking over it. But he nearly always went home that way in the afternoon, for then it fitted into his mood. Back streets were best going back home after a morning in school, because the quiet gave you time to think. The brewery way was good some mornings because the carters would be out with their big drayhorses, and it was nice passing them, and Back Martha Street was a good way going back to school at dinner-time because it was nice to look into the little foundry and watch the men playing cards round a bench and listen to their talk.

There were other reasons, such as the lads one met along the different routes, and the other smells one encountered— the brewery when the hops were boiling up—and the nice bright gable-ends along Back Martha Street, and streets that smelled funny. But he could never think the reasons out for going any special way, and he relied wholly on the inner prompting which said, This way, or Not this way. In fact, if he tried to think out which way to go he could never come to a conclusion. He had only to think of the woman mopping the dentist's doorstep and he knew at once that it was a sin to go that way and have bad thoughts, so that he would then go another way, and it always worked out wrong. This thing had to prompt him without his thinking, and then he always felt safe.

275

After passing Back Martha Street he listened for the voice of the thing which already would have sensed the day and its colour, and the colour of his thought and which would advise him the way to go, and when it didn't speak—as occasionally happened—he crossed Derbyshire Street and went over the brewery ground : I'll be able to exercise with my corks better this way. Half-way across the brewery ground he had a feeling that he hadn't come the right way, and he turned to the left and went down Back Howbert Street. Suddenly he spotted a figure ahead, playing with a ball. Instantly he dropped the corks into his pockets.

' Howgo, Chey,' he called.

Charlie Criddle didn't speak, but caught the ball and approached him. ' " The sledge has withered from the lake ",' he spoke dreamily, ' " an' no brids sing ".'

' The *sedge*, Chey,' he said quickly. ' What the heck's the sledge ? '

' Sedge ? I know what a sledge is—but what the flappin' Nora is a sedge ? '

' Summat on a lake, Chey.'

' Don't be fawse, Mike, it don't become thee. If tha goes round contradictin' folk tha should first know what tha'rt talkin' about.'

' Listen, Chey, a sedge is summat as withers.'

' Scorn withers—is that a sedge ? Tha'rt gettin' all billoxed up an' tha knows it. Did ta hear about that chap in the paper as poisoned his wife with a razor ? '

' Aye, he gave her arsenic.'

' An' no brids sing. An' no brids sing. I were sayin' that all night long, Mike. It hath me infatuated. What comes after " I made a garland for her head " ? '

' " And bracelets too, and fragrant zone——" '

' Oh Christ aye ! " She looked at me as she did love. And made sweet moan." I were cudgitatin' like mad over that bit in bed. I'd have given a fortune to know it. Aye, an' made sweet moan, an' made sweet moan. An' no brids sing, an' no brids sing. An' gave her arse a nick. Who told thee, Mike ? '

276

' It's hairs on, Chey.'

' Ready? ' yelled Charlie, flinging the ball into the air. They both raced after it, and then they began kicking it along the street on the way to school. Charlie stopped three times along the way to turn his head upwards and cry out : ' " And made sweet moan. And made sweet moan." ' The last time he called out : ' That'll plague me tonight, Mike. I can feel it in my veins. " And made sweet moan." '

CHAPTER SIX

A Mucky Doffer

HE SEARCHED EAGERLY along the books on the public library shelf for the name 'Curwood'. There was none, and he felt depressed. Once I read a book I like I hate turning to another author. He opened a number of books, until in one his eye caught the line: '*A vast expanse of virgin snow, white and unbroken, stretched as far as the eye could see.*' That'll do nicely. Deserts, great prairies, glaciers, uncharted oceans—a book to do with anything like that suits me. I can't stand anything to do with pets and kids, or history. I'll have a nice read before I go to Benediction. He walked along the warm streets. June. I'll be fourteen in a week's time. He counted the number of steps he could hold a deep breath. Warm evenings make me think of Ella. I hope I see her walking past the window when I get in, or happen in the street. It makes me go red but it breaks my thoughts up.

Willie was just wheeling his bicycle out the back way.

'Wouldn't it be better, agraw,' said the mother, 'for you to have a nice evening's rest after your long day, instead of going off ridin' the bike now?'

'We're only havin' a spin round Preston,' said Willie.

'That's a great lovely warm evenin',' said the mother, 'but there's a touch of a breeze just the same.'

'Sure you'd think you were back home, Mickyeen,' said Willie, 'back in the dear old bog.'

'Musha that one hasn't the grain of nature, Mickyeen,' she said.

'Do you think we'll ever go back?'

'Well we're goin' on the bikes,' said Willie, 'this June holidays——'

'If God spares ye the health,' said the mother. 'But don't let anyone belongin' us see you in them short trousers.'

278

'It's in them they'll see me,' said Willie, 'an' no shirt.'

'Sure Aunt Kate would reel with joy at the sight of you, surely,' said the mother, 'shirtless or not.'

Willie went off whistling, after giving the mother a kiss. He kissed her too and then sat down on the back doorstep and opened his book.

'I'm a bit worried about your father,' she said. 'He went off at two o'clock an' isn't back yet.'

'Where is he, mother?'

She lowered her voice within the kitchen. 'Gone to the Lilworth pictures,' she said.

'Maybe he stopped for a drink on the way back,' he said.

'God save us, but he hasn't a penny,' she said, 'since he got the ould nystagmus. It's his medical examination tomorrow, an' watchin' the ould pictures sets his eyes ahakin' away, an' the pit doctor won't sign him off then.'

'Would he be better back at work, mother,' he said, 'with the little compensation he gets?'

'He's dyin' to go back,' she said, 'an' it's more agony to watch the pictures for an hour for him than do a day's work. But he's afraid they'll sack him whilst the pit is slack.' Maybe he's blinded altogether—I wonder will I go? I have a feelin' he'll not be long now.

I love seeing a good picture I do, but I can't go, and he hates 'um, but he has to go to make his eyes bad. He'll be sitting there in the front seat—that makes 'um worse. By right he's frauding, and if he were found out I'll bet he could get sent to prison. But they couldn't send us.

'Oh thank God,' said the mother, 'he's here now.'

At once he stood up and put the book away. Willpower. He liked to stop whistling in the middle of a tune, just to test his willpower—then he would offer the pleasure he had missed to God.

The father came into the house quietly. 'Oh you're back then,' said the mother. 'Will you have a supeen of tea before the meal?'

'All I want altogether,' he said softly, 'is a drink of tea. How are you, Mickyeen?'

279

'Well, father,' he said. He went to the dresser and took up the evening newspaper. 'Will you have the paper, father?'

'The flamin' pictures have the sight driven entirely from my two eyes,' said the man.

'God save us,' said the mother, 'you're killed.'

He could sense the man wanted him out of the way. I suppose he can't talk with me there. He looks a bit helpless sitting there without the newspaper at him. How a chap can be that crazy about newspapers I do not know. Look at the money he'd save if he'd only get books from the library. He'll not say much about the pictures till I've gone. I'll wash. When he came out of the kitchen he said: 'I'll be goin', mother.'

'Urra sit down,' said the father mildly.

'I'm going to Confession, father,' he said, 'tomorrow's the first Friday.'

'God give you the health,' said the man.

'God watch you,' said the mother.

He went out, glad to get away. They think I'm holy, but if they knew some of the things that go through my mind! Folk sitting at their doors—you can see it's Thursday. It always has a nice feeling the day before pay day. They never sit out on a Monday. In Back Greenley Street his eye spotted a woman on a box talking to another woman and feeding a baby at her breast. Mother, what's that woman doing? Stop looking—her's only feeding her baby. Mother, will it eat all that?'

The soft and distant touch of the breeze as he reached the open piece of dirt set a longing feeling going inside him. He didn't know what it was he longed for, except that it was something that seemed to be beyond the paved street and houses and factories. It made him feel like crying.

'Howgo, Michael!'

He turned and saw Herbert Duckworth carrying a kite. It was another high blue kite, and it looked like the tall sail of a ship up above Herbert. He seems to have shrunk since he started work in the mill.

'Howdo, Herbert,' he said warmly. 'Ee, what a beauty!'

'She aren't too bad,' said Herbert, raising it aloft. Under his arm he hugged an enormous reel of factory banding. 'I've had the paper ordered a week—it only came in today.'

'Where are you takin' her to get her up, Herbert?'

Herbert looked up at the Wild Goose chimney. 'There might be just enough wind to get her up from The Dirt,' he said, watching the smoke roll quietly away into the distant sky.

'It won't give you much runnin' space, Herbert,' he said.

'If I get a nice puff o' wind,' said Herbert, 'she'll rise. Like to toss her for me, Michael?'

'Yes, Herbert.'

He took the kite nervously.

'Hold a tick,' said Herbert, 'whilst I check the tailin'.' Herbert stretched the long tail out on the pavement, tightening the screws of paper along it. Then he took a big red dinner hanky from his pocket and tied it to the end of the tail. Next he examined the crossband. Then he rolled up the tail. 'I fancy she'll do, Michael. Walk back as far as Wright's midden, an' I'll give thee a wave of my hand when I want her up.'

He walked along, bearing the big blue kite, shimmering and sighing in his hands. At the midden he turned and held it at the base of the standard, whilst Herbert pulled the string fairly taut. It's going to be a tricky toss-up. I hope I don't make a mess of it. They stood facing each other at a distance of a hundred yards. My arm's aching. Is there never going to be a breeze? I'll be late for Benediction. Suddenly Herbert raised his hand and called: 'Right!'

He pushed the kite forcefully into the air, just as the string went tight. The kite rose with a swish, as though an outpouring of breath left its body. It rose swiftly with the breeze and Herbert's quick dash. It went high above the housetops at one go, and then it gave a wild swing to the left, and looked as though it would duck downwards and smash itself on the pavement. He expected to see Herbert relax the tension and allow the kite to sink to the ground, but instead he gave it the breeze, and made it swing as much as it could, until it had either to rise or be smashed. The kite gave a squirm and rose. It went up higher and faster.

'Good lad, Herbert!' he called, running to him.

'Her's pullin' a bit to the left,' said Herbert critically, 'but her's big enough an' her'll have to take it. I can't bring her in now. Her's a shade light in the tailin' too, but her'll steady once her gets up there.' His blue eyes had become light and large.

'I'll see you later, Herbert,' he said.

The women's voices at church eased a little his cut-off pain. In between prayers and Benediction they sang a hymn, and as it was June and the month of the Sacred Heart they sang: *To Jesus' Heart All Burning*. He listened waiting for the chorus: 'Whilst Ages course along, Blessed be with loudest song,' because in that part something in their voices was released, and a high sweet softness filled the church when they came to it. After Benediction he went to Confession. He felt lightened after it and went walking home slowly in the mild light of evening.

Herbert was standing alone in the street holding the kite string. 'How did you get it here, Herbert?' he asked. Herbert said: 'I went up Back Greenley Street an' got Spadger to hold on whilst I brought the bandin' through the entry. They all said it 'ud drop or else the bandin' would break. They were all wrong.'

'Where are they?'

'Gone for a walk up the Long Brook.'

He looked up along the curved string. Herbert said: 'Can tha see it?'

'Aye, but only just,' he said. The massive reel of white factory string was now down to an inch thickness.

'Still letting off, Herbert?' he asked.

'Aye, Michael,' he said, 'she's got to go out of sight.'

He stood beside Herbert and watched. 'She's out of sight, Herbert,' he said. 'I can't see a speck of her.'

'We'll just give her an extra yard,' said Herbert, and then he held the stick.

282

There was the reel of string, wound skilfully on a heavy round stick, held in Herbert's thin hands, and from it the string ran in a curve, up over Back Greenley Street, over Holt's factory, and then right beyond all factories and chimneys, away out of sight in the distant evening sky.

' Herbert! Herbert!' one of his sisters was calling from the doorstep.

' I've got to go to the outdoor licence for my dad's allowance,' said Herbert. ' Michael, would tha hold on till I come back? '

' Hold the kite, Herbert? '

' Aye, she'll be all right. Steady as an eagle, but pullin'. Just hold on an' I'll be back in five minutes.'

He took the stick of string from Herbert and held it. It was a strange sensation to feel the pull of the kite. He looked along the string that went up into the sky and disappeared. It's like there was someone up there pulling at you from another world. It's a lovely wonderful feeling to feel this pull come down to you in the street on a warm evening. He felt someone coming near him and he half-turned. It was Ella Sharley in oily blue factory pinafore. At the sight of her something seemed to burst out of place inside at his heart. He felt a sudden weakness take hold of his four limbs. And as she drew up beside him a frightening flush of blood raced up his chest and throat and up all over his face and about his head. He held hard to the string of the kite.

' Hello, Michael,' she said.

' Hello, Ella,' he said, hurriedly covering over in his ears the echo of her voice, for fear the distraction would show on his face.

' I'm just holdin' Herbert's kite for him till he comes back. He's gone to the off-licence for his dad's allowance. He asked me to hold it.'

They stood together without looking at each other, both staring up along the curve of string that went up into the sky.

' Is it pullin' hard? ' she said.

' Yes, tidy hard,' he said. My voice sounds different from

hers. 'Would—d'you want to feel at how it's pullin'?'

'If you'll hold with me,' she said.

'All right,' he said, 'I'll hold wi' you!'

She put out her hand. It was a bit pale and oily and the glow was gone from the skin. He held out to her the stick with the string on it.

'You'll have to hold,' he said.

'Not by myself,' she said. 'I'm frightened of. It might get away.'

'I'll hold with you,' he said.

Her two factory hands held the round smooth ends of the winding-on stick, and his short hands gripped it together with hers. They neither spoke nor looked at each other, but far away over housetops and beyond the factories and the high chimneys. Gradually he began to smell the cardroom sweat from her, the smell of cotton and humid warmth dried on her, and the smell of oil and secret womanhood. Then he felt a movement of her face, and his eye saw the mouth shut tight on her and a wet tear on her face.

'Why did you never meet me?' she said.

'I did. It was you.' She didn't speak and he went on: 'Yes, on Bonfire Plot night—you went by with all the girls laughing. I was there at the corner of the churchyard.'

'I came back and you weren't there,' she whispered, still looking to the sky. 'I had to go on with them so they wouldn't know. I turned back at Wire's greengrocer's and waited. I waited till twenty-five to seven.'

'Oh Ella! You went by, didn't you——?'

'I looked for you every night at that corner.'

'How did I know, Ella?'

'You could have easily seen me coming from work—I couldn't see you coming from school.'

'I saw you talking to a boy in the Lilworth one night——'

'Did you speak to me?'

'No.'

'No. I'm a mucky doffer, aren't I?'

'Ella! Ella!'

'You wouldn't want a smelly doffer.'

284

'Ella, don't. Herbert's comin'.'

'I can see, an' I don't bloodywell care—' She took her hands from the stick and his, and he held the kite by the string, and whispered: 'Ella! Ella!' But she went up the street. He could sense her presence on the spot where she had stood: a smelly doffer.

'How's she been pullin,' Michael?' asked Herbert, taking over the kite and giving the string a few tugs.

'Strong,' he said, 'her's been pullin' strong. Can tha feel them flecks o' rain, Herbert?'

'Aye, I thought I did feel a drop then.'

'Tha'd better pull in then, eh?'

Herbert looked at the winding-on stick. 'I don't like havin' a kite up,' he said, 'without goin' bare stick.'

'You're not lettin' more off, Herbert?' he asked.

Already Herbert was giving the kite more string.

'Aye,' he said, 'I don't reckon to let my kite up without I give it all the bandin' I've got. It's half-hearted. An' watch it tak' it!' The string was moving swiftly through his hand. Every few seconds he stopped and gave a feeling tug at the kite string. The kite itself was completely out of sight. He stared at Herbert: what faith made him send his great kite even farther into the unknown sky? 'Only a few more yards,' said Herbert, 'bare stick an' then wind in.'

He looked down at the almost emptied stick jiggling on the ground as Herbert allowed the string to pass outward through his hands.

'Almost bare stick, Herbert,' he said. He wanted to see the stick rise from the ground, when suddenly he saw the end of the string leave the stick and rise. The string—grab it!' he screamed.

Herbert made a snatch at the departing string and just missed. They both darted after it as it was pulled swiftly along the pavement, stamping on it with their clogs. They missed it, and ran to the wall of Back Greenley Street, and Herbert struck with his flat hand against the wall to imprison the moving wisp of string. For one moment he held it but then it pulled itself free. He made a grab after Herbert as he saw it rise up the side of the house. It was too late. The string went over the house and disappeared. It'll be falling, falling, falling, far far away. Falling like a great broken bird, far from the street. Herbert's face was strained and grey.

'Well, that's the last I'll ever see of that, Michael.'

'Ee, I'm sorry, Herbert,' he said 'I saw it come up an' I shouted.'

'I'll never understand how that string weren't tied on to the winding-on stick,' said Herbert. 'I've never known it. It's the first thing I do—tie it on. I must have forgot.' He went back and picked up the smooth black stick. 'Here, Michael,' he said, 'that's a good winding-on stick. Thee have it.'

'Ta, Herbert.'

Herbert looked once more upward and beyond the catories to the faraway empty evening sky. 'I wonder,' he said calmly, 'where she fell?'

'Oh, o'er the Pennine Chain, Herbert,' he said. 'Aye, I'll bet, an' beyond.'

'Her pulled a bit to the left,' Herbert said, 'but I wouldn't ha' altered her.' They looked up the street and saw the lads coming down after their walk. The chairs had all gone in and no one had noticed the incident. Herbert said: 'Oh, Michael—'

'Aye, Herbert?'

'Say naught about it.'

'Not a word, Herbert, if tha doesn't want me to.'

'Ta. Well, I'll be goin' in.'

'So will I.'

'Goodnight, Michael.'

'Goodnight, Herbert. An' ta for the stick.'

'Tha'rt welcome, old butty. Goodnight.'

'Goodnight, Herbert.'

CHAPTER SEVEN

School-leaving Day

—

'I WAS TALKING to George Jenkinson down pit last night,' said the father, pausing to stare at the mother and the boy. He waited, the mug of tea in one hand and the newspaper in the other, for the woman to say something. The newly-washed face of the father in the morning looked oddly sane to him, and the eyes such a clean blue and so quick to see, that he felt more uncomfortable than if he had been unwashed.

'Oh, were you now?' said the mother, moving about the room.

'Arra you often heard me speak of the man,' said the father irritably, 'isn't he the under-manager? An' a decenter bloody man than George Jenkinson you wouldn't meet in a day's walk.' He stared at the boy. 'He's a college-educated man,' he said.

The man took a drink of tea, leant back on the rocking-chair, and looked out from the newspaper, opened wide at the middle pages. The two listeners waited for him to speak.

'He was down in our part of the mine over some shot firing. "M'Cloud, you're back then," says he to me. "I am,' says I, "I am, George,"—George everyone calls him—"but," says I, "divil a one of me knows how long I'll stay back."' The man stared hard at the mother, and went silent for a moment to watch her face.

'"Arra why?" says he, "what the hell's on you, talkin' like that?" "Well," says I, "a great many came back after the ould stag eye, George," says I, "but divil a few were let stay more than a fortnight."' His lips drew back in anger. 'The bloody flamers of owners sack nearly every man after he's been off with the nystagmus—for they know well he might have to go off again sometime. That's so they wouldn't have more compensation to pay him, the gets.' It took him some seconds to calm down and go on with the incident. 'He came over to me at that: "There was some of them was no use, M'Cloud," says he, " an' right enough there was nothing for it but they had to go. But listen to me," says he, " as long as there's a job here for me, there's one for you, M'Cloud." '

He stared at them, and then took a hasty sup of tea to hide his emotion. The mother said: 'Isn't that a great thing now!'

'If I never stir out of this chair,' said the man, 'those were his words, " as long as there's a job here for me, there's one for you, M'Cloud." George Jenkinson, the under-manager. That man has a thousand a year.'

The boy waited until the effect of the father's words was dying down, and then he went quietly from the room and into the backyard. He made a leap at a punch-ball hanging from the clothes-line, and hit it with a straight left. It was made up of paper wrapped tightly round a piece of lead, all rammed tightly into an old sock, and when he hit it the ball swung upwards and over the line, and he dodged under and met it coming down on his tensed chest. For a minute he sparred around the yard and then went back into the kitchen. The mother was swilling out the porridge pot at the slopstone.

'Well, agraw,' she said, ' it's a lonesome thought to think this is your last day at the school.'

'It is,' he said sharply, ' an' no job at all got for me.'

'Musha since we managed this long without you workin',' she said, ' we'll manage another week.'

The temper left him. 'It's that folk keep askin' me what I'm startin' at, mother,' he said softly, ' an' I feel such a great big fool when I have to say I don't know.'

'Well that's a queer thing surely,' she said seriously, ' that you could feel you were that.'

He detected the turn of humour in her voice, and he gave her a soft thump on the back. 'There's nothin' on you only streecin' laughin',' he said.

288

'To tell you the truth, my love,' she said, facing up to him, the grey-blue eyes looking at him, and a hand pressing in place her wavy hair that was parted down the middle, 'the tears are near at the thought that this is the last an' final day I'll see you goin' out the door to school.'

'What's that?' called the father from the front room.

'It's Mickyeen's last day at school,' she said, walking in to him.

'Is that so?' said the father. 'Musha the time went quick enough at the heel of the hunt.'

'He's worryin',' said the mother, 'that we haven't work got for him.'

'Arra why bloody worry, man?' asked the father slowly. 'Isn't every day off work another year on your life, the Lord save us.'

'But people do go askin' him—' began the mother.

'Let them bloody ask,' said the father, 'what business is it of theirs? Sure wouldn't they want to know what you ate for your breakfast in this country. I never knew the likes of it. To hell with them! Maybe he could get a nice job as a shopboy—would never need dirty his hands to his dying day, God save us. What have you in mind, Mickyeen?'

'Oh, well, I don't care,' he said, 'I mean I wouldn't mind what it was so long as it wasn't in the mill.'

'Never mind the mill,' said the man,' so long as you keep out of the pit.' 'Well, sure I always thought it was a great place,' said the mother, 'with all the ould guff you had about it.'

He put down the paper and looked at the woman and boy. 'I wouldn't let a bloody flamin' dog belongin' me go down a pit,' he said savagely. 'No, not a poor flamin' innocent dog.' He turned again to the paper, and was silent for a moment, then he looked up and said: 'Did ye hear what Marshall Hall said in court yesterday? He said it cost that poor divil Russell thirty thousand pounds in money for lawyers' bloody fees.' He stared at them both. 'An' now after spendin' all that of money he has to give up the case entirely. Musha that's bloody poor justice.'

'God help the poor man,' sighed the mother, 'whatever came over him, to have his life laid down fernest the world.'

He waited and then said: 'I'll have to be off. Goodbye, father. Goodbye, mother.' He kissed her, and she came to the door and thrust twopence into his hand. 'Since it's the last day,' she said, 'maybe you'd want to treat your companions to sweets.'

It makes you feel daft—the size of you at fourteen, walking down the blooming street going off to school. Little kids not half the size of you working in the mill, bringing home twenty-two an' ninepence a week. Folk stare at you so. You'd think they were keeping you. Still, I'm glad this is the last day. It's this blooming black hair growing above my mouth —folk get the griffin there's something queer going on somewhere. I wouldn't mind getting right away from this neighbourhood—this town, in fact. The frozen north. Distant mountain peaks of the Himalayas. They're not getting me working in the spinning, that's one thing. I know everybody says the same thing, and then when it comes to it they go and work in the dirty snuffy, but not me. When I say a thing I never go back on it. Breathing in dust all day, and working in that heat—not likely. Then finish up with spinner's cancer. Not this kid, tell your mother. Oh, I forgot to wave!

He turned and ran back to the corner. She was still at the door. A smile came to his face when he saw the grin and wink she gave him, and they waved and then she touched a kiss to him with lips and finger. He touched his upper lip. I'll cut 'em off tonight. A job in the open air, that's what I want. Navvy or something. Get thick hands on me like the Irish, red face and great big chest. They always look content after a day's work.

Happen I've not done too bad at school. I'm the cock. Not many lads get to be the cock. It might have been a toss-up between me and Charlie. But I reckon I'd have licked him after all my exercising. I don't know my own strength. Funny, but I was glad to see Charlie leave school at Easter. My best mate at that, but secretly I was glad to see him go. I don't like folk expecting anything of me. I'd enough with Ella. I'm head monitor too. Weigh up all your good fortune and it makes you unhappy.

Nearing the school gate he saw Miss Skegham turn the corner: we'll meet at the gate. He felt a twist at his heart, but only from memory, and it righted itself almost at once. Stare her in the eye: go on.

'Good morning, Miss,' he said loudly.

'Good morning, M'Cloud,' she said, measuring him up with a glance. He wasn't cool, but he didn't flinch. That was cheeky of me, to speak first, he thought, as he allowed her to enter the gate and walk ahead. It comes of having my Sunday shoes on and my best shirt. If I'd had the torn shirt on I'd have been more careful. It's funny how holes in your clothes make you truly humble.

'Help, Mick!' cried Eddie Radford, who was cornered in the yard. He went along, and the boys scattered at his approach. He ducked and caught one of them, lifted him across the back of his neck, and ran forward with him in the air.

'The mighty M'Cloud on the warpath,' shouted a boy. 'Go on, use him as a batterin' ram.'

'A bloomin' dozen of 'um,' said Eddie, 'got on to me.'

He put the boy down gently. Then he looked at Eddie, looked round at the lads, seeming to see all the faces in a new light. I'm very fond of them all. I love 'em. The whistle blew.

He walked calmly across the yard, making his way through the still and silenced figures of the boys, and as the second whistle blew he was round by the urinal and ready to stand on guard at the entry. As the third whistle blew he got ready to raise his leg, hastening the scuttering figures through first. The entry was clear and he put up his leg. Not as stout as Cumberland's, he thought. He pressed his back against the wall.

Three boys came running in through the gate:

'Hy, M'Cloud, M'Cloud, let's through, please! Go on, please!' He looked at them with assumed severity.

'Right. Get through quick.' His leg fell and rose again. The boys ran along the entry and through the urinal. Two more arrived, breathless and in fear.

'Quick,' he whispered, 'pretend you were in the peestone when the whistle blew.' They darted off after the others. A last boy came running through the gate. He'd just time to do it. He dropped his leg, and gave a silent beckon with his thumb. The boy stopped.

'Quick,' he whispered, 'you've just time.' But the boy didn't want to go through.

'I'm late,' he said.

'Get through, man, get through,' and he gave him a push along the entry as the last whistle sounded.

The departing tread of hundreds of clog-shod feet was heard. He stood there, hoping that no other boys would arrive. Mr Victor came along, the long cane at his side.

'None this morning, sir,' he called to him.

The headmaster nodded. He must have seen that last one go through—I can see it in his eye.

'Please, sir, shall I go off for the letters?'

'Yes, M'Cloud,' said the man. Ah, he's decided to say nothing after all. He turned and went off for the letters. I wonder what I'd have said if he'd have asked me had I let that last one through? He didn't bother because I'm on his side. Aye, I'm on the side of law and authority. I'm the head monitor. It felt nice for a moment, but as he walked round by the church to the presbytery door he shed the feeling. He wasn't at home with it, and it made him uncomfortable. The woman down on her knees mopping the presbytery steps was pressing forward. He kept silent for three or four seconds, staring, and then he spoke before she should turn:

'Are there any letters for Mr Victor?' he asked. She turned to him as she dropped the mop-cloth into the steaming bucket at her side.

'I don't think so, love,' she said. He smiled and said:

'Thank you.' There might easily be a letter there, he thought, but she doesn't care and neither do I.

He went into the infants' school and waited in the hall

whilst Sister Angeline spoke to a parent. The mixed voices were chanting catechism answers.

'Why did God make you?'

'*God made me to know Him, love Him, and serve Him in this world, and to be happy with Him for ever in the next.*' It was a singsong response, always with the same rhythm. Across on the other side of the hall another class was told:

'Say the ten Commandments.' '*I am the Lord thy God, who brought thee out of the land of Egypt, and out of the house of bondage. First: Thou shalt not have strange gods before Me. Thou shalt not make to thyself any graven thing, nor the likeness of any thing that is in Heaven above, or in the earth beneath, nor of those things which are in the waters under the earth. Thou shalt not adore them nor——*' he gave a turn as the dark shape drew up close to him.

'Please, Sister, are there any letters?' Her skin was light and pale with fine freckles on it.

'No, none today,' she said.

'Thank you, Sister.'

He walked out of the door and went slowly across the yard in the warm sunshine to the boys' school.

'Duffy, "Will Faith alone save us?"'

'*Please, Miss, "Faith alone will not save us without good works; we must also have Hope and Charity."*'

'Higgins, "What is prayer?"'

'*Please, Miss, "Prayer is the raising up of the mind and heart to God."*' Along the passage and up the stairs.

'How is Baptism given?'

'*"Baptism is given by pouring water on the head of the child, saying at the same time these words: I baptise thee——*' He felt the blood rise to his face. That no one ever knows what goes on within us!—thanks be to God.

He entered the classroom softly.

'Taylor,' said Mr Denning, '"what do you mean by the flesh?"'

'*"By the flesh I mean our own corrupt inclinations and passions, which are the most harmful of all our enemies."*'

'Harmful? I think you mean "dangerous", Taylor.'

'That's right, sir, "dangerous".'

Mr. Denning looked round the class and then his eye settled quietly on him.

'M'Cloud,' he said, 'you appear to do an unconscionable amount of coming and going these days. Now I wonder—' he began to flick over the pages of the catechism. 'Could you tell me which are the seven Corporal Works of Mercy?'

He stood facing the man: 'Sir, "*The seven Corporal Works of Mercy are: To feed the hungry; To give drink to the thirsty; To clothe the naked; To harbour the harbourless; To visit the sick; To visit the imprisoned; To bury the dead.*"'

'I asked you one that you knew,' said the man, 'so now I'll ask you one that you might not know. M'Cloud, "Which are the twelve fruits of the Holy Ghost?"'

'"*The twelve fruits of the Holy Ghost, sir, are: Charity, Joy, Peace, Patience, Benignity, Goodness, Longanimity, Mildness, Faith, Modesty, Continency, and Chastity.*"'

'Perfectly correct, M'Cloud. Do you happen to know any of the less obvious of those fruits? For instance, what is Benignity?'

'Benignity, sir, refers to being benign.'

'And what does benign refer to?'

'Benign, sir, refers to being kind and smiling, sir, like "a benign smile lit up his face."'

'And longanimity, M'Cloud, does that refer to long?'

'Well, sir, to longsuffering.'

'M'Cloud, you may continue to come and go at your own discretion. And you may sit down now.'

'Thank you, sir.'

'Now the rest of you,' he said, 'do you remember that I said to our worthy monitor, M'Cloud, "you appear to do an *unconscionable* amount of coming and going"? Now can any boy tell me where that word "unconscionable" is used in a context that is very famous? One man uses the word in a comment upon himself?'

Wolsey, he thought: 'I am an unconscionable time dying.' But he didn't hasten to answer, for already the flush of that

294

first elation was slipping away, and he half regretted his exchange with Mr Denning. He was examining its effect upon himself. I am no different from what I would have been had I been unable to answer the questions, except that another feeling would have been inside me in place of the one that is now slipping away. The boys about envied and admired me, but I didn't get anything out of that because they were feeling it and not me. If I had my time over again I would rather he had never asked me the questions. If I am asked again I shall be expected to answer, and I hate anything to be expected of me. No, I will not answer.

'King John, sir.'

'King John, Hesley? When did he say it?'

'I shall be unconscious before I sign this, sir.'

'You'll be unconscious, my boy, if you give me another answer like that one. The word is " unconscionable ". Does any boy know what it means?'

'Please, sir, it means someone who isn't thinking.'

'If it does, Peak, then you're unconscionable.'

I will not answer, he thought, but I know what it means. It means it's sort of beyond everything.

'The word refers to something utterly outside conscience or reason, an excess of some kind,' said Mr Denning. 'And the man who used it said : "I fear, gentleman, I am an unconscionable time a-dying." Can any boy tell me who that was?'

Wolsey. But I will not say it.

'Nobody knows? Well, it was Charles the Second.'

Charles the Second; A damn good job I said nowt—I'd only have made a great big fool of myself.

This is the last Catechism lesson in all my life, he thought. This is the last time I shall sit at this desk. This is the last playtime I shall have in this yard. This is the last pee I shall have in here. This is the last time I shall ever hear the whistle. This is the last time I shall see my drawing-book. These are the last sums I shall ever do in my life.

After playtime Mr Denning said : 'If no one has any objections, I think we could forgo the usual geometry lesson this morning and, before we retire to the hall at halfpast eleven, we'll let the school-leavers tell us of their plans. Will those leaving school today step out in front.' Eddie Radford walked out first, and then Carterham, Peak, and himself behind.

'Well, Edward,' Mr Denning, 'perhaps you'll tell us what you intend to do.'

'I'm going to try to get a job at Donkinson's, sir, the ovenmaker's, I'm goin' to serve an apprenticeship there if I get chance.'

'Oh, and why?'

'Because it's a family firm, sir. You can't beat workin' for a family firm.'

'Why not?'

'Because it's in their interest to keep the firm goin', while some of these big companies are better off going bang. Our Ernie works for 'um, sir, an' he gets a lot of overtime. Every Saturday afternoon during the season he has the job of driving 'um to the Wanderers' ground in their car, an' he gets in for nothing, because one of 'um's a director. He does the gardening for 'um on Sundays an' Sat'days in summer, sir. Last year at June holidays he had the job of drivin' 'um on their holidays through Cornwall, an' this year they're goin' to Scotland, an' our Ernie's goin' with 'um. They pay him his full week's wage just as though he'd been working on the bench, an' they give him his keep, an' he gets tips in the bargain. They say he's better off than old Donkinson himself.'

'It certainly sounds like it, Edward. And what do you hope to do there?'

'Our Ernie says he'll teach me to drive, an' any time he's bad I'll be able to drive 'um around. 'Course I'll be working on the bench as well.'

'And a good job you'll make of it, I'm sure, Edward. Now I'd like to wish you good luck,' said Mr Denning, shaking hands with Eddie, 'and I'm sure the class would like to give you a subdued but sincere cheer.'

They gave him a cheer.

'Well, Francis,' he asked Carterham, 'what have you to tell us?'

'I've got a job in an office, sir, at Fitch's in Oathouse Lane, I start on the Monday after the holidays.'

'What time do you start?'

'Nine o'clock, sir.'

The class laughed: 'What a time to start!'

'How much a week do you get?' asked Eddie Radford.

'I don't get anything the first year.'

The class let out groans of contempt. 'Just a moment,' said Mr Denning, 'that's often the case with certain jobs.'

'What about his poor mother, sir?'

'It must be a rotten job where they don't pay you, sir.'

'I'm sure,' said Mr Denning, 'that Francis will make a good job out of it, and that in time he'll be earning as much as any of us.' They shook hands and the class gave him a cheer.

'Yes, William?' he asked Peak.

'I'm startin' as tea lad at the Bentley's forge, sir.'

'Jolly good, too. Are you looking forward to the job?'

'Yes, sir. My dad allus says "the working man is happiest the world over". I wouldn't fancy an office job, sir. The forge brings you out, sir. 'Course it's not absolutely fixed, sir, as I'll get it, but I think it is.'

The bell rang in the corridor. I'm saved, he thought. My voice had gone shaky on me. There was a hurried shaking of hands. 'Well, M'Cloud, I wish you the best of luck.' He looked at the man's face and thought: I'd do anything for you, Mr Denning. I owe you a lot you'll never know. 'Thank you, sir,' he said.

'A cheer for M'Cloud.' It was the loudest cheer. They like me! He thought. The class trooped out of the classroom down to the hall. He was last and he looked behind. It was a draining-out feeling to leave that room for the last time. All the honour won and the place found and now I must leave it all and go and start again. He hurried down the steps and into the hall. They were all shuffling into position for singing the holiday song. He felt sad.

All around him the boys sang loud and free, whilst he made a vague humming sound, trying out an occasional full note when the singing was pitched just right for him. He wondered at the swell of sound around him, how they could sing naturally, whilst his own voice shook with emotion when it was let out. Then Mr Victor raised his cane and conducted the National Anthem. On the wall was a big picture of the King and Queen, he a smallish man with a bearded face and a stiff glassy stare, whilst she beside him was a handsome tall woman, with rows of necklaces binding high her throat. I could get on with her, but he'd be difficult. Someone tugged his sleeve.

'Let's make a dash for it, Mick,' whispered Peak, 'an' we'll get our school leavin' papers before the Education Office shuts.'

As the three cheers were being given he had edged near the door, and he turned to look at the mass of faces. Everybody seems to be getting smaller. Just think of the big lads there were in the school when I first came to it!—looks like there was nobody to take their places. We must be shrinking away. They can't even shout the same. He found himself slipping out with Peak.

'Come on, Mick, we've left. Nob'dy can do anything to us.'

After all these years—you just slip away as though it were any ordinary Friday. He began to trot alongside Peak once he got out into the yard. Every piece of stone, brick and railing touched an intimate moment of his mind.

They got their school-leaving papers from the Education Office. Somehow, they had little to say to each other as they walked homeward from the town, each carrying his certificate. Then as they were parting at the corner of Drooks Street, Peak said: 'I think we should stick together after we leave school, Mick. We've spent the best years together, an' I think it's only right we should stick together.' He was stirred by the look on the other's face, and the strange tone of his voice.

'I agree with that, Billy,' he said warmly. Peak put out his

298

hand: 'Then let's keep it in mind. Let's keep tryin' to keep together. Good luck, Mick.'

'Good luck, Billy.'

'Tha's been a good mate, Mick.'

'So has tha, Billy, a right good 'un. Good luck.'

'Good luck, Mick.' Peak turned: 'And if ever tha needs help,' he said, 'let me know.'

That's funny, he thought, I never knew Peak to look like that before. I never knew he had it in him.

CHAPTER EIGHT

A Man from the Foundry

THERE WAS NO MASSED and orderly flow of factory workers moving with normal dinnertime rapidity along Derbyshire Street as he walked homeward after leaving Billy Peak, but instead there was an excited uncertainty, with women hurrying this way and that carrying parcels and baskets, and men standing hesitantly at shopdoors, staring at caps and ties and shirts, and many faces he noticed were off their usual route, and everywhere the set stolid expressions had given way to eagerness and agitation.

'Keep hold that bottle, Maggie,' called a big blackhaired woman to her friend, ' or else there'll be no footin' today.' And they let out a screech of gay laughter. Weavers from Kilshaw's—they smell different from cardroom women and their skins haven't that oily look. They all look so different today. Except me—in the green painted glass of Tim Yuck's laundry he caught a full look of himself—I'm an odd sod I am. His face pleased him and he gave his reflection a snigger and went on.

Now for a nice dinner of chips and peas from Tibb's. I'll put plenty of salt and alliker on too. Only time you get chance to give 'um a good dowsing is at late dinnertime when the queue's gone. Funny, the vinegar you get at home never tastes as good as that they have in the shop. One thing, the chips always taste better when you buy them just after one o'clock and they've had time to rest in the top pan. Happen they need to rest a bit after being in the boiling fat. Mother'll want a nice piece of plaice—if she's got money put by. Can't understand folk wasting money on fish —there's nothing in it. That plaice tastes just like that whiff you get when the oil-cloth tilts up near the front door and you get a musty mouthful. The front place'll be nice and clean now—that's one thing nice about Friday. I hope she's done the grate and fireirons—I hate the smell of Brasso and Zebra grate polish. Puts me off my food. Happen we'll eat in the kitchen. It'll be nice and cool.

He walked up the street with an open unhurried air—I've got my school-leaving papers in my pocket, I don't care what folk think—and slowing his step at their own door, he squeezed the latch, and let himself relax wholly as he entered. At once he sensed there was a visitor, and he put on his street manner again, and a keen disappointment struck him as he saw Ma Clarkson from the sweet shop, on a chair by the table.

'Oh, hello, ma'am,' he said, smiling at her. I hope she soon goes, I'm hungry.

'Hello, Michael,' she said.

Standing by the dresser was his mother, her face flushed, and drops of sweat and faint tracks of blacklead on her forehead. She smiled at him. That's her putting-on smile—I wonder what's up?

'Hello, mother,' he said.

'Are you home from school, my boy?' she said.

He half bowed to the visitor as he made his way towards the kitchen but he stopped when she spoke to him: 'I'm here on a very unpleasant errand, Michael,' she said in her candid even tone. 'Your mother owes me some money, and has done for some time. The last time I saw her she gave me her word that she would have it all paid up by today—now she tells me she can't pay me. There's four pounds still owing. That's not a nice thing, is it? I don't know what steps to take about it, but certainly I shall take some.'

He didn't follow her words clearly. I've never heard any-one speak against my mother—and in our own home at that. An uncomfortable itch and tingle climbed up his skin and covered his face. O Jesus, Mary an' Joseph, Jesus, Mary an' Joseph! How did it happen? Now mother'll tell her off. She looked at him.

'It's true, agraw,' she said in an odd resigned way, 'every word the decent woman has said. I borrowed and I haven't paid back. And I gave my word and I haven't kept it. And I can't keep it.' There was no way now for him to go from the room and leave the two women. The mother turned to the visitor: 'But on the verth of my oath, ma'am,' she said, 'I'll have that four pounds paid to you before the month of July is out. I'll send my son here down to you this evening with one pound—'

'You promised me the four pounds—'

'I did, I did—and if things had gone right you'd have had the money. But I promise you that within a month today you'll have your money. And my son there is my witness.'

Ma Clarkson stood up. 'I'm very sorry I came round,' she said. 'I don't know what came over me—one worry and another—but I wouldn't have shamed you before him.'

'You only called for what was your own,' said the mother, 'an' you gave me the money when I badly needed it. So don't be sorry for anything—'

'Just the same,' she said, 'I wouldn't have come out with it before Michael.'

He looked at her and saw the start of tears shaking in her old blue eyes.

'You'll sit down now, ma'am,' said the mother, 'an' stay for a cup of tea.'

'I'm sorry—I can't,' said the woman. 'Do forgive me.'

'I have the kettle on.'

'I mustn't miss the dinner-hour custom,' she said. 'Goodbye, Mrs M'Cloud. Goodbye, Michael.'

'Goodbye, ma'am,' he said, opening the door and putting his hand out to her. The mother came to the door: 'Oh look at the lovely day there,' she said, 'the Lord be praised. So long now, ma'am.' She stood at the door, waving and smiling. The neighbours would never guess, he thought, and began to whisper Hail Marys.

She came in and went over and sat down on the side of a chair. 'Money, money, money,' she said, as though she were alone and talking to herself, 'the curse of God in heaven this day on the filthy ould money. Hasn't it all the youth an' pride knocked out of me—the need of a few miserable pounds. It's stuck there on my mind day an' night—what will he give me, an' who will I pay an' who will I miss? There's never a knock on that door but I'm started, an' my heart struck pale, wonderin' who it is wants money, an' me without a penny. The Lord save us, look at the face on me—gone ould an' crooked with schemin'. An' only yesterday didn't I see myself goin' to the shop with my two eyes turned to the ground, for fear I'd meet anyone—who ever before had the smile for everyone I met along the road. It's the pure truth I'm speakin'. O sweet holy Jesus in heaven, that we could be thrust down into such misery an' poverty —all for the sake of the few dirty pounds of money. Robbed of all decency and pride I am before you, my boy.'

He went over: 'Don't, Mother,' he said. He rested his hand on her stooped soft shoulder. She took his other hand, held it in one palm and slapped it.

'Sure you've a hand like my old Uncle Paudric, God rest his soul in heaven today,' she said.

'I've got my school-leavin' papers, mam,' he said.

'Have you so?' she said. 'Musha I'd hate to see your hand go scarred an' thickened the way they do at work. Well, we'll be on the pig's back after all. Musha look at me an' you dead with the hunger. Go to the silver mugeen an' see what you can find to go off to the chip shop with. I'll make the tea. Urra isn't it a hot day! I'm done after all my polishin'. I must wash soon, an' I'll give a dab of Guard's to my hair. Oh b'jaze, look at the white hair on me. Musha I'd drop dead with the shame if anyone from home saw me that way. Run, agraw, before old Tibb would close the door on you.'

After the meal he sat at the bottom of the stairs, with the back-kitchen door open before him, and he looked out into the backyard, and listened to the mother humming and singing as she ironed holiday clothes for Willie. Four pounds— a lot of money. She held up a pair of cycling shorts. 'Arra the people at home will drop dead, God save us,' she said, 'if they see him riding the road in these yokes.'

'Everybody has everything fixed up but me,' he said.

'Is it work worryin' you again?' she asked.

'Not worryin' me,' he said, 'not likely. But no one in this house knows anyone or anything. We've no influence anywhere. An' I must have a damn job.'

'Then maybe,' she said softly, 'you'd give the bicycle a rub over for Willie.'

'Divil a rub!' he said.

'Ah sure, why should you?' she said. 'It's only that he'll be weary after the hard day's work, an' up to Liverpool to catch the boat he must ride along with Ned this evenin'.'

He got up. 'Where's the cloth an' polish?' He wiped the dust and oil off the frame and began to clean it up. Maybe I'd be happier if I was less lazy, he thought, enjoying the rhythm and movement. Thoughts can't get at you the same when you're working. You think folk talk daft when they say that—but you come to see that they're right.

'Himself'll be well shot when he gets home,' she said. 'There's some kind of holiday share-out, so they'll stay an' have a feed of drink. Keep around, maybe he'd treat you.'

'I want no treat,' he said. The thought of the father coming home soon in his best serge suit, a bit drunk after drawing his wages, was depressing. He'll be talking that loud 'twould burst your ear-drums, and no one could get away from the wild stare of his eye. Still an' all, maybe he would give me a shilling or so. It'll depend on whether he's backed a winner. He heard the mother putting the iron to cool on the side of the wash-boiler. She came to the back-door.

'Musha you're makin' a fine job altogether of the bicycle,' she said. 'Willie won't forget it for you.'

'Tell him you did it,' he said.

'I will not,' she said. He turned as he heard her sigh slowly. Then he watched her rest herself on the stairs. She wiped a palm across her forehead and down her cheek. 'I'm feelin' weary,' she said, 'after all hoppin' an' trottin'. One time of day I'd never feel tired.'

'Rest yourself there,' he said, irritable at the feeling of uneasiness her paled face gave him. 'Rest, Mother, love.'

'I was grand up to half a minute ago,' she said, 'an' now I haven't a puff in me.'

'Mother, will I make you a cup o' tea?'

'I'd rather a good bumper of whisky,' she said, 'if it's not the short answer I'm givin' you.'

'Will you sit there whilst I make tea for you,' he said, 'an' for God's sake stop goin' on.'

'Do you think you'll be able to make a good cup?' she asked. 'I'd like it if there was a cup with the fresh track of an egg on it. My mother, God rest her soul, would always pour her tea into the mug that had the track of an egg left in it before fryin'. The taste of the white would bring a nice creamy froth to the tea.'

'Isn't it a great pity, Mother,' he said, stepping over her feet and going to the tap, 'that the Irish are all a bit soft in the head?'

'Musha we are,' she said, 'we are indeed. But just the same I could almost jump on the bike there, at the thought it would get me back home.'

'Don't be daft, Mam,' he said, 'that an' a ship.'

'Before ever I went to America,' she said, 'I used to hear the old ones sayin', the Lord have mercy on them, how they could never understand some Yank wantin' to come home, back to the few ridges an' the bog, when he could have all he wanted in America. But sure I hadn't set foot in the place when my heart was hungry for the sight of the bog. An' many the night was the pillow wet under my head.'

He waited for the water to boil. 'Put plenty tea in, agraw,' she said.

'Will you whisht till I give you the cup!' he said.

'I wouldn't want anyone say you hadn't the decent hand,' she said.

'Don't say I didn't give you the top of the milk,' he said, handing her the cup of tea.

'Sure you could have let it draw another minute,' she said, 'but it's a good cup just the same. Someone passed the window,' she said softly, 'but I didn't hear him pass the door yet.' She waited, listening, and then there was a soft

305

knock. 'I don't know that knock,' she said, standing up slowly and looking uneasy.

'Will I answer it, mother?' he asked.

She hesitated, then nodded. 'Do, do,' she said, blessing herself hurriedly.

What's on her? he thought, going to the door. Standing before him was a short man in foundry overalls, wearing a flattened cap.

'Is this M'Cloud's, luv?' asked the man.

'Yes, sir,' he said.

'I'll bet you're Bill's brother, eh?'

Bill's brother? 'Oh yes,' he said. Inside he could hear her whispering prayers in Irish. Then her voice broke in clearly : 'Bring the gentleman in.'

'Oh come in, sir,' he said.

'Is your mam in?' asked the man.

'Yes she is,' he said.

The mother stopped whispering prayers and came across with a smile and her hand out. 'I'm Danny,' said the man. 'Danny Blackburn.'

'I'm proud to meet you,' said the mother.

'Happen you've heard Bill mention me,' said the man. 'I'm his riveter.'

'Oh often,' she said, 'we've heard great reports indeed of you. You'll have a cup of tea.'

'Aye, I wouldn't mind,' said the man.

He was going into the kitchen to see if he could pour a cup of tea for the man when suddenly he heard the mother's voice ask with low panic :

'Is my boy hurt badly? Tell me, is he?'

What's she saying? She'll show us up! I wish she wouldn't act daft.

'Bill's had a nasty clout,' said the man softly. Has somebody clouted his lug? Not our Willie's! 'Aye, a real nasty clout.' That's different. He's hurt himself. 'They've had to tak' him on to the infirmary.'

Infirmary?—Oh, bandaged up in a bed. Oh, poor Willie. My brother Willie. He won't be able to go away on his

306

holidays. The saving-up money and the bike will be lying there doing nothing and poor Willie in the infirmary. Ma Clarkson—four pounds. Serve her right if I was able to take her the full four pounds in tonight—straight with you. But poor Willie.

'Oh, sweet sweet Jesus in heaven . . .' he heard the mother move a chair and he turned and looked into the room from the kitchen. She was down on her knees, resting forward on the wooden seat of a chair, praying away, falling into Irish whispers and coming back into English again. The man was looking at the oilcloth, his cap held under his armpit. He'll think we're mad. I'll go and pour him a cup of tea. His hand was shaking as he tried to pour the tea. He slopped milk and sugar in it and took it in to the man. 'Here you are, sir,' he said.

'Ta,' said the man, and he drank it off at once.

'Mother,' he said, going over to her.

'We've got firm's car,' said the man. 'It's waitin' at bottom of t'street. Happen you'd like to come.'

She got up on her feet. 'Get my coat,' she said, 'my dark coat. My fine boy. What happened my fine boy, tell me? Where's my shoes? What happened my fine boy, sir?'

'He's had a right bad clout, lady,' said the man. 'I thought as happen you'd come an' see him at t'infirmary. Firm's car's waitin'.'

'Bring me my shoes,' she called.

'They're here, mother,' he said.

'Where's my dark coat. Oh my fine lovely boy. Is he very badly hurt?'

'Nay, not too badly, lady,' said the man.

'Let me fasten your shoes for you, Mother,' he said, going down on his knees and clumsily tying each shoe. She began to wail softly and he felt ashamed before the man.

'Mother!' he said. She turned and looked at him.

'I didn't wave goodbye to him at the corner today,' she said, 'whatever job it was kept me in the kitchen. I ran to the window and drew the curtain then, but the poor ladeen was gone. He must have waited, I thought, and then gone

307

off without the wave of my hand. Out into the world. It was on my mind there all the morning, God forgive me.'

'Will I come with you, sir?' he said to the man, turning from the face of his mother, for fear he might cry the family tears before a stranger. The man nodded.

'Aye, luv, you come. Where's your dad?'

'Gone for his wages,' he said.

The man said: 'What about your front door?'

He turned to his mother and said: 'What about our front door?'

She was just bringing her two hands down from the centre part in her hair and smoothing the hair over her ears.

'What door?' she said. 'Where are my beads? Bring me my beads. I wasn't there to wave him off. What kind of a mother am I at all?' He got her the rosary beads from the mantelpiece. At the feel of them there came back to his mind how he'd held them in bed at night when he was small in Ireland. The man said:

'I fancy the door will be all right.' He turned to the woman. 'Come on, Mother,' he said, 'we're going.'

The neighbours' stares were on them, he felt, as the three walked towards the big shining car. He was glad to see Mrs Chadwick coming towards them.

'Ee, luv,' she said, 'there's nothing wrong, is there?' He said: 'Our Willie's got hurt at work, Mrs Chadwick. Will you tell me father we've gone to the infirmary?'

'Ee, I will that 'an all,' she said. 'What a shame—today of all days. Ee, do take care of your mam, luv. She's taking it bad. She's in a proper daze.'

'Forgive me, ma'am,' said the mother, 'I have a worry just now.' The driver held the car door open. Inside it seemed so big, with the deep seats of polished leather. And when they drove off all the little familiar corners and streets looked so different from inside a moving car, and all the people in the streets looked stunted, and seemed to be hurrying about in a worried way. Every other one looks crippled, bow-legged or knock-kneed. The mother counted her beads all the way and the man Danny kept silent. He tried to pray himself but he couldn't. It's when people I know are near I can't pray, he thought, I can only pray amongst strangers or alone. His eye glanced at the beads between her fingers—the thousands of prayers that had been said on them over the long years his mother had them and her aunt before that. They were worn away with prayers. He wondered why his mother didn't ask the man what had happened. He turned and glanced at her, and seeing the way her praying face made her look smaller inside the dark coat, he had to force down a tear-lump in his throat. He consciously brought to mind the image of Christ with the crown of thorns and blood drops on his face, and this gave him a control over himself. And he forced himself not to look across at his mother again.

The car drove up a gravel path at the infirmary entrance, and stopped at a door over which was the word *Accidents*. Danny got out and stood shyly in the sunshine. The driver went off and they stood waiting till he came back with a nurse.

' Will you follow me, please,' she said. When they reached the door Danny said: ' Happen I'd better wait outside— bein' in these things.' The mother said: ' Please stay with us—I'd like you to.' Then Danny said warmly: ' Aye, I will that an' all, Missis M'Cloud, if you want me to. I didn't want to show you up.'

They waited in a corridor, and the nurse brought a chair. The place was full of a frightening smell.

' If you'll wait there,' said the nurse, ' the doctor will be with you in a minute or two. The name's M'Cloud, isn't it? '

' Yes, nurse,' he said. He could hear the mother's low murmur as she counted her beads and sighed in between.

' It was the stranger had to take you an' care you, my boy, when you was hurt. Yes, the stranger in the strange place.' Outside sounded the tinkle of a newsboy's bell. A man called out:

' What won the last 'un, Jimmy? '

' Silver Sword. Hundred to eight.'

' Has it, b'Christ? Where'd the favourite run? '

'Don' ask me,' was the answer, 'I only know the winners.'

The nurse appeared with a young man in a white coat. The mother got up and hurried towards him.

'Now then,' he said, soothingly, 'now then.'

'How is he?' she asked softly, 'how is my boy?'

'I've not got good news for you,' he said, shaking his head, 'no, I haven't. There was nothing we could do. He died a few minutes ago.'

'Oh my fine boy,' wailed the mother slowly. The doctor took her by the arm.

'Come with me,' he said, 'I'll take you to him.' Willie dead. I can let the tears come now, he thought, it'll look bad if I don't. But they were stuck there, and came only at the sight of Danny's white face.

'Aahe, dun't fret thyself, luv,' said the man, 'it's out of our hands now. Let's wait outside for thy mam.'

CHAPTER NINE

You get used to the Din

───

HE RESTED HIMSELF on the edge of the bed and looked out on to the deserted back street. Folk 'ud be going mad to get their washin' dry of an ordinary Monday, an' there's not a single clothes-line out this afternoon. Back street looks dead. Everybody's gone away. Town's always dead in Holiday Week. I must say I feel sick stuck in this room all the time. Nowt to do. Funeral tomorrow—Ee, I'll be right fain. Head aches. I'm sick of eating Cleeve's Limerick toffee. I could do with a nice ice-cream soda or a Vimto or a sarsaparilla wine. Why not nip off the back way an' get one? Go on. Folk keep skenning at me. I hate folk skenning at me. Sure to see someone. Ee, luv, what a pity about your Willie! Han' they had t'inquest, luv? When is he being fetched home, luv? When's buryin'? He's better in t'mortuary this weather. Ee, what a shame—just when he were goin' off on his holidays. Ee, I feel sorry for your mam, luv. Her's aged this weekend her has. Her's taking it bad.

I used to fancy myself goin' to a funeral, coming out of the house pale-faced in a new dark suit, long pants, and a white shirt and a black tie, an' walkin' between the two lines of folk gathered on the pavement to watch, an' hearin' 'um say, Ee, look at poor Michael—he's takin' it bad. They aren't even got me a new suit. I'm bloomin' neglected I am. I wish mam 'ud come round to her old self an' start cookin' proper. I could eat summat good an' I could sup summat good. Happen her'll settle to normal when the funeral's over. It's not the same as I thought having this room to myself either. You should never wish for anythin'—you don't know how it'll turn out when you get it. Take the bicycle upstairs out of the way, Mickyeen, where your mother won't be seein' it every half-minute of the day. I wonder dare I cock my leg over the saddle? She'd go mad if I did an' she came up an' caught me. They'd think I was glad he'd gone. God knows I'm not. Poor old Willie, God rest his soul. It must have been ordained from the beginning of time he'd die at seventeen. It seems impossible he could have lived another day. I'll kneel an' say three Hail Marys for him. I wonder what they'll do with the bike? If it were painted she might forget it had been his. The melodeon too. And the spring developers and the weights. They can't get rid of them all. It wouldn't be right. I'll come into some clothes too. I'd better have another go at saying them prayers. I'll have to exercise a bit too. I'll be getting consumption the next thing, sitting in this room. Somebody else arrived.

He went to the door and listened to the voices. The drone of the mother's praying about the house ceased as she welcomed someone.

'I sorrow for you in your loss, Delia.' Who was that? The Irish are coming from everywhere. The house'll be crowded. I hate to go down. If I could make myself look like them—gone in grief. But nothing has happened me. I must be sorry, but I don't feel it. It makes you feel rotten when you go down amongst them. I wish mother wouldn't give way to it so much. My face looks no different in the looking-glass. I wish it 'ud show sorrow. Her's doesn't look like her own face at all. I'd like a right good gamble now, a good game of banker or pontoon or a nice little game of brag, feeling the old cards going out an' seeing the lads leaning forward in a ring waiting for their cards.

A car honked passing the end of the back street. He gave a jump and rubbed his cheeks before the looking-glass. It turned up the front street. Youngsters' clogs clipped along in pursuit, and there was a call:

'Come on, they've fetched Bill M'Cloud 'ome.' Oh I'll have to go down. I'll have to go down. What'll I do? What'll I say? Beetle-a-woe, Battle-a-shay, one a white noggin an' mountain cut. It'll be awful if I do or say the wrong thing. Cry, let me cry as soon as I can. I'm tired of crying every time folk say summat. I wish the funeral was over. There's

312

her voice; going off again high like that—it's dreadful. I'll have to go down. O my God because Thou art so good. I wish I were like other folk. Willie 'ud tell me what to do. I'll have to go down. Listen all the voices, I hate going down. He took his handkerchief out and wiped his face. Happen I have caught consumption. I'll go down, I'll go down. Hail Mary fullagrace.

At the bottom of the stairs he came upon O'Sloane going into the yard. The man gave him a friendly thump on the chest.

'Mickyeen,' he said, 'how are you, Mickyeen?' That's fine now, that's fine now, that's fine the way he done that. He had to turn and go to the middle door and into the front room. People were standing and sitting, and two men were kneeling before a coffin that had been set on a table at the window. Uncle John saw him and took him by the shoulder, and gently pressed him towards the window. The mother was standing at the head of the coffin and he turned his eyes away for he didn't like to see her face the way it was, red-eyed and lines all round it and the smooth hair gone dry and white. One man blessed himself and got to his feet, and turned to the mother:

'I'm sorry for ye, in ye're sorrow, ma'am,' he said, taking her hand.

I'd better kneel. He knelt beside the table on which lay the coffin. He made the Sign of the Cross, joined his hands, stooped his head, and pretended to pray. I mustn't rise too soon, nor must I stay down too long and make a show of myself that way. They'll all be watching. I'm the brother. Maybe that would be enough now. A bit longer would do no harm. Maybe I should try to say a prayer. Our Father Who art. I think that would be enough now. He blessed himself and stood up and tried to move away. The mother came to him.

'Come, come, agraw,' she said, 'here's Willie.'

He stood beside her and looked into the coffin. There was the face of the dead brother. He was shocked at how it was exactly like Willie, except that the mouth was pulled a bit to one side. The mother stooped and kissed the face. I have to do it now. He curled up his feelings and bent his head and put his face down into the coffin and put his lips forward until they touched the flesh. He made himself keep still a moment, against the shock of the coldness of the skin and the smell that frightened him. Then he straightened up and began to cry.

Uncle John nudged him into a chair in the far corner of the room. After a time he calmed and watched the callers. The Irish caller dropped to his knees before the coffin at once, and then spoke to the mother and father on rising. The neighbours would stand and look at him.

'Aahe, doesn't he look at peace,' some said. 'It's the same Billy.' It was comforting to listen to their natural talk.

'Our Harry's gone right off his tommy,' said Mrs Greenhalgh—'first time it's ever happened to him.'

Ned Taylor came in.

'Howdo, Mike,' he called across the room. Then he glanced into the coffin and went out without saying another word.

'Yon lad feels it,' said a woman. Two women came in with money they had collected for the street wreath. Then Danny Blackburn and two other men from the firm. The father and O'Sloane went off up the back street and came back with jugs of beer.

'We were wrong not to have pipes an' tobacco, John,' the father kept repeating.

'It was ever the custom. The shops shut, curse them. An' one can't think of every mortal thing. But we should have had them.' After a time he got out of his chair in the corner and made to go out the backyard, but seeing all the men standing round drinking beer, he turned and went to the room upstairs. He sat on the bed again and heard all the talk rising from the men standing round the backyard, drinking and smoking.

'Yon MacMahon's made a good job of Bill,' said a man. 'Tha'd never know a leg were missin' from above the knee.'

'He made a great job,' said the father,' a great job altogether. I'll never forget it for that man. A fine decent man.'

314

'Now is there a leg missin' indeed?'

'Oh aye. He were workin' on the platform, see, wi' his legs astraddle just like that. Slung from the crane's this girder, see, weighin' a good nine tons of solid steel. Ordinary times it 'ud never ha' happened—but it were one in a million as it caught summat it swung. Just like that. An' round it come, an' if it 'ud been a fraction shorter it 'ud never ha' happened. It just chanced to half-turn, an' the very end of it swung just far enough round to hit Bill. His leg were severed from above the knee just like breakin' a matchstalk in two.'

'The poor, poor lad, God rest him.'

'I heard the scream. Thurned mi blood cold for the minute. But I'll swear he couldn't ha' felt anything after that. That one jab—no more.'

'Which leg were it, Dave?'

'On his left 'un. It came across like that.'

'By gow, he scored many a good goal with that leg did young Bill.'

'Ah, an' tell me, was it off entirely?'

'Aye, entirely, mate.' He put his head near the window to catch the next words:

'I know—because I were one as helped bury it.'

'Did you say bury it?'

'Aye, in the foundry yard. Isn't that right, Danny? It's always been the custom, yu' know, that if a chap loses his limb it's got to be buried there in the yard. It were the same in my dad's day an' his dad's afore him. It wouldn't be right if the leg weren't buried there—it 'ud be bad luck. The chaps wouldn't like it.'

'What's that about the leg?' asked the father.

'It's nothin', Mester M'Cloud,' said Danny, 'nothin'. He were a champion rivet lad were Bill—an' a right good holder-up.'

'Arra go on—haven't I a right to know.'

'We buried young Bill's leg,' said the man, 'we buried it in the foundry yard. We wouldn't ha' let anybody tak' it away from where it happened—no good would ha' come of it if we had. Yu' know it's the same down pit, Mester

315

M'Cloud, they've got to bury a bit o' summat—it's only right an' proper. I saw it go under in the foundry yard, an I'd gamble nob'dy could find the spot now.'

'If it's the tradition,' said the father, 'you can never depart from it. It is and it must be. But don't any of ye let the mother hear it.'

'He shouldna let anybody hear it, Mester M'Cloud. It's summat private to the mates in the foundry yard. It's not a thing to be talked about.'

'Nay, nay, Danny,' said the man, 'if my lad had lost a leg I'd want to know what they'd done wi' it.'

'Shut up,' said Danny. 'Art workin' tonight?'

'Aye, that order has to be finished, holiday or no holiday. I'll go on at ten o'clock.'

'Then tha doesn't want to sup too much, Dave.'

'Urra let me fill your glass,' said the father. 'Sup—an' I'll fill. I'm pleased to meet ye, men. But take care would ye let her hear ye. She'd go distracted.'

It's queer how they're all talkin' about him an' he's lyin' there in silence. It was the same when they kept comin' an' goin'—they all sounded a bit daft at times, whilst he looked very wise lyin' there an' sayin' nothin'. Willie, Willie, Willie —someways I always wronged you. I think I'll say my prayers and get into bed. I've got a bloomin' rotten headache with that cryin' an' stuff. It feels better once you get your clothes off. Aye, get into bed. Do a few exercises—seven trunk forward bends. Into bed.

He woke alone in the darkness. Outside the hot night was red with the glare from the foundry. He wiped the sweat from his forehead with his shirt sleeve. A screeching of a wire rose in the night, and a long shackling roll of chains followed, then a fierce groaning of the crane. The night air coming in the window was strangely warm. Somewhere amongst the streets a drunk man was singing:

'*Great big moon is shinin'* . . .' in a voice thick and sad, and oddly childlike. He listened hard to the singing, feeling an affection for the heart behind the voice. Ella will be walking the front at Blackpool, singing and laughing with

316

others. The breeze will be lovely there, smelling of the salt sea. It was good that time when we were in love. You only realise it when it's gone, how comforting it is. He's stopped singing. Ee, I wish he'd start again. In the silence the crane began to whine and pull. Willie's leg is somewhere under all that lot. Beneath the stone and all that red cinder and rusty clinker in the foundry yard is Willie's leg. Oh why can't I feel that proper grief that other folk get? I've been thinking of that rotten four quid, of his weights, his wallet, his jack-knife, his suits. O Blessed Virgin Mary, ask God to give me some proper grief. I'm hungry too. I'll get up. It's rotten lying here.

He got out of bed, asking the Holy Ghost to look after him and protect him from any evil spirit abroad at night. He pulled his trousers on and crept in the darkness down the stairs. He peeped round the partition at the bottom of the stairs. The back kitchen was empty and dark, but the middle door was open and he could see into the front kitchen. The father had fallen asleep in the rocking chair, his head back and a weary drunken look on his open-mouthed face. Uncle John was sitting up in his shirt sleeves, smoking a pipe. Beside him was the man O'Sloane, smoking a cigarette. The mother was standing at the head of the coffin, looking down into it. She was talking to the body inside it, her voice low and clear.

'Will you ever forgive me, agraw, that I let you go out to work the way I did, amongst strangers in the strange place, amongst all the hard machines that were never for the likes of us? You had the hasty death, my son, the first of any belonging us.' She spoke as though comforting a sick child as she stooped down lower over the coffin: 'You're like a little sainteen, with the track of pain there on your mouth. Yes, they have your young red lip twisted, and your four bones crushed, my own son, that was ever fair and lovely.' Her voice was rising, and Uncle John turned and spoke to her:

'Delia,' he said, 'keep a hold on yourself now.'

'Urra how can I keep a hold on myself, John,' she said,

317

'when I think that never again will I hear his two light feet comin' in that door? How could I? How could any woman? Won't the brightest day of summer be blackened for me when my own boy is put down for ever in the cold grave?'

'It will surely,' agreed Uncle John. He prodded a finger into his pipe, and half-turning spoke softly to her: 'Just the same, Delia, you'd be as well rest yourself now.'

'How could I rest,' she said, 'when I see my own son that I brought over from Ireland, struck silent and cold there before me, in the hard and narrow coffin?'

Uncle John waited for a quiet moment and then said: 'Isn't that the end of us all, Delia? . . . the Lord save us. The coffin and the grave, the end of each one of us.'

The mother put her face down and kissed the white forehead.

'The coffin and the cold grave,' she said, 'and the Lord have mercy on us.'

That's the pure grief, he thought as he watched, and why I have none? Am I that mean and bad that God won't give me feeling? It's self with me all the time. He turned to creep back upstairs when he heard Uncle John speak again:

'There's another one, Delia,' he said, 'an' to neglect him would not be right. So will you come away from there now, Delia, an' God rest him.'

'I will, John,' she said, 'I will indeed.'

He turned to the darkness of the stairs and began to creep up. Uncle John meant me. A flood of tears came to his eyes. He meant me. A whimper broke from him as he went into the bedroom, and then he felt the burst of crying and sobbing jerk upward from his throat. He fell into bed and wept and snuffled into his hands. Soon he felt an easing and flowing about his breast and mouth, and the tension went from his head. It seems like my mean little thoughts are being washed away. He was my brother, he thought, and now he is maimed and dead. After the tears he felt calmed.

He heard someone moving and the door opening. He prayed and looked up. The mother came into the room, carrying a bright candle in one hand, and in the other the

318

tin tray, with a mug of tea set in the middle, and about it slices of bread with the thick butter gleaming.

' Are you awake, my child? ' she said. ' I have something here for you.' She sat on the side of the bed, and he sat up and took the tray from her. She's not her proper self yet, he thought. ' I let myself be distracted,' she said, ' and I had you neglected, God forgive me.' The quiet moment in the room was shattered by a sudden clanging from the foundry, and the noise rolled over the roofs, and there was a shiver of the windowpanes. The mother looked out at a piece of sky.

' Back home in Ireland at this hour of the night,' she said, ' there'd be a great silence.' Ee, aye, I'd all but forgot—it was right hushed and still where we come from. ' Eat up,' she said, ' eat up, agraw.' That's her real voice coming back again. It made him feel at ease and he took a big bite of bread. A good cry scours out your head. He chewed away and swallowed. Bread's good. He brought the mug to his lips and drank. Tea's good. You get used to the din.